Time in Kilkenny

Time in Kilkenny

P Hartwell

DEDICATION

To the keepers of whispers, the guardians of forgotten lore, and the souls who find magic in the shadows of ancient stones. This story is woven from the threads of history that bind us to the past, and the enduring power of love that transcends time itself. May you always feel the pull of the unknown, the allure of the unexplained, and the comfort of knowing that some mysteries are worth holding onto. For those who believe that every old castle, every weathered stone, and every quiet corner of the world holds a story waiting to be told, this is for you. To the dreamers, the seekers, and the romantics who understand that the deepest truths often lie hidden, just beneath the surface, waiting for a curious heart to uncover them. To the quiet strength found in unexpected places, and the resilience of spirits that echo through generations. May your own journeys be filled with discovery, wonder, and the enduring magic of connection, much like the one I found in the heart of Kilkenny, amidst its medieval charm and its captivating, enigmatic soul. This is for anyone who has ever felt the inexplicable draw of a place, a person, or a history that whispers to their very core, inviting them into a world far richer and more mysterious than they could have ever imagined. May you find your own Kilkenny, your own Aine, and your own enduring mystery to unravel.

Chapter One: Arrival in the Emerald Isle

TOUCHDOWN IN DUBLIN

The descent into Dublin wasn't a landing; it was a brutal embrace. Pete, a man carved by thirty-five years of relentless routine, felt the visceral gnaw of travel fatigue in his marrow, a tremor that predated the jarring kiss of rubber on tarmac. This wasn't mere weariness; it was a volatile cocktail of bone-deep exhaustion and an almost feral anticipation. The very air of Ireland, he sensed, thrummed with a potent, unspoken promise, a stark defiance to the sterile predictability of Buffalo's pulse.

His guidebook, a testament to weeks of feverish obsession, felt less like a travel aid and more like a talisman, its pages softened and dog-eared from his desperate clawing for a different reality. His passport, worn thin from his touch, was a promise of passage to a kingdom he'd only dared to haunt in dreams. Two weeks. A paltry reprieve, a fleeting sanctuary from the suffocating grey of his existence, a chance to drown himself in Ireland's legendary welcome, its raw, ancient spirit, its impossibly vibrant green.

His expectations were a fragile whisper: the quiet balm of repose, the resonant echo of centuries, perhaps the comforting amber glow of Guinness in smoke-wreathed pubs. He was a man chasing oblivion from the ordinary, a soul adrift, utterly blind to the insidious pull of a current already snagging him, drawing him into depths far more profound and perilous than his most fevered imaginings could conjure. This wasn't just a vacation; it was a descent, and the descent had already begun.

The disembarkation was a brutal baptism, a cacophony of foreign tongues and a frenzy of limbs that threatened to swallow Pete whole. He was a shard of glass adrift in a human tide, a solitary pulse against the overwhelming momentum surging towards the arrivals hall. The air inside the terminal ripped at his lungs, a chilling, alien draft carrying a scent that defied definition. It wasn't the usual metallic tang of exhaust or the sterile rot of recycled breath. No, this was primal, a guttural whisper of peat fires gnawing at the night, of earth, freshly broken and weeping. It spoke of rain lashing against ancient stone, of forests that held their breath for centuries.

His single, worn suitcase felt absurdly light, a pathetic defiance against the weight of this new reality. He plunged into the throng, a hawk's eye scouring the swirling faces for the beacon of a car rental desk. The guidebook, a crumpled talisman in his fist, was his only anchor in this churning ocean of the unknown. Its dog-eared pages were a testament to a meticulously constructed optimism, a naive belief that maps could conquer the untamed. He'd plotted a course, a fragile skeletal structure for his immersion, a concession to the illusion of control, a desperate attempt to impose order on the howling chaos. He'd dared to dream of sun-drenched journeys, of villages whispering secrets from weathered stones, of moments stolen by the mirrored stillness of placid lakes, a quiet communion with a world that now felt vast, and utterly indifferent.

The instant his boots struck the tarmac, a visceral shock coursed through him. The Irish air, far from crisp, was a lungful of wild, untamed dampness that ripped away the stale exhalations of the plane, forcing him into an immediate, almost violent awakening. Overhead, the sky wasn't merely grey; it was a bruised, leaden expanse, a canvas pregnant with the primal threat of rain, yet paradoxically, it bled a soft, ethereal light that leached the sharp edges from the world, imbuing the very earth with an ancient, brooding soul.

The wind, a predatory presence in this land, didn't just tug; it clawed at his jacket, a relentless, murmuring beast whispering secrets in a tongue that resonated deep within his bones, a melody both achingly familiar and chillingly alien. He found the car – not merely a rental, but a squat, unyielding beast of metal, a pragmatic scar on the verdant landscape, its solidity a grounding anchor against the swirling uncertainty of what lay ahead.

Slipping behind the wheel, the sheer, crushing weight of his expectations didn't descend as a gentle reminder, but as a vise gripping his chest. This wasn't a chance to *unplug*; it was a desperate, clawing escape from the asphalt jungle that had threatened to consume him, a desperate bid for a primal, unvarnished *being*. The suffocating chains of his former existence shattered, replaced by the intoxicating, almost terrifying siren song of the unknown – a visceral promise of experiences that would scar and shape him, of sights that would sear themselves onto his retinas, of sounds that would echo in the hollows of his soul.

The tarmac bled into a brutal, breathtaking panorama the moment Pete peeled away from the airport's sterile embrace. This wasn't mere beauty; it was a raw, untamed spirit that clawed at his senses, even on the fringes of civilization. Ancient stone, scarred by a thousand winters, writhed like petrified serpents across the land, their lines a silent, defiant chronicle etched into the very bones of Ireland, whispering of epochs lost to memory, perhaps even the dawn of time. The fields, oh, the fields! They weren't just green; they were an impossible, soul-searing emerald, a hue so potent it seemed to drink the very lifeblood from the heavens, leaving a lingering thirst in its wake. And amidst this overwhelming viridian, the husks of forgotten farmsteads, like skeletal sentinels, stood stark against the sky, their hollow eyes gazing out from a past that refused to die, each weathered stone a ghost of a life, a scream silenced by centuries. Pete, a man who'd seen his share of grit and glory, felt an unnerving resonance, a guttural pull from the sheer, bloody-minded persistence of this land. It didn't just *hold* history; it *bled* it, its very essence a testament to a resilience that gnawed at his own carefully constructed composure.

The asphalt whispered beneath his tires, a low, insistent hum a stark counterpoint to the coiled tension in his gut. Every turn, every unfamiliar signpost, was a test, a subtle accusation. He gripped the wheel tighter, knuckles white, a ghost of caution from some long-forgotten forum hammered into his synapses – *drive left, stay sharp*. The guidebook, a dog-eared sentinel on the passenger seat, bled faint light, its maps a cryptic labyrinth. Kilkenny. The name itself was a phantom on his tongue, plucked from the digital ether, a mere whisper of medieval allure and an *atmosphere* that snagged at his imagination like a forgotten memory. He craved not the predictable clamor of tourist traps, but the hushed secrets of forgotten lanes, the slow unraveling of time.

This wasn't about escape, not entirely. It was a desperate excavation, a silent promise to himself to bury the gnawing anxieties that clawed at his personal life, to let the relentless grind of his career dissolve into the same ephemeral mist that kissed the dawn. No grand quests, no blinding epiphanies awaited him. He wasn't chasing destiny. He was hunting for a breath, a single, ragged gasp of peace, a sanctuary from the ceaseless storm raging within.

The grinding of the carriage wheels was the only constant against the encroaching silence as the world bled from monotonous plains into a landscape that began to twist and breathe. Gone were the gentle slopes, replaced by an earth that bucked and heaved, as if the very ground remembered ancient struggles. Jagged stone walls, weathered by millennia of unforgiving winds, now fractured the horizon, their stern faces occasionally broken by the looming presence of primeval forests. Their canopies, a suffocating, ink-dark mass, clawed at the sky, promising not just shade, but an engulfing darkness, a repository of whispered histories and forgotten sins.

Above, the sky was a relentless, bruised grey, a suffocating blanket that pressed down, mirroring the weight settling in his chest. The wind, no longer a playful caress, became a mournful dirge, snaking through the skeletal remains of sparse trees, its lament carrying a chilling, soul-deep melancholy. Then, like spectral apparitions, villages flickered into existence – huddled masses of stone cottages, their thatch roofs caked with age, thin wisps of smoke curling from their chimneys like tired sighs. Each hamlet was a phantom, a tableau from a life long extinguished, a jarring echo that resonated with an unnerving blend of the utterly foreign and a deeply buried, forgotten kinship. He found himself compelled to brake, his breath catching in his throat, a potent, insatiable curiosity gnawing at him. He craved to be submerged in their hushed aura, to feel the thrumming, ancient heart of these forgotten places, to unearth whatever lay dormant beneath their stony skins.

He stopped once at a small, roadside pub, a weathered building that looked as if it had grown organically from the very earth around it. The sign, almost entirely obscured by ivy, proclaimed it to be

"The Whispering Oak." Inside, the air was thick with the comforting aroma of turf smoke and something sweet, perhaps mulled cider. A few locals sat at the bar, their faces etched with the stories of time, their conversations hushed and low. Pete ordered a coffee, the warmth of the mug a welcome sensation in his hands. He listened to the gentle murmur of their voices, the occasional burst of laughter, feeling like an observer peering into a closely guarded world. There was a sense of community here, a deep-rooted connection to place that he found both intriguing and a little intimidating. He felt like an intruder, a temporary visitor in a world that had its own established rhythms, its own unspoken rules.

The engine roared to life, a primal thrumming against his ribs, mirroring the quickening pulse in his veins. Kilkenny. The very name coiled in his gut, a promise of something visceral, something *old*. His guidebook, a worn, dog-eared confidante, crackled open, spilling its secrets like embers onto the page. Norman conquerors, their iron-clad boots pounding the earth; medieval bishops, their hushed chants echoing through vaulted stone; a folklore so deep it bled into the very air.

He saw it, not just read it. He saw Kilkenny Castle, a brooding titan, its ramparts catching the dying light like a warrior's armor. He smelled the damp, earthy scent of ancient abbeys, the ghost of incense clinging to the air. He felt the bite of the wind whipping through narrow, serpentine streets, streets that had drunk in centuries of laughter and tears, of whispered betrayals and triumphant cries. He pictured himself lost within that labyrinth, the weight of ages a palpable presence, pressing in, suffocating, exhilarating. The stories weren't merely printed words; they were specters clawing at his consciousness, their voices a low, insistent murmur from the very mortar binding the stones. This wasn't just a destination; it was a crucible, a place where the stark, unforgiving present fractured, revealing the pulsing, vibrant heart of the past, a permeable membrane he was desperate to breach.

The further he drove, the more the landscape seemed to conform to his preconceived notions of Ireland. The green intensified, the hills grew more dramatic, and the skies seemed to deepen to a richer, more contemplative shade of grey. He passed a herd of shaggy, unperturbed cows grazing in a field, their forms softened by the mist that had begun to gather. He saw ancient standing stones, silhouetted against the horizon, their purpose lost to the mists of time, and felt a prickle of something akin to awe. This was not just a vacation; it was an immersion, a journey into a place that felt more like a character in a story than a mere geographical location.

The approaching miles bled into Kilkenny's embrace, not with gentle murmurs, but with a guttural whisper. Stone, raw and ancient, began to claw at the periphery, each weathered block a silent testament to forgotten might. Crumbling edifices, like the skeletal remains of giants, erupted from the earth, their shadows stretching, swallowing the fading light. The very atmosphere thickened, not merely with age, but with an oppressive, palpable weight, as if the centuries themselves were pressing down, a living, breathing entity reaching out from the dust.

He inhaled, drawing in the raw, untamed breath of Ireland, a scent that spoke of peat fires and restless earth. It filled him, a visceral jolt that chased away the gnawing weariness, the dull thrum of exertion in his bones. A flicker of something more than a smile – a dangerous, knowing curve – touched his lips. Here, in this land steeped in time, he was an intruder, yes, a phantom drifting between epochs, but the pulse of a thousand untold stories throbbed beneath his skin, a magnetic pull promising revelations that could shatter his very foundations. The escape from the suffocating normalcy had truly begun, the faint whispers of the unknown morphing into a roaring siren song, a challenge hurled across the ages. And he, a creature forged in the crucible of his own hidden past, was poised to surrender.

THE JOURNEY TO KILKENNY

The train carriage clawed forward, a metal beast devouring the horizon, and Pete, adrift in its rumble, felt the world warp. Gone was the confined sting of the car; here, Ireland's emerald heart pulsed, a violent, breathtaking bloom unfurling with a relentless, hypnotic beat. Pete pressed his face against the cool glass, his breath misting the pane as if trying to break through to the raw, untamed beauty. The hills, a relentless surge of green, were not merely rolling; they were sinewy muscles flexing beneath the sky, each crest a visceral gasp, each valley a shadowy, whispered secret.

And the walls. Not just stone, but bone. Ancient, gnarled arteries of the earth, they writhed across the land, their mossy flesh whispering forgotten oaths and the sweat-stained toil of men long turned to dust. Pete traced their impossible, winding paths, feeling the weight of their enduring legacy press down on him, a silent testament to a thousand storms weathered, a thousand hands that had sculpted these stark, defiant lines. It wasn't quiet beauty; it was a primal roar, a verdant, guttural anthem played out in a thousand shades of emerald and the unforgiving, stoic slate of ages. The air itself seemed thick with the scent of damp earth and the ghosts of ancient sorrows, a symphony that resonated not just in his eyes, but deep within his very marrow.

The infernal, hypnotic clatter of the train wheels gnawed at him, a relentless, metallic heartbeat against the crushing, indifferent silence of the world unfurling beyond the grimy pane. Each mile wasn't a gentle tug, but a visceral yank, a gravitational pull dragging him, inexorably, towards Kilkenny. Towards the gnawing, intoxicating promise of what lay hidden in the shadows of that name. He'd abandoned the sterile efficiency of the rental car, a husk of mere utility, the moment the keys left his grasp. This decision, a desperate gamble, was born of a primal need to bleed the journey into his very being, to claw himself free from the tyranny of maps and surrender to the indifferent, rolling oblivion of time and landscape. The rental car had been a cage, a functional lie. But this train... this was a different beast entirely. It was an engulfing, suffocating embrace, a slow, brutal communion with a land that whispered its secrets in the stark geometry of receding hills, in the fleeting, ghost-like impressions of isolated lives etched onto the canvas of his vision – lonely farmsteads, spectral sheep, all swallowed by the encroaching twilight.

He watched a solitary farmer, a silhouette against the vastness, mending a section of dry stone wall, his movements economical and practiced. There was a timelessness to the act, a connection to an ancient craft that resonated deeply with Pete. He'd always been drawn to crafts that required patience and precision, a contrast to the often frantic pace of his own professional life. Here, in the heart of the Irish countryside, such skills seemed not just preserved, but intrinsically woven into the fabric of existence. The train passed through small, unassuming villages, their stone cottages clustered together as if for warmth, wisps of smoke curling from chimneys, promising a glimpse of interior life that remained tantalizingly out of reach. He imagined families gathered, the scent of baking bread mingling with the ever-present aroma of peat smoke, a scene of simple, unadorned domesticity.

The guidebook, resting on his lap, felt almost superfluous at this moment. Its meticulously researched facts and historical anecdotes seemed to pale in comparison to the living, breathing narrative unfolding before his eyes. Kilkenny, a town whispered about in hushed tones of legend, a place he'd chosen on a whim, was beginning to feel less like a destination and more like a culmination. The very name conjured images of medieval grandeur, of ancient cathedrals and bustling marketplaces, a far cry from the quiet solitude he'd initially sought.

He'd come here, he told himself, to escape. To shed the weight of expectation, the relentless demands of his public life, the carefully constructed persona he wore like a second skin. He craved anonymity, the sweet anonymity of being just another face in the crowd. But Kilkenny was proving to be a treacherous siren. Its raw, unvarnished history, so unlike the polished narratives he usually consumed, was beginning to seep into him, stirring a dangerous curiosity. He found himself drawn to the shadows, to the whispers of forgotten rebellions and hidden injustices, moments that the guidebook glossed over in its pursuit of sanitized charm.

This burgeoning fascination felt like a betrayal of his carefully curated peace. His ambition, a creature he'd thought long tamed, was stirring. What if this raw history could be... harnessed? A different kind of story, a more potent narrative than the comfortable tales of kings and queens? The thought sent a jolt of guilt through him. Wasn't he here to *forget* his past, not to excavate new ones, especially ones that hinted at darker deeds? Yet, there was an undeniable allure to this 'medieval capital of Ireland,' a magnetic pull that transcended his initial desire for mere respite, a pull that now whispered of a different kind of power, a power he both craved and feared. He knew, with a sinking certainty, that if he followed this path, he would lose himself even more completely than he had intended.

A memory surfaced: the place was lauded as a nexus of skill and artistic endeavor, a locale where the past wasn't confined to exhibits but pulsed through its stone pathways and craftsman's studios. This vision struck a chord within him, awakening a dormant longing for ingenuity and a bond with something real and lasting. His existence in Buffalo, though secure and pleasant, frequently felt... devoid of vitality. An unvarying loop of appointments, time constraints, and the monotonous cadence of city life. He hungered for unpredictability, for chance meetings, for those instances that shattered the routine and infused his days with a jolt of authentic marvel. Ireland, and particularly Kilkenny, appeared to hold precisely that allure.

As the train continued its journey, the landscape offered further visual feasts. The fields, a vibrant mosaic of greens, were occasionally punctuated by splashes of vibrant purple heather, clinging stubbornly to rocky outcrops. The sheer, unadulterated wildness of it all was breathtaking. It wasn't manicured or contrived; it was raw, elemental, and profoundly beautiful. He found himself captivated by the way the light played on the hills, creating shifting patterns of shadow and luminescence. It was a living landscape, constantly transforming, revealing new facets with every passing moment.

He thought about his initial expectations for this trip – quiet relaxation, gentle historical immersion, a few pints of Guinness. Those expectations now seemed quaintly naive, like trying to capture the ocean in a teacup, a pale imitation of the reality he was wrestling with. The subtle undertow he'd felt upon arrival in Dublin was becoming more pronounced, a gentle but insistent current pulling him towards something more profound. But was this "profound" a calling to enlightenment, or a siren song luring him to a ruin he couldn't fathom?

A part of him, the part that clung to his carefully constructed life, recoiled. It whispered of responsibility, of the predictable comfort he'd left behind. This burgeoning awakening felt less like a liberation and more like a betrayal of the man he'd always been, the man who valued order and control. He craved the simplicity of those initial plans, the predictable rhythm of a tourist's journey. Yet, the insistent pull was undeniable, a visceral ache that mocked his attempts at denial.

He found himself scrutinizing every conversation, every overheard whisper, searching for a confirmation of this unsettling feeling. But the weight of it was also a terrible burden. The possibility of this encounter, this "something extraordinary," demanded a surrender he wasn't sure he possessed. To truly embrace it meant potentially dismantling the foundations of his own self-perception, a prospect that sent a shiver of genuine fear down his spine. He was caught between the familiar safety of his old self and the terrifying allure of a transformation he couldn't yet define, a transformation that might require him to abandon the very principles he'd built his life upon. This journey wasn't just about escaping the ordinary; it was about confronting the potential for an extraordinary self that might be so alien, so ruthless, that he would scarcely recognize himself – and worse, might even despise the man he would become. He wanted the profound, but the cost of it felt like an unbearable price, a sacrifice of his very identity for a truth that might break him.

As the locomotive glided onward, it traversed venerable viaducts, their venerable stone curves elegantly vaulting over meandering waterways that faithfully reflected the muted silver of the heavens. He observed swift, agile martins weaving and dipping with unstudied elegance, their aerial ballet a transient spectacle against the immense canvas above. Every component of the receding panorama appeared to weave itself into an overarching chronicle, a narrative murmured on the breeze, a saga ingrained within the very essence of the territory. A profound sense of expectation began to bloom within him, not the sterile anticipation of a rigid agenda, but a more natural, burgeoning exhilaration, the sort that blossoms from the captivating mystery of the undiscovered.

He settled back into his seat, the gentle rocking of the carriage a comforting lullaby. The faces of his fellow passengers were a mixture of expressions – some engrossed in books, others gazing dreamily out the window, and a few engaged in quiet conversation, their voices a low murmur that blended with the train's constant hum. He felt a sense of camaraderie with them, a shared experience of passage, each of them a traveler on their own unique journey, converging for a brief interlude on this winding path through Ireland.

The air within the metal cocoon was thick, a cloying embrace that clung to his skin. It wasn't merely warm; it was **suffocatingly humid**, laced with a **cloying sweetness** that prickled his nostrils – a phantom floral whisper, maybe the ghost of a forgotten perfume, or the decaying ink of newsprint. It was a **betrayal of the sharp, clean bite of the outside world**, the earthy, invigorating slap he'd experienced stepping from the sterile airport into a reality that finally felt... tangible.

Across the narrow aisle, a shadow moved. A young woman, **lost to the world**, hunched over a **battered, leather-bound tome**. Her brow, a landscape of **unyielding concentration**, was drawn into sharp, **almost painful furrows**. He felt a tremor of something akin to envy, a desperate curiosity to pierce the veil of her focus. What phantom visions did her charcoal scratch into existence? What fleeting, agonizing beauty in this **relentless, unfolding tapestry** had ignited that fierce, consuming fire within her? It was a silent, **stark pronouncement** that beauty wasn't a gift bestowed, but a **battle waged**, each soul wrestling its own unique, visceral truth from the indifferent flow of existence.

As the train slowed for a brief stop at a small, rural station, Pete saw a group of children waving enthusiastically, their faces alight with the simple joy of a passing train. It was a fleeting, but heartwarming, moment, a testament to the enduring fascination that these metal behemoths held, even in the most remote corners of the island. He smiled, a genuine, unforced smile that felt more natural than the polite smiles he often deployed in professional settings.

The unforgiving asphalt surrendered its grip, each mile a desperate plea as the journey gnawed at the land. Suddenly, the placid green bled into a savage drama: colossal cliffs, raw and seething, plunged into the churning maw of the Atlantic. Their obsidian faces, etched by the ceaseless, violent caress of the ocean, stood as defiant sentinels. The verdant pulse of the island persisted, a stubborn, almost defiant, testament to its enduring life, but now it was a fragile counterpoint to the raw, elemental fury of the coastline. A tremor, deep within his very bones, ignited a primal fire, a visceral thrumming that resonated with something ancient, something untamed. This was the Ireland that had sunk its hooks into the souls of poets and painters, the island that whispered of myths and legends, a place where the gossamer veil between the ordinary and the utterly enchanted was not just thin, but practically nonexistent, a breath away from tearing asunder.

With renewed focus, he revisited the worn pages of his travel companion, his digit navigating the intricate lines of the map. Kilkenny's embrace was drawing nearer. The town's allure, vividly depicted through its imposing fortress, its ancient sanctuaries, and its winding thoroughfares, conjured an image of a destination steeped in antiquity, a vibrant echo of Ireland's rich historical tapestry. An irresistible curiosity welled within him, a desire to wander those very lanes, to imprint his passage where legions had walked before, and to absorb the resonant spirit of bygone eras.

The railway carriage served as a peculiar ark, ferrying him not merely over terrestrial distances, but through the corridors of temporal existence. With every depot encountered, every hamlet that blurred beyond the glass, a distinct caesura in a monumental, evolving chronicle seemed to manifest. He consumed this Irish saga with the voracity of a keen bibliophile, each moment fueling a burgeoning eagerness. The unassuming gentleman in pursuit of tranquility was undergoing a profound metamorphosis, his initial humble hopes dissolving in the potent, untainted enchantment of the journey.

The iron beast groaned, its thunderous pulse fracturing into sharp, staccato gasps as it bled into the station. A primal chill snaked through the carriage, thick with the brine-laced breath of the Irish coast, an intoxicating cocktail that tightened Pete's lungs. His knuckles white, he clenched the worn leather of his single suitcase, a tremor running through him – a violent dance of dread and raw anticipation. Kilkenny. The very syllables seemed to vibrate with a hidden power, a siren's call to the unknown.

He launched himself onto the platform, the damp air a chilling kiss against his skin, a premonition of the wildness to come. This wasn't merely travel; it was a seismic shift, a shattering of the ordinary, a sensory bombardment that peeled back the layers of his world, exposing the raw, untamed heart of this emerald isle. The station's murmur, a ghostly symphony, swirled around him, a nascent hum that promised far more than mere arrival. Beneath it, the faintest rustle – the breath of ancient tales, the whispers of forgotten gods. And Pete, a lone figure swallowed by the mist, was finally ready to heed their urgent call. The legends weren't just calling; they were screaming, and he was about to plunge headfirst into their deafening chorus.

FIRST IMPRESSIONS OF KILKENNY

The leviathan of iron **screamed** to a brutal halt, its relentless crawl from the **dreaming, amorphous whisper** of the countryside into the **sharper, yet still seductively understated, throb** of Kilkenny station. Pete, a man whose very stillness hinted at oceans of unexpressed experience, **plunged** onto the platform. The air, still holding the **ghostly kiss** of the Atlantic he'd teased with his eyes earlier, now **assaulted** him with a new, **visceral** scent. It was a primal cocktail: the **guts of damp earth**, the **skeletal tang of ancient stone**, and a **haunting, clinging tendril of smoke**, the **dying breath of peat fires** clinging stubbornly to life in unseen hearths. This was more than an aroma; it was a **raw, guttural declaration** – a testament to **generations etched into the very marrow of this place**, their stories kept alive by the **stubborn, persistent heartbeats of those burning embers.**

Kilkenny hit Pete like a forgotten ghost, its very air thick with the dust of ages. The station wasn't just functional; it hummed with a spectral elegance, a hushed testament to an era when the rumble of the locomotive was a siren song, whispering promises of adventure. Stepping onto the cobbles, the town didn't just unfold – it *raged* into existence, a defiant tapestry of stories etched in stone. Pete's eyes, accustomed to the sterile, predictable geometry of Buffalo, were seized by the sheer, glorious anarchy of the street ahead. Here, buildings didn't stand in mute obedience; they clawed at the sky, a magnificent, crooked embrace of weathered stone, each facade a scarred veteran of countless seasons. They leaned, these ancient structures, not in weakness, but with a defiant intimacy, their very foundations groaning under the weight of centuries, sharing whispered sagas of triumphs and tragedies, their weathered faces a silent, potent plea to be remembered..

The moment his boot struck the cobblestones, a primal jolt shot up his leg. This was no mere pavement; it was a defiant testament to time, a jagged, unforgiving tapestry of rough-hewn rock, a brutal counterpoint to the sterile, soul-crushing asphalt he'd left behind. Each uneven surface bit at his soles, a visceral percussion that echoed the frantic rhythm of his own heart. This wasn't a path; it was a gauntlet, a resonant symphony of clatter and scrape that promised a journey as unpredictable as the shadows dancing around him.

And the light... it was a spectral caress, a ghost of luminescence that clung to the ancient stones, breathing an almost mournful life into their weathered surfaces. It was a light that didn't illuminate, but rather seeped, drawing out the secrets etched into the very marrow of the architecture. It spoke of a past that refused to be forgotten, bathing everything in a honeyed, melancholic glow that stirred a potent, unnamed longing within him. He felt a strange kinship with these stones, a shared burden of history, a silent acknowledgment of lives lived and lost beneath this very sky.

As he began to walk, his single suitcase a manageable weight, the true medieval essence of Kilkenny began to assert itself. The streets weren't wide boulevards; they were narrow, winding passages that beckoned exploration, curving and twisting in ways that suggested organic growth rather than deliberate urban planning. He imagined them as arteries, pulsing with the lifeblood of centuries, each turn promising a new discovery, a hidden courtyard, a tucked-away shop, or a glimpse into a private garden. The sheer density of history was palpable, not confined to museums or designated heritage sites, but woven into the very fabric of the streets, the walls, and the atmosphere itself.

And then, it *erupted* into view, not a gentle unveiling, but a visceral, gut-punching revelation: Kilkenny Castle. It was a brute, a titan that refused to be overlooked. It didn't just dominate the skyline; it *slashed* it, its stone battlements like jagged teeth, its towers raw fists punching at the sky, a defiant roar against time, a testament to the unyielding grip of those who had bled within its confines. Even from this chasm of distance, Pete felt the tremor of its grandeur, its sheer, overwhelming scale a brutal testament to a past carved in blood and iron. This was no mere structure; it was an assertion, a sovereign entity around which the very soul of Kilkenny seemed to have been forcibly hammered into place. The soft Irish light, far from softening its impact, only intensified the drama, bleeding long, skeletal shadows and etching the ancient stone with a thousand whispered atrocities onto Pete's very bones.

He found his guesthouse without much difficulty, guided by the directions he'd carefully printed. Nestled on a quieter side street, away from the immediate shadow of the castle but still within easy walking distance of its commanding presence, it was a building that perfectly embodied the charm he'd already begun to associate with Kilkenny. Its facade was constructed of old, grey stone, the kind that seemed to absorb the very essence of the surrounding landscape. There was a quaintness to it, a sense of cozy solidity. The windows, many paned with multiple small panes of glass, offered glimpses of warm light within. An old wooden sign, bearing the guesthouse's name in elegantly simple lettering, hung above a sturdy, dark-wood door. It exuded a welcoming aura, yet there was also a touch of mystery about it, a feeling that within its walls lay stories and perhaps even secrets, waiting to be discovered by those who stayed.

He pushed open the heavy wooden door and stepped inside, the sound echoing softly in the small reception area. The interior was immediately inviting. The air was warmer now, carrying a faint, pleasant aroma of beeswax polish and perhaps a hint of that ever-present peat smoke, but here it was more domesticated, like the comforting scent of a log fire in a well-loved home. The reception desk was an old, polished oak piece, and behind it stood a woman with kind eyes and a warm smile, her silver hair neatly pulled back. She greeted him with a genuine Irish lilt, her voice a melodic counterpoint to the quiet ambience of the guesthouse.

"Welcome to Kilkenny," she purred, a predatory glint igniting in her emerald eyes, her smile stretching to reveal a flash of something sharp, something far from welcoming. The very air seemed to crackle, thick with the scent of damp earth and something vaguely metallic. "You must be Mr. Peterson?" Her voice, a low thrum against the rising wind, dripped with a knowing insinuation that sent a shiver, not entirely unpleasant, down your spine.

"That's me," Pete replied, the corners of his eyes crinkling, but a flicker of something unreadable danced in their depths. He offered a smile that didn't quite reach them, a fleeting, almost predatory curve of his lips that sent a shiver tracing down her spine. "Pete Peterson." The name, spoken with a low rumble that seemed to vibrate in the air, hung between them, heavy with unspoken stories.

"Indeed, your arrival was anticipated. This particular chamber is an exquisite selection, bathing magnificently in the dawn's rays. I am Fiona," she announced, retrieving a diminutive, gleaming key from its place on the wall. "Should any requirement arise, consider me at your complete disposal."

Upon receiving the key, a profound sense of tranquility enveloped Pete. The initial anxiety of reaching an unfamiliar locale, particularly one so richly endowed with heritage and a pronounced personality, started to recede. In its place bloomed an eager expectation and a deep satisfaction. Even from these nascent moments, Kilkenny resonated with a distinctiveness unlike any place he had previously encountered. This difference transcended mere architectural styles or ambient scents; it was an intrinsic sensation, a palpable feeling of entering a narrative that breathed with life.

He followed Fiona up a gently creaking staircase, his suitcase bumping lightly against the wooden treads. The hallway was lined with framed old photographs, sepia-toned images of Kilkenny in days gone by, of stern-faced families and horse-drawn carriages. It was a subtle but effective immersion into the town's past, a gentle preparation for the experiences that lay ahead.

His room was on the second floor, overlooking a quiet courtyard. It was small but perfectly formed, decorated in a style that was both comfortable and characterful. A wrought-iron bed frame, crisp white linens, and a sturdy wooden dresser gave it a sense of timelessness. The window offered a view of the courtyard below, where a few pots of hardy, brightly colored flowers bloomed against the grey stone walls. He could hear the distant murmur of the town – the occasional clang of a bicycle bell, the low rumble of a passing car, the faint echo of voices – but here, in his room, there was a sense of peaceful seclusion.

He dropped his suitcase by the door and walked over to the window, leaning his forehead against the cool glass. Kilkenny. He was here. The train journey had been a prelude, a gentle easing into the rhythm of the Emerald Isle. Now, he was on solid ground, the medieval heart of Ireland beating around him. He thought back to the rolling green hills, the ancient stone walls, the solitary farmer. Those images were still vivid, but they were now being overlaid with the more immediate, tactile reality of Kilkenny: the cobblestones, the stone buildings, the looming presence of the castle, the scent of peat smoke.

He opened the window, letting in a fresh gust of air that carried with it the distinct smells of the town. The air felt cleaner, fresher, and somehow more alive than the air he'd left behind in his everyday life. He took a deep breath, trying to fully absorb the essence of this new place. He could see the rooftops of other old buildings stretching out before him, a sea of grey slate and weathered brick. The soft, diffused light of the late afternoon cast a golden hue over everything, softening the edges and making the ancient town seem even more enchanting.

Though unpacking and recovering from his travels seemed prudent, Kilkenny's allure proved overwhelmingly potent. An insatiable craving to discover, to meander and allow the town to unfold its character, became an almost unbearable temptation. He experienced an unburdened gait, a liberating sensation he hadn't felt in ages. His initial intention for this venture was a nebulous yearning for tranquility, a subtle evasion of the burdens weighing him down in Buffalo. Yet, as he stood in this delightful chamber, immersed in Kilkenny's sonic and olfactory tapestry, he grasped that this experience was already blossoming into something substantially more significant.

Discovering a miniature town chart tucked away in a repository, he spread it across the chest of drawers. The formidable fortress stood out, a striking landmark situated close to Kilkenny's core. The River Nore meandered adjacent, enriching the locale's topographical and historical narrative. His fingertip followed the intricate veins of the constricted lanes, envisioning his passage through them, surrendering to their circuitous routes. The travel companion, initially perceived as an unnecessary appendage on the journey, now emerged as an indispensable instrument, a beacon to illuminate his exploration of Kilkenny's undeniably complex historical tapestry.

Kilkenny's renown as a hub for artisanal pursuits, a locale where time-honored craftsmanship retained its prestige and vitality, resonated deeply with him. This particular aspect held a potent allure, a counterpoint to his own endeavors, which, despite their mental rigor, often felt devoid of a corporeal, tactile dimension. The prospect of immersing himself in the active presence of craftspeople, of observing the meticulous genesis of objects both aesthetically pleasing and built to last, stirred a profound, hushed anticipation within him. He envisioned entering intimate studios, inhaling the fragrant air of seasoned timber or the sharp, mineral essence of a smithy, and witnessing the masterful dance of practiced fingers transforming unformed matter into vibrant existence.

The softness of the light outside was beginning to deepen, signaling the approach of evening. He knew that the best way to truly get a feel for Kilkenny was to experience it as the day transitioned into night. He put on a light jacket, grabbed the map, and headed back down the stairs. Fiona was still at the reception desk, arranging some fresh flowers in a vase.

"Heading out for a bit, Mr. Peterson?" she murmured, her gaze, sharp as broken glass, pinning him as she rose, a faint, unsettling scent of night-blooming jasmine clinging to the air around her. The question, laced with an unspoken weight that settled heavy in his gut, hung between them, a tangible thing, as if the very silence crackled with anticipation.

"Just to get my bearings," Pete rasped, his voice a low rumble that seemed to vibrate in the very air. He tilted his head back, the raw scent of pine and damp earth clinging to him, and let the overwhelming splendor wash over him. "God, it's... *magnificent*."

"Ah," she purred, a flicker of something ancient and knowing dancing in her eyes, her smile a slow, deliberate unveiling of secrets. "It has its moments, yes. But tread lightly, my dear. These stones... they drink the rain, you see. They gleam with a slick, treacherous beauty, a silent promise of a broken ankle, a ripped hem, a sudden, jarring descent into the shadowed gutters. Feel the chill that seeps from them? It's not just water, you know. It's the memory of every hurried step, every careless stumble. Be wise. Let your instincts guide you, not just your eyes, lest you become another whispered tale in the damp, echoing alleys."

"**A shiver, not entirely unwelcome, traced a path down Fiona's spine.** 'Good to know,' he murmured, his voice a low rumble that seemed to vibrate in her very bones. A flicker of something wild, a predator's nascent delight, danced across his lips, a smile that didn't quite reach the unnerving depths of his eyes. The air, thick with the scent of old paper and something faintly metallic, seemed to hold its breath. 'Thank you, Fiona,' he added, the words a silken thread, both a promise and a subtle, chilling threat."

Emerging back onto the thoroughfare, he found the evening atmosphere invigorated by a refreshingly crisp breeze, now imbued with an inviting, savory aroma – possibly emanating from a nearby establishment – subtly entwined with the enduring, earthy fragrance of peat smoke. The gentle, widespread illumination, while still present, was gradually yielding to a richer, more honeyed hue as the sun descended towards the horizon. The tightly packed lanes, which had exuded a delightful historical charm earlier in the day, now seemed to possess a more evocative, almost enigmatic aura, as the encroaching twilight stretched and intensified the somber shades.

With no set purpose, he began to ambulate, surrendering his direction to the whims of his soles. The aged stones beneath his footwear produced a resonant cadence, a percussive echo that amplified the historic aura of his environment. His gaze frequently ascended, absorbing the stately facades—the slender, lofty apertures, the elaborately carved portals, and the delicate masonry adorning numerous edifices. Each structure appeared to possess its own narrative, its own distinct soul. Arriving at a junction, he lingered, his gaze drawn down an uncommonly confined thoroughfare that seemed to vanish into the encroaching dusk. It presented an alluring prospect, an unspoken invitation to venture deeper into the ancient core.

A primal thrum vibrated through the soles of his boots, the distant echo of music, sharp and alive. It wasn't just a tune; it was a raucous, defiant Irish spirit, a riot of fiddles and bodhráns clawing its way from a shadowed doorway. Beneath that sonic onslaught, a deep, guttural murmur rose – the mingled voices of souls unburdened, punctuated by bursts of uninhibited laughter that snagged at the edges of his carefully constructed reserve. This was the molten core of belonging, a searing counterpoint to the sterile, predictable solitude that had become his armor. He craved this raw, untamed communion, the kind that shattered the meticulously laid bricks of his ordinary existence and ignited something forgotten within him.

Upon navigating a turn, the majestic Kilkenny Castle re-emerged, now considerably nearer and exuding an even greater sense of grandeur. Illuminated by the gentle effulgence of the descending sun, its venerable stone turrets appeared to ascend with regal bearing towards the heavens, forging a commanding outline against the encroaching twilight. Its immense magnitude was profoundly striking, and one could readily sense the palpable gravity of ages emanating from its time-worn ramparts. He paused, captivated by its appearance, striving to internalize its essence and decipher the chronicles harbored within its formidable edifice. Visions of armored warriors and esteemed dignitaries, of relentless assaults and joyous festivities, all played out within those fortifications across the epochs, filled his thoughts.

He consulted his map again, noting the proximity of the castle to other significant landmarks, such as St. Canice's Cathedral and the Medieval Mile, a stretch of historic street that connected many of the town's key attractions. He decided to head in the general direction of the cathedral, drawn by the promise of more ancient architecture and the chance to perhaps gain a higher vantage point of the town.

The labyrinthine avenues meandered and twisted, each revealing a fresh vista, an undiscovered element to embrace. He strolled past charming boutiques showcasing artisanal creations and time-honored taverns with their shadowed, beckoning entrances. A subtle murmur of existence pervaded the atmosphere, a mellow vitality that imbued the settlement with a pulse, a captivating aliveness, even with its venerable roots. A profound sense of belonging began to blossom within him, an assurance that he was gradually, yet irrevocably, integrating into its very cadence.

A siren call, a primal thrum of strings and pipes, beckoned him from the rain-slicked street, a magnetic pull toward the dimly lit promise of 'The Malt House.' A tremor of anticipation, a flicker of something more than mere curiosity, held him captive for a breath. Then, with a decisive step, he breached the threshold, plunging into a visceral symphony of sensation.

The air itself was a living entity, thick and humid, heavy with the primal scent of roasting meat, a dark, earthy perfume that clung to the very timbers. Beneath it, the robust, almost aggressive tang of dark ale, a promise of potent solace. He navigated the throng, a man on a silent quest, his gaze scanning the rough-hewn faces.

In a shadowed alcove, a coven of musicians held court. Their instruments, ancient and weathered, sang with a fierce, unyielding joy, a tapestry of sound that hammered against the ribs, demanding a response. The melody wasn't merely lively; it was a primal dance, a visceral pulse that seized the very soles of his feet. Around him, the patrons were a study in contained rapture. Some were islands of boisterous camaraderie, their laughter a counterpoint to the music. Others, cloaked in a quiet reverence, surrendered to the sonic tide, their faces etched with a profound, almost painful beauty, illuminated by the flickering candlelight.

He found his sanctuary at the bar, an empty stool beneath him, a silent invitation. A pint of Guinness materialized, its dark, obsidian depths mirroring the secrets he carried. As the first wave of its rich, malty current washed over his tongue – a velvety, almost reverent taste – he felt a deep, resonant hum within his own bones. He was not merely observing; he was absorbing, a willing vessel for the raw, untamed spirit of this place, a hunter caught in the intoxicating scent of the hunt.

The air throbbed with a raw, untamed pulse. Not just played, but *wrought* by those possessed souls – fingers a blur of fevered motion, dancing a desperate waltz across the taut strings of a fiddle, coaxing shrieks of raw joy from a tin whistle, hammering out a primal heartbeat on the taut skin of a bodhrán, and weaving it all into a snarling, intricate web with a guitar. The melody wasn't merely complex; it was a wild, intoxicating storm of reels and jigs, a sonic torrent that clawed its way into your very bones, a defiant, exultant spirit that dared you to stand still.

Pete felt it – an involuntary tremor in his thigh, a seismic shift in his chest. His foot, no longer his own, was a captive to the relentless, irresistible rhythm. A smile, pure and unbidden, cracked his face, a fragile bloom in the intoxicating whirlwind. This wasn't the gentle whisper of history he'd half-expected; this was the roaring heart of it, the *true* Ireland he'd hunted, a visceral punch to the soul. Forget dusty ruins and silent stones. This was the fire, the irrepressible, lifeblood pulse of a culture refusing to be contained, a vibrant, defiant flame flickering in the very soul of Kilkenny.

Engaging the establishment's host, a jovial fellow whose face bore the warmth of good health and whose gaze sparkled with an inviting mirth, Pete found an instant rapport. Their discourse flowed effortlessly, encompassing the locale's character, the sonic tapestry of the evening, and the narrative of Pete's travels. Liam, the proprietor behind the counter, proved an invaluable wellspring of regional lore, readily dispensing sagas and suggestions. He enlightened Pete on the prime locations for authentic artisanal creations, delved into the historical resonance of the ancestral fortress, and pinpointed the premier taverns for resonant live performances.

"Liam remarked, polishing the bar, "You've chosen a splendid evening for Kilkenny. While our usual tunes are spirited, they reach a crescendo of excellence on Tuesdays.""

Pete savored another gulp of his Guinness, a broad smile gracing his features. "Truly remarkable," he affirmed, his voice resonating with genuine awe. "This melody is unlike anything I've ever encountered."

As dusk settled, Pete discovered himself increasingly captivated by the pub's genial spirit. Immersed in the melodies, engaged in conversation with Liam and several regulars who congregated at the counter, he surrendered to the comforting embrace and shared fellowship of the establishment. The fatigue that had burdened him from his travels had utterly vanished, supplanted by a surge of renewed vigor and a profound recognition of the profound joy found in genial companionship and resonant tunes.

Emerging onto the thoroughfare, he found the town enveloped in a hushed stillness, the night's gloom fractured by the comforting radiance of streetlamps and the stray illumination escaping from dwelling panes. The atmosphere had grown perceptibly chillier, and a fine dew commenced to descend, bestowing a polished gleam upon the ancient paving stones. Against the nocturnal canvas, the imposing form of Kilkenny Castle stood stark, a sentinel overlooking the slumbering settlement. Veiled by the clinging vapor, its contours appeared gentler, lending it an almost spectral quality, more akin to a phantasm than an edifice of solid rock..

Energized from his memorable outing, he returned to the guesthouse, his gait still buoyant. The moonlit, misty lanes of the sleeping town now seemed even more evocative. Lingering by the guesthouse entrance, he cast a final, appreciative gaze over Kilkenny, the town that had deeply captivated him. It was a place where the ancient and the contemporary pulsed with life, a locale where history wasn't merely preserved but actively permeated the very air. A subtle thrill coursed through him at the prospect of future explorations within this spellbinding medieval gem. As he unlocked the guesthouse door, the comforting aroma of peat smoke embraced him like a familiar spirit. Ascending the stairs to his chamber, he eagerly anticipated the dawn of a new day.

SETTLING IN

The door to his room, number 12, clicked shut behind him, a soft, definitive sound that seemed to seal him within a bubble of quiet anticipation. The room, though modest in size, was bathed in the gentle, muted light filtering through the leaded panes of the window. It overlooked a small, enclosed courtyard, a miniature world of weathered stone walls, a few stubbornly cheerful potted plants that had clearly weathered their own share of Irish seasons, and a solitary, moss-covered bird bath. It was a view that spoke of intimacy and seclusion, a welcome contrast to the sprawling, often impersonal, expansiveness of his life back in Buffalo.

Pete set his suitcase down on the worn Persian rug that lay in the center of the room. The familiar weight of it, a collection of his most essential possessions, suddenly felt incongruous. Inside were the clothes he'd packed with a practiced, almost automatic efficiency, the toiletries he used with the same lack of conscious thought, the worn paperback that had been his intended travel companion. These were the artifacts of his routine, the tangible pieces of a life he had momentarily stepped away from. Unpacking them here, in this quiet, history-steeped room, felt like a deliberate act of translation, a shifting of paradigms.

He opened the suitcase and began to take out his belongings, not with the usual haste of someone trying to get settled, but with a measured deliberation. Each item, as it was placed on the dresser or hung in the small, surprisingly deep wardrobe, seemed to take on a new significance. His favorite worn sweater, a comforting weight against his skin, now felt like a portable piece of familiarity in an overwhelmingly unfamiliar landscape. His toothbrush, mundane in its everyday function, represented a small anchor to the habits that defined his days.

As he unpacked, a profound sense of stillness settled over him. The cacophony of the journey – the rumble of the train, the murmur of conversations, the clatter of his own footsteps on the platform – receded, replaced by a deepening quiet. The objective he had set for himself, the simple, almost desperate need for respite, began to feel less like a distant aspiration and more like an attainable reality. He had envisioned this trip as an escape, a chance to simply breathe and to shed the accumulated pressures of his professional life. And here, in this tranquil room, with the soft Irish light painting the walls, that escape felt tangible.

He ran a hand over the polished surface of the wooden dresser. It was solid, unpretentious, and bore the faint scent of beeswax, a subtle perfume that spoke of diligent care and a certain old-world charm. This wasn't the impersonal, mass-produced furniture of a modern hotel; this was furniture that had likely witnessed decades, perhaps even a century, of comings and goings, of quiet evenings and early mornings. It had a story to tell, if only he were attuned enough to listen.

He walked over to the window and gazed out at the courtyard. The potted plants, small bursts of tenacious color against the grey stone, seemed to embody a quiet resilience. He noticed a small, almost perfectly round stone nestled amongst the soil of one of the pots, worn smooth by time and perhaps by the elements. It was a detail so small, so easily overlooked, yet it held a certain magnetism. It was a testament to the subtle beauty that could be found in the overlooked, the understated.

A gentle breeze rustled the leaves of a small tree in the corner of the courtyard, carrying with it the faint, distinctive aroma of peat smoke that seemed to pervade Kilkenny. It was a scent that was both earthy and comforting, a primal fragrance that spoke of hearth and home, of fires kept burning through generations. It was a scent that felt deeply rooted in the very essence of this place, and as it drifted into his room, it seemed to wrap around him like a warm, familiar embrace.

The initial objective of his trip, that quiet yearning for peace, was undeniably being met. The frantic pace of his work in Buffalo, the endless demands, the constant striving, felt like a distant, almost forgotten memory. Here, there was no urgent email to answer, no pressing deadline to meet, no difficult client to placate. There was only the quietude of his room, the gentle light, and the soft murmur of the town filtering through the thick stone walls.

Yet, as he stood by the window, a nascent curiosity began to stir within him. It was a subtle undercurrent, a quiet tug at the edges of his consciousness, a growing awareness that this place, this medieval city, offered more than just an opportunity for passive relaxation. The history that he had glimpsed on his arrival – the ancient architecture, the cobblestone streets, the imposing castle – was not merely a backdrop; it was an active participant, a presence that beckoned exploration.

He had come seeking stillness, a temporary reprieve. But Kilkenny, with its palpable sense of the past and its subtle, unfolding charm, seemed to be offering him something more. It was a whisper of intrigue, a suggestion that the true essence of his visit might lie not just in the absence of his usual stresses, but in the embrace of something entirely new, something that promised to engage his senses and perhaps even his spirit.

He thought about the guidebook tucked away in his suitcase, a volume he had almost dismissed as unnecessary on the train. Now, it seemed like a key, a potential guide to unlocking the secrets of this medieval labyrinth. He imagined tracing the lines on its pages, following the threads of history that wove through the town, discovering the stories hidden within its ancient stones.

The objective of his trip might have been simple: to find peace. But as he stood there, a sense of quiet anticipation began to build, a subtle shift from mere relaxation to a burgeoning desire to understand, to connect, to truly experience Kilkenny. The initial objective was being met, yes, but it was also, almost imperceptibly, being expanded, enriched by the subtle allure of this enchanting, historic setting. He was settling in, not just physically, but in a deeper, more profound sense, beginning to feel the gentle, inexorable pull of this ancient Irish city. He picked up the small, worn map that Fiona, the guesthouse owner, had provided, its creases a testament to its frequent use by previous travelers. He unfolded it on the dresser, the lines and names of streets and landmarks spread out before him, a silent invitation to venture forth. The castle, prominently marked, seemed to draw his eye, a tangible symbol of the town's rich and storied past. He traced a finger along the river Nore, its path a silver ribbon on the map, imagining its centuries of flow through this very landscape. The narrow, winding streets, depicted as intricate capillaries, held a particular fascination. They promised discovery, the serendipitous unfolding of hidden courtyards and unexpected vistas.

His original intention had been to simply rest, to recharge his batteries after months of relentless work. The idea had been to avoid any strenuous exertion, to allow himself the luxury of doing very little. But as he stood there, the map spread out before him, a different kind of energy began to hum within him. It was a gentle curiosity, a subtle longing to engage with the tangible history that surrounded him. He wasn't looking for adventure, not in the grand, dramatic sense, but for a deeper understanding, a connection to the layers of time that seemed to be etched into the very fabric of Kilkenny.

He thought about the various historical sites mentioned in the guidebook – St. Canice's Cathedral, with its round tower, a beacon of medieval ecclesiastical architecture; the Medieval Mile, a celebrated stretch of street that served as a historical artery, connecting many of the town's most significant landmarks. He had read about Kilkenny's reputation as a hub of traditional crafts, a place where skills honed over generations were still practiced with passion and precision. This resonated deeply with him. His own profession, while mentally stimulating, often lacked a tangible, creative output. The thought of witnessing artisans at work, of seeing raw materials transformed into beautiful, functional objects by skilled hands, held a quiet allure. He pictured himself stepping into a silversmith's workshop, the air thick with the scent of metal and polish, or perhaps a potter's studio, the rhythmic turning of the wheel a hypnotic counterpoint to the creation of form.

The objective of his trip, the initial desire for a simple, unadulterated respite, was still present, a gentle undercurrent of peace. But it was now being interwoven with a nascent desire to explore, to learn, to absorb the unique character of this place. The room, with its quiet charm and its view of the courtyard, had served its purpose beautifully, providing a much-needed sanctuary after his journey. But it was also, in its own way, a starting point, a comfortable base from which to venture out and discover the wider world of Kilkenny.

He knew he could stay in, perhaps read for a while, or simply watch the light change in the courtyard. But the pull of the town, the subtle invitation to step outside and immerse himself in its atmosphere, was becoming increasingly irresistible. The initial objective of relaxation was being met, but in a way he hadn't entirely anticipated. It wasn't just about inactivity; it was about finding a different kind of engagement, a more mindful and appreciative way of experiencing the present moment. Kilkenny, even in these first few hours, was already working its subtle magic, transforming his simple desire for rest into something more nuanced, more enriching. He felt a growing sense of contentedness, a quiet excitement for the unfolding possibilities of his stay. He decided, with a quiet resolve, to take a short walk before the day completely surrendered to evening. The guidebook and map would be waiting for him when he returned, but for now, his own feet would be his guide, allowing the ancient streets to reveal themselves organically. The initial objective of finding peace was certainly being achieved, but he sensed that Kilkenny might offer something even more profound: a rediscovery of simple curiosity and a renewed appreciation for the enduring beauty of history and craft.

AN EVENING STROLL

The lingering light of the afternoon, a soft, buttery hue that clung stubbornly to the horizon, began to yield to the deepening blues of twilight. Pete stepped out of the guesthouse, the click of the door echoing his earlier departure from his room. The air, cool and carrying the faint, comforting scent of peat smoke, greeted him like a familiar acquaintance, despite its foreign origin. His initial intention, a simple stroll to orient himself before the full embrace of night, felt less like a plan and more like an instinct, a gentle tug towards the ancient heart of Kilkenny.

He found himself drawn towards the River Nore, its presence a constant, murmuring companion to the town. The streets, still etched with the echoes of daytime activity, were now softening, the sharp edges of stone and timber blurred by the encroaching dusk. Gas lamps, their mantles glowing with a warm, inviting luminescence, were beginning to flicker to life, casting elongated, dancing shadows onto the cobblestones. Each lamp, a miniature beacon against the encroaching darkness, seemed to imbue the historic architecture with a theatrical grandeur, transforming familiar buildings into silent storytellers of ages past. The meticulous care taken in their placement and maintenance spoke of a deep-seated appreciation for the town's heritage, a commitment to preserving not just the stones, but the very atmosphere they created.

He walked along the riverbank, the water a silken, dark expanse reflecting the deepening sky above. The last vestiges of daylight painted the clouds in hues of bruised purple and fading orange, a painterly display that was both melancholic and beautiful. The Nore, placid and unhurried, flowed with a quiet dignity, its surface occasionally rippled by a stray breeze, breaking the mirror-like reflection into a thousand shimmering fragments. It was a scene of profound tranquility, a stark contrast to the relentless urban rhythm he had left behind. The sounds of the town, the distant murmur of conversations, the occasional clang of a closing shutter, were muted here, softened by the open expanse of the river and the gentle expanse of the riverside path.

As he ambled, his senses gradually attuned themselves to the subtler rhythms of Kilkenny. The solid feel of the worn flagstones beneath his feet, the way the gaslight caught the dew forming on the leaves of the riverside trees, the faint scent of damp earth mingling with the ever-present peat smoke – these were the details that began to weave themselves into the tapestry of his experience. He wasn't actively seeking anything in particular, no specific landmark or historical anecdote. His objective was simpler, more elemental: to simply be in this place, to let its essence seep into him without the filter of expectation or agenda.

Then, drifting on the evening air, he heard it. Faint at first, a delicate melody woven with the resonant tones of a fiddle and the earthy pulse of a bodhrán. It was the unmistakable sound of traditional Irish music, emanating from somewhere nearby, a promise of warmth and conviviality within the ancient stone walls of the town. The music, though still distant, had a magnetic quality, a siren call to anyone seeking a glimpse into the soul of this place. It spoke of community, of shared stories, of a heritage that pulsed with a vibrant, living energy. He found himself gravitating towards the source, his pace quickening slightly, a newfound curiosity piqued by the promise of this auditory invitation.

The music grew stronger as he rounded a bend in the river, leading him down a narrower, more intimate street. The buildings here pressed closer, their facades a tapestry of weathered stone, timber beams, and leaded windows. The gas lamps seemed to glow with an even greater intensity on this street, their light pooling on the cobblestones, creating pools of warm amber that beckuoned him onward. He spotted the source of the music: a small, unassuming pub, its name barely visible above the heavy wooden door, an inscription weathered by time and countless seasons. The sound spilled out from within, a vibrant, infectious counterpoint to the quietude of the river.

He paused for a moment outside the pub, a slight hesitation flickering through him. His intention had been a quiet, solitary exploration. Stepping into a lively pub, especially alone, felt like a departure from that carefully cultivated solitude. Yet, the music was undeniably compelling, and the very anonymity of his presence here, a stranger in a new land, seemed to offer a unique kind of liberation. He could observe, he could listen, and if he chose, he could disappear back into the anonymity of the streets as easily as he had arrived.

He pushed open the heavy door, and the world of the pub enveloped him. The air inside was warm, thick with the mingled aromas of ale, roasted meat, and something indefinably comforting, perhaps the lingering scent of pipe tobacco. Laughter and conversation formed a lively hum, a comforting blanket of sound that immediately dispelled any lingering sense of isolation. The fiddle and bodhrán were at the heart of it all, the musicians clearly lost in their craft, their faces alight with passion. A small, raised platform at one end of the room served as their stage, a simple space that nonetheless held the weight of countless performances.

He found a small, unoccupied table in a corner, out of the main flow of traffic, yet close enough to the music to feel its full impact.

He ordered a pint of the local stout, its dark, creamy head a pleasing contrast to the muted colors of the room. As he sipped the rich, malty brew, he let his gaze wander, taking in the scene. The pub was a microcosm of the town itself, a collection of individuals brought together by shared space and shared experience. There were couples engaged in quiet conversation, groups of friends recounting tales, and solitary figures nursing their drinks, each absorbed in their own world yet part of the collective atmosphere. The walls were adorned with framed photographs, sepia-toned images that hinted at the pub's long history, its patrons and performers from bygone eras. He wondered about the stories held within those frames, the lives that had unfolded within these very walls.

The musicians launched into another tune, this one more up-beat, its rhythm infectious. He found himself tapping his foot, a subtle sway beginning to ripple through him. He watched as a few people spontaneously rose from their seats, forming a loose circle in the center of the room, their movements fluid and uninhibited. It wasn't a formal dance, but a spontaneous expression of joy, a communion with the music that transcended individual performance. He observed their easy camaraderie, the shared smiles and nods of appreciation, and felt a pang of something akin to longing. His life back in Buffalo, while successful by most metrics, often lacked this effortless connection, this communal embrace of simple pleasures.

It was then, as his attention was momentarily drawn to a particularly intricate bowing technique of the fiddler, that he noticed her. She was seated at a table not far from his own, alone, nursing a glass of red wine. Her hair was a deep, rich auburn, pulled back loosely, allowing a few errant strands to frame her face. There was a thoughtful intensity in her gaze as she watched the musicians, a subtle engagement that seemed to set her apart from the more boisterous patrons.

She had a book open on the table in front of her, its pages turned down as if she had been momentarily interrupted in her reading.

He found himself watching her, drawn by an unnameable quality. It wasn't a sudden, overwhelming attraction, but a quiet fascination, a sense that she, too, was an observer, perhaps a fellow traveler in this ancient city, seeking something more than just a fleeting experience. Her stillness, juxtaposed with the lively energy of the pub, created a compelling contrast. She seemed to possess an inner reserve, a quiet strength that intrigued him.

As if sensing his gaze, she looked up, her eyes meeting his across the dimly lit room. They were a striking shade of green, intelligent and perhaps, he thought, a little weary. A faint, almost imperceptible smile touched her lips, a polite acknowledgment of his attention, nothing more, yet it sent a curious flutter through him. He returned the smile, a genuine, unforced gesture, and then quickly looked away, feeling a faint flush creep up his neck. He chastised himself for his unexpected boldness, for breaking his own unspoken rule of unobtrusive observation.

He returned his attention to his drink, but the encounter, however brief, had subtly altered the atmosphere of his evening. The music still filled the air, the laughter still echoed, but now there was a new element in his consciousness, a subtle awareness of another presence, another story unfolding in parallel to his own.

He decided to finish his pint and then continue his walk, his original intention resurfacing. As he rose to leave, he happened to glance back towards her table. She was gathering her belongings, placing the book into a worn leather satchel. For a fleeting moment, their eyes met again. This time, her smile was a fraction more open, a hint of genuine warmth that made him pause.

He stood there, a silent question hanging in the air between them. Should he approach? Should he break his carefully constructed shell of solitude for this fleeting, intriguing connection? The old habits of his professional life, the calculated risks and strategic engagements, warred with the newfound desire for simple, unadulterated experience.

Before he could make a decision, she turned and walked towards the door, her movements graceful and unhurried. As she passed his table, she offered another brief, enigmatic smile, a silent farewell that felt more like an invitation than an ending. He watched her disappear into the night, the heavy door swinging shut behind her, leaving him once again in the quiet hum of the pub.

A sense of mild disappointment settled over him, not a crushing one, but a quiet acknowledgment of a missed opportunity. He had come to Kilkenny seeking peace, a respite from the complexities of his life. But even in these early hours, the city, with its subtle invitations and unexpected encounters, seemed to be nudging him towards something more. The encounter with the woman, however brief, had stirred a nascent curiosity, a reminder of the richness and unpredictability that life offered beyond the confines of his carefully managed routine.

He finished his stout, the taste now imbued with a new layer of experience. The music continued its lively cadence, the pub's warmth still palpable, but his own internal rhythm had shifted. He paid his bill, offered a polite nod to the barkeep, and stepped back out into the cool night air. The gas lamps still cast their warm glow, but the streets now felt different, imbued with the memory of her presence, the echo of her fleeting smile.

He continued his walk, the river now a darker, more mysterious presence in the deepening night. The initial peaceful exploration had, in a way he hadn't anticipated, become the prelude to something else entirely. The encounter, however transient, had planted a seed of intrigue, a quiet question mark in the landscape of his intended tranquility. Kilkenny, he was beginning to realize, was not merely a destination for rest, but a place where the threads of past and present, of solitude and connection, were woven together in ways that were both unexpected and profoundly compelling. He found himself wondering if their paths might cross again, a thought that, surprisingly, did not feel like an intrusion, but rather a gentle, intriguing possibility in the unfolding narrative of his Irish sojourn. The music from the pub, though fading, still resonated within him, a subtle echo of the vibrant life that pulsed beneath the ancient stones of Kilkenny. He realized, with a quiet certainty, that his getaway was already taking a turn he hadn't planned, a turn that promised to be far more engaging, and perhaps more significant, than he had ever imagined. The objective of peace remained, but it was now accompanied by a burgeoning sense of anticipation, a quiet eagerness to see what else this enchanting city, and perhaps its intriguing inhabitants, might have in store for him. The evening stroll, intended as a simple reconnaissance, had already become an unexpected chapter in itself.

Chapter Two: The Enigmatic Áine

A CHANCE ENCOUNTER

The air within 'The Piper's Harp' was thick with a symphony of sounds and scents, a potent elixir of woodsmoke, spilled ale, and the earthy aroma of a hundred conversations. Pete, perched at a small, scarred table in a shadowed alcove, swirled the dark, creamy head of his pint of stout, the bitter-sweet notes a grounding presence. The music, a jubilant reel that seemed to set the very timbers of the pub vibrating, pulsed through him. His initial intention, a quiet observation of Kilkenny's nocturnal pulse, had been irrevocably altered by the sheer, unadulterated life that spilled from this unassuming establishment. He was a solitary observer, yet here, surrounded by the convivial hum, he felt a strange kinship with the unknown faces, a shared experience in the simple act of occupying this space.

It was during a particularly spirited flourish from the fiddler, a cascade of notes that seemed to dance on the very edge of audibility, that his gaze drifted, snagging on a figure seated a few tables away. She was alone, her posture relaxed yet attentive, a half-finished glass of ruby-red wine resting on the table before her. Her hair, a rich, burnished auburn, flowed in loose waves around her shoulders, catching the warm, flickering light of the gas lamps and the candles scattered across the tables, giving it an almost ethereal glow. It was a deep, vibrant hue, the kind that spoke of autumn bonfires and ancient forests. As if sensing his scrutiny, her head turned, and her eyes, a startling, deep emerald green, met his across the room.

There was no awkwardness, no immediate turning away. Instead, a silent, almost imperceptible acknowledgment passed between them. Her gaze was direct, intelligent, and held a depth that seemed to hint at unspoken stories, a world beyond the casual glance of a tourist. It wasn't the overt flirtation of a bar scene, but something subtler, a shared recognition of two souls adrift in the same sea of experience, finding a momentary harbour in the bustling tavern. He felt an immediate, almost visceral pull, a magnetic force that seemed to anchor him to that spot, momentarily eclipsing the music, the chatter, everything else. It was a connection forged in the unspoken, a spark igniting in the charged atmosphere of the pub.

He found himself cataloging the details of her presence: the delicate curve of her cheekbone, the way a stray strand of hair fell across her brow, the thoughtful set of her mouth. She held a book, its cover worn and leather-bound, resting open on the table, its pages turned down as if she had been engrossed in its contents moments before. This detail, in particular, resonated with him. It suggested a mind that sought substance, a companion in solitude that transcended the ephemeral pleasures of the immediate. He, too, carried a book, a well-thumbed copy of a travelogue tucked into his satchel, a familiar comfort in unfamiliar territory.

A slow smile, genuine and unhurried, spread across her lips, reaching her eyes and crinkling their corners. It was a private smile, a gentle amusement at being observed, perhaps, or a simple acknowledgment of shared space. He returned the smile, a hesitant, almost clumsy gesture, and felt a flush creep up his neck, a traitorous warmth betraying his carefully cultivated detachment. He quickly averted his gaze, a flicker of self-consciousness rippling through him. His inclination was to melt back into the anonymity of the crowd, to remain an unseen observer. Yet, the brief exchange had irrevocably altered the tenor of his evening. The pub, which moments before had been a lively backdrop to his solitary exploration, now held a focal point, a presence that imbued the entire space with a new, compelling dimension.

He nursed his stout, his senses now keenly attuned to her presence. He found himself listening not just to the music, but to the rhythm of her breathing, the subtle shifts in her posture. The conversation around him faded into a low murmur, the clamour of the pub receding to the periphery of his awareness. His thoughts, once a steady stream of observations and reflections on the town, now revolved around this intriguing stranger. What was she reading? What brought her to Kilkenny? Was she a local, or another traveler, like himself, seeking solace or discovery in the ancient city?

The musicians launched into a new melody, this one a mournful, lilting ballad, its notes echoing with a timeless melancholy. He watched as a few patrons, caught in the emotional tide of the song, swayed gently, their heads bowed. She, too, seemed affected, her gaze drifting towards the musicians, her expression one of quiet contemplation. There was a stillness about her, a self-contained grace that stood in stark contrast to the boisterous energy of some of the other patrons. She possessed an aura of serene introspection, a quiet confidence that was undeniably captivating.

He imagined approaching her, the words he might say, the awkwardness of the initial introduction. His professional life had been a series of calculated interactions, of navigating complex personalities and unspoken agendas. This felt different, however. There was an innate curiosity that transcended the need for strategic advantage. It was the simple, human desire to connect, to understand. He considered the risk – the possibility of rejection, the embarrassment of a misjudged approach. But the alternative, the regret of a missed opportunity, felt even more daunting.

As if on cue, she began to gather her belongings. She closed her book with a soft thud, slid it into a worn leather satchel, and then reached for her wine glass. Her movements were economical, deliberate, devoid of any haste. Pete felt a prickle of anxiety. This was it, the moment of decision. His heart gave an uncharacteristic thump against his ribs. He could let her leave, another fleeting face in the tapestry of his journey, or he could seize this unexpected moment, this brief window of connection.

He pushed back his chair, the scrape of its legs against the stone floor a jarring sound in the sudden quietude of his internal debate. He took a step, then another, his eyes fixed on her as she stood, preparing to leave. As she turned towards the door, their gazes met once more. This time, her smile was less of amusement and more of a genuine, open warmth. It was a simple gesture, but it held a profound invitation, a silent question that hung in the air between them.

"Excuse me," he began, his voice a little rougher than he intended. He cleared his throat, attempting to regain his composure. "I... I couldn't help but notice your book. It's a rather striking binding." It was a weak opening, he knew, a clumsy attempt to bridge the distance, but it was all he could muster.

She paused, a faint arch to her eyebrows, but her smile didn't waver. "It's an old edition of Yeats," she replied, her voice a low, melodious tone that seemed to weave itself into the pub's ambient sounds. "A favourite."

"Yeats," he repeated, a flicker of recognition. "Of course. I should have guessed." He gestured vaguely towards the book. "He has a way of capturing the spirit of this land, doesn't he?"

"He does," she agreed, her gaze still steady, assessing. "Though sometimes, I think the land speaks for itself, without need for poetic interpretation."

This was it. The conversation had begun. He felt a surge of something akin to exhilaration, a release of pent-up anticipation. "Perhaps," he conceded, a genuine smile returning to his face. "But it's certainly more enjoyable with a guide, wouldn't you say? Especially for someone new to its whispers." He let his gaze linger for a moment, allowing the implication to settle.

She tilted her head slightly, a thoughtful expression settling on her features. "And are you new to Kilkenny's whispers?" she asked, her tone light, yet carrying an undertone of genuine interest.

"Completely," he admitted. "Just arrived this afternoon. Taking it all in, one pint and one street at a time."

"A wise approach," she said, and then, with a slight inclination of her head, added, "My name is Aine."

The name, so perfectly suited to the image, landed with a soft resonance. "Pete," he replied, extending his hand, a gesture that felt both familiar and strangely formal in this setting.

She took his hand, her grip firm and cool. The brief contact sent a jolt through him, a subtle current that underscored the undeniable connection he felt. "It's a pleasure to meet you, Pete," she said, her eyes holding his. "And a pleasure to share a quiet moment with a fellow observer of Yeats and Kilkenny."

He felt a warmth spread through him, an unfamiliar sense of ease. "The pleasure is entirely mine, Aine." He hesitated for a moment, the question forming on his lips. "Are you, by any chance, heading out into the night? Or perhaps you're delaying the inevitable departure?"

Aine's smile widened, a hint of amusement dancing in her green eyes. "I was about to venture out," she admitted. "The night here has its own particular charm, wouldn't you agree? Especially when the moon begins to cast its silver light upon the stones."

He felt a surge of hope. "It does indeed," he said, emboldened by her openness. "I was just contemplating a further exploration myself. Perhaps... perhaps you wouldn't mind some company?" He held his breath, the question hanging in the air, vulnerable and hopeful.

Aine considered him for a moment, her gaze thoughtful. The usual instincts of caution, honed by years of self-reliance, warred within him. He was a stranger, an unknown quantity, and she was a woman of evident discernment. Yet, there was a sincerity in his gaze, a simple desire for companionship that seemed to resonate with her.

"Kilkenny is best explored with a willing companion," she said finally, a gentle smile gracing her lips. "And as you are clearly new to its whispers, perhaps I can offer a little guidance. Lead the way, Pete."

With that, she turned and moved towards the door, her steps deliberate, her satchel swinging gently at her side. Pete, with a renewed sense of purpose and a lightness in his step, followed, leaving the warmth and music of 'The Piper's Harp' behind, stepping out into the cool, moonlit embrace of the Kilkenny night, his solitary exploration unexpectedly transformed into a shared adventure. The faint scent of peat smoke still clung to the air, but now it was mingled with the subtler, more intoxicating fragrance of possibility. The initial spark had ignited, and the enigmatic Aine had ushered him from the periphery of observation into the heart of a new, unfolding narrative. He felt a quiet thrill, a sense of anticipation for the secrets the ancient city, and its captivating guide, might reveal.

FIRST CONVERSATIONS

The resonant chime of the pub door closing behind them seemed to seal the moment, drawing a curtain on the boisterous warmth of 'The Piper's Harp' and ushering them into the cool embrace of the Kilkenny night. The cobblestone street, slick with the residue of a recent shower, gleamed under the diffused glow of the gas lamps, reflecting the nascent moonlight in fractured, silvery shards. Pete found himself walking beside Aine, the initial awkwardness of their transition from strangers to companions surprisingly absent. It was as if a silent, invisible thread had been spun between them in the dim alcove, a thread that now guided their steps and smoothed the path of their nascent interaction.

"It's a beautiful night," Pete ventured, the observation feeling both obvious and necessary. He inhaled deeply, the air carrying the mingled scents of damp earth, distant peat smoke, and something subtly floral that he couldn't quite place, a scent that seemed to emanate from Aine herself.

Aine turned her head, her auburn hair catching the lamplight, and offered a soft smile. "Kilkenny truly comes alive under the moon," she replied, her voice a low murmur that carried easily in the relative quiet. "The stones have a different kind of song then, a more hushed melody." Her words painted a picture, an invitation to perceive the familiar landscape with new eyes, a common theme that was already beginning to weave itself into their dialogue.

They walked at a leisurely pace, their footsteps echoing faintly on the deserted street. Pete, usually reserved, found himself remarkably at ease, the conversational reins held loosely, allowing the flow to be dictated by a mutual curiosity. He asked about her book, about Yeats, and Aine spoke with a quiet passion, her words revealing a deep appreciation for the poet's ability to capture the essence of Ireland. "There's a certain melancholy in his work, wouldn't you agree?" she mused, her gaze sweeping across the shadowed facades of the Georgian buildings. "A reflection of the land's own enduring spirit, perhaps. A resilience born of centuries of stories, both joyous and sorrowful."

Pete nodded, his own thoughts aligning with hers. "I find that too," he said. "He doesn't shy away from the darkness, but he always finds a sliver of light, a spark of something enduring." He hesitated, then added, "It's what drew me to his work, I think. That balance."

"And what brings you to Kilkenny, Pete?" Aine's question was direct, yet softened by a genuine interest that belied any suspicion of mere politeness.

He explained his profession, the transient nature of his work as a freelance journalist specializing in historical sites. He spoke of the allure of ancient places, the stories etched into stone and soil, the desire to connect with the past. He found himself sharing more than he typically would with a casual acquaintance, his usual professional reserve melting away under the gentle probing of her inquiries and the unguarded honesty he sensed in her presence.

"So, you're a seeker of stories," Aine said, a thoughtful expression settling on her face. "That's a noble pursuit. This city is brimming with them. Every lane, every archway, has a tale to tell, if you know how to listen."

"And you seem to know how to listen very well," Pete responded, a genuine smile playing on his lips. Her words resonated with a deep familiarity, a kinship of spirit that surprised him. He felt an instinctive trust, a sense of having found a kindred soul in this ancient city.

Aine's smile widened, a subtle crinkle appearing at the corners of her eyes. "I grew up here, Pete. Kilkenny has always been my anchor. Its stories are woven into the fabric of my own." There was a hint of nostalgia in her voice, a gentle sigh that seemed to carry the weight of memory. Yet, as she spoke of her childhood, of growing up amidst the medieval architecture and the slow rhythm of country life, there was an elusiveness to her narrative, a deliberate vagueness that piqued Pete's curiosity. She spoke of certain places with a particular fondness, of the castle grounds, the medieval mile, the winding paths along the River Nore, but her descriptions often felt more like impressions, like fragments of a larger, unrevealed picture.

As they continued their walk, they passed under the imposing shadow of Kilkenny Castle. Its ancient stone walls, bathed in the ethereal moonlight, seemed to whisper secrets of centuries past. "It's magnificent," Pete commented, his voice hushed with awe. "I've seen photographs, but to stand here... it's something else entirely."

"It has seen many dawns, and many sunsets," Aine said softly, her gaze fixed on the battlements. "It's a silent sentinel, guarding the city's memories." She paused, her brow furrowing slightly. "My grandmother used to tell me stories about the castle, tales of hidden passages and restless spirits. Of course, she was prone to embellishment." A faint smile touched her lips, but there was a seriousness in her eyes that suggested more than just a fanciful recollection.

Pete found himself drawn to these fleeting glimpses of her past, these hints of something more beneath the surface of her calm demeanor. Her connection to Kilkenny felt profound, deeply rooted, yet she spoke of her life there with a certain detachment, as if observing it from a distance, even as she navigated its familiar streets. It was a captivating paradox, one that fueled his fascination.

They reached a small, secluded garden tucked away behind the cathedral, a place of quiet beauty with ancient yew trees and moss-covered stone benches. The air here was cooler, infused with the earthy scent of damp soil and the subtle perfume of night-blooming jasmine.

"This is one of my favourite spots," Aine said, gesturing to a weathered stone bench beneath a large oak tree. "It's a place for quiet reflection. For letting the world catch its breath."

They sat in companionable silence for a moment, the only sounds the gentle rustling of leaves and the distant murmur of the city. Pete found himself watching Aine, the way the moonlight played on her features, the thoughtful tilt of her head as she gazed at the stars appearing in the deepening sky. There was a serene self-possession about her, an inner stillness that he found incredibly alluring.

"What about you, Pete?" she asked, turning her gaze towards him. "What dreams do you carry, beyond the stories of old?"

The question, so personal and direct, caught him slightly off guard. He wasn't accustomed to such open inquiry, especially from someone he had only just met. But with Aine, the usual walls of professional detachment seemed to crumble. He spoke of his desire to unearth forgotten histories, to give voice to the silenced narratives of the past. He spoke of his longing for a sense of belonging, a place to truly call home, a quest that had, in many ways, defined his nomadic life.

"I suppose I'm always searching for a connection," he admitted, the words feeling more honest than he expected. "A way to anchor myself. Maybe that's why I'm drawn to these old places. They feel like they have roots that run deep."

Aine listened intently, her emerald eyes reflecting the starlight. "Roots are important," she agreed softly. "They provide strength, a sense of belonging. But sometimes, even the deepest roots can be disturbed. Or they can lead you down paths you never expected." Her gaze drifted back towards the city, a flicker of something unreadable crossing her features. It was a subtle shift, a fleeting shadow that hinted at complexities he couldn't yet comprehend.

Their conversation meandered through a tapestry of topics – books, music, travels, the nature of memory, the allure of the past. Aine possessed a remarkable ability to draw him out, to elicit thoughts and feelings he often kept carefully guarded. She spoke of her own aspirations, of a desire to create something lasting, something that would outlive her, though the specifics remained frustratingly vague. She mentioned a passion for pottery, for shaping clay into form, and spoke of it with a quiet intensity that suggested it was more than just a hobby. "There's a primal satisfaction in taking something raw and unformed and coaxing it into something beautiful," she'd said, her hands moving as if she were already working the clay. "It's a way of leaving a tangible mark on the world."

Yet, even as he found himself opening up to her, a subtle thread of mystery persisted. Her familiarity with Kilkenny was undeniable, yet it was interspersed with pronouncements that seemed to carry a weight of personal history he couldn't access. She spoke of certain ancient traditions with an insider's knowledge, of local folklore that sounded less like legend and more like lived experience. At one point, while discussing the city's medieval walls, she'd mentioned a particular section, "where the old well still whispers secrets," a phrase that was both evocative and, to Pete, entirely unexplained. When he'd pressed her gently for details, she'd simply smiled and said, "Some secrets are best left to the stones, wouldn't you agree?"

It was this enigmatic quality, this tantalizing glimpse of a hidden depth, that continued to draw him in. Aine was not just beautiful; she was intriguing, a puzzle he found himself eager to solve. Her intelligence was sharp, her insights often profound, and her presence radiated a quiet confidence that was both grounding and captivating. He found himself cataloging her every gesture, the subtle inflections of her voice, the way her eyes seemed to hold an ancient wisdom.

As the night deepened, and the moon climbed higher in the sky, casting longer, more dramatic shadows, they found themselves walking along the banks of the River Nore. The water flowed dark and silent, reflecting the myriad stars like scattered diamonds.

"Thank you, Aine," Pete said, his voice sincere. "This has been... more than I could have expected."

She turned to him, her face illuminated by the moonlight, her smile soft and genuine. "The night is young, Pete, and Kilkenny has many more stories to share. And perhaps," she added, her gaze lingering on his, "we have many more conversations to have."

The unspoken invitation hung in the air, a promise of further discovery. Pete felt a surge of exhilaration. The enigmatic Aine, with her deep roots and elusive secrets, had not only captured his attention; she had begun to weave herself into the very narrative of his journey. He sensed, with a growing certainty, that his time in Kilkenny was about to become far more than a simple journalistic assignment. It was becoming a shared exploration, guided by a woman who seemed as ancient and mysterious as the city itself. The initial spark ignited in 'The Piper's Harp' had now found fertile ground, and Pete was eager to see what bloom would follow. He felt a quiet thrill at the prospect of delving deeper into the enigma of Aine, a mystery far more compelling than any historical site he had ever documented. Her enigmatic nature was not a barrier, but a lure, a siren call that drew him further into the heart of Kilkenny's secrets, secrets that seemed inextricably linked to her own. He was drawn to her quiet strength, the wisdom that seemed to reside in her green eyes, and the subtle hints of a past that she carefully, almost artfully, kept just beyond his reach. This carefully constructed veil only served to intensify his curiosity, turning their initial chance encounter into the beginning of a captivating, unfolding mystery. He found himself wanting to understand the sources of her quiet melancholy, the reasons for the fleeting shadows that sometimes crossed her features. What experiences had shaped her, what hidden depths lay beneath her calm exterior? These were questions that pulsed at the forefront of his mind, eclipsing even the historical narratives he had come to Kilkenny to uncover. Aine was, he realized, the most intriguing story Kilkenny had to offer. The allure was undeniable, a magnetic pull that promised a deeper understanding of both the city and the woman who seemed to hold its ancient heart within her. Their shared walk had transitioned from a casual introduction to an exploration of souls, a tentative dance of shared dreams and unspoken histories, with Aine as both the enigmatic subject and the captivating guide. He felt a profound sense of anticipation for what lay ahead, for the stories that would unfold between them, and for the secrets that Aine, in her own time, might choose to reveal. The night was, indeed, still young, and Pete was ready to listen.

A SHARED HISTORY OF KILKENNY

The familiar scent of damp earth and aged stone, so recently inhaled on their moonlit walk, now seemed to cling to Pete, a tangible reminder of Aine and the city's hushed embrace. As he navigated the narrow lanes, the conversation they'd shared flowed through his mind, a rich tapestry of Kilkenny's past interwoven with Aine's own captivating presence. She hadn't just spoken of history; she had breathed life into it, transforming dusty facts into vibrant, unfolding narratives. Her insights were not the dry pronouncements of a textbook, but the intimate recollections of someone who had grown up with these stories as her constant companions.

"It's as if the very stones here hum with memory, isn't it?" Aine had murmured, her hand lightly brushing against the weathered façade of a building, its intricate carvings almost lost to the shadows. "This was once the home of the Archer family," she'd continued, her voice a low, musical cadence. "They were renowned for their skill with the longbow, and rumour has it, their lineage traces back to the very archers who defended this city during the Norman invasion." Pete had peered closer, trying to discern the faint, almost invisible traces of the Archers' presence, but it was Aine's evocative description, her ability to conjure the clang of steel and the whistle of arrows from the silent stone, that truly brought the past alive. She pointed out a peculiar indentation on the lintel of a doorway, too subtle for an untrained eye. "They say that's where the family crest was carved," she'd explained, "a falcon in flight. It was weathered away centuries ago, but the echo of its form remains."

Her knowledge extended beyond the grand narratives of castles and battles. She spoke of the guilds, the weavers, the goldsmiths, the merchants whose lives had shaped Kilkenny in quieter, yet no less significant, ways. She gestured towards a row of tightly packed houses, their gabled roofs silhouetted against the darkening sky. "These were the homes of the tanners," she'd said, a slight wince passing over her face. "A vital trade, but not a pleasant one. The smell, I imagine, was quite overpowering in its day." She recounted tales of apprenticeships, of families whose fortunes were built on the intricate crafts passed down through generations, and of the vibrant, often rowdy, social life that pulsed within these narrow streets. It was a Kilkenny Pete hadn't encountered in any guidebook, a living, breathing entity shaped by the triumphs and struggles of ordinary people.

What truly set Aine apart, however, was the almost visceral connection she seemed to possess with the city. She didn't merely recount historical events; she seemed to feel them, to carry the weight of centuries within her. When they paused before St. Canice's Cathedral, its ancient round tower standing sentinel against the night sky, she'd spoken of the pilgrims who had once trod these very grounds, their hopes and fears echoing in the vast, silent nave. "Imagine," she'd breathed, her gaze fixed on the tower, "standing there, centuries ago, looking out over this same landscape, knowing that generations before you had done the same. It's a profound sense of continuity." Her words conjured an image of time folding in on itself, of past and present merging in a seamless continuum.

Pete found himself increasingly captivated by her intuitive understanding of Kilkenny. She'd point out architectural anomalies that had escaped his trained eye – a subtly altered window frame, a series of stones laid in a pattern that spoke of a forgotten purpose, a hidden archway half-concealed by ivy. "That arch," she'd said, indicating a narrow passage barely wide enough for a single person, "used to lead to a private chapel, belonging to a wealthy merchant family. They say it was used for clandestine meetings, whispered prayers, and perhaps, even more illicit dealings." Her tone was matter-of-fact, yet there was an undertone of something more, a hint of secrets held close, of knowledge that extended beyond mere observation.

Her descriptions of the families who had once called Kilkenny home were equally rich and personal. She spoke of the Butlers, whose influence had shaped the very fabric of the city, their lineage intertwined with the stones of the castle itself. But she also spoke of lesser-known families, artisans and tradespeople whose names might have faded from official records but clearly remained vibrant in her memory. She described the "Fitzwilliams of Parliament Street," a family of silversmiths whose intricate work was said to have rivalled the finest in Europe. "Their shop," she'd explained, her eyes alight with a quiet passion, "was a treasure trove. They say that even the smallest trinket they fashioned carried a touch of magic, imbued with the skill and dedication of their hands."

As they traversed the medieval mile, a sense of awe settled over Pete. It wasn't just the grandeur of Kilkenny Castle or the solemn beauty of the cathedral that impressed him, but the way Aine wove the city's narrative into a living, breathing entity. She spoke of the old city walls not as mere historical remnants, but as protective embraces, whispering tales of sieges and survival. She described the Black Abbey, its gothic arches soaring towards the heavens, not just as a place of worship, but as a hub of community, a silent witness to centuries of joy and sorrow. Her knowledge was so deep, so intrinsically linked to the place, that Pete found himself wondering if she was simply an exceptionally gifted local historian, or if her connection to Kilkenny ran on a more profound, almost spiritual, level.

There were moments when her words seemed to carry an almost prophetic weight, hints of future events or unspoken consequences woven into her historical anecdotes. When they passed a particularly ancient, gnarled oak tree on the edge of the castle grounds, she paused, her gaze thoughtful. "This tree," she'd said, her voice soft, "has seen so much. It's witnessed the rise and fall of families, the whispers of rebellion, the quiet endurance of generations. They say it's rooted in something ancient, something that remembers everything." Her words weren't a simple observation; they felt like a subtle invocation, a reminder of the enduring power of nature and the deep, hidden currents that flowed beneath the surface of the city.

She possessed an uncanny ability to connect disparate threads of Kilkenny's history, weaving together the lives of medieval nobles, Tudor merchants, and Georgian gentry with an effortless grace. Her understanding of local folklore was not merely academic; it felt like inherited wisdom, a legacy passed down through her own family. She'd mention specific families, their crests, their particular contributions, their feuds and alliances, with a familiarity that suggested she had not merely read about them, but had perhaps known them, or at least, had known those who had known them. It created an intoxicating atmosphere of intimacy, as if Pete were being granted access to a hidden archive, a secret history known only to a select few.

The intensity of her connection to Kilkenny was palpable. It was as if the city itself had imprinted itself upon her, shaping her understanding of the world and her place within it. She moved through the ancient streets with a proprietary grace, her every step imbued with a sense of belonging that Pete, a perpetual traveler, found both envied and deeply intriguing. He found himself looking at the familiar landmarks of Kilkenny through her eyes, seeing not just stone and mortar, but the echoes of lives lived, of stories whispered, of a history that was not merely recorded, but deeply felt. Her passion was infectious, transforming his journalistic assignment into a journey of personal discovery, a deep dive into a past that felt increasingly vibrant and alive, thanks to the enigmatic woman walking beside him. He noticed the way her eyes would linger on certain details, a flicker of recognition, a subtle smile that suggested a private understanding, a shared secret with the ancient city itself. It was this intrinsic connection, this almost mystical bond, that truly set Aine apart, making her not just a guide to Kilkenny, but an integral part of its ongoing narrative. He began to suspect that the true story of

Kilkenny was not to be found in its official histories, but in the intimate knowledge held by women like Aine, women who carried the city's soul within them, their own lives inextricably linked to its enduring legacy.

AN INVITATION TO EXPLORE

The moon, a sliver of pearly luminescence, cast long, dancing shadows across the cobblestones as Aine's suggestion hung in the air between them. Kilkenny, a city already steeped in a rich, almost tangible history, seemed to hold its breath, waiting for Pete's response. The curated tourist trails and well-trodden paths of the medieval mile had offered him a glimpse, a curated taste of the city's past, but Aine's invitation promised something far more intimate, a journey off the beaten track, into the hushed whispers and forgotten corners that only those truly connected to a place could reveal. The very act of her extending the invitation felt significant, a deliberate step away from the expected, a gentle pull into her own curated experience of Kilkenny. He felt a thrill, a surge of anticipation, like a seasoned explorer about to venture into uncharted territory. The academic in him, the one trained to dissect and analyze, was momentarily silenced by the sheer magnetic pull of the unknown, of experiencing the city not as a subject of study, but as a living, breathing entity through the eyes of someone who clearly held it dear.

"I'd like that very much, Aine," Pete replied, his voice steady, betraying none of the quiet exhilaration that had bloomed within him. He met her gaze, a silent acknowledgment passing between them. Her smile, as it returned, was a subtle unfolding, a quiet pleasure that mirrored his own. It was an invitation that transcended mere sightseeing; it felt like a confidence shared, a glimpse into the deeper currents that flowed beneath the surface of Kilkenny, currents that Aine navigated with an effortless, almost instinctual grace. He found himself leaning into the unexpected turn of the evening, the predictable end to their conversation now replaced by the allure of the unscripted, the possibility of stumbling upon something truly unexpected. The air, which had been cooling with the setting sun, seemed to hold a new kind of energy, charged with the unspoken promise of discovery.

As they turned away from the more illuminated thoroughfares, the character of Kilkenny began to subtly shift. The grand facades of the main streets gave way to narrower passages, their entrances almost swallowed by the encroaching darkness. The rhythmic clip-clop of their footsteps on the uneven stones became a more pronounced sound, a solitary beat in the otherwise hushed ambiance. Here, the buildings seemed to huddle closer together, their ancient stone walls bearing the weight of centuries, each weathered brick a testament to countless seasons, storms, and lives lived. Pete found himself instinctively adjusting his pace to match Aine's, his senses sharpening, attuned to the subtle nuances of this less-familiar part of the city. He noticed the way the moonlight caught the dampness on the stone, giving it a soft, almost luminous sheen, and the faint scent of moss and ancient earth that permeated the air.

Aine moved with a quiet confidence, her hand occasionally brushing against the rough texture of a wall as they passed. She didn't point out landmarks or offer historical anecdotes in the same way she had earlier. Instead, her guidance was more organic, a series of subtle gestures and slight shifts in direction that led them deeper into the city's embrace. It felt as though she were drawing him into a secret conversation with Kilkenny itself, a dialogue conducted through shared observation and unspoken understanding. Pete found himself paying closer attention to these subtle cues, the way her gaze would linger on a particular window, the slight pause before she navigated a particularly shadowed alleyway.

"This area," Aine began, her voice low, a soft counterpoint to the stillness, "used to be the heart of the city's artisan community. Before the grander avenues took precedence, these lanes were alive with the sounds of hammers, looms, and the chatter of trade." She gestured towards a row of seemingly unremarkable buildings, their upper floors jutting out over the narrow street, creating a shadowed canopy. "The weavers, the cobblers, the potters – they lived and worked here. Their lives were woven into the very fabric of these streets, just as the threads were woven into their cloth." Pete looked closer, trying to imagine the vibrant activity she described, the bustling energy that must have once filled these now-quiet spaces. He could almost hear the phantom echo of laughter, the ring of metal on metal, the murmur of countless conversations carried on the breeze.

They paused before a particularly sturdy-looking stone building, its doorway framed by a heavy, oak lintel that bore the marks of time and weathering. A faint, almost indecipherable carving was visible, a swirling pattern that Pete would have dismissed as natural erosion if Aine hadn't stopped. "This was a tanner's workshop," she explained, her tone devoid of judgment, simply stating a fact. "It's a trade that's vital, even necessary, but... not one that leaves pleasant memories in its wake. The smell would have been quite something back then." She ran a fingertip over the worn stone, her expression thoughtful. "Yet, even in trades like these, there was artistry. The skill required to treat the hides, to prepare them for use – it was a craft honed over generations. They say the family that owned this place, the O'Connells, were known for their particularly fine leatherwork, their gloves and shoes sought after throughout the region."

As they continued, Pete realized that Aine was not just showing him Kilkenny; she was revealing its layered history, its forgotten narratives, its intimate details. She pointed out a small, almost hidden alcove beneath a protruding stone archway, barely visible in the dim light. "This would have been a place of respite," she murmured, "a spot where someone might have taken a moment to rest, to escape the press of the street. Or perhaps, a meeting place. These narrow passages often held secrets, clandestine encounters." Her words conjured images of hushed conversations, of furtive glances exchanged, of lives lived in the shadows of grander pronouncements. The very architecture of these forgotten spaces seemed to whisper tales of discretion, of moments carefully concealed.

They found themselves near a section of the old city walls, their imposing presence a stark reminder of Kilkenny's defensive past. The moonlight, filtering through the battlements, cast eerie, elongated shadows that seemed to shift and writhe. Aine led him along a less-maintained path that ran parallel to the wall, a narrow track that hinted at infrequent use. "These walls," she said, her voice resonating with a quiet reverence, "are more than just stone. They are the keepers of the city's memory, the silent witnesses to its resilience. Imagine the sentries, pacing these ramparts, their eyes scanning the darkness for any sign of threat. Their vigilance, their dedication – it's all held within these stones."

Pete felt a profound sense of connection to the place, amplified by Aine's insightful commentary. He looked at the rough-hewn stones, the crenellations that still stood testament to their defensive purpose, and could almost feel the weight of responsibility that had rested upon those who had patrolled these heights. Aine's ability to imbue the historical with the personal, to transform a factual account into an immersive experience, was remarkable. She didn't just recite dates and names; she conjured emotions, evoked sensations, and painted vivid pictures with her words. It was as if she were unveiling a hidden layer of reality, a dimension of Kilkenny that existed beyond the visible, a realm of stories and echoes.

She then guided him towards a small, overgrown courtyard, enclosed by ancient, ivy-clad walls. In the center stood a weathered stone well, its opening now partially obscured by a tangle of weeds and moss. "This was once a private garden," she explained, her gaze sweeping across the scene. "Belonging to a family whose fortunes were tied to the wool trade. They say that in times of drought, this well was their only source of water, a lifeline for their household." She knelt by the well, her hand tracing the worn edge of its stone surround. "There are stories, too, of children playing here, of whispered secrets exchanged over its depths. It's a place that has seen joy and hardship, a quiet microcosm of life within these ancient walls."

Pete found himself drawn into the hushed atmosphere of the courtyard. The air was still and heavy, carrying the damp scent of earth and decaying leaves. He imagined the gentle splash of water being drawn, the laughter of children, the quiet conversations that had once filled this space. Aine's presence beside him, her quiet contemplation, added to the sense of intimacy. It felt like a shared moment of discovery, a glimpse into a past that was not just documented, but deeply felt. Her understanding of Kilkenny was not merely intellectual; it seemed to stem from a place of deep, personal connection, as if she carried the city's soul within her.

As they emerged from the courtyard and continued their meandering path, Aine paused beside a particularly old and gnarled oak tree that stood sentinel on the edge of a small, grassy clearing. Its branches, thick and twisted, reached out like ancient arms, their leaves rustling softly in the night breeze. "This tree," she said, her voice taking on a more reflective tone, "is said to be older than the city walls themselves. It has witnessed so much. The passing of generations, the ebb and flow of history, the quiet endurance of life in this place." She looked up at its immense canopy, her expression thoughtful. "There are legends that say it's a guardian, rooted deeply in the earth, a silent observer that remembers everything."

Pete felt a shiver, not of cold, but of something akin to awe. The tree exuded an aura of profound age and resilience, a living monument to the passage of time. He could see why Aine would be drawn to it, why she would attribute such significance to it. It was a tangible link to a past that stretched back beyond human memory, a silent testament to the enduring power of nature and the deep, often unseen, forces that shaped the world. Her words weren't just observations; they felt like an invocation, a gentle reminder of the interconnectedness of all things, of the deep, hidden currents that flowed beneath the surface of everyday life.

She then led him along a section of the wall that was less restored, its stones showing the signs of centuries of exposure to the elements. The moonlight cast dramatic contrasts, highlighting the textures and imperfections of the ancient masonry. "These sections," she explained, "are closer to their original state. They speak of the city's enduring strength, its ability to withstand the forces that sought to diminish it." She touched a stone, its surface rough and uneven. "Each stone has a story, if you know how to listen. The way they are placed, the subtle variations in their colour and form – they tell of the hands that laid them, the skill of the masons, the materials of their time."

Pete found himself captivated by her detailed observations, the way she could perceive so much in what to him was simply ancient stone. It was clear that her knowledge was not confined to the grand historical narratives; it extended to the minutiae, the often-overlooked details that truly brought a place to life. She was revealing Kilkenny in a way no book, no tour guide, no documentary ever could. She was unveiling its soul, its essence, through the intimate lens of her own deep connection. The simple invitation to explore a less-traveled path had, in fact, opened a portal, a doorway into a deeper understanding of Kilkenny, and, Pete suspected, into the enigmatic woman who guided him.

As they continued their walk, the conversation, which had been sparse but meaningful, began to take a more personal turn. Aine spoke of her own childhood, of growing up in Kilkenny, of exploring these very streets and walls with a sense of wonder and curiosity that mirrored his own feelings now. She spoke of family stories, of the whispers of local lore passed down through generations, of a personal history intertwined with the city's own rich tapestry. It was as if she were sharing fragments of her own past, weaving them into the historical narrative, creating a seamless blend of personal experience and collective memory.

"My grandmother," she recounted, her voice soft as they passed a particularly weathered section of the wall, "used to tell me stories about these very ramparts. She'd say that if you listened closely enough on a quiet night, you could hear the echoes of old songs, sung by the soldiers who once stood guard here." She smiled, a touch of wistfulness in her eyes. "I never heard the songs, not exactly. But I always felt a sense of their presence, of the lives they lived, the hopes they held." It was this ability to connect the tangible remnants of the past with the intangible echoes of human experience that made Aine's guidance so compelling. She wasn't just a historian; she was a storyteller, a keeper of memories, someone who understood that history was not just about facts and dates, but about the human lives that shaped them.

The evening was drawing to a close, the moon now higher in the sky, casting a brighter, more defined light. Yet, for Pete, the exploration had only just begun. Aine's invitation, seemingly simple and spontaneous, had opened a door to a deeper, more intricate mystery, one that was only just starting to unfold, drawing him further into the captivating enigma that was Kilkenny, and the equally captivating enigma that was Aine herself. He felt a growing sense of anticipation, a keen awareness that this was not just a walk, but the first tentative step into a narrative that was far more complex and compelling than he could have ever imagined. The city, through her eyes, had transformed from a historical subject into a living, breathing entity, and he, a mere observer, found himself increasingly entwined in its unfolding story, guided by the woman who seemed to hold its very essence within her. He realized, with a growing certainty, that his journalistic assignment had just taken an unexpected and deeply personal turn, a turn that promised to reveal far more than he had initially set out to discover.

THE FIRST HINT OF MYSTERY

Pete found himself increasingly drawn into Aine's curated journey through Kilkenny's less-trodden paths. Her ability to weave personal narratives with historical context created an immersive experience that transcended his initial expectations for a journalistic piece. As they moved away from the more accessible parts of the city, the ancient stones seemed to breathe with a life of their own, each weathered surface a potential repository of untold stories. Aine, with her quiet confidence and insightful observations, acted as both a guide and a conduit, revealing layers of the city that most visitors, and even many locals, would never encounter. It was in these quieter, more shadowed spaces that Pete began to feel the subtle currents of mystery that he suspected were at the heart of his assignment, and more importantly, at the heart of Aine herself.

They paused near a section of the old city walls where the stonework had succumbed to the relentless passage of time and the harsh embrace of the Irish weather. Here, the stones were not merely weathered; they were crumbling, portions of the rampart having sagged inwards, creating a jagged, uneven silhouette against the night sky. Ivy, thick and tenacious, clung to the fissured surfaces, its tendrils probing the very essence of the ancient mortar. Aine gestured towards a particular alcove, a hollowed-out space where the wall had significantly receded. The moonlight, usually a softening presence, seemed to accentuate the decay here, casting deep, unsettling shadows within the recess. "My grandmother used to tell a story," Aine began, her voice dropping to a near whisper, the usual clarity tinged with a newfound hesitancy. "She called this the 'Whispering Nook'."

She didn't offer details of the legend immediately, instead her gaze drifted, seemingly lost in the moon-drenched desolation of the alcove. Pete sensed a shift in her demeanor, a subtle withdrawal that piqued his journalistic instinct. Her usual vibrant engagement seemed momentarily muted, replaced by a pensive stillness. A faint furrow appeared between her brows, a fleeting expression that could have been interpreted as sadness, or perhaps a profound, unspoken sorrow. It was as if a veil had been momentarily drawn across her face, obscuring the depths of her thoughts and feelings. This almost imperceptible change, this flicker of something unarticulated, was the first genuine hint of mystery that Pete had encountered. It was a whisper of a narrative beneath the surface of the city, a story that Aine herself seemed to carry, perhaps even embody.

"She said," Aine continued, her voice barely audible above the gentle sigh of the wind that snaked through the broken battlements, "that on nights like these, when the moon is just so, you can hear... echoes. Not of music, or voices, not in the way you might expect. More like... a resonance. A feeling of something left behind." Her hand, which had been resting on the cool, rough stone of the wall, tightened almost imperceptibly. "She claimed it was a place where lost hopes went to linger. Promises made and broken, dreams that never quite took flight." The vagueness of her words, combined with the melancholy undertone, created an atmosphere of profound intrigue. It wasn't just a historical anecdote; it felt like a personal confession, a glimpse into a family lore that held a significant, perhaps even haunting, weight for her.

Pete felt a prickle of anticipation, the kind that often preceded a significant discovery. He leaned in slightly, his journalist's instinct honed to recognize the subtle nuances of storytelling, the tell-tale signs of a deeper narrative unfolding. "What kind of promises?" he prompted gently, careful not to break the fragile spell she had woven. He knew that pushing too hard too soon could shatter the moment, but he also knew that the seed of a story, once planted, needed careful cultivation.

Aine turned her gaze from the crumbling wall to meet his, and in the dim moonlight, he saw a flicker of something unreadable in her eyes. It was not just sadness now; there was a touch of apprehension, a sense of caution that hadn't been present before. "My grandmother never elaborated," she said, her voice regaining a degree of its usual composure, though the slight tremor remained. "She just warned me, as a child, never to linger too long in the Whispering Nook, especially after dark. She said that while lost hopes might resonate here, sometimes... other things could latch on to them." The implication, veiled though it was, sent a subtle chill down Pete's spine. It was a hint of the uncanny, a suggestion of forces at play that lay beyond the realm of historical fact or folklore.

He looked at the alcove again, the shadows now seeming to deepen, to coalesce into something more substantial than mere absence of light. He imagined the generations of people who had walked these ramparts, the sentries, the lovers, the rebels, each leaving an imprint, an energetic residue. And here, in this specific spot, Aine's grandmother had sensed something more, something that required a warning. It was the first tangible indication that Aine's understanding of Kilkenny, and her connection to its past, was not purely academic or anecdotal. It hinted at a more visceral, perhaps even spiritual, relationship with the city, a relationship that acknowledged the presence of intangible forces.

"Latch on?" Pete repeated, his voice low. "What did she mean by that?"

Aine offered a small, enigmatic smile that didn't quite reach her eyes. "Perhaps she meant that some places hold onto more than just memories," she suggested cryptically. "Perhaps they become conduits for... residual emotions. Intense feelings that, when amplified by places like this, can take on a life of their own." She shook her head slightly, as if dismissing a stray thought. "It's just old wives' tales, I suppose. But she was a very wise woman. And she always seemed to know when something was amiss."

The way she said "amiss" was particularly telling. It wasn't a casual observation about bad luck or minor misfortunes. It carried the weight of a deeper intuition, a sensitivity to the subtle imbalances of the world around her. Pete found himself wondering about the nature of her grandmother's wisdom. Was it a cultural inheritance, a sensitivity passed down through generations of women in Kilkenny, or was it something more personal, a unique attunement that Aine herself might also possess?

As they moved away from the Whispering Nook, the air around them seemed to lighten, the oppressive stillness lifting. Yet, the memory of Aine's words, and the unsettling image of that shadowed alcove, lingered in Pete's mind. This brief, enigmatic exchange had planted a seed of doubt, a subtle questioning of the simple, historical narrative he had come to Kilkenny to uncover. It suggested that Aine was not just a guide to the city's past, but perhaps a keeper of its secrets, a guardian of truths that lay hidden beneath the surface. Her own unspoken emotions, her grandmother's warning – these were the true mysteries, the threads that he now felt compelled to follow.

He found himself observing Aine with a renewed intensity. Her quiet confidence, her deep knowledge, her subtle shifts in mood – they were all pieces of a puzzle he was only beginning to assemble. The fleeting sadness, the veiled apprehension, the cryptic warning about the Whispering Nook – these were not random occurrences. They were deliberate glimpses, perhaps unintentional, into a more complex and perhaps even dangerous facet of her connection to Kilkenny. The city, which had initially appeared as a rich tapestry of historical events and architectural marvels, was now revealing itself to be a place of lingering energies and unspoken histories, and Aine was clearly at its epicenter.

The encounter at the Whispering Nook had served its purpose, not by providing answers, but by posing profound questions. It had confirmed Pete's suspicion that Aine's connection to Kilkenny was far more intricate than he had initially assumed. Her sensitivity to the subtle nuances of the city's atmosphere, her willingness to share fragments of personal lore, her almost instinctive understanding of the unspoken – these were all markers of someone who was deeply entwined with the very soul of the place. The anecdote about the Whispering Nook, with its vague but potent warning, was the first undeniable clue that Aine's own story was as much a part of Kilkenny's enigma as the ancient stones themselves.

As they continued their walk, the conversation gradually shifted back to more familiar historical ground, but for Pete, the landscape had irrevocably changed. The stones of Kilkenny no longer represented just past events; they now seemed to hum with a latent energy, a potential for both illumination and concealment. Aine's brief moment of vulnerability, her grandmother's cautionary tale, had opened a door, revealing a glimpse of a deeper, more complex reality. He realized that his journalistic assignment was no longer simply about documenting history; it was about uncovering the hidden narratives, the whispered secrets, and the personal connections that made Kilkenny, and Aine, so profoundly captivating. The mystery had deepened, and he was now undeniably a part of it, drawn into its intricate web by the enigmatic woman who walked beside him, her presence a constant reminder of the layers of story yet to be revealed. The initial intrigue that had drawn him to Kilkenny had evolved into a genuine curiosity, bordering on a personal quest, to understand not just the city, but the woman who held its secrets so close. He felt a growing certainty that the true story of Kilkenny, the one that mattered most, lay not in the well-trodden paths or documented histories, but in the hushed whispers and shadowed corners that Aine alone seemed to fully comprehend. The subtle shift in her demeanor near the crumbling wall had been more than a momentary lapse; it was the first undeniable clue that Aine's connection to Kilkenny was not merely one of knowledge, but of deep, perhaps even ancestral, resonance. The cryptic warning from her grandmother, hinting at a place where "other things could latch on," was a delicate thread pulled from a much larger, more complex tapestry, a tapestry that Pete was now determined to unravel. It was the first intimation that Aine's relationship with her city might extend beyond the historical and the anecdotal, venturing into territories that skirted the edges of folklore and the unspoken. The fleeting shadow that had crossed her face, the slight tremor in her voice – these were not the markers of a casual observer but of someone intimately acquainted with the emotional currents that flowed beneath the surface of Kilkenny, currents that, on occasion, could become treacherous. This single, poignant moment had elevated his journalistic curiosity into a more profound sense of investigation, hinting at a mystery that was not just about Kilkenny, but about Aine herself, and the legacy she carried within the ancient city.

Chapter Three: Deepening Connections

AINES WORLD UNVEILED

The days that followed the encounter at the Whispering Nook were a testament to Aine's profound connection with Kilkenny. Pete found himself not merely observing, but actively participating in her curated exploration of the city, a journey that felt less like a journalistic assignment and more like an initiation into a hidden world. Aine's introductions to her favored haunts were not just geographical markers; they were portals into her Kilkenny, a version of the city that existed just beyond the gaze of casual tourists. Each place she revealed was imbued with her personal history, her memories, and a subtle understanding that transcended mere intellectual knowledge. It was an intimacy with the city that made Pete feel, at times, like an interloper, a curious outsider peeking through a window into a life and a place he was only beginning to comprehend.

Their mornings often began at a small, unassuming café nestled by the River Nore. It was not the sort of establishment that advertised with bright signs or flashy displays. Instead, its presence was announced by the comforting aroma of freshly brewed coffee that wafted from its doorway, a scent that seemed to beckom those who knew to seek it out. Inside, the walls were adorned with local art, some framed, some simply tacked up with cheerful disregard for convention. The furniture was a mismatched collection of sturdy wooden tables and chairs, each bearing the marks of countless conversations, spilled cups, and shared meals. Aine always ordered the same thing – a strong black coffee and a slice of soda bread, its dense texture a comforting counterpoint to the day's unfolding discoveries. Here, amidst the gentle murmur of conversation and the rhythmic clinking of ceramic mugs, Aine would often share anecdotes about the river, its moods, its historical significance as a lifeline for the city, and the quiet dramas that had unfolded along its banks. She spoke of generations of Kilkenny families who had relied on its waters, of lovers who had met for clandestine meetings beneath its ancient bridges, and of the phantom barge that some claimed still sailed its currents on moonless nights. Pete listened, captivated not just by the stories themselves, but by the way Aine told them. Her voice, usually so clear and measured, would soften, taking on a lyrical quality as she described the play of light on the water, the whisper of reeds in the wind, the enduring strength of the ancient stone bridges that spanned its course. It was as if the river itself was speaking through her, sharing its long and complex history.

One afternoon, Aine led him through a narrow, almost hidden passageway that opened into a secluded garden tucked away behind the venerable walls of St. Canice's Cathedral. The entrance was so unassuming, so easily overlooked, that Pete couldn't believe he had walked past it on numerous occasions without ever suspecting its existence. The garden itself was a small pocket of serenity, a vibrant explosion of color and scent that seemed to exist in its own timeless dimension. Ancient rose bushes, their branches gnarled and twisted like aged storytellers, spilled their fragrant blooms over weathered stone benches. A profusion of wildflowers, their names Aine seemed to know intimately, carpeted the ground beneath the shade of a towering yew tree. In the center of the garden stood a moss-covered sundial, its gnomon casting a long, thin shadow that marked the slow, inexorable passage of time. Aine would often sit here, her gaze thoughtful, as she recounted tales associated with the cathedral, not just the grand historical narratives, but the more intimate, personal stories of the people who had worshipped, worked, and found solace within its ancient embrace. She spoke of medieval monks who had found sanctuary in the cloisters, of parish priests who had ministered to the spiritual needs of the community for centuries, and of the quiet moments of revelation that had occurred in this very garden, when the veil between the mundane and the divine felt thinnest. Pete felt a profound sense of peace here, a stillness that seemed to seep into his very bones. He watched Aine as she traced the intricate patterns of moss on a stone angel, her touch gentle, respectful, as if she were greeting an old friend. Her connection to this place, to the history it represented, was palpable. It was a connection that went beyond knowledge; it was a communion.

Their explorations also led them to a dusty, treasure-filled antique shop on a quiet side street, a place where time seemed to have stalled decades ago. The air inside was thick with the scent of old wood, beeswax polish, and the faint, nostalgic aroma of forgotten lives. Shelves crammed with porcelain figurines, tarnished silver, leather-bound books with brittle pages, and an eclectic assortment of curiosities reached towards the high, shadowed ceiling. Each object seemed to hold a story, a whisper of the past waiting to be coaxed out. Aine moved through the shop with a quiet reverence, her fingers trailing lightly over the surfaces of forgotten treasures. She had a remarkable ability to discern the provenance and the likely history of even the most unassuming items. She would pick up a faded daguerreotype, her eyes alight with speculation as she imagined the life of the person captured within its amber tones, or run her hand over the smooth, worn wood of an old writing desk, conjuring images of letters penned, secrets shared, and dreams conceived. She had a particular fondness for old maps, unfurling them with a practiced grace, her finger tracing the faded lines of ancient boundaries and long-vanished trade routes. For Aine, this shop was not merely a repository of old things; it was a tangible archive of human experience, each object a fragment of a larger, untold narrative. Pete found himself fascinated by her ability to breathe life into these silent witnesses of history. She didn't just see objects; she saw the hands that had made them, the eyes that had beheld them, the lives they had touched.

As Pete spent more time in Aine's company, navigating these hidden corners of Kilkenny, he began to feel a growing sense of being on the outside of a deeply intimate relationship. Aine's knowledge of the city was not merely academic; it was visceral, interwoven with her own personal and familial history. Her insights into the past were often tinged with personal reflections, subtle nods to her own upbringing and the legacy passed down through her family. She spoke of her grandmother, the same woman who had shared tales of the Whispering Nook, with a reverence that suggested a profound influence. It was clear that her grandmother had not just been a storyteller, but a custodian of the city's deeper secrets, a keeper of its soul. Aine's effortless navigation of these less-trodden paths, her instinctive understanding of the subtle energies that seemed to permeate certain places, suggested a connection that was almost inherited, a sensitivity honed over generations. Pete, the seasoned journalist, felt a pang of inadequacy, a realization that his professional objectivity was being challenged by the sheer depth of her personal involvement. He was an observer, meticulously gathering facts and anecdotes, while Aine was a participant, a living embodiment of the city's enduring spirit.

This felt particularly acute when Aine would pause, her gaze fixed on some seemingly unremarkable detail – a weathered carving on a doorway, a peculiar pattern in the brickwork of a wall, a faint inscription on a centuries-old gravestone. In these moments, a stillness would descend upon her, a subtle shift in her demeanor that indicated she was communing with something beyond the immediate physical reality. Pete recognized this as the same quiet intensity he had observed near the Whispering Nook, a flicker of deep connection that she rarely articulated fully. He found himself piecing together fragments of her life, attempting to understand the influences that had shaped her singular relationship with Kilkenny. He learned about her family's long roots in the city, the generations who had lived and worked within its walls, and the oral traditions that had been passed down from mother to daughter. There was a sense, an impression, that Aine carried a living history within her, a direct lineage to the city's past that informed her every observation and interaction.

He noticed how her moods could shift, subtly mirroring the atmosphere of the places they visited. In the vibrant garden, she seemed lighter, her laughter more frequent. In the quiet solitude of the antique shop, a pensive, almost melancholic air would settle upon her. It was as if the city's past wasn't just a subject of study for her, but a palpable presence that affected her deeply. He began to understand that his initial perception of Aine as a knowledgeable guide was too simplistic. She was more than that. She was a conduit, a bridge between the present and the past, and her own emotional landscape was inextricably linked to the stories she unveiled. This made him both increasingly drawn to her and increasingly aware of the subtle boundaries that separated his world from hers. He was a visitor, seeking to understand and document, while she was intrinsically a part of the fabric he was trying to unravel.

The more Pete observed Aine, the more he realized that his journalistic mission was evolving. He had come to Kilkenny to uncover its historical mysteries, but he was increasingly finding himself drawn into the mystery of Aine herself. Her subtle hesitations, her enigmatic smiles, the way her eyes would sometimes cloud over with unspoken thoughts – these were the true enigmas he was encountering. He felt as though he was peeling back layers, not just of Kilkenny's history, but of Aine's carefully guarded inner world. She was a woman who held her city, and its secrets, very close, and he was beginning to suspect that the most compelling stories resided not in the stones or the recorded histories, but within her own quiet intensity. He recognized a pattern in her selective revelations, a gentle way of guiding him through her world without revealing too much, without fully exposing the depths of her own connection. It was a dance of disclosure and reserve, and Pete, ever the observer, found himself captivated by its intricate steps.

He started to anticipate her reactions, to look for the subtle cues that hinted at deeper meanings. When she spoke of a particular historical figure, he would watch her hands, the way they might clench or relax, sensing an unspoken connection or perhaps a quiet judgment. When she described a forgotten corner of the city, he would look for a flicker in her eyes, a momentary stillness that suggested a memory far more vivid than she was willing to articulate. It was as if he were learning a new language, the language of Aine and her Kilkenny, a language spoken in gestures, in silences, and in the subtle resonance of shared spaces. He felt a growing appreciation for her ability to evoke the atmosphere of the past, to make the ancient stones feel alive and present. Yet, with each passing day, the sense of being an outsider only deepened, for her connection was so profound, so intrinsic, that it seemed almost impossible for him to fully grasp its extent. He was like a cartographer trying to map a territory that was constantly shifting, revealing new contours and hidden depths with each turn.

The quiet riverside café, the secluded garden, the antique shop – they were all milestones on a journey that was leading Pete not just deeper into Kilkenny's history, but closer to understanding the woman who was unlocking its secrets for him. He realized that his initial goal of uncovering historical truths was now inextricably linked to unraveling the personal narratives that Aine carried within her. She was not merely a guide; she was a storyteller in her own right, her own life interwoven with the very fabric of the city she so clearly loved. And as he continued to follow her through Kilkenny's shadowed lanes and sun-dappled courtyards, Pete felt an increasing certainty that the most compelling mysteries lay not in the ancient ruins or the documented past, but in the quiet moments, the unspoken words, and the deep, intuitive understanding that Aine possessed. His journalistic curiosity had morphed into something more profound – a quest to understand the woman who held the keys to Kilkenny's soul, and perhaps, in doing so, to unlock a deeper understanding of himself.

WHISPERS OF THE PAST

The rhythmic clatter of the antique shop's bell as they exited was a punctuation mark, not an end. Kilkenny, even as dusk began to bleed through its narrow streets, still held a thousand stories, and Aine, Pete realized, was its most devoted chronicler. Their afternoons, punctuated by Aine's curated revelations, were slowly weaving a new tapestry in Pete's mind, one where the historical landmarks were merely the warp and weft, and Aine herself was the vibrant, enigmatic thread that gave the whole design its life and its mystery. He found himself anticipating not just the places she would lead him, but the subtle shifts in her expression, the particular cadence of her voice when a certain memory surfaced, the almost imperceptible tightening of her hands when a topic veered too close to the personal.

Their conversations, like the winding lanes of the city, often meandered back into the past. Aine possessed an uncanny ability to draw threads from the present and weave them seamlessly into the fabric of Kilkenny's history. Mentioning a particularly intricate carving on a medieval doorway, for instance, would invariably lead her down a path of recollection, not just about the craftsman who had painstakingly carved it centuries ago, but about how her own grandmother had once pointed out a similar, though less ornate, detail on a house on their own street, explaining it as a symbol of good fortune passed down through generations of Kilkenny stonemasons.

These were not mere anecdotes; they were living echoes, transmitted through Aine, imbued with a personal significance that elevated them beyond simple historical fact. Pete, with his journalist's instinct for the story, found himself digging, probing gently, always curious about the source of this deep well of knowledge. He'd ask about her grandmother, seeking to understand the lineage of this inherited wisdom, this intimate understanding of the city.

"Your grandmother," he ventured one afternoon, as they sat on a sun-warmed bench overlooking the medieval walls, the scent of blooming jasmine heavy in the air, "she must have had a remarkable memory, to recall so many of these stories."

Aine smiled, a soft, inward-turning smile that offered little in the way of concrete information. "She had a connection, Pete," she replied, her gaze drifting towards the distant spire of St. Canice's. "A connection to this place. It runs deep in our family, you see. Generations of us have walked these streets, breathed this air, felt the pulse of Kilkenny beneath our feet." She spoke of the continuity, of the shared experiences that bound her family to the city across the centuries, painting a picture of a living, breathing legacy. She described the traditions that had been passed down, the unspoken rules of engagement with the city's past, the subtle ways one learned to read its whispers. There were stories of family gatherings, of evenings spent by the hearth where the past was not just recounted, but relived, where the voices of ancestors seemed to echo in the crackling fire. She spoke of recipes that had been perfected over generations, of festivals celebrated with rituals that had been subtly adapted but never forgotten, of a deep-seated respect for the artisans and the laborers who had built the city.

Yet, when Pete pressed for specifics, for names, for the particular houses her family had called home, for the specific anecdotes that defined her own upbringing within this lineage, Aine would artfully deflect. Her responses were like mist – present, shaping the atmosphere, but impossible to grasp. "Oh, there were so many places," she might say, her eyes twinkling, "each with its own character, its own memories. We were a family that moved with the city, you could say, always finding ourselves drawn to its heart." Or, when asked about her grandmother's particular role in preserving these stories, she might offer, "She was a keeper of the flame, in her own way. She understood that history isn't just in books; it's in the stones, in the soil, in the very air we breathe." These were beautiful sentiments, evocative and poetic, but they offered no tangible facts, no anchors for Pete to moor his journalistic inquiries.

The elusiveness wasn't born of reticence, Pete sensed, but from a profound sense of privacy, a protective shell around a core of deep personal meaning. It was as if her family's history in Kilkenny was so intrinsically woven into the city's own narrative that to isolate it, to dissect it, would be to diminish it. She spoke of her grandmother's hands, often calloused from gardening, but also possessing a surprising delicacy when she handled old objects. She recalled the scent of lavender that always seemed to cling to her grandmother's clothes, a scent that Aine herself now favored. She remembered the stories her grandmother told of the "old ways," of recognizing the subtle signs in the weather, of understanding the language of the birds, of knowing the best spots for foraging wild herbs in the fields surrounding the city. These were glimpses, tantalizing fragments that hinted at a rich and textured life, but always stopped short of revealing the full portrait.

This subtle resistance, this deliberate veil, did not serve to deter Pete; rather, it intensified his fascination. It was like encountering a magnificent sculpture that was partially shrouded, inviting the viewer to imagine the hidden contours, the unseen artistry. He found himself piecing together fragments of Aine's life, not through direct confession, but through her carefully chosen words, her subtle gestures, and the places she deemed worthy of sharing. He learned, for instance, that her grandmother had a particular fondness for the music that played in the older pubs, the traditional Irish tunes that spoke of heartbreak and resilience. Aine, in turn, would sometimes hum a melody as they walked, a melancholic air that Pete felt sure had originated from those same ancestral gatherings. He noticed her quiet reverence for the craftsmanship of old things, her appreciation for the labor and skill that had gone into creating objects that were now considered relics. This, he surmised, was a legacy from her grandmother, a deep-seated respect for the tangible manifestations of human endeavor.

There was a quiet tension that began to thread itself through their growing connection, a subtle friction born of Pete's professional drive to uncover and Aine's innate inclination to protect. He was accustomed to unearthing secrets, to peeling back layers of obfuscation until the truth lay bare. But with Aine, the truth seemed to be a fluid entity, shaped by memory, by emotion, and by a deep, almost spiritual, attachment to her past and to the city itself. He sensed that her family's presence in Kilkenny wasn't a matter of historical record, but of felt experience, a continuous thread of being that defied easy documentation. She was not merely recounting history; she was embodying it, and her own personal narrative was inextricably bound to that broader, more ancient story.

He found himself watching her more closely, trying to decipher the unspoken narratives that flickered across her face. When she spoke of her ancestors' connection to the River Nore, for example, describing how they had relied on its waters for their livelihoods for generations, he would observe the way her gaze softened, the subtle faraway look that suggested she was not just imagining, but remembering. She might mention a specific bridge, not by its historical name, but by a family designation, a marker of a place where generations had crossed, had met, had said goodbye. These were the breadcrumbs he followed, the subtle hints that suggested a deeper reservoir of personal history, a private archive of memories that she was selectively sharing.

"Did your family live by the river?" he asked one blustery afternoon, as they sought refuge in a small, dimly lit bookshop. The air was thick with the comforting scent of aged paper and leather, a fitting sanctuary from the biting wind.

Aine traced the spine of a worn volume of poetry. "We were always connected to its flow," she said, her voice barely above a whisper. "It sustained us, shaped us. It's in our blood, Pete, like the stones of the city itself." She offered metaphors instead of facts, allegories of belonging that were profoundly moving but ultimately unquantifiable. He understood that her family's story wasn't a series of isolated events to be cataloged, but a continuous immersion, a lifelong dialogue with the spirit of Kilkenny.

He learned to appreciate this delicate dance of revelation and reserve. He recognized that his pursuit of information was, in a way, an intrusion into a sacred space. Aine was offering him access to her Kilkenny, a version of the city steeped in personal significance, and he was beginning to understand that this intimacy was a gift, one that required a certain reciprocity of trust and understanding. He found himself drawn to her reticence, seeing it not as a barrier, but as an invitation to engage on a deeper, more intuitive level. Her vagueness about her upbringing wasn't a sign of forgetfulness, but of a profound respect for the intangible aspects of memory, for the emotional resonance of places and people that transcended mere factual recall.

He began to anticipate her hesitations, recognizing them as moments of deep reflection. When she spoke of a certain market square, not just as a historical trading hub, but as the place where her grandfather had first learned the art of bartering from his own father, Pete saw not just a historical detail, but a living connection, a transmitted skill that had shaped a family's identity. He noticed the subtle ways she would pause before speaking about her own childhood, as if carefully selecting the right words, the right memories to share. It was as if she were curating not just her words, but her past, presenting it in a way that was both honest and protective.

"My grandmother used to say," Aine murmured, her gaze fixed on a tarnished silver locket displayed in the bookshop window, "that some stories are best kept close to the heart. They lose their magic when they're shouted from the rooftops." She turned to him then, her eyes holding a gentle challenge. "Some things, Pete, are for knowing, not for telling."

It was in these quiet moments, amidst the whispers of the past that Aine so readily evoked, that Pete began to understand the true depth of her connection to Kilkenny. It wasn't simply that she knew its history; it was that she felt it, that it resonated within her very being. Her elusiveness about her own family wasn't a sign of ignorance, but of a profound understanding that the most potent legacies were often intangible, passed down not in documents, but in feelings, in shared experiences, in the very essence of one's being. He was learning that Kilkenny's secrets, and perhaps Aine's, were not to be unearthed, but to be understood through a shared immersion, a patient observation of the quiet currents that ran beneath the surface of everyday life. The more she shared of Kilkenny, the more he realized he was glimpsing the woman herself, a woman whose own history was as deeply layered and as profoundly captivating as the ancient city she inhabited. This realization, far from diminishing his journalistic curiosity, transformed it into something akin to a respectful inquiry into the soul of a city, and the woman who held its heart.

SHARED EXPERIENCES AND GROWING AFFECTION

The very air within Kilkenny Castle seemed to hum with a history that Aine could translate into a living narrative, and Pete found himself utterly captivated. It wasn't just the grand pronouncements of kings and queens that she spoke of, but the quieter, more intimate moments – the hushed conversations in shadowy alcoves, the rustle of silk skirts on stone floors, the solitary hours spent by a lonely queen gazing out at the rolling green hills. As they walked the ramparts, the wind whipping strands of hair across Aine's face, Pete felt a profound sense of connection, not just to the ancient stones beneath their feet, but to the woman beside him. Her enthusiasm was infectious, her knowledge of the castle's past so deeply ingrained that it felt as though she herself had witnessed centuries unfold.

Imagine," she'd say, her voice rising above the wind's mournful cry, gesturing towards the sprawling grounds below, "the sheer magnitude of the events that have transpired here. Battles fought, treaties signed, lives lived and lost, all within these walls." Pete would watch her, mesmerized, as she traced the outlines of battlements with a gloved finger, her eyes alight with a passion that made the ancient history feel as immediate as a whispered secret. He saw the way her brow furrowed in concentration as she explained the defensive strategies employed by the Normans, the way her smile widened when she spoke of the medieval banquets held in the Great Hall, a smile that held a hint of shared understanding, as if she knew precisely what it felt like to be at the heart of such revelry.

Their exploration of the castle wasn't a mere tour; it was an intimate unfolding of Kilkenny's soul, with Aine as its most eloquent guide. She pointed out the subtle differences in stonework, explaining how each era had left its indelible mark, and then, with a characteristic turn, would link it to a personal anecdote, a story her grandmother might have told about a particular mason or a family legend passed down through generations. "My great-aunt Eleanor swore she heard the phantom footsteps of a medieval page boy near the Watergate Tower," she'd confide, a playful glint in her eye, as they navigated the dimly lit passages. "She claimed he was forever searching for a lost lady-in-waiting." Pete would chuckle, but he also recognized the sincerity in her tone, the genuine belief that the past was never truly gone, merely hidden, waiting to be heard by those who listened closely.

Later, wandering through the meticulously manicured Rose Garden, a riot of color and fragrance against the weathered stone of the castle, the carefully constructed distance Pete had maintained began to crumble. Aine moved with a grace that seemed to echo the timeless beauty of the surroundings, her laughter, light and airy, mingling with the buzzing of bees amongst the blossoms. He found himself drawn to the way she paused to admire a particularly vibrant bloom, her fingers gently brushing a petal, a gesture of profound respect for nature's artistry. It was in these quiet moments, amidst the shared appreciation of beauty, that the romantic currents between them began to surge with an undeniable force.

He noticed the subtle shifts in her demeanor, the way her gaze would linger on his a fraction longer than necessary, the unconscious way she'd lean in when he spoke, as if wanting to absorb every word. The easy camaraderie they had established in the antique shop and on their earlier explorations had deepened into something richer, something that held the promise of more. He found himself anticipating her reactions, the way her eyes would widen with discovery, the way her hand would occasionally reach out to touch his arm in emphasis, a fleeting, electrifying contact.

One particular moment, as they stood overlooking the Nore Valley, the late afternoon sun casting long shadows across the landscape, solidified the shift in their dynamic. A gentle breeze rustled the leaves of an ancient oak tree, and Aine turned to him, her expression soft, contemplative. "It's moments like these," she murmured, her voice barely audible, "when you feel the sheer weight of time, and yet also the enduring beauty of it all. It makes you feel so small, and yet so connected to everything."

Pete, without conscious thought, reached out and gently brushed a stray tendril of hair from her cheek. Her skin was warm beneath his touch, and she didn't pull away. Instead, she met his gaze, her eyes a deep, reflective pool, holding a silent acknowledgment of the unspoken current flowing between them. The world seemed to hold its breath, the distant sounds of the city fading into a hushed reverence. In that suspended moment, surrounded by the grandeur of the castle and the timeless beauty of the valley, the burgeoning romance between them felt as inevitable and as natural as the changing seasons.

As they strolled through the castle grounds, the conversation flowed effortlessly, a blend of historical insights and personal revelations. Pete, usually so adept at maintaining a professional distance, found himself sharing details about his own life, his aspirations, the quiet solitude that often accompanied his work. Aine listened with an attentiveness that made him feel truly seen, her thoughtful questions probing gently, encouraging him to articulate feelings he hadn't even realized he'd suppressed. She, in turn, offered glimpses into her own world, not the carefully guarded historical narratives, but fragments of her personal journey, her love for art, her appreciation for quiet evenings spent reading, her simple joys.

"I've always found solace in stories," she admitted, her voice soft as they sat on a secluded bench, the scent of damp earth and blooming roses surrounding them. "Whether they're etched in ancient stones or whispered in the pages of a well-loved book, they have a way of anchoring us, of reminding us that we're not alone in our experiences." Pete nodded, understanding dawning within him. Her vast knowledge of Kilkenny wasn't just an intellectual pursuit; it was a deeply personal connection, a way of finding her own place within the grand tapestry of human history.

The two weeks they had initially planned for Pete's visit were rapidly dwindling, and the thought of their impending separation began to cast a subtle shadow. What had started as a professional assignment, an opportunity to gather material for his next article, had transformed into something far more profound. He found himself looking forward to their time together with an eagerness that surprised him, an eagerness that extended beyond the historical discoveries. It was the stolen glances, the shared laughter over a particularly absurd historical anecdote, the gentle touch of hands as they navigated a crowded marketplace, that were etching themselves into his memory.

One evening, as they enjoyed a quiet dinner in a small, candlelit restaurant overlooking the River St. Canice, the conversation turned to their lives beyond Kilkenny. Pete spoke of his nomadic existence, the constant travel, the ever-present deadlines. Aine spoke of her rootedness in Kilkenny, her family's deep connection to the city, her own desire to nurture that legacy. There was a moment of quiet contemplation, a shared acknowledgment of the different paths their lives had taken. Yet, in the intimacy of the shared meal, under the warm glow of the candlelight, the differences seemed to fade, replaced by a growing understanding and a palpable desire to bridge any distance that lay between them.

He watched her as she spoke, the subtle animation in her face, the way her eyes sparkled when she was passionate about a subject, the gentle curve of her smile. He realized with a startling clarity that he was falling for her. It wasn't just her intelligence or her charm, but the unique way she inhabited the world, her deep reverence for history interwoven with a genuine warmth and a quiet strength. She had a way of making the past feel alive, and of making the present feel precious.

Later, as they walked along the riverbank, the moonlight painting a silver path across the water, Pete felt an irresistible urge to express the depth of his feelings. The romantic connection between them had solidified, becoming an undeniable force that had woven itself into the fabric of their shared days. He stopped, turning to face her, the gentle murmur of the river providing a soft accompaniment to the beat of his own heart.

"Aine," he began, his voice a little rough, "these past few weeks... they've been unlike anything I've experienced." He saw a flicker of understanding in her eyes, a mirrored emotion that gave him the courage to continue. "I came here looking for a story, for the history of Kilkenny. But I found something much more significant. I found you."

He reached out, taking her hands in his, their warmth a welcome contrast to the cool night air. Her fingers laced with his, a gesture of acceptance, of reciprocation. "You've shown me a Kilkenny I never could have imagined," he continued, his gaze holding hers, "a city that breathes with life and memory. But more than that, you've shown me a different way of seeing, a deeper way of connecting." He felt a profound sense of vulnerability, laying bare his emotions, but it was tempered by the certainty that he was not alone in this journey.

Aine's smile was soft, luminous in the moonlight. "And you, Pete," she replied, her voice a melodic whisper, "have shown me that even the most ancient stones can hold new stories, new possibilities. This 'getaway,' as you called it, has become so much more for me too." She squeezed his hands gently, a silent promise echoing in the gesture. The romantic connection had deepened, transcended mere shared experiences, and was now blossoming into something that felt like the beginning of a profound and enduring romance. The two weeks in Kilkenny were no longer just a vacation; they were the crucible in which a love story was being forged, a testament to the power of shared moments, stolen glances, and the quiet, undeniable pull of two souls finding solace and passion in the heart of an ancient city. The journey into this burgeoning romance felt not like a rapid ascent, but a gentle, persistent unfolding, as natural and as captivating as the ancient city itself.

AN UNEXPLAINED ABSENCE

The late afternoon sun, which had been so warmly bathing Kilkenny in golden hues just hours before, now cast long, melancholic shadows across the cobbled streets as Pete made his way back to the quaint guesthouse. The air, which had previously seemed so alive with the echoes of history and the vibrant presence of Aine, now felt strangely still, almost expectant. He replayed their last conversation in his mind, the casual mention of her needing to attend to a "family matter" that had, without warning, reshaped their entire afternoon. The abruptness of her cancellation, the slight tremor in her voice as she'd quickly finalized their arrangements with a hurried apology, had left him with a peculiar, lingering sense of disquiet. It wasn't just the disappointment of their postponed exploration of St. Canice's Cathedral, a visit he had eagerly anticipated, but something more unsettling.

Aine, with her innate ability to weave the past into the present, to make ancient stones whisper their secrets, had also managed to create a vibrant tapestry of shared moments with Pete. Their connection had deepened with each shared discovery, each lingering gaze, each spontaneous laugh that had rippled through the historic architecture. He had found himself not just admiring her intellect and her passion for Kilkenny, but increasingly drawn to the warmth and genuine kindness that radiated from her. He felt a nascent intimacy, a comfortable ease that had allowed him to shed some of his usual professional reserve, sharing thoughts and feelings he rarely articulated. He had, in short, begun to feel a genuine affection, a romantic pull that had surprised him with its intensity.

Her sudden, almost apologetic, retreat from their planned afternoon felt like a ripple in the otherwise smooth surface of their burgeoning connection. It wasn't a monumental betrayal, not by any stretch, but it was a departure from the open, engaging spirit she had consistently displayed. She had always been so transparent, so eager to share the nuances of Kilkenny's history, and by extension, to allow him glimpses into her own world. Now, a veil, albeit a thin one, seemed to have been drawn. The specifics of this family obligation remained frustratingly vague. "A family matter" was a common enough phrase, a polite buffer against intrusive questions, but coming from Aine, who had so readily unveiled the most obscure historical footnotes, it felt uncharacteristically guarded. He found himself mentally sifting through their conversations, searching for any hint, any unspoken tension that might explain this sudden shift, but found none. Their last meeting had been filled with the usual easy banter and shared anticipation.

He sat by the window of his room, watching as the evening sky deepened to a bruised purple, the streetlights beginning to cast pools of amber light onto the wet cobblestones. He wasn't prone to suspicion, his profession demanding a certain objectivity, a detached observation. Yet, this unexpected shift in Aine's demeanor gnawed at him. He found himself questioning not just her absence, but the nature of her explanation. Had he misinterpreted their connection? Had his own burgeoning feelings led him to project an intimacy that wasn't fully reciprocated? The thought was unsettling. He had allowed himself to be drawn in, to let his guard down, and now, in the face of this subtle evasion, he felt a flicker of vulnerability, a nascent unease that he hadn't anticipated. He replayed her words, her rushed goodbye, the way her eyes had seemed to dart away for a fleeting moment before she'd turned and hurried off. It was a small thing, easily dismissed as mere politeness or a genuine rush, but in the context of their recent shared intimacy, it felt like a deliberate deflection.

The following days unfolded with a quiet rhythm that felt all the more pronounced for Aine's absence. Pete continued his explorations, visiting the Kilkenny Design Centre, browsing through the local craft shops, and revisiting some of the sites they had explored together, but the city felt subtly different, less vibrant, without her by his side. He found himself checking his phone with a frequency that bordered on obsessive, half-expecting a message, an explanation, a resumption of their shared journey. The absence, however, remained. He received a brief, apologetic text the following evening, a reiteration of her regret and a promise to explain soon, but the 'soon' remained undefined, a tantalizingly vague promise that did little to assuage his growing unease.

He tried to focus on his work, on the historical accounts he was meticulously documenting, the photographs he was taking, the narrative he was weaving for his readers. But the story of Kilkenny now seemed inextricably linked to the story of Aine, and her sudden inaccessibility had introduced a narrative thread that felt incomplete, even unsettling. He found himself poring over historical documents, searching for parallels, for patterns of behavior that might shed light on her actions, but history, for all its depth, offered no easy answers to the complexities of human relationships.

The initial pang of disappointment had morphed into a more persistent, gnawing question. He appreciated the nuances of Kilkenny's past, the way generations had left their mark, the layers of history that unfolded with careful study. He understood that people, like cities, had their own hidden depths, their own quiet histories that might not always be readily apparent. But Aine had presented herself as an open book, a guide eager to share all that she knew. This sudden opaqueness felt like a departure from that established truth, and it planted the first seeds of doubt in his mind, not about her character, but about the extent of his own understanding of it. He wondered if the very qualities that had drawn him to her – her deep connection to the city, her almost encyclopedic knowledge – also allowed her to maintain a certain distance, a privacy that he had, perhaps, mistaken for openness.

He recalled their conversations about the complexities of family, the unspoken obligations and loyalties that often shaped people's lives. Perhaps this family matter was indeed something significant, something deeply personal that she was not yet ready to share. He tried to approach it with the same objective detachment he applied to historical research, considering multiple possibilities, acknowledging the limitations of his own perspective. Yet, the romantic connection he felt, the genuine warmth and affection that had blossomed between them, made it difficult to remain entirely dispassionate. Her absence was felt not just as a professional setback, but as a personal void.

He found himself revisiting the Rose Garden, the very place where their connection had truly begun to deepen, where the carefully constructed distance had first begun to crumble. The roses were still in bloom, their petals unfurling in a silent testament to the enduring beauty of nature, but their fragrance seemed to carry a different scent now, tinged with a subtle melancholy. He sat on the same secluded bench, the late afternoon sun casting a different kind of light, one that seemed to illuminate the shadows of doubt that had begun to creep into his thoughts. He had offered her a vulnerability, a glimpse into his own life, and now he was left in a state of quiet uncertainty.

He considered reaching out again, perhaps to her usual place of work, but decided against it. He didn't want to appear demanding or intrusive. It was her prerogative to manage her personal life, and while he was disappointed, he also respected her privacy. Still, the question of transparency lingered. In any relationship, whether professional or personal, a degree of open communication was essential, a mutual willingness to share, to be understood. Her vagueness, however unintentional, had created a small but significant gap, a space where speculation could begin to fill the void.

He wondered if his own assumptions had been too grand, too eager. Had he mistaken polite camaraderie for something more profound? Had he, in his eagerness to find a compelling narrative, projected a romantic entanglement where none truly existed? These were the questions that circled his mind, a subtle undercurrent of disquiet beneath the surface of his objective professional observations. The charm of Kilkenny, so vividly brought to life by Aine, now seemed to hold a certain enigmatic quality, much like the woman herself. He knew that the past, even the recent past, could be interpreted in many ways, and that people's motivations were often far more complex than they initially appeared. Her unexplained absence, coupled with her characteristic vagueness, had planted the first seed of doubt in his mind, making him question not just the transparency of their burgeoning relationship, but the very foundations upon which it seemed to be built. He hoped, with a quiet intensity, that this was merely a temporary detour, a brief interruption in an otherwise promising narrative, and that the woman who had so effortlessly captured his attention would soon re-emerge, her explanations as clear and as illuminating as her historical insights had always been. The story of Kilkenny, and his own story within it, suddenly felt far less predictable, and infinitely more complex, than he had ever anticipated.

PETES GROWING SUSPICIONS

Pete found himself adrift in the quiet ebb and flow of Kilkenny, the vibrant energy that had previously captivated him now tinged with an almost imperceptible undercurrent of unease. The city, once a kaleidoscope of history and burgeoning affection, had begun to feel like a complex manuscript with certain pages deliberately blurred. His initial disappointment at Aine's abrupt departure had, over the ensuing days, coalesced into a more persistent, almost analytical curiosity. He wasn't a man given to facile assumptions, his professional life demanding a rigorous examination of evidence, a dispassionate sifting of fact from fiction. And in the recent interactions with Aine, he felt a growing need to apply that same meticulous scrutiny.

He found himself replaying their conversations, not with the fond nostalgia of someone recalling shared joy, but with the sharp focus of an investigator piecing together a fragmented narrative. He'd catch himself pausing mid-sentence, his mind snagging on a particular turn of phrase, a fleeting expression he'd initially dismissed as irrelevant. For instance, during their exploration of Kilkenny Castle, when he'd casually remarked on the resilience of the medieval stonework, he recalled Aine's unusually sharp intake of breath, a barely perceptible flinch before she'd smoothly redirected the conversation to the castle's later architectural modifications. At the time, he'd attributed it to a momentary distraction, perhaps the vastness of the Black Tower looming overhead. Now, however, it felt like a deliberate, almost instinctive, deflection.

Then there was the incident at St. Francis's Abbey. They had been discussing the effigies, the silent sentinels of a bygone era, when Pete had mused aloud about the enduring nature of memory, how even the most forgotten figures could be brought back to life through diligent research. Aine had been unusually quiet then, her gaze fixed on a particular, weathered tomb. When he'd gently probed, asking if she recognised the effigy, she'd offered a vague, "It's a very old one, Pete. Many stories are lost to time." The response was, on the surface, perfectly reasonable, yet the subtle tremor in her voice, the way her fingers had traced the worn stone as if seeking an answer there herself, struck him as more than mere historical contemplation. It felt like a personal connection, a hesitant acknowledgement of a shared understanding, quickly stifled.

He started to notice a pattern, a subtle hesitancy whenever he ventured too close to certain aspects of Kilkenny's more shadowed past. His interest wasn't morbid; it was rooted in his professional fascination with how societies grappled with their darker histories, their triumphs and their failures interwoven. He'd inquired about the specifics of certain renovations at St. Canice's, wondering about the practicalities of preserving such ancient structures, and Aine had responded with a general overview of the historical periods of repair. But when he'd pressed for details about a particular section, a seemingly minor reconstruction from the early 19th century, her knowledge, usually so encyclopedic, seemed to falter. She'd offered a generalized explanation, a somewhat dismissive comment about the "practical necessities of the time," and quickly steered them towards the more aesthetically pleasing elements of the cathedral's design. It was as if certain historical details were off-limits, shielded by a carefully constructed curtain of vagueness.

His internal monologue became a constant echo chamber of their interactions. He'd mentally dissect her smiles, the subtle shifts in her posture, the moments when her eyes seemed to hold a flicker of something unsaid, something perhaps even anxious. Had he misinterpreted the warmth and openness she'd initially displayed? Had his own burgeoning romantic feelings colored his perception, creating a narrative that didn't align with reality? The thought was unsettling, a quiet tremor beneath the surface of his composure. He was a historian, trained to observe, to analyze, to connect seemingly disparate pieces of information. And the current pieces of the Aine puzzle didn't quite fit.

He found himself increasingly drawn to the Kilkenny Archive Centre, not for his own research, but as a quiet place to sit and reflect, to mentally sift through the fragments of their recent encounters. He'd observe the diligent archivists, their focused intensity, the way they treated each document with a reverence that suggested a deep understanding of its hidden significance. It mirrored, in a way, his own burgeoning need to understand the unspoken narrative surrounding Aine. He felt a growing suspicion, not of malice, but of something far more complex: a carefully guarded secret, a facet of her life or her connection to Kilkenny that she was unwilling or unable to reveal.

He re-read the initial emails they'd exchanged, the polite, professional tone that had gradually warmed into something more personal. There had been no hint of deception, no red flags to warn him. She had presented herself as an enthusiastic local guide, a conduit to Kilkenny's rich tapestry. But now, in the absence of her immediate presence, he began to see the subtle ways she had controlled the flow of information, expertly navigating his questions, revealing only what she deemed appropriate. It was a skill, he grudgingly admitted, that spoke of a deep understanding of human psychology, a talent for managing perceptions.

The unease wasn't a sudden eruption; it was a slow, insidious creep, like ivy gradually obscuring the facade of an old building. He started to question the very nature of their connection. Was it the genuine spark he believed it to be, or was it a carefully orchestrated experience designed for his benefit, a curated glimpse into the city that served a purpose beyond mere historical appreciation? The romantic idealism that had begun to bloom in his heart was now being challenged by a more pragmatic, even cynical, consideration. He felt like a scholar who had discovered an ancient text, only to realize that the most crucial passages had been deliberately expunged.

He found himself revisiting the Rose Garden again, the site of their first truly intimate conversation. The roses were still vibrant, their colours rich and deep, but to Pete, they now seemed to possess a more complex fragrance, one that hinted at secrets rather than simple beauty. He sat on the same bench, but this time, his gaze wasn't fixed on the blooms, but on the distant cityscape, the spires and rooftops that Aine knew so intimately. He tried to see Kilkenny through her eyes, to understand what hidden layers might exist beneath the surface he had been shown.

He wondered if her evasiveness stemmed from a place of genuine fear, or perhaps a sense of obligation that he couldn't comprehend. Kilkenny, for all its historical charm, was still a living, breathing city, with its own contemporary currents and complexities. Perhaps her "family matter" was a genuine crisis, one that required her complete attention and forbade any further distractions. Yet, the historian in him couldn't quite shake the feeling that there was more to it, a deliberate withholding of information that felt... strategic.

He remembered a particular anecdote she'd shared about the Black Abbey, a tale of monastic life and its eventual dissolution. She had spoken with a certain detached reverence, her voice taking on a slightly more formal tone, as if reciting from a well-worn script. When he'd inquired about the specifics of the land ownership changes following the dissolution, the names of the families who had acquired the abbey's holdings, her response had been a swift, "The records are extensive, Pete. It's a labyrinth of legal jargon." Again, a polite brush-off, but one that felt designed to shut down further inquiry.

The more he replayed their interactions, the more he noticed the subtle art of redirection, the way she'd expertly pivot from a potentially revealing detail to a more general, easily digestible fact. It wasn't a conscious act of deception, he told himself, but perhaps a practiced habit, a way of maintaining control over her narrative, and by extension, his perception of her. He realized that his initial enchantment had perhaps made him less discerning, more willing to accept the surface narrative at face value. Now, the surface was beginning to peel away, revealing something less clear, more enigmatic.

He found himself scrutinizing the photographs he'd taken with Aine, searching for clues in her expressions, the way she held herself.

In some, she was animated, her eyes sparkling with enthusiasm. In others, there was a subtle guardedness, a tension around her mouth that he hadn't noticed at the time. He wondered if these were the moments when she was contemplating the "family matter," or when she was actively managing the information she was sharing with him.

The thought that Aine, and by extension Kilkenny itself, might not be precisely what they seemed gnawed at him. He had come to Kilkenny seeking authentic history, unspoiled by the gloss of modern tourism. He had found that authenticity in Aine, or so he had believed. Now, he was forced to consider the possibility that the most authentic narrative was one that remained partially untold, a deliberately obscured chapter. His growing suspicions weren't about doubting her character outright, but about questioning the completeness of the picture she had presented. He felt a strange duality: the lingering affection for the woman he believed he was getting to know, warring with the historian's imperative to uncover the truth, however complex or uncomfortable it might be. The romantic narrative was developing an unexpected subplot, one of intrigue and unanswered questions, and Pete, the detached observer, was finding himself reluctantly drawn into its unfolding mystery. He found a peculiar irony in the situation; he was a historian tasked with uncovering the past, and now he felt he was uncovering a more immediate, personal history that was being carefully veiled from him. The mystery of Kilkenny was deepening, and Aine was at its enigmatic heart.

Chapter Four: Kilkenny's Hidden Layers

EXPLORING THE MEDIEVAL MILE

The morning air in Kilkenny, though crisp and invigorating, carried a different weight for Pete than it had just days before. The initial thrill of discovery, the effortless charm of Aine's guidance, had been replaced by a quiet, almost methodical determination. He needed to understand Kilkenny, not just as a tourist beholding its picturesque facades, but as a historian seeking the deeper strata, the unwritten narratives that even the most passionate local could overlook, or perhaps, deliberately obscure. His mind, still sifting through the subtle evasions and guarded responses of their recent interactions, felt a distinct pull towards a more independent exploration. He decided to walk the Medieval Mile, not as a guided tour, but as a personal pilgrimage into the heart of the city's layered past.

He began at the outset of the Mile, the eastern end where the city's medieval core truly began to assert itself. The familiar stones beneath his feet seemed to hum with a silent energy, a testament to centuries of footsteps that had trod the same path. He'd already visited St. Canice's Cathedral with Aine, but today, he approached it with a renewed sense of purpose. The majestic structure, a formidable testament to Norman and later Gothic influence, loomed before him, its imposing presence a constant reminder of the city's enduring legacy.

He entered the cathedral grounds, the air thick with the scent of old stone and damp earth. The tombstones, weathered and worn, told silent stories of generations past, each inscription a faded whisper from a forgotten life. He lingered, running his fingers over the pitted surfaces, imagining the hands that had carved them, the lives they had commemorated. These were the raw materials of history, tangible links to individuals who had once walked these very grounds.

His gaze, however, was drawn inexorably upwards, to the magnificent round tower that stood sentinel beside the cathedral. It was a structure that had always captivated his imagination, a stark, cylindrical edifice that seemed to defy the passage of time. He remembered Aine's brief mention of its construction, the almost casual way she'd stated it predated the current cathedral, a silent observer to centuries of change. Today, he was determined to climb it, to gain a perspective that only elevation could provide.

The ascent was a journey into the past, each rough-hewn stone step a testament to the skill and labor of its medieval builders. The tower was narrow, the spiraling staircase enclosing him in a tight embrace of ancient masonry. As he climbed, the light grew dimmer, punctuated by narrow slits in the stone that offered fleeting glimpses of the outside world. He imagined the watchmen who had once stood here, their eyes scanning the horizon for approaching threats, their lives intimately tied to the fortunes of this city.

With each upward step, Kilkenny seemed to unfurl beneath him, not as a static postcard, but as a living, breathing organism, its history interwoven with its present. He emerged onto the small, windswept platform at the apex, the panoramic vista unfolding in a breathtaking spectacle. The city lay spread out before him, a tapestry of red-tiled roofs, narrow lanes, and ancient structures, all cradled within the embrace of the River Nore.

From this vantage point, the true essence of the Medieval Mile revealed itself. He could trace its sinuous path, a vibrant artery connecting Kilkenny Castle at one end to the cathedral and its associated monastic buildings at the other. The density of historical architecture was striking. Here, a sturdy medieval tower stood beside a Georgian townhouse, and there, the remnants of an ancient city wall were incorporated into the fabric of a modern building. It was a physical manifestation of history layered upon itself, a testament to the city's resilience and its ability to absorb and adapt rather than discard.

He could see the intricate layout of the old town, the way the streets followed the contours of the land, dictated by needs and considerations lost to the mists of time. The newer buildings, while undeniably present, seemed to nestle within the existing framework, respectful of the ancient bones of the city. It wasn't a jarring juxtaposition, but a conversation across centuries, each era adding its voice to the ongoing narrative.

His historian's eye began to pick out details he hadn't noticed before. The faint outline of a long-vanished city wall, the subtle shifts in stonework that indicated different periods of construction, the clustering of buildings around specific points of historical significance. He could almost visualize the bustling marketplace that would have once animated these streets, the merchants hawking their wares, the citizens going about their daily lives, oblivious to the fact that they were living within a tableau that would, centuries later, be studied and admired.

He noticed the proximity of certain structures, the way St. Canice's and the round tower stood in such close concert with the Dominican Priory (the Black Abbey), though on opposite sides of the Mile. He knew Aine had touched upon the Black Abbey's history, her brief mention of the dissolution of the monasteries still echoing in his mind. From this height, he could appreciate the strategic importance of these religious and civic centres, their placement a deliberate act of urban planning designed to shape the spiritual and temporal life of the community.

The view wasn't just a visual feast; it was a conceptual revelation. He could see how the Medieval Mile wasn't merely a tourist trail, but the original circulatory system of Kilkenny, the locus of power, commerce, and faith. The newer parts of the city, sprawling outwards, seemed almost secondary, an addition to this ancient, enduring core. He could trace the river, its vital role in the city's development evident from this elevated perspective. He saw the castle, a formidable bastion dominating the skyline at the western end of the Mile, and imagined the centuries of political and social drama that had unfolded within its walls.

As he scanned the rooftops, his gaze fell upon a particular area, a cluster of buildings that seemed to possess a denser, more tightly packed historical feel. He tried to recall Aine's commentary on that specific part of the city, but his memory offered only a vague outline, a sense that she had navigated his questions about it with practiced ease, offering generalities rather than specifics. Now, seeing it from above, he felt an intensified curiosity. What stories lay hidden in that particular neighbourhood, what forgotten pathways, what deliberately obscured layers?

He descended from the tower, the sunlight on the ground feeling like a return to a more grounded reality, though his mind was still soaring with the insights gained from his elevated perch. The Medieval Mile, once a straightforward concept, had now revealed itself as a complex palimpsest, a historical document written and rewritten over time, with much still concealed beneath the surface. His independent exploration had already yielded a deeper appreciation for the city's spatial and historical evolution, and it had, in turn, sharpened his focus on the subtle gaps in Aine's narrative. The historian in him was now fully engaged, not just with Kilkenny's past, but with the personal enigma that Aine represented within it. He felt a growing conviction that understanding the city, in its true, unvarnished complexity, was intrinsically linked to understanding her. The walk had been more than just sightseeing; it had been a crucial step in his ongoing investigation, a confirmation that Kilkenny held more secrets than he had initially imagined, secrets that Aine seemed uniquely positioned to both reveal and conceal. He decided to continue his walk, letting the stones guide him, hoping that the ground level held more direct answers than the aerial view.

He continued his stroll along the Mile, now with a more focused gaze, scrutinizing the architectural details, the inscriptions on plaques, the subtle changes in building materials. He passed the Tholsel, a fine example of medieval civic architecture, its imposing structure hinting at the administrative power once wielded within its walls. He paused, imagining the legal proceedings, the public announcements, the vibrant pulse of civic life that had once defined this space. He found himself mentally cross-referencing his observations with his memories of Aine's descriptions, seeking consistency, and finding instead, more subtle deviations. Her account of the Tholsel, he recalled, had been brief, focused on its external appearance, with no delving into its specific historical functions beyond a generalized mention of civic administration.

His route led him towards the heart of the old city, where the narrow laneways branched off the main thoroughfare, inviting exploration. He stepped into one such lane, its cobblestones worn smooth by countless feet. This was where the city's secrets might truly lie, tucked away from the main thoroughfares, accessible only to those who ventured beyond the obvious. He found himself drawn to the remnants of ancient doorways, the shadowy recesses of alleyways, the weathered facades that hinted at stories untold. He was searching for context, for the small details that might illuminate the larger narrative he was trying to construct.

He passed by the Shee Alms House, a beautiful example of Tudor architecture, its ornate facade a stark contrast to the more austere medieval structures he had been observing. He remembered Aine mentioning its charitable purpose, its role in housing the city's poor. But again, her explanation had been a surface-level summary, devoid of the deeper historical context he now craved. Who had built it? What were the specific circumstances that led to its creation? These were the questions that now occupied his mind, questions that seemed to intentionally elude Aine's direct engagement.

He continued his perambulation, the Medieval Mile unfolding before him like a historical map, each building, each street, a chapter in Kilkenny's long and complex story. He found himself lingering near the old city walls, imagining their formidable presence in centuries past, their role in defining and protecting the urban space. He ran his hand over the rough texture of the ancient stones, feeling a tangible connection to the people who had built and defended them. He thought about the strategic placement of these walls, the way they had shaped the city's growth and development, and how their presence, even in fragmented form, still dictated the urban landscape.

His walk brought him back to the vicinity of the Black Abbey, the Dominican Priory he had observed from the round tower. He decided to approach it from ground level this time, to see if a closer inspection would reveal anything new. The ruins were atmospheric, their weathered stones speaking of a turbulent past. He recalled Aine's almost dismissive comment about the land ownership changes following the dissolution, her assertion that the records were a "labyrinth of legal jargon." Now, standing amongst the ruins, he felt a pang of frustration. What specific families had benefited from the dissolution? What legal machinations had transferred these sacred lands into private hands? These were not mere academic curiosities; they were the missing pieces of a puzzle that seemed to connect directly to the fabric of Kilkenny's present and, perhaps, to Aine's own connections to it.

He explored the surrounding area, noticing the proximity of other historical buildings, the way they clustered together, forming distinct neighbourhoods within the larger urban fabric. He saw how the Medieval Mile was not a singular, monolithic entity, but a dynamic network of interconnected spaces, each with its own history and its own secrets. He tried to visualize the original layout, the original functions of these spaces, and how they had been altered and adapted over the centuries.

As he continued his exploration, his historian's instinct for detail was sharpened by his personal quest. He noticed a particular style of window tracery that recurred in several buildings, indicating a common period of construction or influence. He observed the subtle variations in the thickness and composition of the walls, clues to different construction techniques and materials used over time. These were the physical manifestations of Kilkenny's layered history, the silent witnesses to its evolution.

He found himself drawn to the less frequented corners, the areas that seemed to have been overlooked by the usual tourist routes. In these quieter pockets, he felt a greater sense of authenticity, a feeling of stepping back in time more profoundly. He encountered weathered stone archways, remnants of forgotten courtyards, and the haunting beauty of crumbling facades. Each discovery was a small victory, a shard of insight into the city's hidden depths.

He paused by a particularly old-looking building, its stone facade darkened with age and weather. He noticed an inscription above the doorway, partially obscured by lichen. He carefully brushed away the growth, revealing faint lettering that hinted at its original purpose. It was a small detail, easily missed, but it sparked a surge of excitement within him. This was the essence of historical discovery, the uncovering of the unseen, the forgotten.

He continued his walk, the sun beginning its slow descent towards the horizon, casting long shadows across the ancient stones. The Medieval Mile had revealed itself not as a simple historical pathway, but as a complex, multi-layered narrative, a physical embodiment of Kilkenny's past and present intertwined. His independent exploration had deepened his appreciation for the city's historical richness and, more importantly, had intensified his awareness of the carefully guarded secrets that lay beneath its surface. The fragmented insights he had gathered, coupled with the subtle evasions he recalled from Aine, were beginning to coalesce into a more compelling, and at times, unsettling picture. Kilkenny, he was realizing, was a city that revealed its layers only to those who were willing to look beyond the obvious, and his quest to understand Aine was increasingly becoming a quest to understand the city itself, in all its enigmatic complexity. He felt a renewed sense of purpose, a historian's drive to peel back the layers, to uncover the truth, no matter how deeply it might be buried.

THE BLACK ABBEYS SECRETS

The Black Abbey stood as a solemn sentinel, a testament to a past that had weathered centuries of change, its stones whispering stories of devotion, dissolution, and the persistent hum of memory. Pete stepped across the threshold of what remained of the Dominican priory, the cool, still air immediately enveloping him, a palpable contrast to the bustling energy of the Medieval Mile he had just traversed. The silence here was different; it was a resonant silence, filled with the phantom echoes of chanting monks, the rustle of habits, and the steady rhythm of prayer that had once sanctified these grounds. He felt a profound sense of stepping into a hushed, sacred space, even in its ruined state.

He walked slowly, his footsteps soft on the worn flagstones that still bore the marks of countless processions. The surviving architecture, though fragmented, spoke volumes. The soaring arches, reaching towards a sky that now pierced through where a roof once stood, hinted at the grandeur of the original structure. Pete traced the outline of a window with his fingertips, imagining the stained glass that would have once cast kaleidoscopic patterns of light onto the floor, transforming the very air into a devotional spectacle. Each remaining column, each fractured piece of carved stonework, was a fragment of a larger narrative, a puzzle piece he was slowly trying to assemble.

His gaze swept across the nave, the open expanse where the friars would have gathered for services. He could almost picture them, robed figures moving with practiced grace, their voices rising in unison, a spiritual anchor in a turbulent world. The weight of their presence, though long gone, felt heavy, imbuing the air with a sense of solemnity and purpose. This was a place where lives had been dedicated to contemplation, to service, to the pursuit of the divine. He wondered about their daily routines, the simple acts of faith that would have punctuated their days, the shared meals, the studies, the quiet moments of reflection.

He moved towards what would have been the choir, the area where the monks would have been seated. Here, the remnants of the altar and the surrounding stonework were more defined, offering a clearer glimpse into the heart of the monastic worship. He paused, his eyes scanning the walls, searching for any surviving inscriptions or decorative elements that might offer a more direct connection to the past. The stone was cool and unyielding beneath his touch, yet he imagined it had once been animated by the fervent faith of the men who had built and worshipped here.

His attention was drawn to a specific area, a recessed alcove that seemed to have escaped the worst of the ravages of time. There, resting on a low plinth, was an effigy. It was a stone carving of a person, likely a significant figure associated with the abbey, though time and the elements had rendered its features indistinct. The face was worn smooth, the inscription below it a mere whisper of its former self, a series of faint indentations that defied easy deciphering. Pete knelt, his historian's curiosity piqued. He gently brushed away a thin layer of dust and moss, hoping to coax some clarity from the weathered stone.

As he studied the effigy, an odd resonance began to settle over him. It wasn't a direct, intellectual understanding, but a more intuitive connection, a feeling that a silent narrative was embedded within the very stones of this sacred place. The figure, though anonymous now, had once been someone. Someone important enough to warrant such a memorial. He found himself wondering about their life, their contributions to the abbey, their place in the history of Kilkenny. Was this a friar, a benefactor, perhaps someone of noble birth whose piety or patronage had earned them this resting place?

He tried to make out the inscription, his mind working to fill in the gaps, to interpret the worn symbols. It was like trying to read a palimpsest, a text layered over another, with the original obscured by the passage of time and the erosion of memory. He imagined the original carver, meticulously chipping away at the stone, creating a likeness that would endure for centuries. And yet, here it was, nearly erased, a poignant reminder of the transient nature of even the most enduring human efforts.

The silence of the abbey seemed to deepen as he focused on the effigy. He could hear the distant sounds of the city filtering in – the faint murmur of traffic, the occasional cry of a bird – but within the abbey walls, the world outside felt distant, muted. He was enveloped in a pocket of profound stillness, a space where the concerns of the present seemed to recede, replaced by the timeless weight of the past. He thought about the friars who would have passed this effigy daily, perhaps offering a prayer, perhaps acknowledging the legacy of the person it represented.

He continued to study the surrounding area, the surviving walls of the priory's cloister, the remnants of monastic cells. He tried to reconstruct the layout in his mind, to envision the complete monastic complex as it would have stood in its heyday. He imagined the friars walking in the cloister, their daily meditations punctuated by the changing light and the seasons. He considered the practicalities of their lives – the kitchen, the scriptorium, the dormitory. Each stone, each arch, each surviving fragment was a clue, a breadcrumb leading him deeper into the abbey's hidden layers.

He found himself drawn to a particular section of wall where the stonework was particularly rough and irregular. It looked older, more primitive than the refined masonry found elsewhere. Could this be a remnant of an even earlier structure, perhaps on which the Dominican priory had been built? Kilkenny, he knew, was a city of layers, with each era building upon, or incorporating, what had come before. The Black Abbey, founded in the 13th century, was no exception, and the possibility of even deeper historical strata beneath its foundations was a tantalizing prospect.

He thought back to Aine's brief mention of the Black Abbey during their earlier conversation. She had spoken of the Dissolution of the Monasteries, the historical event that had led to the abbey's eventual abandonment and ruin, mentioning it almost as a footnote in the city's grander narrative. She had been dismissive of the intricate legalities surrounding the land transfers, characterizing the records as an impenetrable "labyrinth." Pete's historian's mind, however, saw not an impenetrable labyrinth, but a rich tapestry of legal and social history waiting to be unraveled. Who had been the beneficiaries of this dissolution? Which families had gained control of these vast monastic estates? The questions continued to accumulate, each one a thread pulling him further into the intricate web of Kilkenny's past.

He stood up from his kneeling position, his knees stiff from the prolonged posture. He took a final, lingering look at the effigy, a silent promise to himself to try and uncover its identity. There was something about its near-obliteration that resonated with him, a sense of lost voices and forgotten stories that he felt compelled to bring back to light. The Black Abbey, in its quiet, ruined magnificence, had offered him a profound sense of connection to the past, a tangible link to the lives and beliefs of those who had come before. It was a place that held its secrets close, but not so close that they could not, with patience and persistence, be coaxed out.

As he prepared to leave, his gaze fell upon a weathered stone basin near the entrance, likely part of a lavabo where the friars would have washed their hands before meals. It was a small, functional detail, yet it spoke of the daily rhythms of monastic life, the simple rituals that formed the bedrock of their existence. It was these small, humanizing details that most often captivated him, these glimpses into the ordinary lives lived within the grand sweep of history.

He stepped back out into the sunlight, the transition from the abbey's cool interior to the open air of the city a jolt. The silence of the Black Abbey lingered in his mind, a quiet counterpoint to the ongoing exploration of Kilkenny. He knew that his time here had been more than just a visit to a historical ruin; it had been an encounter with the enduring power of faith, the inevitable tide of historical change, and the persistent mystery of the human story. The effigy, with its nearly erased inscription, remained a focal point, a symbol of the lost narratives that still held the potential to unlock deeper truths about Kilkenny and the people who had shaped its past, and perhaps, its present. He felt a quiet resolve settle within him – the Black Abbey's secrets, like the city's own, were waiting to be unearthed, and he was more determined than ever to be the one to do the uncovering. The weight of centuries felt less like a burden and more like an invitation, a call to delve deeper into the layers of time that made Kilkenny so utterly compelling. He knew, with a certainty that settled deep in his historian's soul, that the Black Abbey held more than just stones and shadows; it held whispers of truth, and he was ready to listen. His gaze drifted back to the weathered facade, a silent promise passing between him and the ancient stones. He would return, armed with knowledge, with questions, and with a quiet determination to decipher the stories etched into its very being.

LOCAL LEGENDS AND FOLKLORE

The chill that had settled in Pete's bones inside the Black Abbey seemed to follow him back out into the crisp Kilkenny air, but it was a different kind of chill now, one tinged with the prickle of an unanswered question. He found himself drawn to a small shop tucked away on a side street, its window a delightful jumble of antique postcards, dusty books, and handcrafted trinkets. The sign above the door, faded and charmingly crooked, read "Aisling's Antiques & Curiosities." It felt like the kind of place where stories, rather than just objects, were preserved.

As he pushed open the door, a small bell tinkled merrily, announcing his arrival. The interior was a cozy labyrinth of towering shelves and overflowing display tables, the air thick with the comforting scent of aged paper and polished wood. Behind a counter laden with silver brooches and intricately carved wooden boxes sat an elderly woman. Her silver hair was pulled back into a neat bun, and her eyes, a startlingly bright blue, twinkled with an intelligence that belied her delicate frame. She wore a knitted shawl, a kaleidoscope of blues and purples, and her hands, gnarled with age, moved with surprising deftness as she sorted through a pile of lace.

"Dia duit," Pete greeted her, his voice a little rough from disuse.

The woman looked up, her smile warm and immediate. "And a very good day to you too, young man. Come in, come in out of the wind. Can I help you find something special, or are you just browsing the echoes of days gone by?"

"A bit of both, I think," Pete admitted, taking a tentative step further into the shop. "I'm exploring Kilkenny, trying to understand its layers."

Her eyes seemed to brighten further at his words. "Layers, you say? Ah, Kilkenny has layers upon layers, like a good stew. Some are plain to see, like the Castle and the Abbey, and some... well, some are tucked away in the whispers of the wind, or the shadows in the corner of your eye." She gestured with a hand adorned with a simple silver ring. "My name is Aisling. And this old place is full of the stories these things carry."

Pete introduced himself and explained his interest in Kilkenny's history, mentioning his recent visit to the Black Abbey. Aisling listened with an attentive nod, her gaze never leaving his face.

"The Black Abbey," she murmured, her voice taking on a softer, more reflective tone. "A grand place it was. And a sad end, like so many of those old houses. But even in ruin, they hold their memories. And their... occupants, some would say."

This piqued Pete's interest. "Occupants? You mean ghosts?"

Aisling chuckled, a dry, rustling sound. "Ghosts, spirits, lingerings, call them what you will. Kilkenny has its fair share. They say the Black Abbey is home to more than just memories of monks. There's a Grey Lady, you know, said to weep for a lost love who never returned from the wars. And sometimes, on a moonless night, you can hear the clatter of chains, though no one knows for sure who it belongs to. Some say it's a friar who tried to escape with forbidden knowledge, others a medieval prisoner held beneath the priory."

Pete leaned against a sturdy oak counter, his historian's mind already whirring. "Is there any historical basis for these stories, or are they purely the product of imagination over time?"

Aisling tapped a finger against her chin, her blue eyes thoughtful. "Oh, the stones themselves hold the truth, if you know how to listen. Take that Grey Lady. There was a knight, Sir Reginald, who was stationed at Kilkenny Castle back in the 14th century. His betrothed, Elara, was said to be as beautiful as the dawn. He went off to fight in France, promising to return swiftly. But he never did. Some say he fell in battle, others that he was captured and died in a foreign prison. Elara waited. She walked the ramparts of the castle, she prayed at the abbey, and eventually, her grief consumed her. They say she died of a broken heart, still waiting. And her spirit, they say, still walks the grounds of the Black Abbey, a sorrowful vigil."

She paused, letting the story hang in the air. "And the chains? Well, there are older tales, before even the Dominicans arrived. This land has seen many things. Druids, chieftains, battles. Some say the chains belong to a chieftain who was betrayed by his own kin and buried alive with his treasure, his restless spirit forever guarding what was stolen from him."

Pete felt a familiar surge of excitement, the thrill of a historical puzzle. "So, the legends are tied to specific individuals or events?"

"Often," Aisling confirmed, her voice gaining momentum. "The old stories, they don't just spring from nowhere. They're like roots, reaching down into the soil of history. There's the tale of 'Mad' Molly, for instance. She lived in a small cottage just outside the city walls centuries ago. They said she could see things others couldn't, talk to the other side. One day, her only child wandered off into the woods and was never found. They searched for days, but it was as if the earth swallowed him whole. Molly claimed he was taken by the 'Little People,' the fairies, who lived in the old dolmens scattered across the countryside. She spent the rest of her days wandering the fields, calling for him, and people would cross themselves when they saw her, muttering about her curse. They say her spirit still haunts those woods, forever searching for her lost son, and that if you stray too far from the path on a misty morning, you might hear her wailing."

Pete jotted down notes in a small leather-bound notebook he always carried. "The Little People... fairies. This connects to a broader vein of folklore, doesn't it? The idea of hidden realms, of beings that co-exist with us."

"Indeed," Aisling agreed, her eyes shining. "Kilkenny, like many ancient places, has always had a strong belief in the unseen. My own grandmother told me stories about the 'Banshee of the Nore.' Not the wailing kind, mind you, but a silent specter that would appear to families on the eve of a great tragedy. She'd be seen standing by the river, her hair flowing like dark water, her face obscured by shadow. If she looked directly at you, it was said to be a sign of impending doom. My grandmother swore she saw her once, just before her brother died in the Great War. She never spoke of it again, but the memory was etched onto her soul."

She continued, her voice a melodic cascade of forgotten lore. "And then there are the curses. Oh, Kilkenny has its share of those too. The tale of the Butcher's Curse is a grim one. A butcher, notorious for his cruelty to animals and his sharp temper, was said to have cheated a local witch out of her payment for a prime cut of meat. In her fury, she cursed him and his descendants. It's said that for generations, every male heir born to his line met a violent or untimely end. Some say the curse was broken when the last of his direct descendants left Kilkenny for good, but others whisper that certain families still bear the mark of that old anger. You can almost feel it, a coldness that clings to certain old buildings in the city, places where his family once lived and prospered."

Pete was captivated. This was precisely the kind of subterranean narrative he suspected lay beneath Kilkenny's polished historical veneer. "These aren't just ghost stories, are they? They feel like cultural memory, ways of explaining the unexplainable, or perhaps cautionary tales."

"They are all of those things, and more," Aisling said, her voice low. "They are the threads that bind the past to the present, the tangible to the intangible. They are how we make sense of loss, of fear, of the sheer randomness of life. When a child went missing, it wasn't just a disappearance; it was the fairies taking them. When a good harvest failed, it was an ancient spirit angered. These stories provided a framework, a way to understand the world when the world itself was often brutal and baffling."

She picked up a small, tarnished silver locket from the counter. "This belonged to a woman named Sarah, who lived in the mid-1800s. Her husband was a sailor, and he was lost at sea. They never found his body. Sarah was heartbroken, but she refused to believe he was gone forever. She would stand on the banks of the Nore, gazing out at the water, convinced he would somehow return. She'd talk to the river, telling it to bring him home. One day, she simply walked into the water, following the current, as if she were being drawn to him. Some say her spirit still walks along the riverbanks, a silent sentinel, eternally waiting for her lost love. They say if you're walking by the Nore late at night and you feel a sudden, inexplicable chill, or hear a faint sigh carried on the breeze, it might be Sarah, still searching."

Pete was struck by the common thread of waiting, of loss, of a desperate hope that defied the finality of death. "It's fascinating how these themes recur. The Grey Lady waiting for her knight, Molly for her child, Sarah for her sailor."

"Because loss is a universal language," Aisling said softly. "And love, even in its absence, leaves its mark. These stories, they are testaments to the enduring power of human emotion, etched into the very fabric of this city. They are the whispers of lives lived, of loves lost, of fears confronted."

She leaned closer, her voice dropping conspiratorially. "But it's not just people who linger. There are places, too, that seem to hold an energy of their own. There's a certain alleyway, near the old city walls, that people avoid after dark. They call it 'Whispering Alley.' The story goes that a pair of lovers, from feuding families, used to meet there in secret. One night, they were discovered by the woman's enraged father and brothers. In the ensuing struggle, both lovers were killed. It's said that on certain nights, you can hear their whispered conversations, their desperate pleas, carried on the wind. Some claim to have seen fleeting figures, spectral lovers locked in an eternal embrace. And if you listen closely enough, they say you can hear the soft weeping of the young woman, her sorrow echoing through the centuries."

Pete found himself drawn to the subtle undercurrent of unease that these tales evoked. They weren't the lurid, sensational kind of ghost stories you might hear elsewhere; they felt more ingrained, more woven into the very identity of Kilkenny.

"And are these stories generally accepted by the people here, or are they more like urban myths?" Pete asked.

Aisling shrugged, her movements fluid and graceful. "Oh, some scoff, of course. They say it's nonsense, old wives' tales. But others... others keep the stories alive. They pass them down from generation to generation. And even those who claim not to believe, well, they might still cross themselves when they pass a certain corner, or feel a shiver down their spine on a particular evening. There's a part of us, I think, that wants to believe in something more, something that transcends the mundane. And these legends, they provide that. They add a layer of mystery, a hint of magic, to the everyday."

She picked up a small, smooth stone, worn almost perfectly round. "This was found near the old ringfort outside the city. They say that if you hold such a stone and whisper a secret into it, then throw it into the River Nore, your secret will be carried away forever. But beware, for if your secret is one of betrayal or malice, the river may not be so forgiving. It might whisper it back to you when you least expect it, in the sound of the water flowing past your ears."

Pete thought about the sheer volume of stories Aisling had shared, each one painting a vivid picture of Kilkenny's hidden emotional landscape. "It sounds like Kilkenny is a place where the past isn't just remembered; it's actively felt."

"Precisely," Aisling confirmed, her gaze intense. "The past here is not a closed book. It's a living, breathing entity. It influences the present in ways we might not always understand. These legends, these whispers of spirits and curses, they are the undercurrents. They are what give Kilkenny its unique character, its depth. They are the hidden layers that make this city so much more than just its stones and mortar."

She gestured around her shop, a silent testament to her words. "Every object here has a story, a history. And the city itself... it has a thousand thousand stories, waiting to be discovered, waiting to be heard. You just have to be willing to listen."

Pete felt a profound sense of gratitude for this unexpected encounter. Aisling, with her sharp memory and her deep well of local lore, had opened a door he hadn't even realized was there. He had come to Kilkenny looking for historical facts, for tangible evidence of the past. But he was finding something more – a sense of the past as a living force, a realm where history and folklore intertwined, where the ordinary brush strokes of everyday life were coloured with the extraordinary hues of the supernatural.

He purchased a small, intricately carved wooden bird from Aisling, a silent thank you for her time and her stories. As he stepped back out into the street, the city seemed different. The ancient buildings no longer just stood as historical monuments; they felt imbued with the spectral presences Aisling had described. The wind whistling through the narrow lanes no longer sounded like mere air currents; it seemed to carry the faint echoes of whispered conversations, of mournful laments, of ancient curses. Kilkenny was revealing itself to him, not just as a city of medieval architecture and historical significance, but as a place steeped in a rich, often uncanny, folklore that resonated with a primal, enduring power. He knew, with a growing certainty, that his exploration of Kilkenny's hidden layers had only just begun. The stories Aisling had shared were not mere curiosities; they were clues, pointing towards a deeper understanding of the city's soul, a soul that seemed to pulse with the echoes of its past, both human and perhaps, something more. He felt a pull, an undeniable draw, to investigate these whispered tales, to see if the tangible evidence could be found to support the spectral narratives. It was a quest that promised to lead him down paths less travelled, into the very heart of Kilkenny's enduring mysteries.

A GLIMPSE OF AINES OTHER LIFE

The late afternoon sun cast long, distorted shadows across the cobblestone streets as Pete continued his meandering exploration of Kilkenny. The tales spun by Aisling in her antique shop still resonated within him, adding an almost spectral dimension to the ancient city. He found himself drawn to the periphery, to the quieter streets where the grand historical pronouncements of the castle and abbey softened into the more intimate narratives of everyday life. It was in one of these unassuming lanes, where the buildings seemed to huddle closer to the ground, that he saw her. Aine.

She was walking with a briskness that was unfamiliar, her usual vibrant energy replaced by a focused intensity. Pete watched from a discreet distance as she approached a modest dwelling, its façade of weathered stone softened by a profusion of climbing ivy. It looked like any other home in this older part of Kilkenny, unassuming, perhaps even a little neglected, but utterly unremarkable to the casual observer. Aine paused at the gate, glancing briefly up and down the street before pushing it open and stepping onto the short path leading to the front door.

Curiosity, a persistent companion on this journey, tugged at Pete. He couldn't quite place why he felt compelled to observe her, but there was an undeniable shift in her demeanour that had pricked his attention. He ducked behind the low wall of a small, overgrown garden opposite, positioning himself for a clearer view without being overtly conspicuous. He watched as Aine knocked, a brief, sharp rap that seemed to echo the tension he now sensed radiating from her. The door opened almost immediately, revealing a figure Pete couldn't quite make out from his vantage point. There was a brief exchange, a few murmured words too low to discern, and then Aine stepped inside.

The door closed with a soft click, leaving the street quiet once more, save for the distant cry of a seagull and the murmur of the River Nore. Pete waited, his gaze fixed on the door, his mind racing through possibilities. Was this a friend's house? A relative? Or was it something else entirely? He recalled their earlier conversation, Aine's easy laughter, her infectious enthusiasm for Kilkenny's vibrant present, her almost dismissive attitude towards the more macabre aspects of its past that Aisling had so readily shared. Had he perhaps misread her? Was her public persona, the one he'd glimpsed at the market and during their brief walks, merely a carefully constructed facade?

The minutes stretched on, each one amplifying the stillness around the house. Pete's historian's instinct, trained to observe and piece together fragmented information, was on high alert. He found himself scrutinizing the house itself, looking for any subtle clues. The windows were small, suggesting an older construction. The paint on the door was peeling in places, and the stone step leading up to it was worn smooth by countless feet. It was a house that seemed to breathe history, but not in the grand, public way of the Black Abbey. This felt more personal, more lived-in, and perhaps, more private.

Then, the door opened again. Aine emerged, and the change in her was striking. The briskness was gone, replaced by a languid, almost weary grace. Her shoulders seemed to slump slightly, and her usual bright spark appeared dimmed, replaced by a subdued introspection. She didn't look back at the house, but instead turned and began walking away, her steps slower now, more hesitant. She didn't seem to notice him, or if she did, she gave no indication. Her gaze was fixed somewhere in the middle distance, her expression unreadable.

Pete's mind, already buzzing with Aisling's tales of hidden spirits and lingering curses, latched onto this observation. This wasn't the Aine he thought he knew. This was someone else, someone with secrets tucked away, compartmentalized from the cheerful guide who had shared her favourite Kilkenny haunts with him. He felt a peculiar sense of unease, a feeling that he had stumbled upon a hidden room in a house he thought he had fully explored.

He waited until Aine had rounded a corner before emerging from his hiding place. He didn't follow her; that would feel too intrusive, too much like an accusation. Instead, he walked towards the house she had entered. He stopped at the gate, the same one she had touched, and looked at the unassuming dwelling. It still offered no obvious clues to the transformation he had just witnessed. The ivy climbed, the stone was weathered, the door was peeling. It was simply a house.

Yet, the impression Aine had made was undeniable. The woman who had emerged was different from the one who had entered. What had transpired inside those walls in the short time she was there? Had she been delivering something? Receiving something? Was it a place of solace, or of burden? The subdued anxiety he had detected in her posture, the quiet weariness that seemed to have settled over her like a shawl, spoke volumes that her words had not.

He leaned against the gate, the cool metal a grounding sensation against his hand. He tried to reconcile this image of Aine with the one he had cultivated in his mind. He pictured her animatedly pointing out architectural details, laughing with a genuine, unforced joy. Had he been so eager to find a connection, so ready to accept her effervescent personality at face value, that he had missed the subtler currents beneath the surface?

A fleeting thought, sharp and unwelcome, surfaced: what if her entire persona in Kilkenny was a performance? What if this encounter was a glimpse into her 'real' life, a life she kept carefully shielded from the casual observer, and from him? The idea felt like a betrayal, not of Aine herself, but of his own perception. He prided himself on his ability to discern the nuances of human interaction, to read between the lines of spoken words and observed actions. This instance, however, left him with a frustrating blank space, a missing piece of the puzzle.

He considered the implications. If Aine had a hidden life, a facet of herself she kept concealed, what did that say about her connection to Kilkenny? Was she, like so many of the city's historical figures Aisling had described, carrying unseen burdens? Were the hushed conversations and the anxious demeanour a manifestation of some internal conflict, or perhaps something more tangible, something tied to the very fabric of the city that held so many secrets?

Pete found himself re-evaluating everything he thought he knew about her. Their conversations about Kilkenny had been largely superficial, focused on the well-trodden paths and the obvious attractions. He had asked about her experiences, her connection to the city, but her answers had always been light, cheerful, and focused on the present. He hadn't pressed further, assuming her enthusiasm was genuine and all-encompassing. Now, he wondered if he had been too easily satisfied, too willing to accept the surface-level narrative.

He looked back at the house, at the unassuming façade that now seemed to hold a silent testament to a life lived in shades of grey, rather than the vibrant colours he had associated with Aine. The knowledge that she could inhabit such a different emotional space, and apparently do so with such practiced ease, was unsettling. It suggested a capacity for self-containment, for managing different aspects of her identity, that was both intriguing and a little disconcerting.

The sun dipped lower, painting the sky in hues of orange and purple, a dramatic flourish that contrasted sharply with the quietude of the lane. Pete felt a growing sense of responsibility, an urge to understand this duality he had glimpsed. It wasn't just about Aine anymore; it was about the city itself, and how it seemed to nurture these hidden layers, these unspoken truths. Aisling had spoken of the city's whispers, its unseen currents. Perhaps Aine was one of those whispers, a living embodiment of Kilkenny's capacity for concealed depths.

He knew he couldn't simply ignore what he had seen. This brief, unsettling encounter had introduced a new element into his investigation, a human variable that was far more complex and potentially more revealing than any ancient artifact or crumbling monument. Aine, in her quiet transformation, had become a mystery in her own right, a puzzle piece that refused to fit neatly into the picture he had been so diligently constructing. He felt a strange mixture of disappointment and renewed purpose. The comfortable narrative he had been building was shattered, replaced by something far more compelling and, he suspected, far more representative of the true Kilkenny. The city, it seemed, was not content with offering up its history easily; it also demanded that one unravel the complexities of its present, and the people who inhabited it. And in Aine, he sensed a significant key to unlocking those deeper, more elusive layers. His path had taken an unexpected, and perhaps more profound, turn. The curated cheerfulness was a mask, and he was now more determined than ever to understand what lay beneath it. The question wasn't if there were hidden layers to Kilkenny, but how deep they ran, and what they revealed about the people who called this ancient city home. Aine's fleeting, altered demeanour was a stark, silent testament to that depth, a quiet ripple that suggested a vast, unseen current flowing beneath the surface of her familiar, amiable presence.

THE UNSPOKEN UNDERCURRENT

The late afternoon sun, once a friendly beacon, now seemed to cast a more discerning, almost accusatory light on Pete's observations. His encounter with Aine had been more than just a fleeting moment of curiosity; it had been a seismic shift, a crack in the polished veneer of Kilkenny's charm. He had always believed that to truly understand a place, one had to understand its people, and Aine, in her sudden, almost ethereal withdrawal, had presented him with a puzzle far more compelling than any ancient manuscript. The incident at the ivy-covered house had ignited a new line of inquiry, one that led him not to dusty archives, but to the hushed conversations of Kilkenny's older inhabitants.

He found himself drifting through the narrower streets again, the same ones where he had first seen Aine's transformed demeanor. This time, his intent was not casual exploration, but deliberate, subtle interrogation. He sought out the familiar faces he had encountered during his initial days in the city, those who possessed the steady gaze of long acquaintance with Kilkenny's rhythm. He started with Mr. O'Connell, the retired librarian whose encyclopedic knowledge of local history had been so invaluable. Pete found him tending to his small, immaculately kept garden, the scent of damp earth and roses filling the air.

"Mr. O'Connell," Pete began, pitching his voice to a casual, friendly tone, "I was thinking about Aine the other day. She's such a vibrant part of Kilkenny, isn't she? Always so full of life and knowledge about the city." He watched the older man's reaction closely, looking for any flicker of recognition, any subtle alteration in his posture.

Mr. O'Connell straightened slowly, his weathered hands pausing their work. He offered a small, almost imperceptible nod. "Aye, Aine. She's... a spirited young woman." The words were polite, perfectly innocuous, yet Pete detected a slight hesitation, a careful selection of adjectives that felt less like an endorsement and more like a measured description. The eyes, behind his spectacles, held a depth that suggested more was being held back than expressed. "She's got a good way with people, that's for sure."

"She was telling me about some of the older parts of the city, the more... lived-in histories," Pete continued, weaving his question subtly into the conversation. "Do you know her family well? Have you known her for a long time?"

Mr. O'Connell resumed his weeding, his movements deliberately slow. "Been in Kilkenny all my life," he said, his gaze fixed on a persistent dandelion. "Seen a lot of faces come and go. Aine's family... they've been here a while, like most." The evasion was skillful, a masterclass in polite dismissal. He offered no specifics, no anecdotes, no warmth. It was as if Aine's personal history was a subject best left unexamined, a tapestry of which only the outermost threads were visible.

Pete sensed the invisible barrier being erected, the unspoken agreement among some of the older residents to maintain a certain level of privacy, particularly when it came to certain individuals. He thanked Mr. O'Connell for his time and moved on, a growing certainty solidifying within him. Aine wasn't just an acquaintance; she was a presence that evoked a specific, guarded response.

His next stop was Mrs. Doyle, a woman whose sharp eyes and even sharper wit had charmed him during a chance encounter at the market. He found her in her small cottage on the outskirts of the city, surrounded by knitting and the comforting aroma of baking bread.

"Mrs. Doyle, hello!" Pete greeted, trying to recapture the easy rapport they had shared. "I'm still enjoying the fruits of Kilkenny, though the weather's turning a bit." He paused, then steered the conversation. "I was hoping you might have some insight for me. I've been speaking with Aine... you know, the young woman who runs the craft shop down by the river?"

Mrs. Doyle's hands, busy with a skein of wool, stilled for a fraction of a second. Her head tilted, a gesture that seemed to weigh his question before she answered. "Aine," she repeated, her voice softer, less effervescent than he remembered. "Yes, I know of her." There was no effusive praise this time, no shared anecdote. Instead, a subtle tension seemed to coil in the air around them.

"She's so knowledgeable about the city's past," Pete pressed, his historian's curiosity piqued by the subtle shift. "I was wondering if you'd known her family long, perhaps her grandmother? I seem to recall her mentioning a grandmother who was quite a character." He was fishing, using a vague memory of a past conversation to prompt a more specific response.

Mrs. Doyle's eyes met his, and in their depths, Pete saw it again – that same guarded flicker he had observed in Mr. O'Connell. It wasn't suspicion, not exactly, but a kind of knowing reticence, a silent understanding that the surface narrative was not the whole story. "The past is a long and winding road, Mr. Davies," she said, her voice taking on a slightly more formal tone. "Many families have their own stories, their own... private paths. Aine is a good girl, she is." The affirmation felt perfunctory, a shield against further inquiry. "She's a hard worker, that's clear."

The emphasis on her work, on her public persona, was a clear indication that Mrs. Doyle, like Mr. O'Connell, was unwilling to delve into anything beyond what was publicly known, or perhaps, what was deemed acceptable for an outsider to know. It was as if Aine's name, when spoken by these older residents, acted as a signal for a subtle, collective retreat, a shared unspoken pact to protect certain narratives.

Pete persisted, his mind piecing together the fragments. He found himself in conversation with a retired schoolteacher, a kindly woman named Eleanor, who had a reputation for her sharp memory and her deep roots in Kilkenny. He approached her as she was leaving the local post office, her basket laden with what looked like groceries.

"Miss Eleanor, good afternoon," Pete began, his smile genuine. "I'm Pete Davies, we met briefly at the Kilkenny Castle tour last week. I'm finding so much to love about this city, it's truly captivating."

Miss Eleanor paused, her brow furrowing slightly as she tried to place him. "Ah, yes, the gentleman with the keen interest in masonry," she recalled, a faint smile gracing her lips. "Yes, Kilkenny has a way of holding onto its stories, doesn't it?"

"It does indeed," Pete agreed, seizing the opportunity. "And speaking of stories, I've been spending some time with Aine, from the craft shop. She's been a wonderful guide to some of the hidden corners." He waited, his gaze steady. "I was curious, do you know her family? I feel as though there's so much history intertwined with the people here, and I'm trying to understand those connections better."

Miss Eleanor's smile wavered, and her eyes, which had been alight with friendly recollection, grew a shade more serious. She didn't immediately dismiss his question, but there was a distinct shift in her demeanor. It was as if a subtle alarm had been tripped, prompting a more guarded response. "Aine," she mused, her voice softer now, tinged with a hint of something Pete couldn't quite decipher – was it pity, caution, or simply a profound, unshareable knowledge? "She's a... resilient young woman." The word "resilient" hung in the air, loaded with unspoken implications.

"Resilient?" Pete echoed, his interest intensifying. "In what way?"

Miss Eleanor hesitated, her gaze drifting towards the imposing silhouette of St. Canice's Cathedral in the distance. "Kilkenny isn't always an easy city for everyone, Mr. Davies," she said, her voice barely above a whisper, as if imparting a secret. "It has its shadows, its old ways. Some people... they carry the weight of it more than others." She turned back to him, her eyes earnest, yet still holding that characteristic Kilkenny reticence. "Aine is one of those who carries a weight, I believe."

The implication was clear, and it resonated deeply with Pete's earlier observations. The house, the hurried entry, the subsequent weariness – it all began to coalesce into a more coherent, albeit unsettling, picture. The polite evasiveness of Mr. O'Connell and Mrs. Doyle now seemed less like indifference and more like a deliberate choice, a collective unspoken agreement to keep certain truths shielded from outside view. Miss Eleanor, with her more direct, yet still veiled, comment, had inadvertently confirmed his growing suspicion.

Pete felt a surge of both frustration and exhilaration. The easy narrative of Kilkenny, the one he had been so readily embracing, was proving to be a thin veneer over something far more complex. Aine, whom he had initially perceived as a bright, uncomplicated presence, was clearly at the center of a hidden current, a story that the city's elders either couldn't, or wouldn't, articulate.

He continued his subtle probing throughout the rest of the afternoon, engaging with shopkeepers and locals who had spent most of their lives in Kilkenny. Each conversation, while seemingly innocent on the surface, chipped away at the edifice of Aine's public persona. He asked about the history of her family's shop, about the area where he'd seen her enter the house. The responses were invariably polite, sometimes even friendly, but always skirted around any specifics that might reveal too much about Aine herself.

He learned, for instance, from a baker who had known Aine since she was a child, that her family had indeed been in Kilkenny for generations, a fact that only deepened the mystery. "They're quiet folk, the O'Neills," the baker had said, dusting flour from his apron. "Always have been. Keep to themselves, mostly. Good people, though. Good people." Again, the "good people" felt like a preface to an unsaid caveat, a subtle acknowledgment of something that set them apart, something that required a certain understanding.

The underlying unease, the collective reticence, was palpable. It wasn't a conspiracy of silence, but rather a shared, ingrained instinct to protect what was personal, to maintain a delicate balance between the city's rich public history and the more private, often more burdensome, histories of its inhabitants. Pete began to understand that Kilkenny's layers weren't just historical; they were deeply personal, woven into the fabric of the present day, and guarded by those who understood their true weight.

He found himself thinking about Aisling's tales in a new light. The antique dealer had spoken of the city's "lingering energies," its "unseen currents." Pete had initially dismissed some of it as colorful storytelling, an embellishment of Kilkenny's already rich past. But now, listening to the hushed tones and the carefully chosen words of the locals when Aine's name surfaced, he felt a prickle of understanding. These weren't just stories; they were lived experiences, reflections of a city that demanded more than just surface appreciation.

The guarded responses weren't born of malice, he realized, but of a deep-seated respect for privacy, and perhaps, a gentle warning to an outsider who might not fully grasp the subtleties of their community. They were offering him not answers, but a direction – to look beyond the easily accessible narrative, to acknowledge the unspoken undercurrents that shaped both the city and the lives within it. Aine, with her vibrant outward demeanor and her hidden moments of weariness, was a living testament to this intricate, often veiled, reality. His quest to understand Kilkenny had irrevocably shifted, leading him to a more profound, and perhaps more challenging, truth: that some of the city's most significant stories were not carved in stone, but whispered in the guarded glances and the carefully chosen words of its people. He had come to Kilkenny seeking history, but he was finding humanity, in all its complex, often hidden, glory. The unspoken undercurrent was not just a feature of Kilkenny's past, but a vital, breathing element of its present, and Aine was its most compelling, enigmatic current bearer

Chapter Five: Unraveling Clues

A MYSTERIOUS PHOTOGRAPH

Pete found himself drawn back to the small antique shop nestled between a bustling pub and a quiet bookbinder's. It was a place he and Aine had stumbled into during one of their earlier explorations, a treasure trove of forgotten trinkets and faded memories. The scent of beeswax polish and aged paper was a comforting balm, a stark contrast to the subtle unease that had begun to permeate his thoughts regarding Aine. He'd initially dismissed the evasiveness of the locals as a general Kilkenny trait, a polite way of keeping an outsider at arm's length. But the recurring pattern, the almost imperceptible closing off whenever Aine's name, or her family's history, was mentioned, had begun to feel less like politeness and more like a deliberate, collective act of preservation.

He meandered through the aisles, running his fingers over the worn velvet of a Victorian chaise lounge, the cool porcelain of a forgotten doll. The shopkeeper, a stout man with a perpetually flour-dusted apron and a kindly smile, nodded a greeting from behind his counter, his hands busy with a delicate silver locket. Pete had exchanged pleasantries with him before, the man a font of local gossip, though, as Pete had discovered, carefully curated. It was a familiar dance, a polite inquiry met with a cordial, yet ultimately unrevealing, response.

His gaze drifted to a shelf laden with old photograph albums, their leather covers cracked and their pages yellowed with age. He'd always had a soft spot for old photographs, windows into lives long past, each sepia-toned image a silent narrative waiting to be deciphered. One album, bound in dark, unadorned leather, seemed to beckon him. Its pages felt heavier, its contents perhaps more substantial. He pulled it down, the clasp groaning in protest.

As he began to leaf through the album, a cascade of faces, fashions, and forgotten landscapes unfolded before him. There were portraits of stern-faced Victorian families, candid snapshots of children playing on cobbled streets, and sweeping landscapes of the surrounding countryside. He paused at a particularly arresting image, a stiffly posed group shot in front of what was unmistakably Kilkenny Castle. The architecture was familiar, yet the surrounding grounds seemed subtly different, less manicured, more wild. The clothing, too, was a giveaway – high collars, bonnets, and long, voluminous skirts spoke of a time long past, perhaps the turn of the century, or even earlier.

But it wasn't the historical context that seized Pete's attention. It was the woman standing slightly apart from the group, her posture relaxed, her gaze directed slightly off-camera, as if caught in a fleeting thought. There was something about her face, a certain tilt of the head, the curve of her jawline, and then, it hit him with the force of a physical blow – her hair. It was a vibrant auburn, a shade that Pete knew intimately, the same shade that framed Aine's face.

And her eyes, though muted by the passage of time and the sepia tones, seemed to possess a familiar intensity, a spark that he had seen in Aine's own green eyes.

He stared at the photograph, his heart hammering against his ribs. It was uncanny. The resemblance was more than just a fleeting similarity; it was a deep, almost unnerving echo. He leaned closer, straining to discern any further details. The woman's dress was simpler than those of the other figures in the photograph, a practical, almost almost bohemian style, a stark contrast to the stiff formality of the era suggested by the other attire. It was the kind of dress that suggested a degree of independence, a spirit that chafed against convention.

He flipped through the album more quickly now, his earlier casual browsing replaced by a frantic, almost desperate search. Were there others? Other glimpses of this woman, this spectral doppelganger of Aine? But the album seemed to contain only a handful of photographs from that particular era, and the one he had found was the only one that featured her so prominently. It was as if she had deliberately, or perhaps accidentally, been captured in a moment of singular focus.

The shopkeeper, sensing Pete's unusual absorption, ambled over. "Find something interesting there, sir?" he asked, his voice a gentle rumble.

Pete carefully closed the album, his hand trembling slightly. "This photograph," he began, his voice a little hoarse. "This woman... she looks so much like someone I know. It's quite remarkable." He gestured towards the album. "Is there any information about who these people are?"

The shopkeeper peered at the photograph, his brow furrowed in concentration. He tilted his head, stroking his chin thoughtfully. "Ah, yes. That particular album... it belonged to the O'Connell family, a rather prominent family in Kilkenny's history, though I believe they've long since moved on. They were collectors of sorts, amassed quite a few interesting pieces over the years." He tapped a finger against the glassine page. "As for the people in the photo... it's difficult to say without any identifying marks. Many of these old albums are a bit of a mystery, even to the families who owned them."

He paused, his gaze lingering on the woman's face. "She does have a certain... presence, doesn't she? A look that suggests she knew her own mind." He offered a small, knowing smile, the kind that hinted at a depth of understanding he wasn't quite ready to share. "This city, you see, it holds onto its stories. And sometimes, those stories are hidden in plain sight, waiting for the right eyes to see them."

Pete's mind raced. The O'Connell family. He'd spoken to a Mr. O'Connell, the retired librarian. Could there be a connection? The subtle reticence he'd encountered from him now seemed to take on a new hue. Was it possible that this photograph, this uncanny resemblance, was a piece of a puzzle that the older generation was reluctant to fully reveal?

"Do you know if the O'Connells had any particular branch of the family that was known for... distinctive features?" Pete asked, choosing his words carefully. "Perhaps a family trait that's passed down?"

The shopkeeper chuckled, a warm, rumbling sound. "Well, sir, families are like old oak trees. They have their roots, their branches, and sometimes, a few particularly distinctive leaves. I wouldn't be privy to the specifics of their family tree, I'm afraid. But it's true what they say, isn't it? The eyes, the hair... sometimes, a striking resemblance can cross generations. It's the way of things, I suppose."

He then turned his attention back to the silver locket, leaving Pete with a host of unanswered questions. The shopkeeper's words, while seemingly innocuous, only served to deepen the mystery. The striking resemblance wasn't just a coincidence; it was a familial echo, a visual testament to a shared lineage. But if this woman was a relative, how was it that Aine had never mentioned her, or shown him any photographs? And why did the older generation, like the shopkeeper and the people he'd spoken to previously, become so guarded when her name arose?

Pete felt a growing sense of bewilderment. He had come to Kilkenny seeking historical narratives, the tangible remnants of the past. He had found them in the stones of the cathedral, the walls of the castle, the archives of the library. But the more he delved into the city's present, the more he found himself encountering fragments of a hidden history, a narrative that seemed to be carefully guarded, its most crucial pieces concealed.

He purchased a small, intricately carved wooden bird, a purely symbolic purchase, as his mind was miles away. He thanked the shopkeeper, his gaze lingering on the album of photographs. He knew, with a certainty that settled deep within him, that this sepia-toned image was not just an interesting historical artifact. It was a clue, a significant one, pointing towards a past that was inextricably linked to Aine's present.

Stepping back out onto the bustling street, the late afternoon sun still casting long shadows, Pete felt a renewed sense of purpose, albeit tinged with a growing unease. The guarded conversations, the subtle evasions, the uncanny resemblance in the photograph – they were all pieces of a larger, more complex puzzle. A puzzle that, he suspected, had Aine, and her hidden family history, at its very heart.

He stopped by a small, independent bookshop, a place that always had a curated selection of local history and folklore. He browsed the shelves, hoping for any mention of prominent Kilkenny families or any historical accounts that might shed light on the

O'Connells or families with similar prominent features. He found a detailed history of Kilkenny Castle, filled with architectural drawings and anecdotes of its famous inhabitants. He poured over its pages, looking for any mention of individuals who bore a resemblance to the woman in the photograph, or any hints of unusual family connections within the castle's storied past. The book was a rich tapestry of documented history, but the threads he was seeking, the personal, unrecorded histories, remained elusive, hidden within the broader narrative.

Later, sitting in a quiet corner of a dimly lit pub, nursing a pint of Guinness, Pete pulled out his phone. He scrolled through the few photographs he had taken of Aine – candid shots, moments of her laughing, her eyes sparkling with life. He held the phone next to a mental image of the sepia-toned photograph. The auburn hair, the shape of the eyes, the gentle curve of the mouth – the similarities were undeniable. It was like looking at a faded copy of a vibrant original.

He considered contacting Aine, confronting her directly with his discovery. But the thought was quickly dismissed. The careful way she had deflected his earlier questions, the subtle weariness he had observed, suggested that this was not a simple matter of sharing old family photos. There was a weight attached to this resemblance, a history that she, for reasons he couldn't yet fathom, was keeping hidden.

He decided to revisit the house where he had seen Aine disappear so abruptly. He approached it with a new perspective, no longer just an observer of a peculiar incident, but a seeker of answers. The ivy still clung to the walls, the gate still stood slightly ajar, as if waiting for a hesitant return. He looked for any plaques, any markers that might indicate the history of the dwelling or its former occupants. There was nothing visible, no indication of its age or any notable past residents. It was just another old house on a quiet street, yet it felt imbued with a significance he hadn't grasped before.

As he stood there, trying to piece together the fragments of his investigation, he found himself observing the other houses on the street. They were a mix of old and new, some well-maintained, others showing signs of neglect. He noticed a small, almost unnoticeable detail on the house adjacent to the one Aine had entered – a faded blue ribbon tied to the doorknob, a seemingly innocuous decoration. He also observed an elderly woman tending to her window boxes across the street, her movements slow and deliberate. He considered approaching her, but the familiar hesitation returned, the ingrained caution he had begun to recognize in the older residents of Kilkenny. They were a community that guarded its secrets, not with hostility, but with a quiet, ingrained protectiveness.

His thoughts kept returning to the photograph and the woman in it. Who was she? A great-aunt? A grandmother? Or someone even closer, someone whose legacy cast a long shadow? The fact that Aine's family had been in Kilkenny for generations, as the baker had mentioned, only amplified the enigma. It suggested a deep-rooted history, a connection to the city that went far beyond a simple business ownership.

He decided to delve deeper into the O'Connell family history. He returned to the library, this time seeking out the local history section, the less-trafficked aisles that held the more obscure records. He found old city directories, genealogies, and chronicles of Kilkenny's prominent families. He spent hours poring over dusty volumes, his eyes scanning names and dates, searching for any mention of an O'Connell who might have a connection to the woman in the photograph.

He found a brief mention of the O'Connell family in a book detailing Kilkenny's merchant families from the late 19th century. It noted their success in the textile trade and their residence in several properties around the city. There was a brief description of a Mrs. Eleanor O'Connell, a woman known for her charitable work and her patronage of the arts. The description was accompanied by a small, grainy photograph, too indistinct to be conclusive, but the hair colour, if the reproduction was accurate, seemed to match. However, the dates associated with Mrs. Eleanor O'Connell placed her firmly in a generation earlier than the woman in the antique shop's album. This O'Connell wasn't the direct link he was looking for, but it suggested a lineage, a presence that had endured through the decades.

He then stumbled upon a small, privately published booklet on Kilkenny's vernacular architecture, which included photographs of various historical buildings. One of the images, a shot of the exterior of Kilkenny Castle from the early 20th century, featured a small group of people posing near the entrance. And there, partially obscured by a pillar, was a woman with a familiar cascade of auburn hair, wearing a simple, unfussy dress. The angle was poor, and the resolution low, but the profile, the general build, it was undeniably the same woman. This second sighting, in a different context, confirmed that this was no mere accidental resemblance to Aine. This woman was a recurring figure in the city's visual history, yet her identity remained a tantalizing mystery.

The weight of these discoveries pressed down on him. The sepia-toned photograph from the antique shop was no longer an anomaly; it was a confirmed piece of evidence, pointing towards a deep, and perhaps deliberately obscured, connection between Aine and a woman from Kilkenny's past. The careful preservation of this past, he realized, was not just about respecting history; it was about safeguarding a present that was intimately bound to it. He felt like he was on the cusp of understanding something profound about Aine, about her family, and about the very fabric of Kilkenny itself. The city, he was learning, was not just a collection of ancient buildings and documented events; it was a living entity, its secrets held not in stone, but in the hushed tones and guarded glances of its people, and in the faded images preserved in dusty albums.

A FORGOTTEN FAMILY NAME

Pete's steps echoed a newfound urgency as he made his way towards the Kilkenny Historical Society. The building itself was an edifice of quiet dignity, a testament to the city's enduring heritage, its stone facade weathered by centuries of sun and rain. He carried the antique album with him, the sepia photograph of the auburn-haired woman a tangible link to the deepening mystery. Inside, the air was thick with the scent of old paper and a hushed reverence for the past. Dust motes danced in the shafts of sunlight filtering through tall, arched windows, illuminating rows upon rows of meticulously cataloged documents and artifacts.

He approached a woman with kindly eyes and silver hair pulled back in a neat bun, who sat behind a large, polished oak desk. She greeted him with a warm, professional smile. "Good afternoon. Can I help you?"

"Good afternoon," Pete replied, placing the album gently on the counter. "I was hoping you might be able to help me identify someone in this photograph. It's from an old album I recently acquired, and I believe the family might have been from Kilkenny."

The archivist's eyes lit up with professional curiosity. She carefully opened the album, her movements precise and respectful. As she turned the brittle pages, her gaze landed on the photograph Pete had flagged. A subtle shift occurred in her demeanor, a flicker of recognition, or perhaps, a veiled professional caution. She leaned closer, her brow furrowing slightly.

"This woman," she murmured, her voice soft. "She has a rather distinctive look." She paused, then turned to a nearby computer terminal, her fingers flying across the keyboard. "Do you have any other information about the album, or the family name mentioned?"

"The shopkeeper mentioned it belonged to the O'Connell family," Pete offered, watching her intently. "But he wasn't able to provide much detail."

The archivist's search continued, a quiet symphony of keystrokes and rustling paper. Minutes stretched, punctuated only by the distant chime of a grandfather clock. Finally, she looked up, her expression a mixture of intrigue and something else, something harder to define.

"The O'Connells," she began, her tone measured. "That is a name that has... faded from our records over time. They were a notable family in Kilkenny, particularly in the late 18th and early 19th centuries. Involved in trade, primarily wool and textiles. They were quite prosperous."

She navigated through digital archives, displaying old census records and property deeds on her screen. "However," she continued, her voice dropping slightly, "their presence in Kilkenny seems to have abruptly ceased. There are no records of them leaving, no accounts of their demise here. It's as if they simply... vanished."

Pete felt a prickle of unease. "Vanished? What do you mean?"

"Just that," she replied, tapping a finger on the screen. "One generation, they are prominent figures in the city's records, owning several properties, actively involved in civic life. The next, there's no trace. No wills filed, no property transferred, no further mention in any official capacity. It's a historical anomaly, a rather perplexing one.'"

She then focused on the photograph again. "And this woman... if she is indeed an O'Connell, her appearance is certainly striking. Let me cross-reference some genealogical records and local histories from that specific period. We have some private collections, family trees compiled by enthusiasts over the years, which might hold more personal details."

The archivist's dedication was unwavering. She delved into dusty binders filled with handwritten family trees, meticulously cross-referencing names and dates. Pete watched, a growing sense of anticipation building within him. He felt like he was peeling back the layers of a very old, very carefully constructed onion.

After a considerable amount of searching, the archivist let out a soft exclamation. "Ah! Here we are. In a privately compiled genealogy, a Mr. Seamus O'Connell, a descendant of a distant branch of the family, made notes about a particular lineage of his family who were known for their distinctive auburn hair and striking green eyes. He refers to them as 'the forgotten branch.'"

She pointed to a faded entry in a thick, leather-bound volume. "According to this, the woman in your photograph is likely Elara O'Connell. Born in the 1790s. She was the daughter of a prominent merchant, but the notes become... vague, after her marriage. The marriage record itself is difficult to trace, as if it were deliberately obscured."

Pete leaned closer, his eyes scanning the spidery script. "What else does it say about her? Or her family?"

"It mentions that Elara was considered... unusual," the archivist said, choosing her words with care. "There are whispers, anecdotal accounts, passed down through oral tradition rather than recorded history, suggesting she had a deep affinity with the natural world.

Some even referred to her as having a certain 'understanding' of the old ways, the ancient traditions of the land."

She paused, her gaze distant for a moment. "These kinds of stories often arise around families who live apart from the mainstream, who hold onto older beliefs. It doesn't necessarily mean anything concrete, of course, but in the context of their sudden disappearance..." She trailed off, her professional tone faltering slightly, replaced by a hint of genuine curiosity, perhaps even a touch of awe.

"Disappearance," Pete repeated, the word echoing the archivist's earlier sentiment. "So, they didn't just move away?"

"It appears that way," she confirmed. "The O'Connell name, and any associated property, simply cease to be recorded after the early 1800s. It's as if the entire family line, or at least the Kilkenny branch, was excised from the historical record. The 'forgotten branch,' as this genealogy calls them, seems to have truly been forgotten."

Pete thanked the archivist profusely, his mind a whirlwind of new information. Elara O'Connell. The forgotten branch. Vanished. The words resonated with a chilling familiarity, aligning with the subtle evasiveness he had encountered from the locals. It wasn't just a reluctance to discuss Aine's family; it was a deep-seated, generational silence, a collective amnesia that seemed to have been deliberately cultivated.

He left the Historical Society with the album clutched tightly in his hand, the image of Elara O'Connell imprinted on his mind. He decided to revisit the antique shop, hoping the owner might recall more, now that Pete had a name, a potential connection. The familiar scent of beeswax and aged paper greeted him as he stepped back inside. The shopkeeper, the same kindly man with the flour-dusted apron, looked up from polishing a brass candlestick.

"Back again, sir?" he said, his smile unwavering.

"Yes," Pete replied, his voice low. "I've been doing some digging, and I believe the family connected to this album might be the O'Connells. Specifically, a woman named Elara O'Connell."

The shopkeeper's hands stilled. The smile on his face faltered, replaced by a sudden, almost imperceptible tension. His eyes, which had been twinkling with good humor, now held a flicker of something akin to apprehension. He looked down at the album Pete had placed on the counter, then back at Pete, his gaze sharp and searching.

"O'Connell, you say?" the shopkeeper's voice was quieter now, the geniality replaced by a certain wariness. He wiped his hands slowly on his apron, as if stalling for time.

"Yes," Pete confirmed, watching the subtle shift in the man's demeanor. "I was told they were a prominent family, but they seem to have disappeared from Kilkenny's records. The archivist at the Historical Society mentioned it's quite a mystery."

The shopkeeper's eyes darted around the shop, as if checking for eavesdroppers, though the only other sound was the ticking of a distant clock. He leaned closer across the counter, his voice dropping to a conspiratorial whisper. "O'Connell... aye, I've heard the name. Not spoken of much, mind you. Not for a very long time."

He paused, his gaze locking with Pete's. "There are stories, sir. Old stories. The kind folks in Kilkenny tend to keep to themselves. Tales of the O'Connells, particularly Elara." He lowered his voice further, the whisper barely audible. "They say the family... they dabbled in things. Things best left undisturbed."

Pete's breath hitched. "What kind of things?"

The shopkeeper hesitated, his gaze flicking towards the door. "Ancient powers," he murmured, the words barely forming. "The old magic of the land. They say Elara O'Connell had a connection to it, a way of understanding the whispers of the stones, the secrets of the earth." He shivered, despite the warmth of the shop. "Some say they didn't disappear. They say they... transcended. Or perhaps, they were taken. For meddling where they shouldn't have."

He leaned back, his expression grave. "My own grandmother used to tell me stories. She lived in the countryside, near where the O'Connells were said to have had their ancestral lands. She'd warn us children not to stray too far, especially after dusk. Said the air there felt different, older. She spoke of the O'Connells with a mixture of fear and respect. Said they were tied to the very spirit of this place, for better or for worse."

The shopkeeper picked up the brass candlestick again, his hands now trembling slightly as he polished it. "It's not for me to say, sir. I'm just a purveyor of old things. But when a family name is associated with such tales, and then disappears without a trace... well, it makes a man think. Makes him wonder what truths lie hidden beneath the polished surfaces of history."

Pete left the shop, the shopkeeper's hushed words echoing in his mind. Ancient powers. Magic of the land. It was a far cry from the historical accounts he had been pursuing, yet it felt eerily congruent with the pervasive sense of unease and the carefully guarded silence he had encountered. The O'Connells hadn't just faded from Kilkenny; they had become a cautionary tale, a whispered legend shrouded in the mystical.

He walked through the cobbled streets, the late afternoon sun casting long, distorted shadows that seemed to twist and writhe with the O'Connells' story. He found himself looking at the old buildings with new eyes, imagining them not just as historical structures, but as silent witnesses to a past that was far more complex and perhaps, far more dangerous, than he had ever anticipated. Elara O'Connell, the woman with the auburn hair and the unusual affinity, was no longer just a face in a photograph; she was the focal point of a narrative that seemed to weave itself through the very fabric of Kilkenny, a narrative that hinted at forces beyond mortal comprehension. The connection to Aine, he now understood, was not merely familial; it was perhaps something deeper, something rooted in the very essence of this ancient city and the enigmatic O'Connell lineage. The mystery had deepened, taking a turn into the unknown, and Pete felt a chill that had nothing to do with the evening air.

AINES EVASIVE ANSWERS

The midday sun, usually a source of warmth and cheer, seemed to cast a pall over the bustling market square. Pete found Aine by the familiar stall selling artisanal cheeses, her presence a stark contrast to the ordinary transactions happening around her. He'd rehearsed this moment a dozen times in his head, each scenario ending with a confession, a shared secret, a clearing of the air. But as he approached, the carefully constructed script began to unravel, replaced by a gnawing apprehension.

He held the antique album, its worn leather cover a tangible anchor to the past. The sepia photograph of Elara O'Connell, her auburn hair a vibrant echo against the muted tones of the image, felt heavier than usual. He stopped a few feet from Aine, the scent of aged paper and lingering perfume mingling in the air between them.

"Aine," he began, his voice a little rougher than he intended.

She turned, a bright smile gracing her lips, a smile that didn't quite reach her eyes. "Pete! I didn't expect to see you here. Lost in the labyrinth of Kilkenny's finest?" She gestured playfully towards a pyramid of Gouda.

He didn't return the smile. He held up the album, letting it rest on his palm. "I wanted to show you something."

Her gaze dropped to the album, and for a fleeting second, Pete saw it – a flicker of something raw, unguarded. It was gone as quickly as it appeared, replaced by that practiced, almost imperceptible shift in her posture, a subtle drawing inward. Her fingers, which had been idly tracing the rim of a cheese wheel, stilled.

"What is it?" she asked, her tone betraying a carefully manufactured nonchalance.

He opened the album to the page with Elara's photograph, holding it out to her. "This woman. I believe she might be an ancestor of yours. The O'Connell name came up."

Aine's eyes widened, not with recognition, but with something that looked alarmingly like fear. It was a fleeting expression, a shadow that crossed her face before being expertly smoothed away. She took a step back, almost imperceptible, and her hand instinctively went to her throat.

"O'Connell?" she repeated, her voice a shade too high. "I... I don't think so, Pete. I've never heard that name associated with my family. My grandmother was a Byrne, and before that, the lineage is... quite distant. Nothing that rings a bell."

Pete watched her, the subtle evasion hitting him like a physical blow. It wasn't just a denial; it was a deflection. Her carefully constructed composure felt like a dam built against a rising tide, and he suspected that tide was about to break. "Are you sure, Aine? Because the similarity is quite striking. And the O'Connells were a significant family here, centuries ago. They seem to have just... vanished from the records."

He laid out the fragmented narrative he had pieced together – the archivist's account of a family that ceased to exist in official documentation, the shopkeeper's hushed whispers of ancient magic and clandestine disappearances. He spoke of Elara, the woman with the auburn hair, and the chilling echoes of her story in the very fabric of Kilkenny. He watched Aine's face as he spoke, searching for a crack in her carefully maintained façade.

Her reaction was a study in controlled panic. Her fingers tapped a nervous rhythm against her thigh, her gaze darted around the square as if seeking an escape route. "Pete, this is... fascinating, I'm sure, from a historical perspective. But honestly, I don't see how it connects to me. My family history, as far as I know, is quite ordinary." She forced a small laugh, a brittle sound that didn't quite land. "Perhaps you're seeing things because you want to. You've been so invested in this... historical detective work."

"But the resemblance, Aine," Pete pressed, his own voice steady, though his heart pounded against his ribs. "Look at it. The eyes, the set of the jaw... it's uncanny. And the name O'Connell... it feels right, doesn't it? Doesn't any part of you feel a pull towards it?"

She finally met his gaze, her eyes hard, a chillingly deliberate mask of polite dismissal. "Pete, I'm flattered you're so interested in my family, truly. But I'm afraid you're on a wild goose chase. My lineage is not tied to any mysterious vanished families with dramatic stories." She reached out, her hand briefly touching his arm, a gesture that felt more like a warding off than an affectionate touch. "Let's leave the dusty archives and the whispered legends behind for now. How about we forget about all this and enjoy our afternoon? I was thinking we could get that coffee we talked about."

Her attempt to steer the conversation back to their burgeoning romance felt like a desperate maneuver, a flimsy shield against the truth. He saw it clearly now: the evasiveness wasn't a casual omission; it was a deeply ingrained pattern, a protective mechanism honed over years, perhaps generations. Her family, or at least a significant part of it, was indeed connected to the O'Connells, and she was actively, deliberately, hiding it.

"I can't just forget about it, Aine," Pete said, his voice quiet but firm. "This isn't just some historical footnote; it's your history. And it feels like it's intertwined with what's happening now, with the... the unease I've been feeling around Kilkenny, around your family."

He saw a flicker of something – irritation? – cross her face before it was masked again. "Unease? Pete, you're letting a few old stories get to you. Kilkenny is a beautiful, ancient city. It has its share of myths and legends, but that's all they are. Myths."

"But the way people react when I mention certain things," Pete countered, his gaze unwavering. "The way

you react. You said yourself your family history was 'distant.' That's not a neutral term, Aine. That's a carefully chosen word to keep people at arm's length."

Aine finally pulled her hand away, crossing her arms. The casual warmth had completely evaporated, replaced by a cool, appraising look. "Perhaps I'm just private, Pete. Some things are best kept within the family. Especially when the family has no desire to dredge up old, potentially uncomfortable truths for the sake of a romantic story."

The implication hung heavy in the air between them. He was not only digging into history, but he was also intruding on her personal life, her family secrets. Her words were a clear dismissal, a boundary drawn in the sand. Yet, he couldn't ignore the tremor in her voice, the subtle clenching of her jaw. She was defensive, not because the history was untrue, but because it was a truth she desperately wanted to keep buried.

"So, you're not going to tell me anything?" Pete asked, the disappointment a bitter taste in his mouth. "You're not going to acknowledge that this woman, Elara, could be related to you? Or that the O'Connells, who seem to have vanished from Kilkenny, might be your ancestors?"

Aine finally broke eye contact, turning her back to him and fiddling with a display of artisanal jams. "As I said, Pete, I don't know anything about it. My grandmother never spoke of such things. It's best to leave the past undisturbed." Her voice was clipped, final. "Now, if you'll excuse me, I really must be going. I have... other arrangements to attend to."

She didn't wait for his response. With a final, curt nod, she turned and walked away, her figure quickly absorbed by the milling crowds. Pete watched her go, the photograph of Elara O'Connell a silent testament to the secret she carried. Her evasiveness wasn't a passive act of ignorance; it was an active, deliberate concealment. And in that moment, Pete knew with a chilling certainty that Aine wasn't just connected to Kilkenny's past; she was a living, breathing part of its deepest, most guarded secret. The carefully woven tapestry of their budding romance had just been ripped asunder by the threads of a centuries-old mystery, a mystery that Aine, the woman he was falling for, was desperately trying to keep hidden. The implication of her heritage was far more profound than a mere family tree; it suggested a legacy, a connection to something ancient and perhaps, dangerous, that she was determined to keep from him, and perhaps, from the world. His pursuit of the O'Connells had now become a direct confrontation with Aine herself, and the realization that she was actively shielding her past only solidified his resolve to uncover the truth, whatever the cost. Her carefully constructed walls of denial only served to make him more determined to find the cracks. The unanswered questions about her family, coupled with the lingering unease in Kilkenny, painted a picture of a lineage far more complex and shadowed than Aine was willing to admit. The photograph of Elara O'Connell was no longer just a clue; it was a silent challenge, a harbinger of the deeper, more personal layers of the mystery that were yet to be unraveled. He realized that his attraction to Aine was now inextricably linked to the enigma of her family, a connection that was becoming increasingly complex and potentially perilous. Her reaction, the fear masked by composure, the swift denial, was the most telling clue of all. It confirmed his suspicion that Aine's reticence was not born of ignorance but of a deep-seated need to protect a legacy she perhaps didn't fully understand herself, or worse, a legacy she feared. The ordinary charm of the market square had dissolved, replaced by the cold, hard reality of secrets and evasion. He was left standing there, the album a weight in his hand, the image of Elara O'Connell a stark reminder of the woman who held the key to a past he was determined to unlock.

THE OLD MILLS SHADOW

The afternoon sun, once a cheerful companion, now offered little solace as Pete drove towards the river. Aine's casual mention of the old mill, nestled somewhere along its meandering course, had felt like a sudden, unexpected diversion from their tense conversation in the market square. She'd described it as a place of "sentimental value," a phrase that, given her earlier evasiveness, now carried a weight of unspoken history. He suspected it was a place she frequented to escape, perhaps even to commune with the past she so fiercely guarded. He knew it was a long shot, this solitary pilgrimage, but the image of Elara O'Connell, her stoic gaze from the sepia photograph, urged him onward. He felt a growing conviction that the answers he sought weren't confined to dusty archives or whispered tavern tales; they were etched into the very landscape of Kilkenny, into the forgotten corners where the O'Connell lineage might have left its true mark.

He found the turn-off Aine had vaguely described, a barely-there track that led away from the main road and plunged into a dense, overgrown copse. Branches scraped against the car's paintwork, a prelude to the encroaching wildness. The air grew cooler, damper, as he ventured deeper, the sunlight filtering through the thick canopy in dappled, shifting patterns. The silence here was different from the hushed reverence of the library or the cheerful din of the market; it was a profound, almost suffocating quiet, broken only by the murmur of the nearby river and the rustle of unseen creatures in the undergrowth. It felt like a place that had been deliberately forgotten, a secret whispered only to the wind.

Finally, the trees parted, revealing a sight that simultaneously saddened and intrigued him. There it stood, the old mill, or what remained of it. It was a skeletal ruin, its stone walls crumbling, choked by ivy and moss. The waterwheel, once a proud, rhythmic heart, was now a broken, rotting skeleton, its timbers splintered and bleached by time and weather. A melancholic beauty clung to the desolation, a testament to resilience in the face of decay. The river, a ribbon of grey-green water, flowed past it, its current swift and indifferent, as if carrying away the mill's memories with its relentless flow.

Pete parked the car and stepped out, the scent of damp earth and decaying wood filling his nostrils. He walked towards the mill, his footsteps crunching on scattered stones and fallen leaves. The atmosphere was heavy, charged with an unspoken narrative. It wasn't just the decay that lent it this weight; it was a palpable sense of lingering presence, as if the mill's stones themselves held the imprint of those who had once worked within its walls, of those who had perhaps sought refuge or engaged in practices far removed from the mundane milling of grain. He could almost hear the ghostly echo of turning wheels, the faint cries of seabirds, and the murmur of voices lost to centuries.

He circled the structure, his eyes scanning the weathered stonework. The mortar between the stones was crumbling, the granite worn smooth in places by the relentless touch of time. It was then that he noticed them – the symbols. Etched deep into the ancient stone, almost hidden by the creeping moss, were markings that seemed both familiar and utterly alien. They were geometric, intricate, with a certain fluidity that suggested they weren't merely decorative carvings. Some resembled stylized spirals, others sharp, angular patterns, and one, in particular, seemed to depict a coiled serpent or a knot of impossible complexity.

He ran his fingers over the cool, rough surface of the stone, tracing the lines of the symbols. They felt... significant. They resonated with a deep, primal energy, a resonance he'd felt before, though he couldn't quite place it. It was the same feeling he'd experienced when the shopkeeper at the antique store had spoken of the 'old ways,' of 'places where the veil between worlds grew thin.' The shopkeeper had mentioned symbols, cryptic sigils used in ancient rituals, meant to ward off evil or, conversely, to draw power from unseen forces. Could these be those very symbols?

He pulled out the small notebook he'd been using to jot down his findings, the one containing the sketches he'd made from the shopkeeper's descriptions. Flipping through the pages, he found them – crude, hasty reproductions of symbols he'd seen in old books, symbols that were said to be part of a lost Celtic tradition, whispers of pagan beliefs that persisted long after the arrival of Christianity. And there, among them, was a symbol uncannily similar to the coiled serpent he'd found on the mill's wall.

He felt a shiver, not of cold, but of a thrilling, terrifying recognition. This wasn't just an old mill; it was a place of power, a place imbued with a history that stretched back to the very roots of Kilkenny's ancient past, a past that was inextricably linked to the O'Connells. He looked around, his gaze sweeping over the surrounding landscape. The river curved sharply here, its waters eddying around the mill's foundations. The trees pressed in, creating a sense of enclosure, of secrecy. It was a secluded spot, perfect for clandestine meetings, for rites performed away from prying eyes.

He explored the interior of the mill, stepping carefully over fallen beams and debris. The interior was open to the sky, the roof long gone. Sunlight streamed in, illuminating dust motes dancing in the air. The stone grinding stones, once massive and central to the mill's function, lay askew, like fallen monuments. It was here, amidst the detritus of its former life, that he found something else. Tucked into a crevice in the wall, almost entirely hidden by a thick curtain of ivy, was a small, flat stone. It was different from the rough-hewn granite of the mill itself, smoother, darker, and bearing a single, deeply carved symbol.

This symbol was the spiral, the very first one he'd noticed on the outer walls, but rendered with a precision and artistry that suggested a deliberate, ceremonial purpose. It was perfectly formed, almost hypnotic in its symmetry. As he held the stone, feeling its coolness against his palm, a strange sensation washed over him. It was a feeling of profound connection, of an ancient awareness stirring within the very earth beneath his feet. He felt a faint echo of what might have been. Were these rituals conducted here? Were the O'Connells involved in practices that transcended the ordinary, practices that might explain their abrupt disappearance from the records?

He spent hours at the mill, meticulously documenting the symbols he found, sketching them in his notebook with renewed urgency. He noted their placement, their variations, their proximity to different parts of the structure. He discovered more of them, scattered on doorways, on window frames, and even on the remnants of the water channel. Each discovery deepened the mystery, solidifying his belief that this place was more than just a derelict building; it was a forgotten sanctuary, a nexus of something ancient and powerful.

As the afternoon wore on, the light began to fade, casting long, distorted shadows across the ruins. The wind picked up, rustling the leaves in the trees, and the river seemed to grow louder, its murmur deepening into a low, resonant hum. The sense of presence intensified, no longer just an impression but a tangible feeling. He felt as if he were being watched, not by human eyes, but by something older, something that had witnessed the mill's rise and fall, its secrets and its silence.

He imagined Aine here, perhaps as a child, drawn to the solitude and the mystery, or perhaps as an adult, revisiting a place that held a powerful, perhaps even dangerous, connection to her lineage. The 'sentimental value' she'd spoken of now seemed to hint at a deeper, more complex relationship with this place, a relationship woven with threads of ancestral memory and hidden truths. If Aine herself was unaware of the true significance of these symbols, of the potential rituals that might have taken place here, then her family had done an exceptional job of keeping their history buried. But if she did know, then her earlier denial in the market square felt all the more deliberate, all the more desperate.

He carefully placed the small, inscribed stone into a protective pouch he carried for significant finds, tucking it away with the photograph of Elara O'Connell. The two artifacts felt intrinsically linked, two pieces of a puzzle that was slowly, agonizingly, coming together. The symbols on the mill's walls, the ancient carvings, the whispered folklore – they all pointed towards a lineage that was not just historically significant, but potentially steeped in practices that were considered arcane, even heretical, in their time. The O'Connells had not merely vanished; they had, perhaps, intentionally withdrawn, leaving behind only these enigmatic markers as silent testament to their existence and their beliefs.

He lingered for a while longer, the fading light painting the ruins in hues of purple and gold. The old mill stood silhouetted against the darkening sky, a silent sentinel guarding the river and its secrets. It was a place steeped in an atmosphere that transcended mere dilapidation, a place where the past felt not only present but palpably alive. He knew he would have to return, to spend more time deciphering the markings, to try and understand the context of their use. But for now, standing in the deepening twilight, with the wind whispering through the broken stones, he felt a profound sense of having touched something ancient, something vital, something that lay at the heart of the O'Connell mystery. This place, this forgotten ruin, was a testament to a history that Aine could no longer afford to keep hidden, a history that was now, irrevocably, entwined with his own quest. The melancholic beauty of the mill, its desolation speaking volumes, had revealed a truth far more compelling than any spoken word – that the O'Connells, and whatever they represented, had left an indelible mark on Kilkenny, a mark etched in stone and carried by the whispering river, waiting patiently for someone to finally read its forgotten language.

A PATTERN EMERGES

The worn leather of his notebook felt familiar and grounding beneath Pete's fingers as he sat by the riverbank, the last rays of the setting sun painting the water in streaks of amber and rose. The silence of the old mill had been profound, a silence that seemed to absorb sound, leaving only the thrum of his own thoughts. He'd spent hours there, tracing the cryptic symbols etched into the ancient stone, his initial confusion slowly giving way to a dawning, disquieting realization. It wasn't just a haphazard collection of ancient markings; there was a deliberate placement, a recurring motif that spoke of purpose, of ritual, of a language only partially understood. The spiral, the coiled serpent, the knot of impossible complexity – they weren't random graffiti. They were signposts.

He pulled out the photograph of Elara O'Connell again. Her gaze, as steadfast as ever, seemed to hold a quiet knowing. He'd dismissed her as a mere historical footnote, a face from a bygone era. Now, holding the small, inscribed stone he'd found tucked away in the mill's crevice, a stone bearing the perfectly rendered spiral, he saw her differently. He saw her as a keeper of secrets, a member of a lineage that deliberately shrouded itself in enigma. The guardedness he'd encountered in Aine, her almost visceral reluctance to discuss her family's past, no longer seemed like simple reticence. It felt like a learned behavior, a practiced art of omission passed down through generations, a necessity for survival in a world that might not understand, or worse, might condemn, the beliefs and practices her ancestors held dear.

The local legends he'd initially filed away as colorful folklore now took on a sharper edge. The tales of unusual gatherings by the river, of peculiar lights seen in the woods, of whispers of those who could 'see beyond the veil' – they weren't just stories. They were fragmented echoes of a deeper reality, a reality that the O'Connells, it seemed, had actively participated in. He recalled the old fisherman in the pub, his gruff dismissal of the O'Connell name, his muttered words about "trouble and the old ways." At the time, he'd thought it mere superstition, the ramblings of a man steeped in local lore. But now, standing where the O'Connells had seemingly practiced ancient rites, the fisherman's words resonated with a chilling prescience. The O'Connells weren't just a family who had fallen on hard times or moved away; they were a family who had been different, who had walked a path divergent from the mainstream, a path marked by symbols that hinted at a connection to forces beyond the ordinary.

He carefully compared the sketches in his notebook with the symbols on the mill walls and the stone he held. The uncanny resemblance between the coiled serpent carving and the one depicted in the shopkeeper's book was undeniable. The shopkeeper, a man who seemed to possess a singular, almost unsettling knowledge of Kilkenny's hidden history, had spoken of sigils used for protection, for invocation, for communion with what he'd vaguely termed 'the ancient energies of the land.' He had been quite specific about the spiral, describing it as a symbol of journey, of transformation, of the cyclical nature of life and death, often associated with places of power and spiritual convergence. The mill, situated on the riverbend, a natural confluence of waters and a place where the land itself seemed to hum with a low, constant energy, fit that description perfectly.

The thought that Aine's connection to Kilkenny was not merely a matter of birthright, but of a lineage deeply embedded in the town's mystical undercurrents, began to take root. Her evasiveness, her subtle shifts in conversation whenever the topic veered too close to her ancestry, felt like a conscious effort to keep a powerful secret buried. He wondered if she understood the full implications of her heritage, if she had ever been privy to the true significance of the symbols or the rituals that might have been performed at the mill. Or was she, like him, merely on the precipice of discovery, her family history an inheritance she hadn't yet fully claimed or comprehended? The phrase 'sentimental value' took on a new meaning, suggesting not just nostalgia for a place, but a connection to a legacy, a spiritual inheritance that could be both a blessing and a burden.

He remembered the way Aine's eyes had flickered when he'd shown her the O'Connell photograph, a fleeting, almost imperceptible change in her expression. He'd attributed it to the natural curiosity of seeing a distant relative. Now, he suspected it was a deeper recognition, a subconscious acknowledgment of a shared ancestral thread, a thread that was being tugged by his questions. Her attempts to deflect, to steer the conversation away from the O'Connells and towards the more mundane aspects of Kilkenny's history, were not just about privacy; they were about safeguarding something vital, something perhaps even dangerous. The O'Connells hadn't just vanished; they had deliberately woven themselves into the fabric of Kilkenny's hidden history, leaving behind a trail of breadcrumbs for those who were meant to find them, or perhaps, for those who were destined to stumble upon their secrets.

The river continued its relentless flow, a constant, murmuring presence that seemed to carry the whispers of centuries. The symbols on the mill, the photograph, the hushed legends – they were no longer isolated fragments. They were coalescing, forming a pattern that was as intricate and complex as the knot symbol carved into the mill's ancient stones. This pattern suggested a deliberate concealment, a generations-long effort to obscure a truth that was fundamental to the O'Connell identity. It wasn't just about a family's past; it was about a way of life, a belief system that had found a haven in the secluded corners of Kilkenny, a system that utilized the very land as a conduit for its power.

Pete closed his notebook, the faint scent of damp earth and old paper clinging to him. The weight of the inscribed stone in his pocket felt significant, a tangible link to a past that was no longer merely academic but deeply personal, at least in his pursuit. He had stumbled upon more than just a historical anomaly; he had uncovered a lineage that had deliberately cultivated its own mystique, a family that had left its indelible mark not just on the town's register, but on its very soul, etched in stone and whispered on the wind. The O'Connells were not merely a mystery to be solved; they were an enigma to be understood, a legacy that was now inextricably woven into his own narrative. He knew, with a certainty that settled deep within him, that Aine's guardedness was not a barrier to his investigation, but a testament to the profound, ancient power that her family represented, a power that was now beginning to reveal itself, one cryptic symbol at a time. The pattern was emerging, and it was more profound, more ancient, and more captivating than he could have ever anticipated.

Chapter Six: Trust and Deception

A DIVIDED HEART

The setting sun, which had moments ago bled across the river in hues of molten gold, now surrendered to the encroaching twilight. Pete watched the last sliver of orange vanish below the horizon, a tangible sense of his own internal landscape mirroring the fading light. The quiet introspection by the water's edge had been a welcome respite, a moment to process the swirling revelations that Kilkenny seemed determined to unearth. Yet, even in the deepening shadows, the central conflict remained, stark and unavoidable. His heart, a stubborn organ that refused to be governed by logic alone, was increasingly occupied by Aine.

He traced the rim of his empty mug, the faint warmth still clinging to it a ghost of the shared intimacy he'd experienced earlier that day. Aine's smile, the way her eyes crinkled at the corners when she laughed, the easy cadence of their conversation – these were not things he could easily dismiss. He found himself replaying snippets of their time together, the casual touches that lingered a fraction too long, the shared glances that seemed to communicate volumes. There was a warmth in her presence, a grounding effect that had begun to subtly recalibrate his internal compass. He'd arrived in Kilkenny on a quest for historical truth, a detached observer seeking to piece together a forgotten narrative. He hadn't anticipated, hadn't even considered, the possibility of becoming entangled in the present, of finding himself drawn to one of the very people he was trying to understand.

This growing affection, however, was becoming increasingly difficult to reconcile with the persistent questions that shadowed his every thought. The O'Connell lineage, once a mere academic curiosity, now felt like a veil drawn across the woman he was coming to care for. He remembered the brief, almost imperceptible tightening of her jaw when he'd steered the conversation towards her family's history in the pub, her quick redirection towards the more palatable topic of the local harvest festival. It wasn't just a desire for privacy; it felt like a practiced, deliberate deflection, a skill honed over years, perhaps even generations, of knowing when and how to obscure the truth. He found himself studying her expressions more intently now, searching for clues, for any flicker of recognition or denial that might betray the secrets she held.

Was it possible that the laughter they shared, the comfortable silences that punctuated their conversations, were all part of a carefully constructed facade? The thought was a cold, unwelcome intrusion, a serpent coiling in the nascent warmth of his burgeoning feelings. He valued honesty, transparency. His own life, in its own way, had been built on a foundation of openness, of pursuing knowledge without reservation. To discover that the woman who had so effortlessly captured his attention might be living a life veiled in carefully guarded secrets was a deeply unsettling prospect. It forced him to re-examine his own judgment, to question the very foundation upon which this budding connection was being built.

He found himself revisiting their earlier discussions, dissecting her words, searching for inconsistencies, for hidden meanings. Had her casual mentions of growing up in Kilkenny been entirely truthful, or had they been a skillful curation of details, omitting the parts that might lead too close to the truth? He remembered her insistence that her family had no particular historical significance, no lingering influence on the town's present. It was a statement delivered with a disarming sincerity, yet now, armed with the knowledge of the symbols, the whispers of ancient rites, and the very tangible presence of the inscribed stone in his pocket, her words took on a different hue. They sounded less like a statement of fact and more like a carefully rehearsed narrative.

The contrast between the Pete who had first arrived in Kilkenny, a man driven by an academic pursuit, and the Pete sitting here now, wrestling with the complexities of human connection, was stark. He had been prepared for historical enigmas, for the challenge of deciphering ancient texts and forgotten traditions. He had not been prepared for the emotional entanglement, for the delicate dance of attraction and suspicion. He felt like a man caught between two worlds, the tangible reality of his research pulling him in one direction, and the magnetic pull of Aine drawing him in another, a direction fraught with the uncertainty of deception.

He remembered a specific moment from their walk through the old town earlier that day. They had passed by a small, unassuming cottage, its windows shuttered and its garden overgrown with a riot of wildflowers. Aine had paused for a moment, her gaze fixed on the weathered facade, a peculiar expression on her face – a mixture of longing and something akin to apprehension. When he'd asked if she knew the place, she'd simply shaken her head, offering a vague response about how some houses in Kilkenny just had a certain melancholic air about them. But her eyes, for that brief instant, had held a depth of knowledge, a recognition that belied her casual dismissal. It was a subtle cue, easily overlooked, but now, it felt like a significant breadcrumb, leading him down a path he was increasingly afraid to follow.

The question of motive loomed large. If Aine was indeed aware of her family's involvement in practices that, by modern standards, might be considered unusual, even dangerous, why would she conceal it? Was it a matter of shame, a desire to distance herself from a past that might invite judgment? Or was it something more, a conscious effort to protect a legacy, to safeguard a tradition that was meant to remain hidden? The shopkeeper's words echoed in his mind – the emphasis on 'ancient energies,' on 'places of power.' If the O'Connells were indeed connected to such things, then concealment might not just be a matter of personal preference, but a necessity for survival.

He found himself caught in a peculiar paradox. The more he learned about the O'Connells, the more he understood why Aine might feel compelled to remain guarded. Yet, that very guardedness, that air of mystery, was also what made her so compelling, so intriguing. It was a siren call, a challenge that resonated with the part of him that craved discovery. He yearned for the trust that genuine affection demanded, the open sharing of vulnerabilities and histories. But every instinct, every piece of evidence he'd uncovered, suggested that such openness with him, regarding her family's past, was unlikely, if not impossible.

The weight of the inscribed stone in his pocket felt heavier now, a tangible symbol of the hidden truths that lay beneath the surface of Kilkenny, and perhaps, beneath the surface of Aine herself. He imagined her family through the generations, weaving their lives into the fabric of the town, their secrets passed down like heirlooms, their practices shrouded in the mists of time. Were they practitioners of forgotten arts, keepers of ancient knowledge, or simply a family with a rich and complex history that they chose to keep private? The ambiguity was a constant source of internal conflict, a battle between the heart that yearned for connection and the mind that demanded certainty.

He knew, with a growing sense of dread and fascination, that he was approaching a precipice. The path of his investigation was no longer purely academic; it was becoming deeply personal. The lines between observer and participant were blurring, and the potential consequences of his discoveries were no longer confined to historical records but extended to the fragile, yet burgeoning, relationship he shared with Aine. He had to decide whether to press forward, risking the potential loss of what he was beginning to value, or to retreat, leaving the deepest secrets of the O'Connells, and perhaps of Aine herself, undisturbed. The twilight had fully settled now, casting long shadows that seemed to stretch from the ancient stones of Kilkenny, reaching out to touch the very core of his divided heart. The silence of the approaching night was not empty; it was filled with the unspoken questions that hung between him and the woman he was falling for, questions that threatened to unravel everything. He stood at a crossroads, the familiar comfort of his notebook no longer enough to anchor him against the swirling tides of suspicion and affection. He had to find a way to navigate this treacherous terrain, to seek the truth without sacrificing the fragile hope of genuine connection, a hope that, with each passing moment, seemed to grow more precious and more precarious.

THE ANTIQUE DEALERS WARNING

The bell above the door of 'The Gilded Relic' gave a faint, almost apologetic chime as Pete pushed it open. The air inside was thick with the scent of aged wood, beeswax, and something indefinably older, a perfume of forgotten centuries. Mr. Silas, the proprietor, was perched on a stool behind his counter, polishing a tarnished silver locket with a practiced, almost ritualistic slowness. He looked up, his eyes, magnified behind thick spectacles, registering Pete's presence with a flicker of recognition, and perhaps, a hint of wariness. Pete's previous visit, his pointed questions about local history and specific families, hadn't gone unnoticed, and the antique dealer's quiet, evasive responses had only fueled Pete's growing suspicions.

"Back again, are we?" Silas's voice was a low rumble, like stones shifting in an ancient riverbed. He placed the locket down, his movements deliberate, as if measuring the weight of each word he was about to utter. He'd always possessed an air of knowing more than he let on, his shop a repository not just of objects, but of unspoken histories, of the town's layered secrets.

Pete nodded, stepping further into the dimly lit space, the scattered artefacts seeming to watch him with a silent, collective gaze. "I was hoping you might have some more insights, Mr. Silas. About Kilkenny's past, specifically certain families." He hesitated, then decided directness was the only path, however fraught with potential misunderstanding. "I'm particularly interested in the O'Connells."

Silas's hands stilled on the counter. A subtle tension entered his posture, a tightening around the eyes that was barely perceptible, yet utterly unmistakable to Pete, who was becoming adept at reading the nuances of guarded behaviour. The dealer picked up a velvet cloth and began to polish an ornate, dark wood box, his gaze now fixed on its intricate carvings.

"The O'Connells," Silas murmured, the name rolling off his tongue with a careful neutrality. "A long-standing name in Kilkenny, of course. Like many old families, they have their roots deeply entwilled with the town's history." He paused, then added, almost as an afterthought, "And its... peculiarities."

The word 'peculiarities' hung in the air between them, charged with an unspoken significance. Pete leaned forward, his academic detachment beginning to fray at the edges, replaced by a more visceral curiosity, a sense of being on the precipice of something significant. "Peculiarities? What kind of peculiarities are we talking about, Mr. Silas?"

Silas sighed, a soft exhalation that seemed to carry the dust of ages. He set down the cloth and the box, turning his full attention to Pete, his expression one of cautious consideration. "Kilkenny, you see," he began, his voice dropping lower, "is a town where certain... understandings have persisted through the generations. Traditions that aren't always written down in the official histories, but are felt, observed, passed down through whispers and subtle cues."

He gestured vaguely around the shop, as if the very objects within were silent witnesses to these 'understandings'. "Some families, for reasons of their own, have become custodians of these understandings. They are the ones who... maintain a certain balance, you might say. Who ensure that particular paths remain open, or perhaps, remain closed."

Pete felt a prickle of unease crawl up his spine. He'd come seeking historical facts, genealogical lines, perhaps even a forgotten document. He hadn't anticipated a conversation that felt less like historical research and more like an initiation into a clandestine society. "And the O'Connells are one of these families?"

Silas met Pete's gaze directly, his magnified eyes holding an unnerving depth. "The O'Connells," he confirmed slowly, deliberately. "Their association with these matters is... notable. They are known to be keepers of old ways. Not in a way that is ostentatious, mind you. They are discreet. Their role is often tied to the preservation of specific energies within the town, to maintaining certain... ancient agreements."

The phrase 'ancient agreements' struck Pete with a peculiar resonance, echoing the subtle but persistent feeling that Kilkenny itself held a hidden purpose, a secret life. He remembered the symbols etched into the stone, the shopkeeper's earlier mention of 'places of power'. "Agreements with whom, Mr. Silas? Or with what?"

Silas steepled his fingers, his gaze drifting towards a shadowed corner of the shop, where a collection of antique maps lay unfurled. "That, my young friend," he said, his voice laced with a knowing weariness, "is the question that has occupied many minds in Kilkenny over the centuries. Some would say it is an agreement with the land itself, with the ancient forces that reside here. Others speak of... guardians, of entities that require acknowledgment and respect. The O'Connells, and families like them, are seen as intermediaries, those who understand the necessary rituals, the proper deference to be shown."

He picked up a small, intricately carved ivory comb, turning it over and over in his hand. "It's a burden, of course," he continued, his tone softening. "To carry such knowledge, such responsibility. It shapes their lives, their interactions, their very lineage. It's why, as you may have observed, they tend to be guarded. Their secrets are not merely personal; they are generational imperatives."

Pete's mind raced, piecing together the fragments of information, Silas's veiled allusions, Aine's subtle deflections, the pervasive sense of an underlying current beneath the surface of Kilkenny life. If Aine's family was indeed involved in such a deeply entrenched tradition, her guardedness wasn't just about privacy; it was about a profound, inherited duty. It explained the faint hesitation he'd sensed, the almost imperceptible flinch when certain topics arose. She wasn't just keeping a secret; she was upholding a pact.

"So, their role is to preserve these 'understandings'?" Pete probed, trying to get a clearer picture of this inherited responsibility. "Does that mean they actively... do things? Perform rituals, perhaps?"

Silas gave a slow nod. "In a manner of speaking. It's not necessarily about grand ceremonies, though there may have been times for that. More often, it's about maintaining the flow, ensuring that the natural energies of certain places remain undisturbed, or are channeled in the correct way. It's about knowing the cycles, the seasons, the celestial alignments that hold significance. It's a form of custodianship, a delicate dance with forces that the uninitiated cannot comprehend."

He looked directly at Pete again, a hint of something akin to concern in his expression. "And it's a path that is not without its dangers. For those who disrupt these ancient understandings, or who fail to show the proper respect, there can be... consequences. Kilkenny has a long memory, and it has a way of reminding those who forget its older ways."

The warning was clear, delivered with an almost paternalistic gravity. Silas wasn't just a purveyor of antiques; he was a conduit for the town's unspoken lore, a keeper of its deeper currents. He was hinting that Pete's investigation, his very presence asking these questions, might be seen as a disruption.

"So, the O'Connells... they're protectors? Or perhaps wardens?" Pete ventured, trying to translate Silas's cryptic pronouncements into more tangible terms.

"Perhaps 'stewards' is a better word," Silas replied, his gaze softening as he ran a thumb along the smooth, cool surface of a jade pendant. "They steward something precious, something vital to the town's equilibrium. It's a role that demands vigilance, discretion, and an understanding that extends far beyond the material world. It's a responsibility that is woven into the very fabric of their existence, a legacy passed from parent to child."

He paused, his eyes scanning Pete with an assessing look. "You ask many questions, Mr. Hayes. More than most visitors. There's a sharp intellect behind your inquiries, but also... a certain intensity. A desire to uncover what lies beneath. I sense you're not content with the surface. But be warned, some beneath the surface is best left undisturbed. The past in Kilkenny is not always a pleasant thing to excavate."

The implication hung heavy in the air. Pete felt the familiar academic thrill of discovery warring with a growing sense of apprehension. He was not just researching history; he was treading on ground that was actively, deliberately maintained, a sacred territory guarded by families like the O'Connells. His fascination with Aine was no longer a simple matter of burgeoning affection; it was intrinsically linked to the secrets she, and her family, were sworn to protect. The antique dealer's words had painted a picture of a responsibility so profound, so ancient, that it shaped not just a lineage, but the very character of the town.

"I understand," Pete said, his voice a low murmur. "But I need to understand. If their family has this... this role... it must have shaped their history, their lives. And perhaps, it connects to why certain things have happened here, or why certain knowledge has been lost or suppressed."

Silas inclined his head, a small, almost imperceptible nod. "Indeed. The threads are many, and they are deeply intertwined. The O'Connells, through their custodianship, have likely influenced many aspects of Kilkenny's development, its fortunes, and its misfortunes. Their actions, however subtle, have ripple effects. And often, those effects are not readily apparent to the casual observer." He picked up a small, silver key, its head intricately shaped like a coiled serpent. "Some families carry burdens, Mr. Hayes, that are not easily explained by conventional means. They are tied to the land, to its ancient energies, to the subtle currents that govern the ebb and flow of life and power in places like Kilkenny. It is a clandestine role, a silent guardianship that can, at times, be a lonely existence."

He offered the key to Pete, not to take, but to examine. "Look at this," he said. "A simple key, perhaps. But what does it unlock? A chest? A door? Or perhaps, something more abstract? A secret passage? A forgotten truth? Families like the O'Connells are the keepers of such keys, the ones who know what they open, and why they must remain locked for most. Their vigilance is what keeps the balance, what ensures that the older ways are not entirely forgotten, nor are they exploited."

Pete looked at the key, then back at Silas, a dawning realization of the depth of the secrets he was uncovering. This wasn't just about a family with a rich history; it was about a family with a living, breathing responsibility, one that permeated every aspect of their existence and, by extension, the town of Kilkenny itself. The antique dealer's warning was a stark reminder that he was venturing into territory where the rules were ancient, unspoken, and potentially perilous. He felt a strange mix of apprehension and exhilaration. He was closer than ever to the truth, but the path ahead was becoming increasingly shadowed, and the stakes, he suspected, were far higher than he had initially imagined. The very air in the shop seemed to thicken, charged with the unspoken weight of generations of duty and secrecy. Silas's words had served as a potent, if unsettling, confirmation: the O'Connells were not merely inhabitants of Kilkenny; they were its custodians, its silent guardians, and their legacy was a profound, and perhaps dangerous, mystery.

AINES VULNERABILITY

The late afternoon sun cast long, distorted shadows across the cobblestone street as Pete found himself once again at Aine's doorstep. The scent of damp earth and the faint, lingering aroma of sea salt, carried on the gentle breeze from the nearby coast, seemed to wrap around the small cottage like a comforting embrace. He'd come, not with a barrage of questions, but with a quiet desire to simply be present, to offer a different kind of presence than the one he had been investigating.

Aine opened the door, her expression a delicate blend of surprise and hesitant welcome. The day's earlier frostiness seemed to have thawed, replaced by a more open, though still guarded, warmth. Her eyes, usually so bright and observant, held a subtle weariness, a shadow that hadn't been there when he'd last seen her. It was a weariness that spoke not of physical exhaustion, but of something deeper, something etched into the very fabric of her being.

"Pete," she murmured, her voice softer than usual. "I... I wasn't expecting you." She stepped aside, a silent invitation for him to enter. The interior of the cottage was a stark contrast to the bustling antique shop. It was simple, uncluttered, filled with the soft glow of lamplight and the comforting presence of well-loved books and worn, comfortable furniture. It felt like a sanctuary, a space where the weight of the outside world might, for a brief moment, be set aside.

He entered, the door closing softly behind him, sealing them in a bubble of shared quietude. He didn't press her for answers, didn't try to unravel the mystery that clung to her like a second skin. Instead, he simply looked at her, his gaze conveying a quiet understanding, a silent acknowledgment of the unspoken burdens he sensed she carried.

They sat by the hearth, the fire crackling merrily, casting dancing patterns on the stone walls. Aine poured them both cups of herbal tea, her movements economical, almost practiced, yet there was a tremor in her hand as she handed him his. He noticed it, of course, the subtle betraying of an inner turmoil. He wanted to reach out, to offer a reassuring touch, but he hesitated, aware that he was still an outsider, a visitor in a world she held so tightly guarded.

"It's been a... difficult few days," she began, her voice barely above a whisper, her gaze fixed on the swirling steam rising from her cup. "There are times when the weight of it all... it feels immense."

Pete nodded, his heart aching with a sympathy he hadn't anticipated. He'd arrived seeking answers, armed with theories and deductions, but in this quiet moment, all that seemed to matter was the palpable sadness in her eyes, the subtle tremor in her voice.

"The lineage," she continued, choosing her words with extreme care, as if treading on thin ice. "It's not just a name, Pete. It's... a responsibility. Something passed down, generation after generation. And sometimes," her voice cracked slightly, "sometimes it feels like it's consuming everything."

She didn't offer details, no names, no specifics of what this 're-sponsibility' entailed. It was a confession veiled in vagueness, a cry for understanding without the explicit revelation of the cause. He sensed a deep-seated weariness, a profound exhaustion that went beyond the mundane. It was the weariness of someone who had carried a burden for too long, a burden they couldn't articulate, perhaps even couldn't fully comprehend themselves.

"Is it... is it something you want to do?" he asked, his voice gentle, seeking to understand the agency she possessed within this inherited role.

Aine looked up, her eyes meeting his, and for a fleeting moment, he saw a flicker of raw pain, a vulnerability that stole his breath. "Want?" she echoed, a wry, sad smile touching her lips. "Want is a luxury, Pete. For those of us... born into certain lines, there are duties. Sacrifices. It's not about what we want. It's about what we must do."

She looked away again, her gaze drifting towards the window, as if seeking solace in the deepening twilight. "There are times," she confessed, her voice laced with a profound melancholy, "when I just... I wish I could be someone else. Someone who didn't have to carry this. Someone whose choices weren't dictated by the past, by the echoes of what came before."

He realized then, with a clarity that both illuminated and troubled him, that her secrecy wasn't necessarily born of malice, or a deliberate intent to deceive him. It stemmed, perhaps, from a profound sense of duty, a deep-seated fear of repercussions if she were to betray the confidences of her lineage, or worse, a fear of what might happen if the 'balance' her family was sworn to protect were ever truly disrupted. It was the burden of custodianship, as Silas had hinted, a responsibility so ancient and all-encompassing that it had shaped every facet of her existence, leaving her with little room for personal desire or open expression.

"What kind of sacrifices?" he ventured, his question a quiet probe, not demanding, but seeking to offer a space for her to share, if she so chose.

Aine's shoulders stiffened almost imperceptibly. The brief flicker of openness seemed to recede, replaced by a renewed layer of that familiar, carefully constructed reserve. She took a slow sip of her tea, her gaze downcast.

"The sacrifices of a life," she murmured, her voice regaining some of its earlier guarded tone. "Of opportunities. Of... knowing peace, perhaps. Of being entirely free to choose one's own path, without the weight of obligation pressing down."

She paused, then added, her voice laced with a hint of desperation, "It's like... like living under a perpetual shroud. You can see the world, but you can never quite touch it, never fully immerse yourself in it, because there's always this... this other thing. This duty that pulls you back, that demands your attention, your allegiance."

Pete leaned forward, his empathy a tangible thing in the quiet room. He saw not a woman withholding information out of spite, but a soul wrestling with an inheritance that felt more like a curse. Her vulnerability was not a sign of weakness, but of the immense pressure she was under.

"Aine," he said, his voice earnest, "I don't need you to tell me everything, not if it's not something you're ready to share. But I want you to know that I... I see that you're struggling. And I want to help, if I can."

She finally looked at him again, a faint blush coloring her cheeks. There was a flicker of gratitude in her eyes, quickly masked by a renewed wave of her customary reticence. "You are kind, Pete," she said, her voice soft, almost wistful. "But some burdens are meant to be carried alone. And some secrets are too deep, too old, to be easily shared, even with someone you... trust."

The word 'trust' hung in the air between them, heavy with unspoken meaning. He had earned a sliver of it, he knew, but the chasm of her lineage and its secrets remained vast. Her vulnerability was a tantalizing glimpse behind the curtain, a confirmation of the immense forces at play within her family, and within Kilkenny itself. It made him wonder if her evasiveness wasn't a betrayal of him, but a fierce, almost desperate attempt to protect not only herself, but the very foundations of her ancestral duties. The weight she felt was real, palpable, and it made him question his own role in potentially disturbing a delicate, centuries-old balance. He realized that his pursuit of truth was now inextricably linked to her struggle, and the delicate dance between them would require more than just intellectual curiosity; it would demand a profound understanding of loyalty, burden, and the quiet strength found in vulnerability. The secrets she carried were not just historical artifacts; they were living, breathing entities that shaped her very existence, and in their shared quietude, he felt the undeniable pull of their intertwined destinies.

He recognized the weariness in her voice, a resonance with the stories he'd pieced together from Silas and the hushed whispers of the townsfolk. It wasn't a weariness born of simple fatigue, but of a deep, soul-level exhaustion, the kind that comes from carrying an unspoken weight for an entire lifetime, a weight inherited from generations before her. It was the weariness of a lineage that demanded constant vigilance, a constant subtle sacrifice of personal freedom for the sake of maintaining a fragile, ancient equilibrium.

"It's the feeling," Aine continued, her voice barely audible, her gaze fixed on the flickering flames in the hearth, as if drawing some arcane strength from their dance, "that you're constantly... treading carefully. That one wrong step, one careless word, could have repercussions that echo far beyond yourself. It's like being born with invisible chains, chains forged not of metal, but of duty and expectation."

Pete watched her, his academic curiosity now tempered by a profound sense of empathy. He saw the flicker of pain in her eyes, the almost imperceptible clench of her jaw as she wrestled with emotions she was clearly reluctant to fully express. Her vulnerability was not a ploy, not a calculated move to elicit sympathy, but a genuine outpouring of a soul burdened by an inheritance she had not chosen.

"Do you ever feel... resentful?" he asked, his voice low and gentle, choosing his words with care. He didn't want to push her, but he felt a desperate need to understand the true cost of her family's role.

Aine considered the question for a long moment, a faint frown creasing her brow. "Resentful?" she mused, the word tasting unfamiliar on her tongue. "Perhaps. Sometimes. When I see others, free to pursue their dreams, unburdened by... such ancient responsibilities. But mostly," she sighed, a soft, sorrowful sound, "it's more a sense of... inevitability. A recognition that this is my path, whether I wish it to be or not. And within that inevitability, there's a constant struggle to... to honor it, without being consumed by it."

She reached out, her fingers tracing the rim of her teacup, her gaze distant. "My grandmother," she began, her voice gaining a new, softer cadence, "she was a woman of immense strength, of quiet dignity. She carried the weight with such grace. She taught me that it wasn't a burden to be resented, but a legacy to be respected. But there were times, I know, when even she felt the strain. I saw it in her eyes, the moments when the mask of composure would slip, revealing the profound weariness beneath."

Pete felt a wave of understanding wash over him. Silas's words about the O'Connells being custodians, stewards of ancient agreements, now resonated with a deeper, more personal meaning. Aine wasn't just the keeper of secrets; she was the heir to a profound, and perhaps lonely, responsibility. Her guardedness wasn't a barrier to him out of malice, but a shield against a world that could never truly comprehend the intricacies of her lineage, and perhaps, a shield to protect something precious that she was sworn to safeguard.

"So, this... legacy," Pete ventured, "does it require you to make difficult choices? To perhaps... avoid certain things, or people, for the sake of maintaining... whatever it is you're meant to maintain?"

Aine's gaze snapped back to him, a sharp, almost pained expression flashing across her features. "Choices are made for us, Pete," she said, her voice hardening slightly, the brief vulnerability receding once more behind a wall of practiced reserve. "The path is often laid out, and deviations are... discouraged. Strongly."

The implication was clear, though the specifics remained shrouded in mystery. She was caught in a current, a tide of ancestral obligation that dictated not just her actions, but her very choices. Her reluctance to reveal details wasn't a sign of deceit, but of a deeply ingrained understanding of the consequences of oversharing, of the potential dangers inherent in betraying the confidences of her lineage.

"I can't... I can't explain everything," she continued, her voice dropping again, laced with a tremor of unspoken emotion. "It's too... complicated. Too deeply woven into the fabric of who I am, and who my family is. But I want you to know," she met his gaze directly, her eyes holding a raw, unvarnished plea for understanding, "that it's not about keeping you at arm's length out of a desire to deceive. It's about a responsibility that is as ancient as the stones of this town. And sometimes, that responsibility requires a certain... distance. A certain degree of secrecy."

She paused, a faint flush rising to her cheeks, a sign of her own discomfort at revealing so much. "There are moments," she confessed, her voice barely a whisper, "when I question it all. When I wonder if the sacrifices are worth the... the preservation. But then I remember what my grandmother told me. That some things are too important to let go. Too vital to the world's delicate balance."

Pete felt a profound sense of empathy surge within him. He saw now that Aine's guardedness wasn't a reflection of her feelings towards him, but a manifestation of the immense, inherited burden she carried. Her vulnerability was a potent testament to the sacrifices demanded by her lineage, a silent plea for understanding in a world that could never fully grasp the weight of her ancestral duties. He realized that her secrets were not born of malice or intent to deceive, but from a deep-seated sense of obligation, a need to protect something far greater than herself. The brief glimpse into her inner turmoil, the raw emotion in her voice, deepened his empathy immeasurably, making him wonder if her secrecy was a shield forged from fear, or a testament to her unwavering commitment to protecting a legacy she held sacred. His understanding of her shifted, from that of an enigmatic figure with something to hide, to that of a young woman grappling with a profound and ancient responsibility, a responsibility that shaped her every interaction, and her every silent sacrifice. The quiet confession had not unraveled the mystery, but it had illuminated the deeply human struggle at its core, a struggle that made her all the more compelling, and her secrets all the more understandable.

THE UNVEILING OF A SECRET

The air in the guesthouse library was thick with the scent of aging paper and the faint, comforting aroma of beeswax polish. Dust motes danced in the slivers of sunlight that pierced the heavy velvet curtains, illuminating rows upon rows of leather-bound volumes. Pete had sought refuge here, a temporary reprieve from the gnawing questions that circled Aine like a persistent storm. He'd come with the intention of losing himself in a forgotten tale, to momentarily escape the oppressive weight of his current investigation, but as his fingers brushed against the spine of a particularly aged tome, a flicker of something – curiosity, perhaps, or a subconscious pull – drew him in.

It was a diary, bound in worn, cracked leather, its pages brittle and yellowed with the passage of centuries. The script, though faded, was remarkably legible, a graceful, looping cursive that spoke of a meticulous hand. The first page bore no name, only a date: 1748. An oddity, he thought, for a diary. Most people, even then, would have at least marked their name. He settled into a plush armchair, the silence of the library amplifying the rustle of the pages as he turned them.

The initial entries were mundane, chronicling the daily life of a woman named Elara. She wrote of the changing seasons, the harvest, the small joys and sorrows of a life lived in Kilkenny. But as Pete delved deeper, the entries began to shift, taking on a more introspective and, dare he think it, familiar tone. Elara's observations about the town, its undercurrents, its subtle shifts in energy, mirrored so many of the things he'd felt himself, things that Aine had alluded to in their hushed conversations. There was a recurring theme, a subtle undercurrent of guardianship, of a deep, innate connection to the very soul of Kilkenny.

"The hum," Elara wrote on one particularly striking page, "it is stronger this eve. A resonance that vibrates not in the ears, but in the very marrow of my bones. The veil thins, and the whispers grow bolder. It is time for the wards to be renewed."

Pete paused, his brow furrowed. The 'hum'? The 'veil thinning'? These were not the words of a simple farmer's wife. He flipped through more pages, his heart beginning to beat with a growing sense of anticipation. Elara described a cyclical duty, a responsibility passed down through her maternal line, a lineage tasked with maintaining a delicate balance within the town. It was a stewardship, she wrote, a silent pact with the land itself, ensuring its continued vitality and warding off unseen threats.

"My mother, bless her weary soul, spoke of it as a sacred trust," Elara confided, her pen scratching with a certain urgency. "A legacy woven into our very blood. She showed me the places, the points of convergence, where the earth breathes its secrets. And she taught me the old words, the protective syllables that bind and shield."

He read of rituals performed under the cloak of darkness, of herbs gathered under specific lunar phases, of ancient symbols etched into hidden places. These were not merely quaint superstitions; they were presented with a solemnity, a deep-seated conviction that spoke of generations of practice. Elara's descriptions of these rites were detailed, almost reverent, hinting at a profound understanding of forces that lay beyond the mundane. She spoke of a specific well, a place of great power, and the intricate ceremonies performed to appease whatever lay within its depths, to ensure its benevolent influence on the town.

"The wellspring," she penned, her hand trembling slightly, "is the heart of it all. A conduit between worlds. The duty falls to us to keep its waters pure, its influence steady. When the cycle turns, and the shadows lengthen, it is our vigilance that prevents the darkness from seeping through and staining the heart of Kilkenny."

Pete felt a chill crawl up his spine, a prickle of recognition that was both exhilarating and unsettling. Elara's descriptions of her duties, her subtle references to a 'hidden essence' of the town, the very idea of a lineage bound to its well-being – it all resonated with Aine's own veiled pronouncements, her hesitations, her profound weariness. Could this Elara be a distant ancestor? Was Aine, in her own quiet way, continuing a tradition that stretched back centuries, a tradition of safeguarding Kilkenny from unseen dangers?

He continued to read, his initial intent of escape vanishing entirely, replaced by a fervent need to uncover the full truth. Elara's diary was a map, a historical echo of the very mysteries that now surrounded him. She wrote of a recurring cycle, a rhythmic ebb and flow of power and vulnerability that afflicted the town, a phenomenon she attributed to its unique spiritual constitution.

"The tremors return with the turning of the seasons," Elara noted in an entry dated autumn of 1749. "A faint disquiet that settles upon the folk, a growing unease that no amount of sunlight can dispel. It is then that the old ways are most vital, the ancient protections most necessary. The townsfolk feel it, though they know not its source, attributing it to ill fortune or the whims of the weather."

She spoke of the importance of maintaining certain 'points of resonance' within the town, locations that acted as anchors or conduits for the town's energy. These were not marked on any map, their significance known only to those who carried the lineage. Elara's descriptions were tantalizingly vague, hinting at ancient structures, hidden groves, and perhaps even subterranean passages.

She wrote of specific stones, worn smooth by time and touch, that held a certain power, and the need to ensure they remained undisturbed.

"The standing stone by the old mill," she wrote, "its surface warmed by my touch, hums with a low thrum. It is a sentinel, a guardian. Its presence is essential for the containment of the fluctuations, for the anchoring of the town's spirit. I must ensure its roots remain firm, its purpose unforgotten."

Pete's mind raced. He'd seen peculiar stones, weathered and ancient, in various parts of Kilkenny, often dismissed as mere remnants of a forgotten past. Could these be the very anchors Elara spoke of? And if so, what were they anchoring? What were they protecting against? The diary hinted at more than just a general sense of well-being; it spoke of active, deliberate protection against something malevolent.

"There are whispers in the wind," Elara confided in a particularly chilling entry, "not of the natural sort, but of things that slither and seek to enter. They are drawn to the imbalance, to the cracks in the veil. The bloodline, though it may waver and change, must remain vigilant. For the sake of Kilkenny, and for the sake of those who dwell within its embrace, we must stand firm."

The similarity to Aine's own veiled warnings, her deep-seated sense of unease and responsibility, was too striking to be a mere coincidence. It was as if Elara, centuries ago, was speaking directly to Aine, and through her, to Pete. The diary was a testament to a legacy of custodianship, a tradition of safeguarding that had been passed down through generations, a secret passed from mother to daughter, cloaked in the mundane details of daily life.

Pete's gaze drifted to a passage where Elara described her deepest fears. "The weight of this knowledge," she wrote, "it is a solitary burden. To see what others cannot, to feel what others do not, and to bear the responsibility of acting upon it, often in silence. It is a lonely vigil. And sometimes, I wonder if the sacrifices demanded will ever cease, if the vigilance will ever find its rest."

This, Pete knew, was the crux of Aine's own struggle. The weariness he'd seen in her eyes, the guardedness, the subtle tremor in her hands – it all stemmed from this ancient, inherited duty. Elara's diary wasn't just a historical document; it was a profound validation of Aine's lived experience, a testament to the immense pressure she was undoubtedly under. The 'lineage' was not a metaphorical concept; it was a tangible, historical reality, a responsibility that had shaped the lives of women in Kilkenny for centuries.

He found himself looking at the diary not as a historical curiosity, but as a key, a Rosetta Stone that could unlock the deeper mysteries of Aine and her family. The cryptic pronouncements, the evasive answers, the palpable sense of her struggle – it all began to fall into place. Aine's secrecy wasn't a sign of distrust towards him, but a deeply ingrained reflex, a learned behavior born of centuries of carrying a profound and potentially dangerous secret. She was bound by a duty that transcended personal inclination, a commitment passed down through blood and tradition.

As he turned another page, he noticed a faint, almost imperceptible smudge of what looked like dried, dark ink near the bottom of one of Elara's more anxious entries. It was irregular, unlike the precise strokes of her pen, and seemed to have been made with a fingertip. He leaned closer, a sudden thought striking him. He remembered Silas, his hushed mentions of the O'Connells' role as "stewards," and the almost reverent way he spoke of their ancient duties. Was this diary part of that legacy? Had it been hidden away in the guesthouse library, waiting to be discovered by someone who could understand its true significance?

Elara's writing grew more fragmented as the diary progressed, filled with a sense of foreboding. She wrote of a specific time of year, a convergence of events that made the town particularly vulnerable. She alluded to a 'great test' that her lineage had faced periodically, a challenge that required immense strength and unwavering resolve.

"The moon will be at its zenith," she wrote, her script becoming almost frantic, "and the air will crackle with unseen energies. This is the time when the old pacts are tested, when the boundaries are thinnest. The rituals must be performed with absolute precision, lest the wards falter and the gateway... opens."

Gateway? The word sent a shiver down Pete's spine. What gateway was she referring to? Was it a physical passage, or something more... metaphysical? He looked at the diary, at the faded ink and the brittle pages, and felt an overwhelming sense of connection to this woman, Elara, who had lived and loved and feared in the very same town centuries before him. Her life, her struggles, her unshakeable sense of duty – they were mirrored in Aine, a living echo across time.

He realized that Aine's guardedness wasn't a rejection of him, but a manifestation of the very lineage described in this diary. It was a testament to the power of tradition, to the weight of inherited responsibility. The O'Connells weren't just a family; they were custodians of a secret that had shaped Kilkenny's history, a secret that demanded sacrifice, vigilance, and a profound understanding of the unseen forces that governed their world. The diary was a revelation, a tangible link to the past that illuminated the present, and in doing so, it deepened Pete's resolve to understand not only the mysteries of Kilkenny, but the burdens carried by the woman at its heart. He closed the diary, the weight of its contents settling heavily upon him, a silent testament to the unveiling of a secret that had been buried for centuries, a secret that was now inextricably woven into the fabric of his own investigation. The pieces were beginning to fall into place, forming a picture far more complex and ancient than he had ever imagined.

THE DILEMMA OF TRUTH

The library, once a sanctuary, now felt like a cage, the silence amplifying the turmoil churning within Pete. Elara's diary lay on the velvet-draped table, a tangible link to a past that was disturbingly, undeniably present. He'd come seeking distraction, an escape from the gnawing questions that clung to Aine like the Kilkenny mist. Instead, he'd found a testament to a legacy, a chronicle of a duty that stretched back centuries, a lineage of custodianship that now, it seemed, rested upon Aine's shoulders. The realization was both exhilarating and terrifying.

He traced the worn leather of the diary, the faint indentation where Elara's fingertip had pressed years ago. It wasn't just a historical curiosity; it was a mirror, reflecting the very struggles he saw in Aine. Her guardedness, her moments of profound weariness, the subtle tremors in her hands – they weren't signs of an unreliable witness, but manifestations of an inherited burden, a responsibility whispered down through generations. The O'Connells weren't merely a family; they were stewards, guardians of Kilkenny's unseen soul, tasked with maintaining a balance Pete was only beginning to comprehend.

This understanding, however, presented him with a stark and agonizing dilemma. He held in his hands the proof, the historical validation of Aine's cryptic pronouncements, her veiled warnings, her deep-seated anxieties. He knew, with a certainty that resonated deep within him, that her life was inextricably bound to the secrets Elara had so meticulously, and often fearfully, documented. The temptation to confront Aine, to lay the diary before her and demand the unvarnished truth, was almost overwhelming. He imagined the relief it might bring her, the burden shared, the walls between them finally crumbling.

But then, a more chilling thought intruded. What if his demand for truth, his need for absolute clarity, was precisely what could shatter the delicate trust they had managed to build? Elara's diary spoke of isolation, of the solitary nature of their duty. "The weight of this knowledge," she had written, "it is a solitary burden." Pete saw that same solitude in Aine, a quiet self-imposed exile from the ordinary, a necessary shield against a world that couldn't, or wouldn't, understand. To push too hard, to demand the complete unveiling of a secret generations had died to protect, could be a betrayal of that very legacy. It could be seen not as an act of solidarity, but as an invasion, a violation of the sanctity of her inherited trust.

He pictured Aine's face, the way her eyes would sometimes cloud over with an ancient sadness, the almost imperceptible flinch when a certain topic was broached. Her life was not his to dissect, her secrets not his to pry open with a blunt instrument. He was an outsider, albeit one who had stumbled upon a truth far deeper than he'd ever anticipated. Did he have the right to demand she lay bare the entirety of her existence, to expose herself to potential danger or misunderstanding for his sake?

The alternative was to accept her partial revelations, to continue their relationship with the unspoken acknowledgment of her hidden life, her inherited responsibilities. It meant living with the uncertainty, the unanswered questions, the nagging sense that a significant part of her remained shrouded in mystery. It meant accepting that their connection, as deep as it might feel, would always have an unspoken boundary, a veil that she, for reasons of self-preservation and duty, had to maintain. This path, while less confrontational, felt like a form of quiet surrender, an admission that some truths were too profound, too dangerous, to be fully grasped or shared. It meant walking a tightrope, balancing his desire for honest connection with the respect for her intrinsic need for discretion.

He remembered the way Silas had spoken of the O'Connells, his hushed reverence for their "stewardship." Silas, too, seemed to understand the weight of their lineage, the almost sacred nature of their role. He hadn't pressed for details, hadn't sought to unravel the intricacies of their duties. He had simply acknowledged their significance, their quiet influence on the fabric of Kilkenny. Perhaps that was the way forward – to acknowledge, to respect, and to trust that when and if Aine was ready, she would share what she could.

But the investigator in him recoiled at the thought of settling for partial truths. His entire career had been built on peeling back layers of deception, on exposing the hidden motives, on unearthing the facts, no matter how uncomfortable. To consciously choose ignorance, to accept a narrative deliberately curated for his benefit, felt like a dereliction of duty, not just to himself, but to the pursuit of truth itself. Was he willing to compromise his own principles for the sake of a relationship, however precious it was becoming?

He closed his eyes, picturing the various points of resonance Elara had alluded to, the ancient stones, the hidden groves. These were places of power, places that demanded respect, places that held secrets not meant for casual observation. Aine, he realized, was such a place. Her guardedness was a form of protection, a bulwark built around a core of ancient knowledge and inherent danger. To breach that bulwark without invitation, without a clear understanding of the consequences, was a gamble he wasn't sure he was willing to take, not yet.

The thought of Aine carrying this immense burden alone was a powerful one. Elara's diary had revealed a lineage not just of guardianship, but of sacrifice. It was a legacy that demanded vigilance, often in silence, often in isolation. Could he stand by and watch her bear that weight, knowing what he now knew, and offer only a partial understanding, a hesitant hand reaching across an unacknowledged divide? It felt like a betrayal of the very connection he felt growing between them, a connection that seemed to transcend mere circumstance.

He considered the implications of each choice. If he confronted Aine, he risked alienating her, destroying the trust that was still so fragile. He might be met with further evasion, or worse, outright rejection, leaving him with more questions than answers and the gnawing regret of having pushed too hard, too soon. But if he chose to accept her carefully constructed narrative, he would forever carry the knowledge of what lay beneath, a silent observer to her hidden life. He would have to live with the unanswered questions, the constant awareness of the unspoken, the understanding that she held a part of herself back from him, a necessary but painful exclusion.

The weight of Elara's diary felt immense, not just the physical weight of the aged pages, but the symbolic weight of the truth it contained. It was a truth that implicated him, that drew him into the ancient currents that flowed beneath Kilkenny's surface. Aine was at the center of those currents, and he was now irrevocably drawn into her orbit.

He opened his eyes and looked out the library window. The sunlight had shifted, casting longer shadows across the manicured gardens. The world outside continued, oblivious to the revelations contained within these hallowed walls. He could feel the subtle, almost imperceptible hum Elara had described, a faint resonance that seemed to emanate from the very stones of the guesthouse, from the ancient heart of Kilkenny itself. It was a reminder that the world was far more complex than it appeared, that beneath the veneer of the mundane lay forces and traditions that had shaped human lives for centuries.

Pete realized that his dilemma wasn't just about Aine; it was about his own capacity for trust and his willingness to accept the limitations of his understanding. Was he prepared to trust Aine's judgment, her need for discretion, even if it meant a degree of uncertainty in their relationship? Or was his need for definitive answers so great that he would risk fracturing the very bond he was beginning to cherish? The path ahead was unclear, shrouded in the same mist that often enveloped Kilkenny, a mist that concealed as much as it revealed. He knew one thing for certain: the discovery of Elara's diary had irrevocably altered the landscape of his investigation, and more importantly, his burgeoning feelings for Aine. He was no longer just an observer; he was a participant, caught in the currents of a legacy that demanded a profound and personal choice. The truth, he understood, was not always a simple unveiling, but often a delicate negotiation between what is known, what is revealed, and what must, for the sake of something greater, remain respectfully veiled. The choice he faced was not merely intellectual; it was deeply emotional, a test of his willingness to embrace the complexities of a world far richer, and far more perilous, than he had ever imagined. He picked up the diary, its weight a tangible reminder of the path he had to tread. He could not unlearn what he had discovered, and he could not unfeel the connection he felt to Aine. Now, he had to decide how he would proceed, navigating the treacherous waters of trust and deception with a newfound understanding of the deep, enduring currents that shaped both Kilkenny and the woman at its heart. The question remained: would he choose the certainty of a potentially fractured intimacy, or the uncertainty of a shared, albeit incomplete, truth?

Chapter Seven: The Heart of the Mystery

KILKENNYS ANCIENT HEART

The library, once a quiet haven for research, now felt like a claustrophobic chamber, the silence amplified by the thrumming unease in Pete's chest. Elara's diary, a weathered testament to a bygone era, lay open on the table, its fragile pages whispering secrets he was only beginning to decipher. He had come to Kilkenny seeking a respite, a distraction from the unsettling ambiguities that clung to Aine like the persistent, damp mist. Instead, he had unearthed a legacy, a chronicle of a duty passed down through generations, a custodianship that had, by some invisible thread, now fallen to Aine. The realization was a disquieting blend of exhilaration and dread.

His fingers, calloused from years of sifting through evidence and grappling with the often-unpleasant realities of his profession, traced the faded script on the page. Elara's words weren't just historical footnotes; they were reflections, mirroring the very struggles he'd observed in Aine. Her reserved demeanor, the weary shadows that sometimes flickered in her eyes, the almost imperceptible tremor that sometimes stole across her hands – these weren't the hallmarks of an unreliable witness, but rather the visible manifestations of an inherited weight, a responsibility that had been whispered, perhaps even burdened, down the lineage of the O'Connells. They were not merely a family, Pete now understood with a chilling clarity, but custodians, guardians of Kilkenny's unseen essence, tasked with maintaining a delicate equilibrium that he was only just beginning to grasp.

This burgeoning understanding presented him with a deeply unsettling quandary. He held in his possession the undeniable proof, the historical validation of Aine's cryptic pronouncements, her veiled warnings, her deeply entrenched anxieties. A profound certainty had settled within him: her life was inextricably entwined with the secrets Elara had so meticulously, and often fearfully, committed to paper. The urge to confront Aine, to lay the diary at her feet and demand an unvarnished truth, was almost overpowering. He could almost envision the relief it might bring her, the catharsis of shared understanding, the potential dismantling of the invisible barriers that had sprung up between them.

However, a more disquieting consideration intruded, casting a shadow of doubt over his impulse. What if his insistent pursuit of truth, his desperate need for absolute clarity, was precisely the catalyst that would shatter the fragile trust they had painstakingly cultivated? Elara's diary spoke voluminously of isolation, of the inherently solitary nature of their sacred duty. "The weight of this knowledge," she had written, her penmanship betraying a profound weariness, "it is a solitary burden." Pete recognized that same pervasive solitude in Aine, a self-imposed exile from the ordinary ebb and flow of everyday life, a necessary shield against a world that was either unwilling or unable to comprehend the depth of her commitment. To push too aggressively, to demand the complete revelation of a secret that generations had guarded with their very lives, felt like a profound betrayal of that very legacy. It risked being perceived not as an act of solidarity, but as an intrusion, a violation of the sanctity of her inherited trust.

He found himself replaying the image of Aine's face, the way her eyes would occasionally cloud over with an ancient, inexplicable sadness, the almost imperceptible flinch that would ripple through her when certain subjects were broached. Her life was not his to dissect, her secrets not his to pry open with the crude instruments of his profession. He was, by definition, an outsider, albeit one who had inadvertently stumbled upon a truth far more profound and pervasive than he had ever anticipated. Did he possess the inherent right to demand that she lay bare the entirety of her existence, to expose herself to potential danger, misunderstanding, or even judgment, solely for his own intellectual satisfaction?

The alternative was to accept her carefully curated narrative, to continue their burgeoning relationship with the unspoken acknowledgment of her hidden life, her inherited responsibilities. It meant navigating a path paved with uncertainty, a landscape dotted with unanswered questions, a constant awareness that a significant portion of her remained shrouded in an impenetrable mystery. It meant accepting that their connection, however deeply felt, would forever be demarcated by an unspoken boundary, a veil that she, for reasons of self-preservation and an unwavering sense of duty, was compelled to maintain. This path, while undoubtedly less confrontational, felt akin to a quiet surrender, an acknowledgment that some truths were simply too profound, too inherently dangerous, to be fully apprehended or openly shared. It was the choice to walk a precarious tightrope, attempting to balance his intrinsic desire for an honest, unadulterated connection with a profound respect for her fundamental need for discretion and privacy.

He recalled the reverent tone Silas had adopted when speaking of the O'Connells, his hushed admiration for their long-standing "stewardship." Silas, too, seemed to possess an innate understanding of the weight of their lineage, the almost sacred nature of their generational role. He hadn't pressed for intrusive details, hadn't sought to unravel the intricate tapestry of their duties. He had simply acknowledged their significance, their quiet yet undeniable influence on the very fabric of Kilkenny. Perhaps, Pete mused, that was the more appropriate path forward – to acknowledge, to respect, and to cultivate a trust that, when and if Aine felt it was the right time, she would share whatever she felt able to.

But the ingrained instincts of an investigator, honed by years of relentless pursuit, recoiled at the very notion of settling for partial truths. His entire professional existence had been dedicated to the painstaking process of peeling back layers of deception, to exposing hidden motives, to unearthing the unvarnished facts, regardless of how uncomfortable or inconvenient they might be. To consciously choose ignorance, to accept a narrative that was deliberately curated for his benefit, felt like a profound dereliction of duty, not merely to himself, but to the very core principle of truth-seeking that had guided his career. The question loomed large: was he truly prepared to compromise his own deeply held principles for the sake of a burgeoning relationship, however precious it was rapidly becoming?

He closed his eyes, picturing the various points of resonance that Elara had alluded to in her diary – the ancient stones, the secluded groves, the places where the veil between worlds seemed Thinnest. These were not merely geographical locations; they were sites of palpable power, places that demanded a deep and abiding respect, places that harbored secrets not intended for casual observation or idle curiosity. Aine, he realized with a growing sense of conviction, was such a place. Her guardedness was not a sign of evasiveness, but a form of protection, a meticulously constructed bulwark erected around a core of ancient knowledge and inherent danger. To breach that bulwark without explicit invitation, without a clear and comprehensive understanding of the potential repercussions, felt like an incalculably high-stakes gamble, one he wasn't entirely convinced he was prepared to take, not yet, at least.

The image of Aine bearing this immense, inherited burden alone was a powerful and persistent one. Elara's diary had illuminated a lineage not merely of guardianship, but of profound sacrifice. It was a legacy that demanded constant vigilance, often enacted in silence, frequently undertaken in profound isolation. Could he truly stand by and passively witness her carrying that immense weight, armed with the knowledge he now possessed, and offer only a superficial understanding, a hesitant hand reaching out across an unacknowledged, and perhaps unbridgeable, divide? It felt like a betrayal of the very nascent connection he felt blossoming between them, a connection that seemed to transcend the mundane circumstances of their meeting, reaching back into the mists of time.

He meticulously weighed the potential ramifications of each potential course of action. If he confronted Aine directly, he risked alienating her irrevocably, potentially shattering the delicate and still-fragile trust that had begun to form between them. He might be met with further, more entrenched evasion, or worse, outright rejection, leaving him adrift with even more unanswered questions and the profound, lingering regret of having pushed too hard, too soon, and ultimately, too carelessly. Conversely, if he chose to accept her carefully constructed narrative, he would be forever burdened by the knowledge of what lay hidden beneath the surface, a silent, complicit observer to her clandestine existence. He would have to reconcile himself to living with the persistent gnawing of unanswered questions, the constant awareness of the unspoken truths that lay between them, the understanding that she held a fundamental part of herself back from him, a necessary but undoubtedly painful form of exclusion.

The sheer weight of Elara's diary felt immense, extending far beyond the physical heft of its aged pages. It was the symbolic weight of the truth it contained, a truth that implicated him directly, that irrevocably drew him into the ancient, unseen currents that flowed silently beneath Kilkenny's surface. Aine, he now understood with absolute certainty, was situated at the very epicenter of those currents, and he was now inextricably caught within her powerful orbit.

He opened his eyes, his gaze drifting towards the library window. The sunlight had subtly shifted, casting elongated shadows across the meticulously maintained gardens. The world outside continued its oblivious progression, entirely unconcerned with the profound revelations contained within these ancient, hallowed walls. He could almost feel it now, the subtle, almost imperceptible hum that Elara had described in her diary, a faint, resonant vibration that seemed to emanate from the very stones of the guesthouse, from the very ancient heart of Kilkenny itself. It was a visceral, undeniable reminder that the world was a far more intricate and multifaceted place than it often appeared on the surface, that beneath the placid veneer of the mundane lay potent forces and deeply rooted traditions that had shaped human lives and destinies for countless centuries.

Pete realized with a startling clarity that his current dilemma extended far beyond the singular focus on Aine; it was, in fact, a profound test of his own capacity for trust and his willingness to acknowledge and accept the inherent limitations of his own understanding. Was he truly prepared to place his faith in Aine's judgment, in her deeply ingrained need for discretion, even if it meant accepting a degree of inherent uncertainty in their developing relationship? Or was his unyielding need for definitive, irrefutable answers so overpowering that he would risk fracturing, or even shattering, the very bond he was beginning to cherish so deeply? The path ahead remained obscured, shrouded in the same ethereal mist that so frequently enfolded Kilkenny, a mist that served to conceal as much as it promised to reveal. He knew, with a certainty that resonated deep within his soul, that the discovery of Elara's diary had irrevocably altered the landscape of his investigation, and, perhaps more significantly, the trajectory of his burgeoning feelings for Aine. He was no longer merely an observer; he had, by the twists of fate, become an active participant, ensnared in the powerful currents of a legacy that demanded a profound, deeply personal, and ultimately, defining choice. The truth, he was beginning to understand, was not always a straightforward unveiling, but often a delicate, nuanced negotiation between what is already known, what is cautiously revealed, and what must, for the preservation of something far greater, be respectfully veiled. The choice that lay before him was not simply an intellectual exercise; it was a deeply emotional crossroads, a formidable test of his willingness to embrace the inherent complexities of a world far richer, far more ancient, and undoubtedly, far more perilous than he had ever previously imagined. He picked up the diary once more, its worn weight a tangible, almost physical reminder of the arduous path he now had to tread. He could not simply unlearn what he had discovered, nor could he unfeel the profound connection he felt forging with Aine. Now, the critical decision he faced was how he would proceed, how he would navigate the treacherous, unpredictable waters of trust and deception with this newfound, albeit unsettling, understanding of the deep, enduring currents that shaped both the ancient city of Kilkenny and the enigmatic woman who stood at its heart. The central question remained, echoing in the quiet library: would he choose the perceived certainty of a potentially fractured intimacy, or the inherent uncertainty of a shared, albeit incomplete, truth?

He stood by the window, the aged parchment of the diary cool beneath his fingers. The late afternoon sun cast long, dramatic shadows across the cobblestone lanes visible below. Kilkenny wasn't just a collection of ancient buildings and storied landmarks; it was a living, breathing entity, its very stones imbued with the echoes of centuries, its air thick with the palpable residue of lives lived, loves lost, and secrets guarded. The notion that certain families, families like the O'Connells, could be so intrinsically bound to its fate, to its very essence, began to make a profound, almost unnerving, sense. It suggested a relationship that transcended mere residence, a connection that bordered on the symbiotic, a deep-seated intertwining of lineage and land, of duty and destiny.

He saw it now in the way the light fell upon St. Canice's Cathedral, in the stoic resilience of the round tower that had stood sentinel for over eight hundred years, in the very texture of the stones that formed the ancient city walls. There was a resonance here, a low hum of ancient energy that seemed to vibrate through the earth itself. It was the accumulated weight of history, the spectral presence of countless individuals who had walked these paths before him, their hopes, their fears, their triumphs and their tragedies all imprinted upon the very fabric of the place. Kilkenny wasn't merely a backdrop for his investigation; it was an active participant, an ancient consciousness that influenced the lives of those who were attuned to its whispers.

This new perception shifted his understanding of Aine dramatically. Her reticence, her occasional moments of what he had previously interpreted as anxiety or aloofness, now seemed less like personal quirks and more like an innate response to the pervasive energies of her ancestral home. She was not simply a resident of Kilkenny; she was, in a way he was only beginning to comprehend, a part of it. Her family's long-standing role as custodians wasn't a quaint historical footnote; it was a living, breathing responsibility, a commitment that likely demanded a constant vigilance, a deep attunement to the subtle shifts and currents that flowed beneath the surface of ordinary life.

He thought of Elara's descriptions of "thin places," of moments when the veil between the physical and the spiritual seemed to shimmer and recede. Were these places more concentrated in Kilkenny? Did the city itself act as a perpetual nexus, a point where the past and the present, the seen and the unseen, were in constant, dynamic interplay? And if so, what did that mean for Aine, for the keeper of its deepest secrets? Her position, he realized, was not merely one of safekeeping information, but of actively participating in the maintenance of a delicate balance, a balance that likely involved forces and energies that lay far beyond the realm of conventional understanding.

The thought sent a shiver down his spine, not of fear, but of a profound, almost reverential awe. He was no longer just investigating a cold case or a family mystery; he was touching upon something far older, far more elemental. The history of Kilkenny, as documented in dusty tomes and etched into ancient stones, was merely the visible manifestation of a deeper, more potent narrative. And Aine, he understood, was not just a character within that narrative, but a vital, living conduit, her life and well-being intrinsically linked to the continued existence and stability of Kilkenny's ancient heart.

He imagined the weight of that responsibility, the constant awareness of a duty that extended not just to the present, but to all the past and all the future generations who would call this place home. It was a burden that would necessitate a certain detachment, a careful guarding of oneself, lest the immense energies of the place overwhelm or consume. Aine's guardedness, her deep-seated anxieties, her moments of profound weariness – these were not weaknesses, but the understandable consequences of living with such an extraordinary, and perhaps perilous, inheritance. Her life was a testament to a lineage of service, a quiet, unwavering commitment to safeguarding something precious and ancient.

This realization brought a fresh wave of empathy, a softening of the professional detachment he usually maintained. He saw Aine not as a potential suspect or an unreliable witness, but as a guardian, a sentinel bound to a duty that was both magnificent and daunting. The mystery wasn't simply about uncovering what had happened in the past; it was about understanding the profound, almost mystical, connection between a woman, her lineage, and the ancient city that held them both in its embrace. Kilkenny's ancient heart was not just a geographical location, but a living force, and Aine was its beating, enduring pulse. He understood, perhaps for the first time, that the secrets she guarded were not merely personal or historical, but were woven into the very essence of the place, intrinsically linked to its ongoing existence, its very soul. This wasn't just a mystery to be solved; it was a legacy to be understood, a sacred trust to be respected, and a woman, deeply entwined with it all, to be seen with new eyes.

THE SYMBOLISM OF THE CASTLE

The towering stone edifice of Kilkenny Castle, once a mere backdrop to the unfolding narrative, now loomed in Pete's mind with an entirely new significance. It wasn't just a remnant of Norman conquest or a testament to centuries of aristocratic lineage; it was rapidly becoming the physical anchor for the intangible currents he was beginning to sense swirling beneath the placid surface of Kilkenny. He'd spent hours poring over local histories, dusty volumes unearthed from the very library where Elara's diary had offered its first tantalizing glimpses into Aine's world. The castle's story, a grand sweep of conquest, consolidation, and domestic drama, now seemed less like a historical account and more like a veiled chronicle of a deeper, more elemental purpose.

He'd learned of its origins, of the strategic earthwork fortress erected by Richard de Clare, the Earl of Pembroke, commonly known as Strongbow, in the wake of the Norman invasion. But it was the subsequent transformation, the stone stronghold that began to rise in the 12th century under William Marshal, that truly captured his attention. Marshal, a knight of legendary prowess, had recognized the strategic importance of the site, commanding a bend in the River Nore. The castle was not merely a military stronghold; it was a declaration of power, a physical manifestation of the dominance the Normans sought to impose. Pete found himself tracing the historical accounts of its construction, imagining the sheer grit and determination required to raise such a formidable structure in an age of limited technology. The sheer scale of it, the thick stone walls, the imposing keep, all spoke of an intention that went beyond mere habitation. It was designed to endure, to project strength, and to command respect.

As he delved deeper, the castle's story became a tapestry woven with the threads of its various inhabitants. The Butlers, Earls of Ormond, held sway for centuries, transforming it from a grim fortress into a grander residence, reflecting their growing wealth and influence. Pete pictured the grandeur of their era, the opulent balls, the political machinations played out within its walls, the quiet hum of domestic life that must have once filled its vast chambers. Yet, even in these descriptions of domesticity and refinement, he detected an undercurrent of something more. Were these noble families merely living within the castle, or were they, in some way, also part of its enduring purpose? Elara's diary had spoken of 'guardianship,' of a duty passed down through generations. Could the Butlers, in their long tenure, have been unknowingly, or perhaps knowingly, playing a role in this ancient stewardship?

The legends surrounding Kilkenny Castle were even more compelling. Tales of hidden passages, of spectral figures glimpsed in the moonlight, of unexplained phenomena that had long been whispered about by the locals, began to coalesce in Pete's mind. He found accounts of Lady Eleanor Butler, the alleged mother of Piers Butler, the 8th Earl of Ormond, and her rumored involvement in witchcraft and dark arts. These were dismissed by most historians as mere folklore, embellishments born of superstition and a fear of powerful women in a patriarchal society. But Pete, armed with the unsettling revelations from Elara's diary, saw a different narrative emerging. Lady Eleanor's legend, however embellished, spoke of a woman who wielded influence, who was perceived to possess knowledge beyond the ordinary. Was it possible that her "witchcraft" was, in fact, an early manifestation of the very custodianship Elara had documented?

He imagined Aine walking through those same grounds, perhaps even within the castle itself, her own guarded nature a reflection of the ancient forces that seemed to emanate from its very core. The castle, he began to theorize, was not merely a historical monument; it was a focal point. A nexus for the hidden power that coursed through Kilkenny, a physical manifestation of the protective wards that Elara had hinted at. The very stones, weathered by centuries of rain and wind, seemed to absorb and retain the ambient energies of the land. And at the heart of this ancient edifice, Pete suspected, lay the key to understanding the intricate web of responsibility that had ensnared Aine.

He revisited the castle's history, focusing not on the political shifts or the changes in ownership, but on the enduring aspects, the elements that had remained constant through the ages. The stout defensive walls, the strategic layout, the very choice of location – these were not arbitrary decisions. They spoke of an awareness of the land, of its inherent energies, and of a need to both harness and protect them. Kilkenny, nestled in its fertile valley, was a place of ancient significance long before the Normans arrived. Pete found references to pre-Christian rituals performed in the area, to sacred groves and ancient burial sites that predated the castle by millennia. The Normans, in building their stronghold, had, perhaps unknowingly, erected their structure upon a foundation of even older power.

The castle, therefore, was more than just a Norman stronghold; it was a layer built upon layers of history, each stratum imbued with its own unique resonance. The pagan reverence for the land, the Norman assertion of dominance, the aristocratic grandeur of the Butlers, and now, the quiet, persistent duty of the O'Connells – all these threads converged within its imposing walls. Pete began to see the castle as a kind of energetic amplifier, a structure designed, either intentionally or by virtue of its placement, to channel and contain the spiritual essence of Kilkenny.

He recalled Elara's cryptic notes about "thin places," and it struck him with a sudden, chilling clarity that Kilkenny Castle itself might be one of the most significant of these. A place where the veil between worlds was not just thin, but perhaps, intentionally permeable, allowing for the flow of certain energies, or perhaps, for the very purpose of containment. The legends of Lady Eleanor Butler, the tales of spectral sightings, could these be manifestations of the energies that were either being channeled or, conversely, kept in check by the castle's ancient architecture?

He imagined Aine's role in this intricate system. Was she a guardian of the castle itself, or of something that resided within its depths? Elara's diary had spoken of a "heart," a central point of power that needed constant vigilance. Could this 'heart' be located within the castle, perhaps in its deepest dungeons, or beneath its ancient foundations? The thought sent a tremor of excitement, mixed with a palpable sense of unease, through him. He was venturing into territory that defied rational explanation, yet every piece of evidence, every whispered legend, seemed to point towards this monumental structure as the epicenter of the mystery.

He found himself drawn to the physical details of the castle that were often overlooked in historical accounts. The specific types of stone used in its construction, the orientation of its various towers, the layout of its inner courtyards – all these elements, he theorized, might hold clues to its true purpose. Was the castle's design a deliberate attempt to create a containment field, a sophisticated system for managing energies that were both powerful and potentially dangerous? The sheer robustness of its construction, the thickness of its walls, the impregnability of its design, all suggested a need for protection, not just from external enemies, but perhaps from something internal as well.

He remembered Elara's reference to the castle as a "silent sentinel," and the phrase echoed in his mind with a newfound resonance. A sentinel was a guard, a watcher. Was the castle, in its very permanence, tasked with a continuous watch over something significant? And if so, what was it watching? The narrative of Aine's family, the O'Connells, as custodians, now seemed intrinsically linked to the castle's own enduring presence. They were not just its inhabitants or owners; they were, in a profound sense, its caretakers, responsible for maintaining its ancient function.

Pete's investigation, which had begun with a desire to understand a potentially simple domestic disturbance, was rapidly evolving into something far grander, far more ancient, and infinitely more complex. Kilkenny Castle, once just a tourist attraction, now represented the physical embodiment of the mystery that ensnared Aine. It was the silent witness to centuries of secrets, the repository of ancient power, and the likely focal point of the protective wards that Aine was bound to maintain. He felt a growing conviction that to truly understand Aine's burden, he needed to understand the castle, its history, its legends, and its enduring, enigmatic purpose. The key, he suspected, was not just in the words written on fragile pages, but in the very stones of Kilkenny's most formidable and storied landmark.

He imagined the castle at different points in its history. The raw, imposing fortress of William Marshal, designed for defense and assertion of power. The more refined, yet still formidable, residence of the Butlers, who, while enjoying its comforts, would have been acutely aware of the underlying strength and history of the edifice. Then, perhaps, a period of subtle shift, a transition of understanding where the custodianship became more consciously tied to the castle's deeper significance. This was where the O'Connells entered the picture, their role evolving from mere inheritors of property to inheritors of a profound responsibility. Elara's diary offered glimpses into this transition, detailing the increasing weight of this duty, the subtle but persistent unease that accompanied it.

Pete felt a growing certainty that the castle was not just a passive structure. It was an active participant in whatever was happening in Kilkenny. Its design, its materials, its very location, all suggested an intentionality that transcended mere architectural ambition. He speculated about the possibility of specific chambers within the castle being designed to amplify or dampen certain energies, or perhaps to serve as focal points for the protective wards. Could the famed "long gallery" have served a purpose beyond displaying art? Were the deep, forbidding dungeons more than just cells for prisoners? Each question led to more speculation, but each speculation felt grounded in a growing, albeit unconventional, understanding of the forces at play.

He found himself scrutinizing old maps and architectural plans of the castle, looking for anomalies, for features that seemed out of place or unusually designed. He was searching for the subtle signs of a purpose that was deliberately concealed, a function that was masked by centuries of evolving use. The legends of hidden passages, dismissed by most as fanciful tales, now seemed to take on a new dimension. Could these passages have been conduits for energy, or secret routes for maintaining the delicate balance that Aine was now responsible for?

The concept of protective wards, mentioned in Elara's writings, began to take on a tangible form in his mind, anchored by the physical presence of the castle. He imagined the castle as the central anchor point for these wards, its ancient stones acting as conduits, channeling and perhaps even radiating the protective energies that kept Kilkenny safe from... what, precisely? The answer remained elusive, shrouded in the same mist that perpetually clung to the valley. But the castle, he was convinced, was the mechanism, the very heart of this ancient, unseen defense system.

He envisioned Aine, not just as a woman haunted by her family's past, but as a living embodiment of this custodianship. Her reserved nature, her occasional moments of profound sadness, her deep-seated anxieties – these were not personal failings, but the understandable reactions of someone who bore the immense weight of protecting not just a legacy, but the very essence of a place. Kilkenny

Castle was the physical manifestation of that legacy, and Aine was its living guardian.

The sheer scale of the castle, its enduring presence against the ever-changing tides of history, spoke of a power that transcended human dominion. It was a silent testament to a continuity that ran far deeper than recorded history. And within its imposing walls, Pete was convinced, lay the heart of the mystery he had been drawn into, a mystery intrinsically bound to the ancient stones, the whispered legends, and the solitary woman who carried its burden. He felt a profound sense of purpose solidifying within him; his investigation was no longer just about uncovering the truth of a past event, but about understanding and perhaps even aiding in the maintenance of something ancient and vital, something that had its physical locus within the very heart of Kilkenny Castle. The implications were staggering, and as the sun began to set, casting long, dramatic shadows across the grounds, Pete knew his journey into the heart of Kilkenny's mystery had only just begun, and its most significant landmark stood silent, yet eloquent, before him.

AINES FAMILIAL BURDEN

The air in the small, cluttered sitting room of Aine's cottage was thick with unspoken words, each one a hesitant breath drawn before the plunge. Pete watched her, his own anticipation a taut string in the quiet space between them. The scent of drying herbs, familiar and comforting, seemed to hold its breath too, as if acknowledging the weight of the confession about to be laid bare. He had come to Kilkenny seeking answers, armed with Elara's fragmented diary and a growing conviction that the town's history held a deeper, more resonant chord than any guidebook could reveal. But he hadn't anticipated that the melody would be sung by Aine herself, her voice a fragile instrument carrying the burden of generations.

"It's... it's not just a feeling, Pete," Aine began, her gaze fixed on the worn rug beneath her feet, as if the pattern held some ancient, coded message she was trying to decipher. "This connection I have to Kilkenny, this sense of responsibility... it's real. It's inherited." She finally met his eyes, and the depth of weariness and ancient knowledge she held within them was startling. "My family, the O'Connells, we're not just residents of Kilkenny. We're its custodians."

Pete leaned forward, the casual curiosity that had propelled him thus far deepening into a profound, almost reverent, attention. Custodians. The word, so simple and mundane, hung in the air like a pronouncement. Elara's diary had alluded to a duty, a guardianship, but Aine's quiet, measured tone lent it a gravity that Pete had only begun to suspect. "Custodians of what, Aine?" he asked, his voice low, careful not to break the delicate thread of her confession.

Aine took a slow, shaky breath, her fingers twisting the worn fabric of her skirt. "Of the essence, Pete. Of the... balance." She paused, searching for the right words, for a way to translate the intangible into something he could grasp. "Kilkenny, it's built on something ancient. Older than the Normans, older than the stones of the castle. There are... currents here. Energies. Sometimes they run strong, and sometimes they... shift. They can become unstable."

He remembered Elara's fragmented notes, her cryptic references to 'thin places,' to a palpable sense of being watched, to a protective force that seemed to emanate from the very land. He had initially dismissed them as the ramblings of someone under stress, perhaps even delusional. But Aine, grounded and seemingly rational, was weaving those same threads into a coherent, if unbelievable, tapestry.

"You mean like... supernatural? Ghosts? Magic?" The questions sounded almost absurd as they left his lips, a jarring intrusion of the mundane into the mythic space Aine was opening.

She offered a faint, almost sad smile. "Not exactly like in the stories, perhaps. It's more... elemental. Like the earth itself has a heartbeat, and Kilkenny is a place where that heartbeat is particularly strong. And sometimes," her voice dropped, becoming almost a whisper, "sometimes, that heartbeat falters. Or something tries to disrupt it."

Pete felt a chill, not of fear, but of a profound, unexpected recognition. The castle, the ancient sites, the legends that clung to the town like the persistent mist from the Nore – they weren't just relics of the past. They were integral to this 'balance' she spoke of. "And your family... you're meant to... maintain it?"

"We are," Aine confirmed, her gaze unwavering now. "It's a responsibility passed down through every generation. My mother, her mother, and so on, back to the very beginning. We're watchers. Protectors. We ensure that the energies remain stable, that nothing from... elsewhere, or nothing from within the deepest layers of Kilkenny's own history, disrupts the natural flow." She finally looked directly at him, her eyes holding a universe of inherited duty. "It means always being aware, always observing, always being ready to... intervene, if necessary."

"Intervene how?" Pete pressed, his mind racing, trying to reconcile the image of the quiet, reserved woman before him with the idea of a guardian capable of intervening in unseen forces.

"It varies," she said, her voice tinged with a weariness that spoke of countless nights spent in vigilance. "Sometimes it's about reinforcing existing wards, using knowledge passed down through ancient texts and rituals. Sometimes it's about understanding the subtle shifts in the land, in the very atmosphere, and acting to counteract them. It's a constant vigilance, a living connection to the town's very soul." She gestured vaguely towards the window, towards the sprawling landscape that lay beyond. "Elara... she understood some of it. She saw the patterns, felt the unrest. That's why she sought me out, I think. She felt the same pull, the same obligation, even if she didn't fully grasp its scope."

The pieces began to slot into place with a dizzying, almost overwhelming, sense of clarity. Aine's evasiveness, her reluctance to engage fully with the world beyond her immediate duties, her deep, almost spiritual, connection to Kilkenny – it all made a terrible, beautiful sense. She wasn't being difficult or aloof; she was simply living a life dictated by a commitment that predated her by centuries.

"So, this 'disturbance' that Elara was investigating..." Pete began, the implications dawning on him. "Was it a threat to this balance?"

Aine nodded, her expression grave. "It was. Something was trying to exploit the weaknesses, to create a tear, a disruption. It felt... wrong. A deep disharmony. And it was growing, feeding on the ambient energies. Elara was trying to understand it, to find its source, so that I could act." She hesitated, then added, "She got too close. The forces she was investigating... they reacted."

The casual tragedy of Elara's death, the unanswered questions that had driven Pete's investigation, now felt imbued with a cosmic significance. Elara hadn't just stumbled upon a secret; she had been caught in the crossfire of an ancient conflict. And Aine, burdened by her inherited duty, had been left to bear the weight of that loss, and the ongoing threat.

"This knowledge... it's a heavy burden, Aine," Pete said, the words a simple acknowledgement of the profound weight she carried.

"It is," she agreed, her voice barely audible. "It's been the burden of my family for as long as anyone can remember. We don't live for ourselves, not entirely. We live for Kilkenny. We ensure its peace, its stability, even when the cost is immense." She finally looked up, a flicker of something akin to desperate hope in her eyes. "Elara's diary... it was a cry for help. A way to reach out, to find someone who could understand, who could perhaps even help. She knew she was in danger, and she knew that if anything happened to her, the knowledge she had gathered needed to be passed on. To someone who could continue the work."

The unspoken implication hung heavy in the air: that 'someone' was him. Pete, the outsider, the investigator, was now being drawn into a lineage of guardianship he could never have imagined. He thought of the castle, of its enduring presence, its silent watch. It wasn't just a historical monument; it was a symbol, an anchor for the very forces Aine was sworn to protect. The Norman strength, the Butler grandeur, and now, the quiet, unyielding vigilance of the O'Connells – all intertwined around the heart of Kilkenny.

"So, the 'thin places' Elara wrote about... they're points where this balance is most vulnerable?" Pete ventured, trying to process the vastness of this revelation.

"They are," Aine confirmed. "Places where the veil between our world and... other influences is thinner. The castle itself is one of the strongest anchors, but there are others, scattered throughout the town and the surrounding countryside. Ancient sites, places of natural power. My family's duty is to maintain the integrity of these places, to ensure the wards are strong, that the energies are channeled correctly."

He recalled the numerous times he'd felt an inexplicable sensation of presence while exploring Kilkenny, a prickling on his skin, a sudden shift in the air. He had attributed it to the town's ancient atmosphere, its rich history. Now, he understood. It wasn't just history; it was the constant, subtle hum of a force at work, a protective energy being maintained by generations of women, culminating in Aine.

"And the threat?" Pete asked, the question still feeling both impossibly real and utterly fantastical. "What exactly was it? What were you fighting against?"

Aine's shoulders tensed. "It's... difficult to describe. It's not a person, not in the way we understand it. It's more like a force, a corruption, that seeks to feed on instability, to sow discord. It thrives in the shadows, in the forgotten places, and it was drawn to the power inherent in Kilkenny, seeking to twist it, to break the balance for its own ends." She shivered, despite the warmth of the room. "Elara discovered its origins, or at least, its current manifestation. It was linked to a specific site, a place of ancient power that had been disturbed."

The words 'disturbed' and 'ancient power' echoed in Pete's mind, bringing him back to his own investigations into Kilkenny's pre-Norman past, to the whispers of forgotten rituals and sacred groves. Had his own curiosity, his own digging into the town's deepest secrets, inadvertently played a part in this disturbance? The thought was a heavy one, adding another layer to his growing sense of responsibility.

"And your role now, Aine?" he asked, his voice gentle. "What do you need to do?"

"I need to understand the full scope of the threat," she said, her gaze resolute. "Elara's notes were incomplete. She was interrupted. I need to find the missing pieces, to understand the nature of the disturbance and how to counter it. And I need to be vigilant, to watch for any signs of its resurgence." She looked at him, a new question forming in her eyes. "Elara trusted you. She believed you could help. I... I don't know how you fit into this, Pete, but if you are willing, if you can help me understand what Elara discovered, then perhaps, together, we can ensure Kilkenny's safety."

The invitation, spoken with such quiet earnestness, was more than just an offer of collaboration; it was an invitation to step into a world he had only glimpsed through the pages of a diary, a world of ancient duty and unseen forces. The familial burden of the O'Connells, which had been a mere whisper of mystery, now stood revealed as a profound, life-altering commitment. Aine's story wasn't just about her family; it was about the very soul of Kilkenny, a soul she was sworn to protect. And in that moment, Pete knew his journey had taken a turn he could never have anticipated, a turn that would lead him deep into the heart of Aine's ancient trust, and the enduring mystery of Kilkenny. He nodded, his decision made not by logic, but by the palpable sense of truth and the quiet strength he saw in the woman before him. The silence in the room now felt less like hesitation and more like a shared understanding, a silent pact forged in the face of an ancient, unfolding threat. He was no longer just an investigator; he was, in a way, a potential ally in a battle he was only beginning to comprehend.

THE SIGNIFICANCE OF THE OLD MILL

The weight of Aine's confession settled over Pete, transforming the familiar charm of Kilkenny into something far more profound, far more potent. He had come seeking historical facts, fragments of a forgotten life, but he had stumbled into a living legend, a generational commitment woven into the very fabric of the town. His mind, trained to seek logical explanations, grappled with the immensity of what Aine had shared – the concept of 'custodians,' of maintaining an unseen 'balance,' of energies and currents flowing beneath the surface of everyday life. It was a narrative that dwarfed any historical account he had ever encountered.

"The old mill," Pete murmured, the words a tentative bridge back to tangible reality, a grounding point in the swirling implications of Aine's revelation. He pictured the weathered stone, the giant wooden wheel now long dormant, the gentle murmur of the River Nore flowing past. It had always struck him as a place steeped in a quiet melancholy, a forgotten sentinel on the edge of town. He'd felt an unusual stillness there, an almost watchful quietude during his initial visit, an impression he'd filed away as atmospheric. Now, it clicked into place with a chilling clarity. "You said... it's important. Not just to your family's history, but to your duties?"

Aine nodded, her gaze distant, as if her thoughts were already tracing a path back to that familiar, yet now profoundly significant, landmark. "The mill," she began, her voice gaining a measure of steadiness, a return to the focused intent that characterized her. "It's more than just an old building, Pete. For generations, it's been a nexus. A place where the natural energies of the land converge, where the flow is particularly strong, and therefore, particularly sensitive." She paused, searching for the precise language. "Think of it as a... confluence point. A natural amplifier for the very forces I've been tasked with safeguarding."

Pete leaned closer, the scent of drying herbs in the small cottage suddenly seeming to carry the faint, earthy aroma of damp stone and flowing water. "A confluence point for what, exactly?" he asked, his investigative instincts reasserting themselves, albeit now directed towards a far more esoteric set of 'facts.'

"For the life force of Kilkenny," Aine explained. "The river, the ancient ley lines that crisscross this region, the very earth beneath our feet – they all contribute to a subtle, constant flow of energy. The mill, due to its location and the way it was built, amplifies this. It channels it. It's a natural monument, yes, but it's also a deliberate focal point for maintaining the town's... energetic health."

He thought back to his solitary exploration of the mill. He'd climbed the worn stone steps, run his hands over the pitted wood of the wheel, peered into the dark, silent races. There had been no overt signs of anything unusual, no spectral apparitions, no echoing whispers. Yet, there had been a palpable sense of something more, a quiet hum beneath the surface that he'd attributed to the sheer weight of history. "You felt this energy when you were there?"

"Always," Aine confirmed without hesitation. "Even as a child, I felt it. It's like a low, steady thrumming, a sense of deep peace, but also of immense power held in reserve. It's a place of grounding. But," her voice dropped, a shadow crossing her features, "it's also a place that requires constant attention. Like any living thing, it needs to be tended."

He recalled a specific detail he'd noticed, something that had seemed out of place, yet he'd dismissed it as mere structural anomaly or perhaps some forgotten graffiti. "There were... symbols," he ventured, trying to conjure the image from his memory. "Etched into the stone, near the water intake. They looked old. Intentional."

A faint smile touched Aine's lips, a shared understanding passing between them. "Ah, yes. The wards. They are ancient. Older than the mill itself, in a way. They were there before, on the original site, and when the mill was built, the builders, who were themselves aware of the land's significance, incorporated them, reinforced them. They are part of the ancient protective rituals passed down through my family."

"Rituals?" The word felt both foreign and strangely resonant. He had expected history, perhaps folklore, but not active, ongoing ritual. "What kind of rituals?"

"They are designed to harmonize the energies," Aine explained, her gaze becoming intense, as if she were re-enacting them in her mind. "To ensure the flow remains pure, unobstructed. They are not about conjuring or banishing in the dramatic sense you might imagine. They are about reinforcement, about guiding, about ensuring that the natural currents are not diverted or corrupted by external influences. The symbols you saw are specific to Kilkenny, to this particular confluence. They are what my ancestors called 'binding marks,' meant to stabilize the energetic field, to create a barrier against any disharmony that might seek to infiltrate."

Pete felt a shiver trace its way down his spine, a sensation entirely separate from the cool air of the cottage. He remembered the unsettling feeling he'd had, the subtle disorientation, the sense of being on the threshold of something vast and unknown. It wasn't just the age of the mill; it was the palpable presence of something else, something ancient and watchful, that had made him feel so acutely aware of his own insignificance in the face of it. "So, that feeling... that unease I had when I visited the mill..."

"Was your intuition sensing the concentrated energy," Aine confirmed. "And perhaps, if there were any subtle shifts happening at that time, any nascent instability, you would have felt that too. It's a place of immense power, Pete. And where there is great power, there is always the potential for it to be misused, or to be disturbed."

He pictured the mill again, no longer a quaint relic but a vital node in a network he was only beginning to comprehend. The weathered stones, the groaning timbers, the ceaseless flow of the Nore – they were all part of a grand, hidden mechanism, a living entity that Aine and her lineage were sworn to protect. The 'disturbance' Elara had been investigating, the disruption she had feared, was therefore directly tied to this place, to its function as a conduit.

"Elara," Pete said, her name a quiet echo in the charged atmosphere of the room. "She knew about the mill? About these symbols?"

Aine's expression softened, a hint of sorrow touching her eyes. "Of course. She grew up hearing the stories, seeing the subtle signs. She understood, at least in part, the significance of our family's role. She often spoke of the mill with a reverence that went beyond mere appreciation for its historical architecture. She felt its importance, its connection to the town's deeper pulse. She would have recognized the symbols, understood their purpose. And it is likely that whatever disturbance she was investigating was connected to this place, to its vulnerability."

The pieces were falling into place with a dizzying speed. Elara, driven by her own curiosity and perhaps a latent connection to Kilkenny's hidden energies, had likely been drawn to the mill, seeking answers, perhaps even attempting to observe or understand the wards herself. The fact that Aine's family had a direct, active role in maintaining these ancient protections cast Elara's research in a new light. She wasn't just an amateur historian; she was delving into a sacred trust, a secret guardianship that stretched back through centuries.

"It's the heart of it, isn't it?" Pete mused aloud, the concept solidifying in his mind. "Kilkenny's enduring nature, its resilience, its... essence. It's protected by these places, and by your family's constant vigilance."

"That's a poetic way of putting it, but yes," Aine agreed, a rare hint of something akin to pride in her tone. "The mill is one of the primary anchors. But there are others, smaller nodes, equally important in their own way, scattered throughout the town and the surrounding countryside. Each one has its own particular resonance, its own set of wards or guardians who understand its unique function.

My family's role has always been focused on this primary nexus, the mill, and its immediate vicinity, but our understanding extends to the interconnectedness of it all."

He thought about the sheer scope of this inherited responsibility. It wasn't a hobby or a historical curiosity; it was a living, breathing duty, passed from mother to daughter, demanding constant awareness, an intimate knowledge of the land and its unseen currents. It explained Aine's quiet reserve, her deep connection to the town that seemed almost symbiotic. She wasn't just a resident; she was an integral part of Kilkenny's energetic ecosystem.

"So, when Elara found something... dangerous... was it a threat to the mill itself, or to the energy it channels?" Pete inquired, trying to refine his understanding of the adversary.

"It was a threat to the balance that the mill helps to maintain," Aine clarified. "Think of it as a parasite, or a corrosive element, that seeks to disrupt the natural flow of energy. Elara discovered that this particular entity, this force, was drawn to places of significant power, like the mill, and it was attempting to corrupt or drain that power, to create an imbalance that would ripple outwards and destabilize the entire region. It was a direct assault on the very essence of Kilkenny's vitality."

The image of a subtle, insidious corruption taking root in a place of such ancient power sent a fresh wave of unease through Pete. It was a far more terrifying prospect than any boogeyman or tangible villain. It was an abstract threat, yet one that had very real consequences for the town and its inhabitants. Elara's investigation, then, was an attempt to identify the source of this corruption, to find its weak point, so that Aine, as the custodian, could act to neutralize it.

"And her notes," Pete said, his gaze meeting Aine's. "She was trying to pass on what she learned, to give you the information you needed to fight it."

"She was," Aine confirmed, her voice low. "She understood the danger she was in, and she knew that if she failed, the knowledge would be lost, and the threat would continue to grow unchecked. She trusted me to understand, to continue her work. And she trusted you, Pete. She believed that your perspective, your methodical approach, could help unravel what she had started."

The weight of that trust, the implicit burden of Elara's unfinished mission, now felt immense. Pete had entered Kilkenny with a simple aim: to understand Elara's fate. Now, he was being drawn into a far grander, more complex narrative, a struggle for the very soul of the town, a battle fought not with swords and shields, but with ancient knowledge and vigilant custodianship. The old mill, once a point of passive curiosity, had become a focal point, a symbol of the interwoven history and unseen forces that defined Kilkenny. His earlier visit there, the intangible feeling of being observed, the strange resonance of the place, was no longer just a passing impression; it was a direct link to Aine's ancestral duties, a testament to the enduring significance of the old mill. He understood now that his fascination with Kilkenny was not merely an academic pursuit; it was an echo of a deeper, more fundamental connection, a resonance with the town's ancient heart that he was only just beginning to comprehend, a heart that beat strongest at the old mill.

A CHOICE TO BE MADE

The air in Aine's cottage, once merely evocative of drying herbs and the gentle scent of woodsmoke, now seemed to carry the very essence of Kilkenny's hidden life. Pete felt it clinging to him, an invisible residue of ancient energies and generational duty. He looked at Aine, her face illuminated by the soft glow of the oil lamp, her expression a complex tapestry of weariness, resolve, and a vulnerability she rarely allowed to surface. He had sought historical truths, tangible facts to fill the gaps in Elara's fragmented research. Instead, he had been handed a legacy, a responsibility that stretched back through centuries, anchored by the silent, watchful presence of the old mill.

The narrative Aine had unveiled was one that his rational mind struggled to fully integrate. 'Custodians,' 'energetic currents,' 'confluence points' – these were not terms found in any historical archive he had ever consulted. Yet, the sheer conviction in her voice, the quiet certainty with which she spoke of safeguarding the town's life force, resonated with an undeniable truth. It was a truth that had begun to reveal itself subtly, even to him, during his solitary explorations. That pervasive stillness at the mill, the almost imperceptible hum beneath the surface of everyday reality, now had a context, a purpose. It wasn't just atmospheric; it was the pulse of something vital, something actively tended.

He replayed the memory of the mill in his mind: the weathered stone, the great, unmoving wheel, the ceaseless murmur of the River Nore. He remembered the strange sense of being observed, a prickling on his skin that he had dismissed as the product of isolation and the weight of history. Now, he understood. It was his intuition, Aine had said, sensing the concentrated energy, perhaps even the nascent instability that Elara's investigation might have inadvertently stirred. The symbols etched into the stone, the 'wards' Aine called them, were not random markings but ancient fortifications, binding marks designed to stabilize and protect. They were part of a ritualistic maintenance, a continuous effort to ensure the purity and integrity of the town's energetic flow.

Elara. Her name echoed in the quiet space between them, a poignant reminder of the tragedy that had set him on this path. She had known. She had understood the significance of the mill, the ancient responsibilities of Aine's lineage. Her research, her deep dive into Kilkenny's past, had undoubtedly led her to the very heart of this hidden world, and in doing so, had placed her directly in its path. Pete felt a pang of sorrow, a renewed sense of urgency. Elara had been trying to protect them all, to arm Aine with the knowledge she needed to confront whatever threat had emerged. Her final, desperate act had been to entrust him, a stranger to this profound secret, with the task of bridging the gap, of ensuring that her work, and Aine's vital custodianship, would not be in vain.

He looked at Aine again. The woman who had been, for him, a subject of historical inquiry, a source of local lore, had revealed herself to be so much more. She was a guardian, a linchpin in a cosmic balance he had never conceived of. And with that revelation came a stark, unwelcome choice. He could retreat, shaken by the sheer magnitude of what he had discovered, by the potential dangers that lay hidden beneath Kilkenny's charming façade. He could return to his world of quantifiable facts and verifiable evidence, leaving Aine to her solitary vigil.

But the thought of leaving, of severing this connection, felt like a betrayal. Not just of Elara, but of something deeper, something that had begun to stir within him the moment he'd set foot in Kilkenny. His feelings for Aine had evolved far beyond the professional curiosity that had initially drawn him here. He found himself captivated by her quiet strength, her unwavering dedication, the subtle grace with which she carried the weight of her inherited duty. There was a profound connection between them, forged in shared grief and the slow unfolding of a truth that transcended the ordinary. The idea of walking away, of leaving her to face these unseen threats alone, was no longer conceivable.

"This is... a lot, Aine," Pete began, his voice rough with emotion. He felt adrift, caught between the tangible reality of his former life and the bewildering, yet undeniable, existence she inhabited. "I came here looking for answers about Elara. I thought I was just an observer, a historian documenting her research. I never... I never imagined this." He gestured vaguely, encompassing the cottage, the town beyond, the invisible forces she described. "A living legend. A secret guardianship."

Aine met his gaze, her eyes steady, offering a silent understanding. "I know it's difficult to comprehend, Pete. It's not something most people ever have to confront. But Elara... she believed in you. She saw something in you, a certain clarity, a willingness to look beyond the surface. She believed you could help."

"Help how?" Pete's question was laden with a genuine fear of the unknown, but also a burgeoning sense of purpose. The methodical approach he'd honed as a researcher, his trained ability to dissect complex problems, suddenly felt like a potential asset, not a hindrance, in this alien landscape. "I don't have your knowledge, your connection to this... this energy."

"You have questions," Aine said softly. "And you have a fresh perspective. You can see things that I, perhaps, have become too accustomed to. Elara's notes are filled with observations, with potential avenues of investigation that she was pursuing. She was piecing together a puzzle, trying to identify the nature of the threat, its origins, and its weaknesses. My family's duty is to maintain the balance, to reinforce the protections. But understanding the enemy, truly understanding it, is a different kind of task. It requires a different kind of mind."

He thought of Elara's notebooks, filled with her meticulous observations, her cryptic drawings, her increasingly urgent scribbles. He had seen the progression of her fear, her determination to uncover the truth. Now, he understood that her research was not merely an academic exercise. It was a vital act of reconnaissance, a desperate attempt to arm the custodian with the intelligence needed to protect Kilkenny.

"She was looking for something specific, wasn't she?" Pete probed, trying to anchor himself in the concrete details of Elara's work. "Something that indicated the nature of the threat, or how it operated."

Aine nodded, her expression growing more serious. "She believed the entity she was investigating was not a natural phenomenon, but something... introduced. Something that sought to exploit Kilkenny's unique energetic signature for its own purposes. She was tracking subtle anomalies, distortions in the natural flow that shouldn't have been there. Her focus was on identifying the vector, the point of ingress, and the mechanism by which it was attempting to corrupt the energy."

"And she found something at the mill?" Pete's mind raced back to his own visit, to the feeling of a subtle wrongness, a discordance beneath the mill's ancient harmony.

"She documented increased activity there," Aine confirmed. "Unusual fluctuations in the readings she was taking, subtle shifts in the patterns of the wards that suggested a pressure being applied, an attempt to undermine their integrity. She suspected that the mill, as the primary nexus, was not just a target, but potentially a key to the entity's larger objective. If it could corrupt the source, it could destabilize the entire network."

Pete's gaze drifted to the window, to the dark shapes of the Kilkenny rooftops against the night sky. The town he had come to know, with its winding medieval streets and its quiet charm, now seemed to hold a hidden depth, a secret life that pulsed beneath the surface. He had been drawn into a world where history and myth intertwined, where the fate of a town rested not on political machinations or economic forces, but on the careful tending of unseen energies.

This was the choice. To step back, to preserve his own sense of order and understanding, or to step forward, into this nebulous, yet profoundly real, struggle. The potential risks were considerable. If Elara had been in danger, what might await him? He wasn't a guardian, merely a scholar, a man of books and archives. Yet, the thought of leaving Aine to bear this burden alone, to face these threats without any support, felt like an abdication of a responsibility he now felt, however reluctantly, bound to.

He remembered Elara's face in the photographs, her bright, intelligent eyes filled with a passion for uncovering hidden truths. She had dedicated herself to this cause, and her pursuit had ultimately cost her her life. To abandon it now, to let her sacrifice be in vain, felt unthinkable. And more than that, there was Aine. The quiet strength of her commitment, the way she spoke of her ancestors and her duty, had ignited something within him, a respect that had deepened into something far more personal. He cared for her, truly cared for her, and that feeling made the choice, while terrifying, also strangely inevitable.

"I understand," Pete said, his voice low but firm, cutting through the silence. He looked directly at Aine, his gaze unwavering. "I can't just walk away. Not now. Not after everything you've told me, and not after what happened to Elara." He paused, gathering his thoughts, the decision solidifying within him. "I want to help. I want to understand. And I want to finish what Elara started."

He saw a flicker of relief, swiftly followed by a renewed intensity, in Aine's eyes. It was as if a burden had been momentarily lifted, only to be shared. "Pete," she said, her voice a soft breath. "Are you sure? This isn't like researching old documents. The stakes are... different."

"I'm sure," Pete affirmed, the conviction in his voice surprising even himself. He had always been a man of reason, of logic, of tangible evidence. But the profound reality of Aine's life, the palpable presence of something ancient and powerful that she guarded, had shifted his perspective entirely. He was no longer just a historian; he was, however unwillingly, a participant. And in that participation, a new purpose was beginning to take shape, a purpose that involved protecting not just the memory of Elara, but the very essence of Kilkenny, embodied by the quiet strength of the woman sitting before him.

"Elara believed we could find a way," Pete continued, a sense of resolve hardening within him. "She believed that by understanding the threat, by uncovering its weaknesses, we could neutralize it. I have her notes, her research. I can help you analyze them, look for patterns, for inconsistencies that I might be able to spot with my... detached perspective." He hesitated, searching for the right words. "It's not the kind of help you're used to, I know. But it's what I can offer."

Aine extended a hand, her fingers brushing against his. The touch was electric, a simple gesture that conveyed a world of unspoken gratitude and shared commitment. "Thank you, Pete," she whispered. "Elara would have been so pleased."

The warmth of her hand lingered on his, a tangible anchor in the swirling uncertainty of their shared future. He had made his choice. The path ahead was fraught with peril, shrouded in the same ancient mystery that had drawn him to Kilkenny in the first place. But he was no longer alone, and he was no longer merely an observer. He was part of something larger, something vital, and for the first time since Elara's death, a flicker of hope, however fragile, ignited within him. He would face this new reality, not with the detached curiosity of a historian, but with the determined purpose of someone who had found something worth fighting for, someone who had, in the heart of Kilkenny, found a connection that transcended time and expectation. The old mill, the nexus of this hidden world, now represented not just a historical site, but a battleground, a focal point for a conflict that would require all his intellect, all his courage, and all the burgeoning trust he had placed in Aine.

Chapter Eight: Whispers of Danger

AN UNSETTLING OBSERVATION

As Pete settled into the uncomfortable reality of Aine's revelations, he found himself constantly scanning his surroundings. The quaint cobbled streets of Kilkenny, which had initially charmed him with their medieval authenticity, now felt like a stage set, a carefully constructed façade that hid something far more sinister. He noticed the way certain figures lingered in doorways, their faces obscured by the deepening twilight, the way shadows seemed to stretch and twist unnaturally in his peripheral vision. It was a subtle shift in perception, a growing awareness that he was no longer just a visitor but a subject of observation, perhaps even of more direct scrutiny.

During his solo explorations, seeking out the various historical markers Elara had mentioned in her notes, Pete developed a heightened sense of unease. He'd be walking along the Nore, the river's gentle murmur usually a soothing sound, but now it seemed to carry a disquieting undertone, as if whispering secrets he wasn't meant to hear. He'd catch a fleeting glimpse of movement among the trees on the riverbank, a shape that detached itself from the natural patterns of light and shadow just long enough to register as something other than a stray dog or a passing bird. He'd stop, straining his ears, but the sound would always dissipate, leaving him with nothing but the rustling of leaves and the ceaseless flow of water.

One afternoon, while examining the weathered stones of the old city walls near St. Canice's Cathedral, Pete felt a distinct sensation of being watched. He turned abruptly, his heart thumping against his ribs. A few yards away, a man stood by a shop entrance, ostensibly admiring the window display of antique books. But the man's posture was rigid, his gaze fixed not on the books, but in Pete's general direction, though subtly angled away as if to avoid direct eye contact. The man wore a nondescript grey coat, and his features were unremarkable, almost deliberately so, as if designed to blend into any backdrop. Pete met his eyes for a fleeting moment, and in that instant, he saw not mere casual observation, but a calculated, assessing gaze. The man then turned away, melting back into the pedestrian traffic, leaving Pete with a cold knot of apprehension in his stomach. It wasn't just his imagination; this was tangible, a subtle but undeniable presence that felt like a coiled snake, ready to strike.

This sensation of being under surveillance wasn't confined to chance encounters. As he spent more time with Aine, poring over Elara's meticulously documented research, the feeling intensified. He noticed a recurring pattern: whenever he and Aine discussed specific aspects of Kilkenny's energetic history, particularly those pertaining to the mill or the ancient ley lines that supposedly converged there, a subtle shift would occur in the town's ambient atmosphere. It was as if their whispered conversations were being amplified, not by sound, but by a network of unseen listeners. He'd sometimes feel a phantom prickle on his skin, as if unseen eyes were tracking his movements, even when he was indoors.

He found himself retracing his steps, checking over his shoulder with increasing frequency. The quiet lanes that had once seemed so inviting now felt claustrophobic, potential ambush points. He started to feel a disconnect between the mundane reality of Kilkenny—the tourists milling about, the shopkeepers going about their business—and the hidden currents of energy and danger that Aine described. It was like living in two parallel worlds, one serene and familiar, the other humming with an unseen, potentially hostile, intelligence.

The urgency of Elara's fate, coupled with Aine's solemn warnings about the nature of the entity she was safeguarding against, lent a new gravity to these unsettling observations. What had initially felt like abstract historical intrigue was rapidly morphing into something far more immediate and concrete. The 'threat' Elara had been investigating wasn't just a theoretical disruption of Kilkenny's energetic flow; it was an active, perhaps even sentient, force that was aware of their probing, and potentially capable of retaliation.

Pete recalled a particular incident when he had been walking back to Aine's cottage after a late afternoon spent exploring the grounds of Kilkenny Castle. He had taken a slightly different route, a narrow alleyway that ran behind some of the older merchant houses. The passage was dimly lit, and the air was thick with the scent of damp stone and decaying mortar. As he passed a particularly deep recess, he heard a faint scuffing sound, like a shoe dragging on the ground. He paused, his senses on high alert. He saw a flicker of movement at the far end of the alley, a hunched figure slipping around a corner. It was too quick, too indistinct, to be anything other than deliberate evasion. He called out, "Hello? Is anyone there?" but received no reply, only the echoing silence of the narrow passage.

He continued on, his pace quickening, the alley suddenly feeling far more menacing. He emerged onto a more open street, blinking in the fading light, and cast a nervous glance back. The alley remained empty, a dark maw swallowed by the encroaching night. But the feeling persisted, a cold certainty that he had been observed, perhaps even followed. It was as if the very fabric of the town was watching him, its ancient stones and hidden pathways acting as eyes and ears for something he couldn't yet comprehend.

This growing awareness of being observed was amplified by Aine's own caution. She rarely ventured out alone after dusk, and when she did, it was with a quiet alertness that suggested she was constantly attuned to her surroundings. She had mentioned, in hushed tones, that certain individuals in town, those who were sensitive to Kilkenny's deeper currents, had also noticed a subtle shift, an increase in what they described as "unsettling energies." Some had reported fleeting glimpses of figures that didn't belong, of shadows that moved with an unnatural gait, or of an pervasive feeling of being constantly monitored.

"It's as if the veil has thinned," Aine had explained, her voice barely a whisper, as they sat in the dimly lit parlor, the oil lamp casting dancing shadows on the walls. "Elara's work, her probing into the mill's secrets, it's like she stirred something that was dormant. And now, whatever it is, it's aware of us. It knows we're looking."

Pete found himself studying Aine more closely, noting the slight tension in her shoulders, the way her eyes would dart towards the windows at the slightest sound. She was accustomed to this vigilance, this constant awareness of potential threats, but for Pete, it was a jarring, unsettling introduction to a world where danger was not always overt but often subtle, insidious, and deeply ingrained in the very essence of the place.

The feeling of being watched wasn't always accompanied by specific sightings. Sometimes, it was a more pervasive sense, a general unease that settled upon him like a physical weight. He'd be walking through the market square, the cheerful bustle of vendors and shoppers a stark contrast to his inner turmoil, and he'd feel a prickling sensation on the back of his neck, a conviction that unseen eyes were cataloging his presence. He'd try to shake it off, attributing it to stress, to the overwhelming nature of his new understanding of Kilkenny. But the feeling persisted, a constant, low-level hum of anxiety that underscored every moment he spent outside the relative safety of Aine's cottage.

He began to analyze Elara's notes with a new intensity, searching not just for historical facts, but for any mention of surveillance or overt interference in her research. He found passages where she alluded to "unwanted attention," to "feelings of being followed," and to "subtle attempts to misdirect her inquiries." One entry, written in a hurried, almost frantic hand, spoke of a late-night encounter near the river where she felt she was being deliberately tracked, though she couldn't identify her pursuer. "The shadows moved with their own volition," she had written. "It was not human."

This cryptic remark, coupled with Pete's own experiences, painted a chilling picture. The threat Elara had uncovered wasn't just a passive force; it was actively monitoring them, reacting to their attempts to understand it. The stakes, which had already felt incredibly high, now seemed to have escalated dramatically. Kilkenny wasn't just a town with a hidden history; it was a place where that history was actively resisting discovery, and the guardians of its secrets, including Elara and now himself, were in its sights.

He had to be more careful. He had to learn to see what Elara had seen, to understand the subtle signs of surveillance, the almost imperceptible shifts that indicated a watchful presence. It was a terrifying realization, but also a necessary one. He couldn't afford to be blindsided. The history he was trying to uncover was alive, and it was watching. The whispers of danger were no longer just metaphorical; they were the subtle rustlings in the shadows, the unnerving sense of being observed, the chilling certainty that he was treading on ground that was actively defended. And the more he learned, the more he realized that Kilkenny's deepest secrets were guarded not just by ancient wards and hidden energies, but by something far more immediate and menacing. He was no longer just a historian seeking lost truths; he was a target, and the game had very real, very dangerous consequences. The unsettling observation was no longer just an observation; it was a warning.

AINES GROWING APPREHENSION

The weight of what he had uncovered pressed down on Pete, a tangible pressure that settled in his chest and made each breath a conscious effort. The revelations Aine had shared were not abstract historical footnotes; they were living, breathing truths that permeated Kilkenny's very stones, its very air. He felt the shift in her demeanor, the subtle tightening around her eyes when he spoke of his own observations, his own growing unease. It was a shared anxiety, a mutual understanding of the precariousness of their situation, yet Aine's was laced with a deeper, more ingrained weariness. She was the custodian, the one who had lived with the whispers of danger for her entire life, and now, he was being drawn into that perpetual vigilance.

"You need to be more careful, Pete," she said, her voice a low murmur that barely disturbed the quiet of her cottage. The oil lamp cast a flickering glow, painting shifting shadows across her face, highlighting the nascent lines of worry that etched themselves around her mouth. She was mending a tear in an old linen tunic, her movements precise and economical, but Pete could see the slight tremor in her hands, the way her gaze would occasionally lift from her needlework to fix on some unseen point beyond the window. "Not everyone in Kilkenny is as they seem. And some... some are not what they seem at all."

Pete nodded, folding one of Elara's notebooks and placing it carefully on the small table between them. He understood her unspoken plea for discretion. He had already learned that not all curiosity was welcomed, and that some questions, particularly those that brushed against the town's hidden currents, could attract unwanted attention. He had felt it himself – the prickling sensation of being watched, the fleeting glimpses of figures that seemed to melt into the shadows, the unsettling feeling that his presence was being cataloged by an unseen intelligence.

"I'm trying, Aine," he replied, his own voice tinged with a frustration he was trying to keep in check. "It's just... when I see something, or feel something, I want to understand it. Elara's notes are so full of cryptic observations, and I feel a responsibility to decipher them, to find the patterns she was so desperately seeking." He paused, choosing his words carefully. "But I can't shake the feeling that by digging, we're not just uncovering history, we're provoking something. Something that doesn't want to be uncovered."

Aine sighed, setting aside her needlework. She reached across the table, her fingers gently touching the worn cover of Elara's notebook. Her touch was lighter than usual, almost tentative, as if she were afraid of disturbing something within the book, or perhaps within him. "Elara believed that understanding was the only true defense," she said, her gaze distant, lost in a memory of her predecessor. "She believed that knowledge could disarm it, could reveal its vulnerabilities. But she also knew the risks. She wrote to me, in her last letters, about feeling a distinct pressure, as if unseen forces were trying to steer her research in a different direction, to cloud her judgment."

Her eyes, when they met his, were filled with a profound, unsettling gravity. "Pete, you've seen how the town changes when we speak of these things, how the air itself seems to thicken. It's not just your imagination. Whatever Elara disturbed, it's sensitive. It's aware. And it doesn't like being investigated." She leaned forward, her voice dropping to a near whisper, the intimacy of the moment amplified by the surrounding silence. "There are people in Kilkenny, individuals who have lived here for generations, who have their own ways of sensing these shifts. They know when the currents are disturbed. Some of them are wary, others... others are complicit, in ways you might not understand."

The implication hung in the air between them, heavy and suffocating. Complicit. The word itself conjured images of hidden alliances, of a network of eyes and ears working in concert to protect Kilkenny's secrets, or perhaps, to serve the very force they were trying to understand. He thought of the man by the bookshop, his deliberately averted gaze, the cold assessment in his eyes. Had he been one of those people? Or something else entirely?

"What do you mean, complicit?" Pete asked, his voice barely audible. He felt a chill creep up his spine, unrelated to the cool evening air. The quaint charm of Kilkenny, the veneer of historical authenticity he had initially been so drawn to, was beginning to peel away, revealing a far more complex and dangerous reality.

Aine's brow furrowed. "There are those who benefit from the status quo, Pete. Those who have always benefited. Their livelihood, their influence, it's all tied to the stability of this place, to the energies that flow through it. If those energies are corrupted, if the balance is upset, their own positions are threatened." She paused, searching for the right words, the ones that would convey the depth of her concern without overwhelming him. "They might not understand the full nature of what we're dealing with, but they sense the disruption. And they will act to protect what they perceive as their own."

She picked up a small, intricately carved wooden bird from the mantelpiece, turning it over and over in her hands. "Elara had a few... allies," she continued, her tone carefully neutral. "People who understood, or at least suspected, what she was investigating. But even they were cautious. They warned her about asking too many questions of the wrong people, about drawing too much attention to herself." Aine's gaze met his again, a silent plea for him to heed those same warnings. "You need to trust your instincts, Pete. If a situation feels wrong, if a person seems... off, then retreat. Don't push. Don't try to force an answer where one isn't readily offered."

He understood. His scholarly instinct, his ingrained desire to pursue every lead, to dissect every anomaly, was a luxury he could no longer afford. Kilkenny was not a library; it was a living, breathing ecosystem, and he was an intruder, a disruptor. And in this ecosystem, the predators were not always obvious.

"I've noticed it too," Pete admitted, his voice a little rougher than he intended. "The way certain people react when I mention the mill, or when I ask about the town's older history. It's like a switch flips, a wariness that wasn't there a moment before." He thought of a conversation he'd had with a local shopkeeper a few days prior, an elderly man who had initially been eager to share anecdotes about Kilkenny's past. But the moment Pete had inquired about the specific architectural details of the old mill, the man's demeanor had shifted abruptly. His eyes had become guarded, his answers clipped and vague. He had abruptly ended the conversation, citing a need to attend to customers, though the shop had been nearly empty.

"They're being warned, or they're already under its influence," Aine said, her voice barely above a whisper. "The entity, whatever it is, it has a network. It's subtle, it's pervasive. It doesn't need to shout to be heard. A sideways glance, a hushed conversation that stops when you approach, a sudden silence from someone who was just speaking freely – these are its methods." She leaned back, her hands resting on the table, her gaze fixed on Pete. The anxiety in her eyes was no longer a subtle undercurrent; it was a palpable wave.

"And your safety, Pete," she continued, her voice laced with a raw vulnerability that struck him more deeply than any of her previous pronouncements. "It's becoming a very real concern. Elara was already... exposed. Her research made her a target. You, by continuing her work, by associating with me, you're placing yourself in the same precarious position." She hesitated, her gaze flicking towards the window as if expecting something to materialize from the darkness. "I can't protect you in the way I protect the mill. My duty is to the energy, to the balance. I can guide you, I can warn you, but I can't stand between you and whatever is out there, watching."

The weight of her words settled on him, heavy and cold. He had come to Kilkenny seeking answers about Elara, about her fragmented research. He had found a legacy, a responsibility, and now, a very real danger. He was no longer merely a detached observer, an academic interested in historical enigmas. He was a participant, inextricably linked to Aine and her ancient duty. And the unseen forces that had claimed Elara's life were now, it seemed, setting their sights on him.

"I understand," Pete said, the words feeling inadequate, but the sincerity behind them was absolute. He met Aine's anxious gaze, trying to project a calm he didn't entirely feel. "I'll be more discreet. I'll trust my instincts, and I'll remember what you've told me about the people here." He paused, the sheer magnitude of their undertaking beginning to truly dawn on him. "But I can't stop. Not now. Elara didn't. And I won't let her sacrifice be in vain."

A faint, almost imperceptible nod from Aine was his only immediate reply, but in that subtle gesture, he saw a flicker of hope, a shared resolve that transcended their mutual fear. The shadows in the cottage seemed to deepen, and the gentle murmur of the wind outside took on a more sinister tone, as if Kilkenny itself was holding its breath, waiting to see what they would do next. He knew, with a chilling certainty, that their investigation had moved beyond the realm of academic curiosity and into a dangerous, uncharted territory where every step was fraught with peril, and every whisper of danger was a harbinger of a conflict yet to unfold. The weight of

Aine's apprehension was now a shared burden, a constant reminder that the secrets of Kilkenny were not merely buried in the past, but actively guarded by present, unseen threats.

THE ENIGMATIC OUTSIDER

The cobblestones of Kilkenny, usually a comforting echo of centuries past, now felt like a stage set for an unfolding drama, and Pete was acutely aware that he was no longer merely an observer. The unease Aine had so carefully articulated was beginning to manifest, a subtle but persistent prickle of awareness that every interaction, every casual stroll, was under scrutiny. He'd felt it before, of course – the lingering stares, the hushed conversations that died with his approach – but this was different. This was a focused attention, a deliberate probing that felt less like accidental observation and more like a calculated assessment.

It began innocently enough, as these things often do. He was browsing the dusty shelves of a small antique shop on Parliament Street, drawn by a display of old nautical charts. The proprietor, a wiry man with eyes that seemed to miss nothing, was initially welcoming, offering a brief history of the shop and its wares. Then, a new figure entered, a man who didn't quite fit the usual Kilkenny demographic. He was younger than most of the locals Pete had encountered, his clothes neatly pressed, his bearing confident, almost too polished for the worn, historic setting. He didn't browse; he seemed to scan, his gaze sweeping over the patrons and the merchandise with an unnerving efficiency.

The man drifted towards Pete, his approach smooth and unhurried. "Fascinating place, isn't it?" he commented, his voice a low, pleasant baritone that carried an almost rehearsed quality. "So much history layered upon history."

Pete offered a polite nod. "It certainly is. I'm trying to get a sense of it all."

The man's eyes, a startlingly pale blue, met Pete's with an unnerving directness. "Oh? And what aspect of Kilkenny has captured your interest so keenly?" He gestured vaguely around the shop. "The architecture? The folklore? Or perhaps something... more specific?"

The casual phrasing, the seemingly innocent question, was laced with an undertone that set Pete's teeth on edge. It felt like a test, a subtle attempt to gauge his knowledge, his intentions. "I'm a historian," Pete replied, keeping his tone deliberately vague. "I'm interested in the town's development over time, its social fabric."

The man smiled, a brief, almost predatory baring of teeth. "A historian. Of course. And are you finding the 'social fabric' as intricate as you'd hoped? Sometimes, the threads can be rather... elusive." He paused, his gaze flicking towards the proprietor, who had discreetly retreated to the back of the shop, his hands suddenly busy with some unseen task. "I've noticed you around. You seem to be quite thorough in your research."

Pete's mind raced. How much did this man know? Had he seen Pete with Aine? Had he overheard conversations? The implication of being 'noticed' was chilling. "I try to be," Pete said, his voice carefully even. "There are so many stories here, it's easy to get lost in them."

"Indeed," the man agreed, leaning slightly closer. "But one must be careful not to get too lost, mustn't one? Especially when those stories involve certain... sensitivities. Some narratives, you see, are best left undisturbed." His pale eyes seemed to bore into Pete, searching for any flicker of recognition or fear. "Kilkenny has its guardians, you know. Individuals who are deeply invested in maintaining the town's... equilibrium."

Guardians. The word resonated with Aine's earlier pronouncements about complicity and vested interests. Was this man one of them? Or was he an agent of something else entirely, someone tasked with monitoring those who might upset the delicate balance?

"Guardians?" Pete echoed, feigning a mild curiosity. "I haven't encountered anyone who has presented themselves in that capacity."

The man chuckled, a dry, rasping sound. "They don't often announce themselves. They operate in the periphery, observing, assessing. They understand the currents that run beneath the surface of this place. They know when they are being... agitated." He straightened up, his expression shifting back to one of polite indifference. "But that's merely conjecture, of course. The ramblings of an interested observer." He gave Pete a brief nod. "I wish you well with your research. Do be careful, won't you? Kilkenny's past is a powerful thing."

With that, he turned and exited the shop as smoothly as he had entered, leaving Pete with a gnawing sense of unease. The antique shop, moments before a haven of historical curiosity, now felt charged with an unsettling energy. The proprietor, when Pete glanced his way, offered a fleeting, unreadable expression before returning to his work, his movements now seeming furtive rather than simply busy.

Pete left the shop, the man's words replaying in his mind. "Some narratives are best left undisturbed." "Kilkenny has its guardians." "Be careful." It was a thinly veiled warning, delivered with an unnerving civility. This was not the subtle pressure Aine had described; this was direct, albeit veiled, intimidation. The encounter felt like a calculated move, a clear signal that his presence and his investigation had not gone unnoticed by the town's hidden protectors.

He walked towards the river, needing the open air, the familiar flow of the water to try and clear his head. The man's appearance confirmed his deepest fears: his probing into Elara's research, his association with Aine, had indeed painted a target on his back. But who was this man? And what was his connection to the town's deeper, more guarded secrets? The pale blue eyes, the carefully chosen words – they spoke of someone who was not merely a local with a vested interest, but perhaps someone with a more organized agenda.

The next few days were a subtle escalation of this newfound vigilance. Pete found himself constantly scanning his surroundings, attributing significance to every unfamiliar face, every prolonged glance. He'd always possessed a certain academic detachment, a scholar's ability to observe without emotional entanglement. But Kilkenny was forcing him to shed that detachment, to become a more primal observer, attuned to threats, to anomalies.

He noticed the same man again, this time lingering near the entrance to St. Canice's Cathedral, his posture casual, his gaze seemingly fixed on the ancient stonework. But Pete saw the almost imperceptible way his head turned, the flicker of his eyes as Pete passed. He was being tracked, his movements cataloged by this 'interested observer.'

Then there was the incident at the market. Pete was examining some local crafts when he felt a presence behind him. He turned, and there was the man again, ostensibly examining a display of knitted woolens, but his attention was clearly on Pete.

"Still at it, I see," the man said, his voice carrying a hint of amusement. "Immersed in the local colour?"

Pete forced a smile. "Just enjoying the atmosphere."

"The atmosphere can be... deceiving," the man replied, picking up a brightly coloured scarf. "It can conceal as much as it reveals. Especially when one is looking for things that aren't meant to be found." He let the scarf drape over his arm. "Are you meeting anyone today? A guide, perhaps? Someone to show you the... less obvious attractions of Kilkenny?"

The question was pointed, a direct probe into his connection with Aine. Pete felt a surge of anger, quickly suppressed. "I'm exploring on my own," he stated firmly. "Kilkenny has plenty to offer a solo explorer."

The man's pale eyes held Pete's. "Indeed it does. But some explorations are best undertaken with... companionship. Or at least, with a clear understanding of who else is exploring the same territory. The paths can be dangerous for the unprepared." He gave Pete a look that was almost pitying. "Some paths lead to enlightenment, others to... entanglement. It's important to know which is which, wouldn't you agree?"

He then moved away, melting back into the flow of the market crowd, leaving Pete with a palpable sense of being both warned and manipulated. The man wasn't just interested; he was actively trying to steer Pete's investigation, to subtly intimidate him into abandoning his quest, or perhaps to control the narrative he was uncovering.

Pete returned to Aine's cottage that evening, the encounter weighing heavily on him. He recounted the interactions, the man's unnerving presence, his pointed questions.

Aine listened intently, her brow furrowed with concern. She recognized the pattern. "He's one of them," she murmured, her voice barely audible. "One of the watchmen. They're not always direct, but when they feel the currents are being significantly disturbed, they will intervene."

"Watchmen?" Pete asked, leaning forward. "Who are they? What are they watching for?"

Aine shook her head, her gaze distant. "They are a collective, of sorts. Their lineage stretches back centuries, intertwined with the history of Kilkenny, with the mill, with the energies. They believe themselves to be its protectors, its custodians. They are the ones who ensure the 'equilibrium' remains, as he put it." She paused, her expression grim. "They don't always understand the true nature of what they're protecting, but they are fiercely loyal to the status quo, to the traditions that have kept Kilkenny seemingly unchanged for so long."

"And this man I met..." Pete pressed. "He's not just a casual observer?"

"No," Aine confirmed. "He's a scout, a tester. He's assessing the threat you pose. He's trying to understand your intentions, your allegiances. And he's trying to sow seeds of doubt and fear." She met Pete's gaze, her eyes filled with a familiar weariness, but also with a steely resolve. "He's letting you know that you are being monitored, that your actions have consequences in this town, consequences that extend beyond academic discourse."

"He mentioned guardians," Pete recalled. "And that some paths lead to entanglement."

"He's trying to isolate you," Aine said, her voice low and urgent. "To make you feel alone, vulnerable. He wants you to believe that you are being watched by unseen forces, that your every move is being judged, and that if you stray from the approved narrative, you will be 'entangled.' It's a psychological tactic. They want you to pull back, to retreat before you uncover something they deem too dangerous."

Pete thought of the sheer effort required to maintain such a network of surveillance, the coordination it would imply. "It's a sophisticated operation," he mused aloud. "This isn't just a few concerned locals whispering amongst themselves."

"It's deeper than that," Aine agreed. "It's a societal conditioning, a generational inheritance. They have their ways of communicating, of passing down information. They are woven into the fabric of Kilkenny, as he said. And their methods are subtle, often indistinguishable from the natural rhythms of the town. A polite warning, a discouraging word, a seemingly coincidental encounter – these are their tools."

"What if he's more than just a watchman?" Pete ventured, the thought of a more direct threat lingering in his mind. "What if he's meant to be an obstacle, or even... a consequence?"

Aine's jaw tightened. "The watchmen have... varying degrees of influence. Some are merely observers, tasked with reporting. Others are more proactive. They can influence events, subtly redirecting individuals, creating situations that discourage further investigation. And some, the more fervent among them, have been known to act more decisively when they feel the core of Kilkenny is truly threatened." She hesitated, her eyes fixed on Pete. "Elara's letters mentioned them. She referred to them as 'the silent shepherds,' always present, always guiding the flock away from the precipice. But she also noted that their guidance could become quite forceful when the flock strayed too far."

The image of the pale-eyed man, his unnervingly smooth demeanor, now took on a more sinister hue. He wasn't just a peripheral figure; he was a manifestation of the resistance Pete was encountering, a tangible embodiment of Kilkenny's determination to keep its secrets buried. He represented the organized, institutionalized effort to maintain the status quo, an effort that transcended individual fear or curiosity and operated with a cold, calculated purpose.

"He knew I was meeting you, didn't he?" Pete asked, a realization dawning.

Aine's gaze softened with a hint of sympathy. "It's highly probable. They have eyes and ears everywhere, Pete. They are accustomed to knowing who is associating with whom, especially when it concerns the mill or its history. Your presence here, your research, it's all a disruption they are actively trying to manage."

The implication was clear: his association with Aine was a significant factor in their assessment of him as a threat. He wasn't just an academic dabbling in history; he was a known quantity, linked to the current custodian of the mill, and therefore, a direct point of contact with the very energies they sought to control.

"So, what do I do?" Pete asked, the question raw with a dawning apprehension. He had braced himself for resistance, for historical puzzles, but not for this level of organized, personal scrutiny.

Aine met his gaze, her own reflecting a deep understanding of the dangerous game they were playing. "You do exactly what Elara did," she said, her voice firm. "You acknowledge the watchmen, you understand their presence, but you do not let them deter you. You continue your research, but with greater discretion. You trust your instincts, and you do not engage with them directly unless absolutely necessary. Their goal is to make you feel observed, but your goal is to ensure that observation does not impede your progress."

She picked up another of Elara's notebooks, its pages filled with meticulous, if cryptic, observations. "Elara learned to move in the shadows, even when she was in plain sight. She learned to compartmentalize, to speak in code, to shield her true intentions. You must do the same."

Pete nodded, absorbing her words. The pale-eyed man, the 'watchman,' was a stark reminder that his academic pursuit had morphed into something far more perilous. He was no longer just uncovering facts; he was navigating a landscape of hidden agendas and watchful eyes, where every interaction could be a test, and every question a potential trap. The enigmatic outsider, with his chillingly polite demeanor and probing questions, was the first clear sign that his presence in Kilkenny had not only been noted but actively registered by the town's clandestine guardians. He was not merely a visitor; he was an unwelcome element, a variable in their carefully guarded equation, and they were determined to ensure he did not destabilize the delicate, ancient balance of their hidden world. The whispers of danger had found a new, more tangible voice, and Pete knew, with a chilling certainty, that he had to learn to listen very carefully indeed.

A MINOR INCIDENT ESCALATES

The weight of the watchman's words, those unsettling pronouncements about guardians and hidden paths, settled over Pete like a shroud. His heightened awareness, initially a defensive reflex, now seemed to amplify every mundane detail, twisting it into a potential threat. Kilkenny, once a charming tapestry of history and tradition, began to reveal a darker, more intricate pattern beneath its surface, and Pete found himself struggling to discern what was real and what was a construct designed to unnerve him. The subtle shifts in the town's atmosphere were no longer mere academic observations; they were personal, and deeply unnerving.

It started with something as trivial as his room at the guesthouse. He'd been meticulous about tidying up, a habit ingrained from years of academic life, where order was paramount. Yet, he found his research materials – his carefully annotated copies of Elara's journals, his own notes on Kilkenny's industrial past – rearranged on his desk. It wasn't a violent disruption, nothing seemed to be missing, but the subtle alteration was enough to send a jolt of adrenaline through him. His spectacles, which he'd left perched on the edge of his notebook, were now neatly placed beside his lamp. A bookmark that had been marking a particularly dense passage in Elara's text was moved to a different chapter altogether. These were not the actions of a cleaner merely tidying up; they were too precise, too pointed. It felt like a message, a silent commentary on his intrusion into these private documents.

He found himself scrutinizing the guesthouse staff, their pleasant smiles and polite inquiries now imbued with a new, unsettling significance. The proprietor, Mrs. Doyle, a woman whose warmth had seemed genuine, now appeared to possess eyes that saw a little too much. Had she, or someone acting on her behalf, entered his room? The thought was intrusive, a violation of privacy that felt chillingly deliberate. He began to double-check his locks, to arrange his belongings in a specific order each night, a ritual born of suspicion. The guesthouse, a place of supposed respite, had become another node in the network of observation he was beginning to perceive.

Then there were the occurrences on his walks. He found himself retracing steps, taking different routes through the city's ancient lanes, but the feeling of being watched persisted. One afternoon, as he was examining the intricate stonework of the old city walls near the Medieval Mile, he noticed a small, antique silver locket lying incongruously on the moss-covered stones. It was open, revealing faded, indecipherable photographs. He felt a primal urge to pick it up, to examine it, but the watchman's words echoed: "Some paths lead to entanglement." Was this a lure? A test to see if he would deviate from his intended path, if he would engage with a seemingly innocuous found object that might hold some hidden significance, or perhaps be a trap? He resisted the urge, his gaze sweeping the area, searching for any sign of the pale-eyed man, or anyone who might have placed it there. The locket remained untouched, a silent, enigmatic marker on his path.

Later that same day, as he strolled along the River Nore, enjoying the serene beauty of the swans gliding across the water, he noticed a book left unattended on a park bench. It was a well-worn copy of a local history, its pages dog-eared and marked with annotations in a spidery, unfamiliar hand. He approached cautiously, his heart thumping a little faster. He recognized the title; it was a book he'd been meaning to find, a comprehensive study of Kilkenny's monastic past. He sat on the opposite end of the bench, pretending to admire the river, his senses hyper-alert. The book remained there, an open invitation, yet a palpable sense of unease prevented him from reaching for it. Was this another test? An attempt to draw him into an interaction, to perhaps engage him in conversation about the book, to glean information about his own research? He could almost feel the unseen eyes watching his reaction. He eventually rose and walked away, the book a silent, unopened enigma at his back.

These were not the overt threats of the watchman's direct approach, but something far more insidious. They were designed to create a subtle erosion of his confidence, to sow seeds of doubt about his own perceptions. Were these genuine coincidences, or orchestrated events meant to unnerve him? The line between paranoia and legitimate concern was becoming increasingly blurred. He found himself questioning the very nature of his presence in Kilkenny. He had come seeking historical truth, armed with academic rigour and a genuine curiosity about Elara's life and work. Now, he felt like a character in a carefully constructed narrative, his every move observed, every action potentially interpreted and used against him.

The isolation began to creep in. He was wary of engaging with locals, of striking up conversations, for fear that any casual remark could be twisted or reported back. The friendly faces that had charmed him initially now seemed to hold hidden depths, their smiles potentially masking a watchful, assessing gaze. He felt a profound loneliness, cut off from his usual support systems, relying only on Aine, and even then, with a growing sense of her own vulnerability. He worried about her. If they were monitoring him this closely, how much did they know about her and her connection to Elara?

The realization that his research was not merely an academic pursuit but a potentially dangerous excavation into Kilkenny's carefully guarded secrets began to dawn on him with increasing clarity. Elara's fate, whatever it might have been, was now inextricably linked to the watchful eyes he felt upon him. He thought of the subtle warning he'd received: "Be careful." It was a simple phrase, but delivered with the watchman's unnerving composure, it had carried the weight of a profound threat. He was no longer just a visiting scholar; he was an anomaly, an outsider who dared to delve into the town's hidden currents, and the guardians of those currents were making their presence known.

The placid surface of Kilkenny had developed ripples, and Pete was now acutely aware that he was the stone that had been cast into its waters. The minor incidents – the rearranged notes, the discarded locket, the unattended book – were not isolated events. They were carefully placed breadcrumbs, designed to lead him down a path of uncertainty, to make him question his sanity, to isolate him, and ultimately, to discourage him from continuing his investigation. He was being played, and the stakes were far higher than he had initially imagined. The peaceful facade of the town was dissolving, revealing a landscape where danger lurked not in outright aggression, but in the insidious manipulation of perception and the chilling certainty of being constantly observed. The whispers of danger had amplified, and they were now a constant, disquieting murmur in the background of his every thought. He had to find a way to navigate this treacherous terrain without succumbing to the manufactured unease, to keep his focus sharp and his resolve unbroken, even as the very air of Kilkenny seemed to conspire against him. The watchmen had made their intentions clear: they were not going to allow him to disturb their equilibrium. And he, in turn, was determined not to be swayed. The game had truly begun.

THE BURDEN OF KNOWING

The weight of this nascent understanding pressed down on Pete with a physical force. It wasn't merely about piecing together Elara's fragmented story or understanding Kilkenny's obscure historical footnotes anymore. His arrival, his insatiable curiosity, had seemingly stirred a dormant power, a silent, vigilant force that perceived his quest as a threat. The subtle rearrangements in his room, the strategically placed locket and book – these weren't the idle pranks of a bored local or a simple misunderstanding. They were deliberate signals, carefully calibrated to instill a sense of unease, to subtly steer him away from the truth. He was no longer an observer; he was an active participant, whether he liked it or not, in a narrative that had clearly been ongoing for generations. The whispers of danger had coalesced into a clear, undeniable hum beneath the surface of Kilkenny's charming facade.

He found himself replaying conversations, not just with the watchman, but with anyone he'd spoken to since arriving. Had he revealed too much? Had a casual remark about Elara's journals, or his interest in a particular historical period, been misconstrued or noted by an unseen listener? The guesthouse proprietor, Mrs. Doyle, with her perpetually kind smile, now seemed to possess an unnerving perceptiveness. Her innocent questions about his research, about his day, felt less like polite small talk and more like gentle probing, attempts to gauge the extent of his discoveries. He started to feel a prickle of unease every time he saw her, a subtle shift in his perception of her warmth, which now felt like a carefully constructed facade designed to disarm. The guesthouse itself, once a sanctuary, now felt like a monitored space, its walls potentially permeable to eyes he couldn't see. He'd begun the habit of double-checking the locks on his door, not out of any genuine fear of petty theft, but as a symbolic act of asserting some semblance of control over his rapidly eroding privacy.

His walks, too, had transformed from contemplative explorations into tense reconnaissance missions. The ancient lanes of Kilkenny, once picturesque, now seemed to stretch out before him like carefully laid-out traps. The same narrow alleyways that had initially charmed him with their historical atmosphere now felt claustrophobic, potential vantage points for unseen observers. He found himself instinctively checking parked cars for tinted windows, scanning rooftops for any sign of movement, his gaze constantly flicking over faces in the sparse crowds, trying to discern any flicker of recognition or undue interest. The watchman's earlier warning – "Some paths lead to entanglement" – echoed in his mind with unnerving frequency. He recalled the small, antique silver locket he'd spotted on the city walls, its presence an anomaly that had both intrigued and repelled him. He'd resisted the urge to touch it, his academic curiosity battling a sudden, visceral instinct for self-preservation. Now, he wondered if that very act of resistance had been observed, noted, and perhaps even judged. Was his caution interpreted as fear, or as a sign of his potential to be manipulated? The book left on the park bench, a local history he'd been eager to consult, now seemed less like a fortunate find and more like a deliberate bait, a test of his willingness to engage with potentially compromised information. He'd walked away from it, the feeling of being watched a tangible presence at his back, a silent confirmation that his presence in Kilkenny was far from being an anonymous academic endeavor.

This growing sense of being scrutinized, of navigating a landscape fraught with unseen dangers, began to take a toll. The initial excitement of his research was slowly being eclipsed by a gnawing anxiety. He found himself overthinking every interaction, dissecting casual remarks for hidden meanings, and second-guessing the intentions of everyone he encountered. The warmth he'd initially felt from the locals, the friendly banter and easy smiles, now seemed to carry a double edge, potentially masking a deeper, more watchful agenda. He was becoming isolated, not by choice, but by a creeping, pervasive suspicion that made genuine connection feel like a risky proposition. The comforting routines of his academic life – late nights in libraries, collaborative discussions with colleagues, the simple act of sharing a coffee with a friend – felt like distant luxuries, replaced by a constant, low-grade hum of vigilance.

The realization that his research into Elara's life wasn't just an intellectual pursuit but a genuine entanglement in a potentially dangerous lineage was a sobering one. He remembered Aine's quiet unease when he'd spoken of his progress, the subtle way she'd sometimes averted her gaze when he pressed for details about her family's past. He had, in his single-minded pursuit of historical truth, inadvertently drawn Aine into this web of unspoken threats. Her family, he now understood, had likely been custodians of these secrets for generations, their lives perhaps shaped by the very forces he was now encountering. He'd dismissed the watchman's initial warnings as the eccentric ramblings of a lonely old man, a colourful local character. But the increasing precision of the "coincidences," the undeniable feeling of being observed, had forced him to reconsider. The simple instruction, "Be careful," delivered with such quiet intensity, now carried the weight of a grave prophecy. He wasn't just uncovering history; he was walking a path that had been deliberately obscured, a path guarded by those who wished to keep its secrets buried.

The implications of this were profound. His relationship with Aine, which had begun as a shared interest in Kilkenny's past, now felt like a dangerous liability. If those who were watching him were indeed connected to the guardians Elara had alluded to, then Aine, and by extension her family, could be seen as part of the very 'guardianship' he was disrupting. He pictured her quiet strength, her intuitive understanding of Kilkenny's unspoken rhythms, and felt a surge of protective anxiety. Had her family always lived under this shadow of surveillance? Had they learned to navigate it, to blend in, to protect themselves through generations of subtle concealment? And now, through him, had that carefully maintained balance been disturbed? The thought was a heavy one, compounding the personal danger he was beginning to feel with a deep-seated concern for the people he was growing to care about.

He looked at Elara's journals again, their pages filled with her elegant, spidery script. Her accounts of Kilkenny's hidden history, her musings on ancient traditions and guarded knowledge, were no longer just historical curiosities. They were a testament to a lineage of individuals who had grappled with these same forces, who had perhaps faced similar threats. He saw her descriptions of clandestine meetings, of veiled warnings passed between individuals, and realized he was not alone in his experience, though his specific situation was undeniably unique. Elara's life, he now suspected, had been a constant negotiation with these unseen guardians. Her dedication to documenting her discoveries, even in the face of what must have been significant resistance, spoke volumes about her courage and her belief in the importance of the knowledge she possessed.

Pete traced a line of text with his finger, a passage where Elara described feeling an "impenetrable wall of silence" whenever she attempted to probe too deeply into certain historical events. She wrote of "shadows that watched from the periphery," of a pervasive sense of being "gently, but firmly, discouraged." He recognized the echoes of his own experiences in her words, the subtle discouragement, the feeling of being gently steered away from forbidden territory. The difference, of course, was that Elara had been a direct descendant, intrinsically tied to Kilkenny's legacy, while he was an outsider, an interloper whose very presence challenged the established order.

He understood, with a clarity that was both terrifying and exhilarating, that he had stumbled into something far larger than a historical research project. He was now part of a narrative that had been unfolding for centuries, a narrative of secrets, of guardianship, and of a silent, persistent resistance to those who sought to expose what was meant to remain hidden. The knowledge he was acquiring wasn't just academic; it was a form of power, a power that others were actively working to contain. And in his pursuit of that knowledge, he had inadvertently become a threat to that containment.

The watchman's words about "guardians" and "hidden paths" now resonated with a deeper, more ominous significance. These weren't metaphorical constructs; they were real people, real forces, actively preserving a particular version of Kilkenny's history. He thought of the watchman's pale eyes, the unnerving stillness that had emanated from him, and a shiver ran down his spine. This was not a game of intellectual pursuit; it was a confrontation, albeit a subtle and insidious one, with custodians of secrets who wielded a quiet but formidable power. He had to navigate this carefully, not just for his own sake, but for Aine's. The knowledge he sought, the truth he was determined to uncover, had become a dangerous commodity, and he was now inextricably linked to its fate. The whispers of danger were no longer just whispers; they were the low, persistent hum of a system in place to protect its secrets, and he had inadvertently activated it.

Chapter Nine: Confronting the Past

THE ANCIENT TEXTS

The musty air of the subterranean chamber clung to Pete like a damp shroud, a stark contrast to the crisp autumn air he'd left behind on the cobbled streets above. Aine, her silhouette a steady presence in the dim light cast by a single, flickering gas lamp, moved with a quiet familiarity through the rows of ancient chests and tightly packed shelves. This was not a place for casual visitors, nor one for the faint of heart. The silence here was not an absence of sound, but a profound, weighty stillness, pregnant with the accumulated weight of centuries. It was a silence that had clearly been cultivated, a deliberate buffer against the intrusive noise of the outside world, and now, Pete understood, against his own burgeoning curiosity.

"This is it," Aine whispered, her voice barely disturbing the quiet. "The heart of it all." She gestured towards a heavy, oak desk, its surface scarred with the marks of countless scribes and scholars. Upon it lay a collection of leather-bound volumes, their covers worn smooth by time and countless hands. They were not merely books; they felt like living artifacts, repositories of a history far more potent than any he had encountered in the public archives or dimly lit corners of the city library.

He approached the desk, his footsteps unnaturally loud on the stone floor. The sheer volume of material was staggering. Journals filled with delicate, almost ethereal script, interspersed with crudely drawn maps and diagrams that hinted at complex, perhaps even arcane, geometries. There were scrolls tied with faded ribbons, their parchment brittle and yellowed, promising revelations that had lain dormant for generations. This was Aine's inheritance, a legacy of guardianship passed down through her bloodline, a secret history meticulously preserved, hidden away from prying eyes and questioning minds.

"My family," Aine began, her voice gaining a quiet strength as she reached for the topmost volume, "has been tied to Kilkenny for as long as anyone remembers. Not just as residents, but as... caretakers. Custodians." She opened the book, its pages brittle and smelling faintly of dried herbs and something indefinable, something ancient and elemental. "These texts," she continued, her finger tracing a line of elegant, looping script, "are our chronicles. They detail our duties, our rituals, and the delicate balance we are sworn to maintain."

Pete leaned closer, his gaze drawn to the intricate lettering. It wasn't just a historical record; it was a testament to a profound commitment, a lifelong dedication to preserving something unseen, something fundamental to the very essence of Kilkenny. He saw references to "the ebb and flow of the town's spirit," to "resonances that must be harmonized," and to "pacts forged in shadow and moonlight." The language was poetic, steeped in metaphor, yet it carried an undeniable weight of purpose.

"The 'balance' you mentioned," Pete prompted, his voice a low murmur, trying to absorb as much as he could from the charged atmosphere. "What exactly does that mean? What are you balancing?"

Aine's gaze met his, her eyes reflecting the flickering lamplight. "It's the unseen energies, Pete. Kilkenny is built upon layers of history, not just of human events, but of elemental forces, of echoes from the very land itself. There are currents, frequencies, that can be influenced. Sometimes for good, sometimes for ill. We, my ancestors, and now I, are tasked with ensuring those currents remain stable. We prevent the darker ones from gaining too much power, and we nurture the ones that bring harmony and prosperity to the town, even if those involved are unaware of our influence."

She carefully turned a page, revealing a detailed illustration of a complex circular diagram, interwoven with symbols that Pete did not recognize. "This," she explained, "is a depiction of the town's energetic lattice. Our role is to maintain its integrity. When there are disruptions – significant historical events, or even powerful emotional surges from the populace – the lattice can become disturbed. We perform rituals, specific sequences of actions and intentions, to realign it. It's a constant vigilance."

The concept was both alien and strangely familiar. He thought of the subtle unease he'd felt since arriving, the feeling of being watched, the uncanny 'coincidences.' Could these be manifestations of a disturbed balance? Were these unseen forces reacting to his presence, his probing questions, seeing him as another disruption?

"So, Elara," Pete began, his mind racing, "her journals. She was part of this? Was she a guardian too?"

Aine nodded, her expression tinged with a sadness that mirrored the ancient feel of the room. "Elara was indeed one of us. She understood the weight of our lineage. Her fascination with Kilkenny's hidden history wasn't just academic; it was an intrinsic part of her being.

She documented everything, not just the events themselves, but the subtle shifts, the atmospheric changes, the whispers of unrest. She was a gifted observer, acutely sensitive to the energetic currents."

She opened another volume, this one bound in dark green leather, its pages filled with Elara's familiar handwriting, but now imbued with a new context. "Listen to this," Aine said, reading aloud. "'October 14th, 1888. The resonance along the river is discordant today. A chill wind, unseasonable and unsettling, sweeps through the town. I felt a pull, a subtle draining, as if something ancient and hungry stirs beneath the surface. The wards feel strained. I performed the necessary rites at dusk, but the feeling of unease lingers. The balance is precarious.'"

Pete listened, a growing sense of awe and trepidation filling him. Elara's words were not the musings of a historian; they were the reports of a sentinel, a guardian actively engaged in a silent, unseen battle. He saw now that his initial interpretation of her writings as mere historical accounts was profoundly mistaken. They were operational logs, records of a clandestine, generational effort to maintain a delicate equilibrium.

"She was aware of the dangers," Aine continued, her voice hushed. "She wrote of feeling watched, not by people, but by something... older. Something that responded to her attempts to understand the deeper layers of Kilkenny. She mentioned feeling 'discouraged' from pursuing certain lines of inquiry, a gentle but persistent pushback from forces she couldn't quite define but inherently understood were tied to the town's hidden energies."

"And the pacts?" Pete asked, remembering the mention from the first journal. "What sort of pacts?"

Aine closed the book with a soft thud, the sound resonating in the quiet. "The pacts are multifaceted. Some are with the land itself, acknowledging its ancient spirit and promising to respect its rhythms. Others are with certain entities, beings of immense power that reside within or beneath Kilkenny, who have agreed to coexist with the human population as long as the balance is maintained. These aren't necessarily malevolent forces, but they are powerful, and their influence can be detrimental if not properly managed. The pacts are an agreement to mutual respect, a codification of boundaries, ensuring that neither side encroaches upon the other's domain."

She picked up a small, intricately carved wooden box from the desk. Opening it, she revealed a collection of smooth, dark stones, each inscribed with a unique, abstract symbol. "These are talismans," she explained. "Each imbued with a specific protective or harmonizing energy, used in our rituals. They are keyed to the town's energetic grid. My family has always collected and maintained them."

Pete looked at the stones, feeling a strange hum emanating from them, a subtle vibration that seemed to resonate with his very bones. He could almost feel the intent, the centuries of focused energy that had been poured into their creation and use. It was tangible, undeniable.

"The lore," Pete prompted, eager to understand the full scope of what he was uncovering. "What forgotten lore are we talking about?"

"Kilkenny has a history far older than its recorded past," Aine said, her gaze distant, as if peering into a forgotten age. "Before the castles and the cathedrals, there were different peoples, different beliefs. Their understanding of the land, of its inherent energies, was far more profound and less mediated by structures. They understood how to interact directly with the natural forces. Some of that knowledge, the techniques, the songs, the ways of sensing and channeling, has been passed down, often in fragmented forms, through generations. It speaks of a time when the veil between our world and others was thinner, when the natural world was more... sentient. My family's role was also to preserve these fragments, to ensure that this older wisdom was not entirely lost, as it holds keys to understanding the deeper workings of the town's energetic makeup."

She gestured to a large, unfurled parchment that lay beside the journals. It was a detailed celestial chart, but unlike any Pete had ever seen. It depicted not just the stars and planets, but also a series of interlocking circles and lines that seemed to correspond with specific locations within Kilkenny.

"This map," Aine said, her voice hushed with reverence, "shows the alignment of certain celestial bodies with Kilkenny's energetic nodes. My ancestors believed that specific astronomical events could amplify or disrupt the town's natural energies. They developed ways to predict these conjunctions and prepare accordingly, often through rituals performed at key locations marked on this chart. The cyclical nature of these events, and our attempts to influence them, forms a significant part of our ongoing duty."

Pete traced a line on the map, his mind struggling to grasp the sheer depth and complexity of what he was seeing. This wasn't just a historical discovery; it was an immersion into a secret cosmology, a hidden layer of reality that existed beneath the mundane surface of Kilkenny. Aine's family wasn't just preserving history; they were actively participating in a continuous, living tradition that shaped the very fabric of the town, whether its inhabitants knew it or not.

"So, all of this," Pete said, gesturing around the archive, "your family's history, the rituals, the lore, the pacts – it's all designed to maintain this 'balance' and protect Kilkenny from what, exactly?"

Aine paused, her brow furrowed in concentration as she returned to one of Elara's journals. She found a passage and read it with a quiet intensity. "'The greatest threat,' Elara wrote, 'is not external invasion, nor even overt malevolence. It is the slow erosion of that balance, the subtle unraveling of the energetic weave. When the town's inherent rhythms are ignored, when its deeper currents are left untended, there is a tendency for discordant energies, ancient and primal, to gain purchase. These are not entities with conscious malice, but forces of chaos, drawn to imbalance. Left unchecked, they can manifest as widespread apathy, societal decay, or even unseen maladies that plague the populace without a discernable cause. Our duty is to be the subtle counter-force, the quiet harmonizers, preventing that descent into entropy.'"

Pete absorbed her words, the implications chilling him to the bone. The true danger wasn't a visible enemy, but a slow, insidious decay, a spiritual and energetic rot that could undermine the very foundations of the town. His research, his quest for knowledge, had inadvertently brought him face-to-face with the guardians who stood against that decay.

"And what happens," Pete asked, his voice barely a whisper, "if the balance is not maintained? What are the consequences of failure?"

Aine's gaze was steady, unwavering. "The texts speak of cyclical periods of darkness, of Kilkenny becoming a place where only the most resilient or the most desperate could thrive. They speak of a draining of vitality, a suffocating malaise that would grip the hearts of its people. Elara believed that the town's prosperity, its very charm and liveliness, was intrinsically linked to the health of these unseen energies. When they falter, so does the town."

He looked at Aine, truly seeing her for the first time not as a helpful local historian, but as a living conduit to an ancient lineage, a keeper of profound and secret responsibilities. Her quiet demeanor, her intuitive understanding of Kilkenny, her subtle warnings – they all began to coalesce into a single, powerful narrative. She wasn't just telling him about her family's past; she was revealing a living, breathing tradition that was vital to the town's continued existence.

"This is... immense," Pete finally managed to say, the word feeling woefully inadequate. He felt a profound sense of humility, realizing how little he truly understood about the world, about history, and about the hidden forces that might shape it. His academic pursuits had led him down a path far more extraordinary and perilous than he could have ever imagined. He was no longer just a researcher; he was a witness to a secret history, a history that was still very much alive, and he was standing at the precipice of its deepest truths, held in the hands of Aine and her ancestors. The ancient texts weren't just records of the past; they were a blueprint for the present, a guide to the unseen forces that continued to shape Kilkenny, and his own destiny within its ancient walls.

AINES ANCESTORS STORY

The journal lay open on the desk, its pages worn to a soft, leathery texture that spoke of countless hours of contemplation. Aine's fingers, delicate yet firm, brushed over the faded ink, her gaze fixed on a particular entry. The script, though archaic, possessed a familiar flow, a cadence that Pete recognized from other ancestral records. But this one, this one felt different. There was an intensity to the handwriting, a raw emotional undercurrent that transcended the mere transcription of events.

"This is Morwenna," Aine began, her voice hushed, a reverence in her tone that immediately drew Pete in. "She was one of my great-great-great aunts, I believe. The resemblance... well, you can see it, can't you?"

Pete nodded, studying the accompanying sketch. Indeed, the woman depicted – her high cheekbones, the determined set of her jaw, the deep-set eyes that seemed to hold a flicker of both fierce intelligence and profound sorrow – bore an uncanny resemblance to Aine. It was as if he were looking at a reflection from another time, a ghost superimposed upon the present.

"Her journal," Aine continued, her voice gaining a low hum of gravity, "covers a period of great discord in the late 1700s. Kilkenny was a different place then, more superstitious, more... volatile, perhaps. And Morwenna writes of a profound disturbance in the town's energetic lattice, a threat unlike anything documented before."

She began to read, her voice a low murmur that filled the cavernous chamber. "'October 3rd, 1789. A disquiet settles upon the town, a chill that no hearth can dispel. The river's song is discordant, a mournful dirge rather than its usual cheerful burble. My senses are assailed by a pervasive unease, a feeling of being watched, not by earthly eyes, but by something far more ancient and insatiable. The wards shimmer with an unusual strain; the ancient stones beneath the High Street groan as if in pain. I fear the tendrils of the Shadow-Weave are tightening their grip.'"

Pete listened, the words painting a vivid, unsettling picture. The Shadow-Weave. The term itself conjured images of encroaching darkness, of insidious corruption. "What is the Shadow-Weave?" he asked, his voice barely a whisper, afraid to break the spell of the narrative.

Aine met his gaze, her eyes mirroring the dim lamplight. "It is the antithesis of the balance we strive to maintain. Think of it as a void, a parasitic force that feeds on discord and negativity. When the town's energetic currents become unbalanced, when fear or despair gain a foothold, the Shadow-Weave finds an opening. It doesn't have a form, not in the way we understand it, but it can influence, amplify, and distort. It can feed upon the town's vitality, leaving it listless, susceptible to all manner of ills, both physical and spiritual."

She turned another brittle page. "Morwenna describes her efforts to counter this growing influence. She speaks of lengthy vigils, of intricate rituals performed under moonless skies, of drawing upon the very essence of the land to bolster the town's defenses. But her entries are also laced with a deep sense of isolation. She felt the burden acutely, the knowledge that she was the sole guardian against an encroaching darkness, with no one else in the town truly understanding the nature of the threat."

Aine paused, taking a slow breath. "Listen to this: 'October 17th, 1789. The villagers speak of a miasma hanging over the lower wards, of crops failing inexplicably, of a pervasive weariness that grips even the most robust. They attribute it to ill fortune, to the wrath of God, to anything but the truth I perceive. They are unknowingly suffering the effects of the weakening weave. My own strength wanes. The rituals are draining, and the constant vigilance wears upon my soul. I feel as though I am standing against a tidal wave with only a flimsy shield.'"

The emotional weight of Morwenna's words pressed down on Pete. He could feel her desperation, her weariness, her profound sense of responsibility. It was a mirror, he realized, to Aine's own solitary struggle, albeit on a different scale. The sheer magnitude of the task, the silent battles waged against unseen forces, and the crushing weight of legacy – these were not abstract concepts for Aine; they were her lived reality.

"She mentions a specific location," Aine continued, tracing a passage with her fingertip. "The old mill by the River Nore. She believed it was a nexus point where the Shadow-Weave's influence was particularly strong. She writes of having to perform a particularly potent ritual there, one that required a significant personal sacrifice."

A wave of apprehension washed over Pete. "Sacrifice? What kind of sacrifice?"

"Her journal is not explicit," Aine admitted, her gaze troubled. "She refers to 'laying down a piece of herself,' of 'offering a fragment of her own light to mend the tear.' Later entries suggest a profound personal loss, a diminishment of her own spirit that she never fully recovered from. She managed to restore the balance, to push back the encroaching darkness, but the cost was immense. She writes of feeling 'hollowed out,' of a perpetual shadow that clung to her even in the brightest sunlight."

Aine's voice dropped to a near whisper. "It's the part that always gets me, Pete. The personal cost. My ancestors were guardians, yes, but they were also women, with lives, with emotions, with the capacity for joy and sorrow. To bear the weight of protecting an entire town, to face down forces that no one else can even perceive, and to do so with such immense personal risk... it's almost unbearable to contemplate."

She turned another page, revealing a detailed, if somewhat rough, sketch of the old mill. Its waterwheel was depicted as broken, its timbers sagging, a stark image of decay. Alongside it, Morwenna had drawn a series of symbols, intricate and unsettling, that seemed to pulse with a dark energy even on the page.

"Morwenna believed that the Shadow-Weave fed on despair," Aine explained. "And in that particular period, there was a great deal of it in Kilkenny. Harvest failures, a bout of fever that swept through the poorer districts, growing unrest due to political tensions in the wider world – all these external pressures created fertile ground for the darkness to take root. Her struggle was not just against the Shadow-Weave itself, but against the collective despair of the town, which inadvertently fueled the very threat she was trying to combat."

She paused, her brow furrowed as she reread a passage. "

'I see now the insidious nature of this foe. It does not always announce itself with thunder and lightning. More often, it creeps in like a fog, a subtle erosion of hope, a whisper of futility that paralyzes the spirit. And the more the people succumb to this despair, the stronger the tendrils become, the more tightly the Shadow-Weave constricts.'"

Pete found himself drawn to the intricate symbols Morwenna had drawn. They were unlike anything he had seen in any historical texts or occult literature he'd ever encountered. They seemed to possess a latent power, a complex language that spoke of forgotten rites and ancient pacts.

"What are these symbols?" he asked, pointing to them.

"Morwenna was exceptionally skilled in the ancient methods of energetic manipulation," Aine explained. "These are not mere sigils; they are complex constructs, designed to channel specific energies, to create a sort of energetic scaffold that could resist the Shadow-Weave's corrosive influence. She adapted some of the older, more elemental protections, weaving them with her own intent and the specific vibrational frequencies of Kilkenny itself. It was a deeply personal and dangerous art."

She continued reading, her voice taking on a more urgent tone. 'November 5th, 1789. The influence is palpable now. I feel it pressing in, a physical weight upon my chest. The light within the town seems to dim, not in the eyes of the people, for they are accustomed to their hardships, but in its very essence. The stones of St. Canice's hum with a low, discordant frequency. I must act, and I must act decisively. The ritual at the mill is the only recourse. The materials are gathered, the incantations prepared. May the ancient powers grant me strength, and may Kilkenny be spared.'"

Aine looked up from the journal, her gaze meeting Pete's. There was a profound sadness in her eyes, a reflection of the centuries that had passed, and the echoes of Morwenna's struggle that resonated within her own heart. "She knew the risk," Aine whispered. "She knew that performing such a ritual, in such a place, at such a time, would demand a great deal from her. She was essentially drawing upon her own life force to act as a conduit, to anchor the town's defenses at a critical juncture."

Pete felt a chill that had nothing to do with the subterranean chamber. He was witnessing the raw, unvarnished truth of Aine's lineage – a history of quiet, often painful, heroism. Elara had been a sentinel, meticulously documenting the town's hidden currents. Morwenna, it seemed, had been a warrior, actively engaged in repelling a direct assault on Kilkenny's spiritual and energetic well-being.

"Did she succeed?" Pete asked, his voice tight with anticipation.

Aine turned another page, and Pete's breath hitched. The pages that followed were sparser, the handwriting more shaky, almost desperate. There were fewer detailed accounts of rituals and more fragmented entries, filled with a profound weariness.

'November 10th, 1789. It is done. The darkness recedes, like a tide drawn back to a hungry sea. The air feels lighter, the river's murmur more harmonious. But the cost... the cost is grievous. A part of me remains tethered to that place, to that struggle. The light I once felt within me is... diminished. I am left with a great emptiness, a lingering echo of the void I faced.'"

Aine closed the journal with a soft, deliberate sound that seemed to reverberate through the stillness. "She succeeded, Pete. She saved Kilkenny from what she described as a 'spiritual blight.' The

Shadow-Weave was repelled, its tendrils severed. But as she wrote, the personal cost was immense. She lived for another twenty years, but she never truly recovered her former vitality. Her journals become increasingly melancholic, filled with observations about the fleeting nature of light and the persistent encroachment of shadow, even after the immediate threat had passed."

Pete looked at the journal, then at Aine. He saw the parallels starkly. Morwenna's struggle against the Shadow-Weave in the late 18th century, her personal sacrifice to maintain the balance – it was a narrative that resonated deeply with the challenges Aine herself was facing now. The same town, the same underlying forces, and the same extraordinary burden placed upon a descendant.

"It's as if history repeats itself," Pete murmured, the realization dawning on him with a chilling clarity. "The same threats, the same responsibilities... passed down through generations."

Aine nodded slowly, her expression a complex mixture of sorrow and determination. "It does. And Morwenna's story is a stark reminder of what that responsibility can entail. It's not just about knowledge or ritual; it's about willingness to sacrifice, to endure hardship, to face down darkness even when it seems overwhelming. She preserved Kilkenny, but she also paid a profound personal price for it."

She picked up another, slimmer volume, its binding of faded blue silk. "This is her personal correspondence, mostly with her sister. Even in these more intimate writings, the weight of her duty is palpable. She writes of feeling drained, of struggling to find joy, of the constant anxiety that the balance might shift again. She expresses a profound loneliness, knowing that her true work, the true nature of her burden, could never be shared with the people she was protecting."

Aine began to read from this new journal, her voice softer now, more intimate. 'My dearest Eleanor, the harvest has been poor again this year. The people whisper of curses and ill omens. I try to offer comfort, to speak of hope, but a coldness has settled within me, a shadow that I cannot banish. I fear I am not strong enough to continue. Sometimes, I envy you your simple life, your ability to find solace in the everyday. My own world is cast in perpetual twilight.'"

Pete listened intently, the raw emotion in Morwenna's words striking him deeply. It was a testament to the human toll of such an inherited duty, a reminder that behind the ancient rituals and the custodianship of hidden energies, there were individuals who experienced fear, loneliness, and profound personal loss.

"She wrestled with her faith, with her own resilience," Aine explained, her voice catching slightly. "She questioned whether the sacrifices were worth it, whether she could continue to bear the burden. It's a question that I think many of my ancestors, and perhaps even I myself, have had to confront at some point."

She looked at Pete, her gaze steady and unflinching. "Morwenna's story isn't just a historical account, Pete. It's a warning, and it's also a testament to the enduring strength of those who have undertaken this guardianship. It shows the cyclical nature of the challenges Kilkenny faces, and it underscores the personal cost involved. Her struggle, her sacrifice, her eventual success in preserving the town's vital energy – it all resonates deeply with what I am facing now. It's a part of my past, yes, but it feels remarkably present."

The air in the chamber seemed to thicken, charged with the weight of centuries of inherited responsibility and the echoes of Morwenna's profound sacrifice. Pete understood now, with a clarity that was both illuminating and deeply unsettling, the true depth of Aine's lineage, the silent battles fought, and the enduring legacy of vigilance and personal cost that had been passed down through her family, a legacy that now rested squarely upon her shoulders. The resemblance between Aine and Morwenna was more than superficial; it was a shared destiny, a mirrored struggle against the unseen forces that sought to diminish Kilkenny's spirit.

THE NATURE OF THE THREAT

The weight of Morwenna's words, of her quiet heroism and profound sacrifice, settled upon Pete like a shroud. He understood, then, the true, terrifying nature of the threat Aine and her ancestors had faced, and continued to face. It wasn't merely a matter of ancient lore or historical curiosities; it was a tangible, insidious force that preyed on the very essence of a place, a force that, left unchecked, could drain the lifeblood from Kilkenny itself. The Shadow-Weave, as Morwenna termed it, was not a creature with claws and teeth, but something far more chilling: a void, an emptiness that sought to consume all vibrancy, all hope, all light. Its power lay not in direct confrontation, but in subtle manipulation, in the amplification of despair, in the slow, insidious erosion of a community's collective spirit.

Aine, sensing his dawning comprehension, continued to elaborate, her voice low and resonant, filling the cavernous space with the gravitas of her ancestral burden. "Morwenna's account is a testament to the fact that the forces we contend with are not always obvious, or even comprehensible, to the uninitiated. The Shadow-Weave, for example, doesn't manifest as a single, identifiable entity. It's more akin to a parasitic infestation of the town's energetic field. Think of Kilkenny's vitality, its inherent essence, as a complex tapestry of interwoven energies – the flow of the Nore, the ancient ley lines that crisscross the surrounding landscape, the collective hopes and fears of its inhabitants, even the very bedrock upon which it's built. The Shadow-Weave seeks to unravel this tapestry, to introduce discord and chaos, to fray the threads until the whole structure collapses."

She gestured towards the journal, her eyes reflecting a deep, ingrained understanding of these abstract concepts. "Morwenna's descriptions of 'tendrils tightening their grip' and the 'groaning of the ancient stones' weren't metaphorical exaggerations. She was sensing the tangible strain placed upon the town's energetic lattice by this encroaching negativity. When the collective mood of a town dips – due to hardship, famine, disease, or social unrest – that despair becomes a beacon, a signal that the Shadow-Weave can latch onto. It amplifies those negative emotions, turning a collective sigh of weariness into a resonating hum of hopelessness, and that hum, in turn, draws more of the Shadow-Weave into the fabric of the town."

Pete tried to visualize this, to grasp the abstract made real. He imagined the energetic field of Kilkenny as a living organism, and the Shadow-Weave as a subtle poison, slowly seeping into its veins. "So, when Morwenna talks about the villagers attributing their misfortunes to 'ill fortune' or 'the wrath of God,' she's saying they were mistaking the symptoms for the cause?"

"Precisely," Aine confirmed, a flicker of grim acknowledgment in her eyes. "They were experiencing the effects of the Shadow-Weave's influence – the failing crops, the pervasive weariness, the general malaise – but they lacked the awareness, the ancestral knowledge, to understand its true origin. They looked for earthly explanations, for divine intervention, for anything but the subtle, unseen force that was actively draining their vitality. And that lack of understanding, that inability to identify the true enemy, was itself a vulnerability. It meant that the burden of defense fell entirely upon the shoulders of those few who could perceive it, like Morwenna."

She traced the faded sketch of the old mill with her finger, her touch reverent. "The mill, as she identified it, was a nexus point. In older times, such places, where natural energies converged or were harnessed, were often considered sacred. But when corrupted, or when a strong negative influence took hold, they could become conduits for something far more dangerous. Morwenna's ritual wasn't just about casting out a shadow; it was about reasserting the town's inherent energetic signature, about reinforcing the very foundations of its well-being against an active, malevolent force."

The concept of personal sacrifice, however, continued to gnaw at Pete. "She mentioned 'laying down a piece of herself,' 'offering a fragment of her own light.' What did that actually entail? What was the nature of that sacrifice?"

Aine's gaze grew distant, shadowed by the weight of generations of similar burdens. "The details are, as she herself admitted, difficult to articulate without personal experience. But based on her later writings, and the accounts of other ancestors who undertook similar difficult tasks, it's about becoming a living conduit. When you're fighting a force that feeds on negation, on void, you have to counter it with something inherently positive, something powerful. For Morwenna, it meant channeling her own life force, her own spiritual luminescence, into the compromised energetic field of the town. It was like taking a piece of her own inner light and using it to cauterize a wound, to mend a tear in the very fabric of reality."

She paused, her voice growing softer, laced with a profound empathy for her ancestor. "Imagine holding a burning ember in your hand, not to warm yourself, but to cauterize a wound on someone else. You absorb the immediate pain, the searing heat, to achieve a greater good. Morwenna essentially did that with her own spirit. She absorbed a portion of the Shadow-Weave's emptiness, its nihilistic pull, into herself. She became the anchor, the point of resistance, that allowed the town's natural energies to reassert themselves. But in doing so, she diminished herself. She created a small, internal void where her own light had been, a space that could never be fully replenished."

Pete felt a cold dread creep into his bones. He looked at Aine, at the quiet strength that resided within her, and he began to understand the true cost of her inheritance. This wasn't a legacy of comfortable wealth or inherited titles; it was a legacy of profound personal struggle, of unseen battles, of a constant, quiet erosion of the self in service of others. "So, she essentially became a battery, a shield, that absorbed the damage meant for the town?"

"In essence, yes," Aine confirmed, her voice barely above a whisper. "And the more potent the threat, the greater the sacrifice required. Her struggle against the Shadow-Weave in 1789 was particularly severe because, as she noted, the town's collective despair was at a high point. The confluence of failed harvests, illness, and a general sense of unease created an environment where the Shadow-Weave could gain a significant foothold. She had to draw deeply from her own reserves, from the core of her being, to counter that level of influence."

She turned another page, her brow furrowed as she focused on a passage detailing Morwenna's efforts to bolster the town's defenses. "Here, she describes reinforcing the existing wards. These aren't just physical structures; they are energetic boundaries, woven from intention and ancient knowledge. She writes about 'recharging them with lunar essence' and 'imbueing them with the earth's steadfastness.' But even these methods were insufficient against the growing power of the Shadow-Weave. It was like trying to hold back a flood with a sieve."

The symbols she had drawn alongside the sketch of the mill became more significant in Aine's explanation. "These symbols," Aine explained, her finger hovering over the intricate designs, "are not mere decorative elements. They are complex diagrams, akin to energetic blueprints. Each line, each curve, represents a specific flow of energy, a precise manipulation of forces. Morwenna was a master of what we call 'sympathetic resonance' – the ability to create energetic links between disparate elements. She was using these symbols to draw upon specific energies, perhaps from the river, from the earth, even from the celestial bodies, and to focus them into a cohesive shield against the Shadow-Weave."

She continued, her voice resonating with a deep respect for her ancestor's skills. "It was a dangerous art, requiring an intimate understanding of Kilkenny's energetic landscape. She had to know precisely where to draw power from, how to channel it without causing further disruption, and how to anchor it effectively. The Shadow-Weave, being a force of negation, would actively try to corrupt these channels, to turn the very energies Morwenna sought to use against her. It was a constant, draining battle of wills, played out on an energetic plane."

Aine then read from another entry, the words filled with a growing sense of urgency and dread. 'November 5th, 1789. The influence is palpable now. I feel it pressing in, a physical weight upon my chest. The light within the town seems to dim, not in the eyes of the people, for they are accustomed to their hardships, but in its very essence. The stones of St. Canice's hum with a low, discordant frequency. I must act, and I must act decisively. The ritual at the mill is the only recourse. The materials are gathered, the incantations prepared. May the ancient powers grant me strength, and may Kilkenny be spared.'"

"The stones of St. Canice's," Aine murmured, her gaze unfocused as she recalled the ancient cathedral, a landmark steeped in centuries of history and spiritual significance. "Even a place of such sacredness could not entirely resist the Shadow-Weave's pervasive influence when the town's energetic balance was so severely compromised. It's a testament to the insidious nature of the threat."

Pete understood now that the threat was not an isolated incident; it was a recurring challenge, a cyclical struggle that ebbed and flowed with the town's fortunes. Morwenna's fight was a precedent, a clear indication of the nature of the forces at play and the immense personal cost involved in repelling them. He saw in her writings the raw, human element of this ancient guardianship – the fear, the isolation, the sheer exhaustion that must have accompanied such a solitary battle.

"She knew the risk," Aine reiterated, her voice tinged with a profound sorrow. "She wasn't naive. She understood that to perform such a ritual, in such a compromised location, would require her to become the focal point of the struggle. She was essentially offering herself as a living conduit, a sacrificial beacon to draw the darkness away from the town and into herself, thereby mending the fractured energetic weave."

The casual observer might have seen Kilkenny as a charming historical town, its past merely a backdrop for tourism. But Pete now understood the deeper, more perilous reality. Kilkenny possessed a unique energetic signature, a vibrancy that made it both beautiful and vulnerable. And for centuries, certain individuals within Aine's lineage had been tasked with safeguarding that vibrancy, acting as silent sentinels against forces that sought to exploit or extinguish it. Elara had been a meticulous chronicler, documenting subtle shifts and potential dangers, while Morwenna had been a warrior, a frontline defender who had actively engaged and repelled a direct assault.

The final entries in Morwenna's journal were a stark testament to the physical and spiritual toll her actions had taken. The handwriting became shaky, the entries more fragmented, interspersed with long periods of silence. Pete read the penultimate entry, a confession of exhaustion and a deep sense of loss: 'November 10th, 1789. It is done. The darkness recedes, like a tide drawn back to a hungry sea. The air feels lighter, the river's murmur more harmonious. But the cost... the cost is grievous. A part of me remains tethered to that place, to that struggle. The light I once felt within me is... diminished. I am left with a great emptiness, a lingering echo of the void I faced.'"

Aine closed the journal, the soft thud echoing in the charged silence of the chamber. "She succeeded, Pete. She pushed back the Shadow-Weave, severed its hold on Kilkenny. The town was saved from what she termed a 'spiritual blight.' But as she so eloquently put it, the personal cost was immense. She lived for another two decades, but the vibrant spark that had defined her earlier years was dimmed. Her later writings are filled with a profound melancholy, a pervasive sense of loss, and a lingering awareness of the shadow that had touched her, a shadow that never fully retreated, even after the immediate danger had passed."

Pete looked at the worn journal, then at Aine. The parallels were undeniable, chillingly clear. Morwenna's struggle in the late 18th century mirrored Aine's current predicament with an unnerving precision. The same town, the same underlying existential threats, and the same profound burden of inherited responsibility now rested upon Aine's shoulders. It was a legacy of courage, yes, but also a legacy of immense personal sacrifice, a constant struggle against forces that were largely invisible and incomprehensible to the outside world.

"It's as if history is a repeating echo," Pete murmured, the realization settling in his gut with a cold, heavy finality. "The same dangers, the same duty... passed down through blood, through generations."

Aine nodded, her expression a complex tapestry of sorrow and an unyielding resolve. "It does. And Morwenna's story is a stark, unavoidable reminder of what that duty truly entails. It's not merely about possessing knowledge or performing rituals; it's about the willingness to endure hardship, to face down darkness even when you feel utterly alone and overwhelmed, and to accept the personal cost that comes with protecting something vital. She preserved Kilkenny's spirit, but she paid a grievous price for it, a price that resonates through the ages, a price that now, perhaps, I too must pay."

The slimmer volume, bound in faded blue silk, spoke of an even more intimate aspect of Morwenna's life. Aine opened it, her voice softening as she began to read from her ancestor's personal correspondence. 'My dearest Eleanor, the harvest has been poor again this year. The people whisper of curses and ill omens. I try to offer comfort, to speak of hope, but a coldness has settled within me, a shadow that I cannot banish. I fear I am not strong enough to continue. Sometimes, I envy you your simple life, your ability to find solace in the everyday. My own world is cast in perpetual twilight.'"

The raw vulnerability in Morwenna's words was palpable, a testament to the profound human toll of such an inherited responsibility. It was a reminder that behind the stoic facade of the guardian, behind the arcane knowledge and the ancient rituals, there were individuals who grappled with fear, loneliness, and the crushing weight of their unique burden. They experienced moments of doubt, of profound exhaustion, and a yearning for the simplicity denied to them by their lineage.

"She wrestled with her faith, with her own resilience," Aine explained, her voice catching slightly, her gaze fixed on the worn pages.

"She questioned whether the sacrifices were truly worth it, whether she could continue to bear the immense weight of her duty. It's a question that I believe many of my ancestors, and indeed, I myself, have had to confront at various points in our lives. The sheer persistence of the threat, the constant vigilance required, can be overwhelming."

She then looked directly at Pete, her gaze steady and unflinching, the shared knowledge between them forging an unspoken bond. "Morwenna's story isn't just a historical account, Pete. It's a profound warning about the nature of the challenges Kilkenny faces, and it's also a testament to the enduring strength and resilience of those who have accepted this guardianship. It demonstrates the cyclical nature of the threats Kilkenny has faced throughout its history, and it underscores, in the starkest possible terms, the immense personal cost involved. Her struggle, her sacrifice, her eventual triumph in preserving the town's vital energy – it all resonates with an unnerving clarity with what I am facing now. It's an integral part of my past, certainly, but it feels astonishingly, terrifyingly present."

The air in the subterranean chamber seemed to thicken, charged with the accumulated weight of centuries of inherited responsibility and the echoes of Morwenna's profound, almost unbearable, sacrifice. Pete's understanding of Aine's lineage had deepened immeasurably. It wasn't just about preserving history; it was about actively engaging in a perpetual, silent war against unseen forces that sought to diminish Kilkenny's very soul. The uncanny resemblance between Aine and Morwenna was no mere coincidence; it was a mirrored destiny, a shared struggle against the encroaching darkness that now, with chilling certainty, Pete knew was once again stirring in the ancient heart of Kilkenny.

PETES ROLE AND CHOICE

The weight of Morwenna's sacrifice, the echoes of her struggle against the Shadow-Weave, still hung heavy in the air, a palpable testament to the burdens Aine carried. Pete had seen the faded ink, felt the tremor of ancestral fear, and understood, with a clarity that chilled him to the bone, the true nature of the guardianship passed down through Aine's family. It wasn't a passive stewardship of historical artifacts or quaint traditions; it was an active, perilous engagement with forces that operated beyond the veil of ordinary perception. He had glimpsed the profound personal cost, the erosion of self, that such a legacy demanded. But as he absorbed Aine's explanation, a new, disquieting realization began to dawn, a realization that shifted the focus of his concern from the past onto their shared present.

"Morwenna's story... it's extraordinary," Pete began, his voice raspy, the enormity of it all settling upon him. "Her strength, her sacrifice... it's hard to even comprehend. And you, Aine, you're living with that same legacy, facing the same... shadow." He looked at her, at the quiet resilience etched onto her features, a resilience forged in the crucible of ancestral duty. "But my being here, my involvement... does it... does it affect that? Does it change anything for you, or for what you have to do?"

Aine met his gaze, her eyes, pools of ancient knowledge and quiet sorrow, holding his. A subtle tension, almost imperceptible, rippled through her posture. She hesitated, a flicker of something akin to apprehension crossing her face, before she spoke, her voice pitched low, as if reluctant to voice the truth. "Pete, the path my family has walked for generations is one that has always required a degree of...

separation. An isolation. It's not a choice made out of preference, but out of necessity. The energies we interact with, the very nature of the threats we guard against, demand a certain solitude. It's a way to shield ourselves, and to prevent any... unintended ripples."

She turned slightly, her gaze drifting towards the ancient stones that surrounded them, as if drawing strength from their enduring presence. "Think of it like this: we are, in many ways, trying to maintain a delicate equilibrium. Like a skilled weaver, constantly mending the tears in a vast, intricate tapestry. Introducing any outside element, even with the best intentions, can sometimes... alter the tension, shift the threads in ways that are difficult to predict or control. And my ancestors learned, over time, that drawing others too close, involving them too deeply, could create vulnerabilities."

Pete felt a prickle of unease. He had been drawn into this world, into Aine's world, not as an observer, but as a participant. He had felt the subtle shifts, the growing connection between them, and now he understood that this very connection, this burgeoning intimacy, might be a complication, a potential disruption to the carefully guarded sanctuary her lineage maintained. "Vulnerabilities? What kind of vulnerabilities?" he pressed, his mind racing, trying to grasp the implications. Was it about being compromised? About revealing secrets? Or something more... profound?

"It's about the focus," Aine explained, her voice gaining a quiet intensity. "The Shadow-Weave, and other such forces, they are drawn to points of disruption, to chaos, to anything that might destabilize the existing balance. My family's work is about maintaining a steady, consistent resistance. When there's a strong emotional or energetic connection to someone outside of this lineage, someone who isn't attuned to these subtle forces, it can create a new focal point. The darkness might perceive it as a weakness, a way to infiltrate, or perhaps simply as a distraction from the primary defense."

She paused, her gaze returning to him, heavy with unspoken concern. "Morwenna, in her journal, alluded to this. She spoke of the burden of her duty sometimes isolating her even from those she loved. She mentioned the 'need for a clear channel,' unburdened by the complexities of personal relationships that could 'cloud the intent' or 'divert the flow of protective energies.' It was a practical consideration, born from centuries of experience. When you are constantly working with subtle forces, with energies that can be easily swayed or corrupted, you have to be incredibly disciplined, incredibly focused. Any external entanglement, as benign as it might seem, introduces variables."

Pete's stomach tightened. He had envisioned their relationship as a source of strength, a shared anchor in the face of the inexplicable. He hadn't considered that his presence, his growing feelings for Aine, might be perceived as a liability, a destabilizing factor in her ancient and precarious work. "So, you're saying that... my being here, that we are... a problem?" The words felt hollow, a betrayal of the hope that had blossomed between them in the shadowed depths of the past.

Aine reached out, her fingers brushing lightly against his hand, a gesture that was both reassuring and tinged with a deep regret. "It's not that simple, Pete. And it's not that I don't cherish our connection, or that I don't find strength in your presence. You have a unique perspective, a clarity that many within my lineage, perhaps myself included at times, have lost. But the reality is, my family's duty is not just about fighting the darkness; it's about managing the town's energetic health, which is an ongoing, delicate process. And that process has always been conducted with a degree of carefully maintained distance from the wider populace, and certainly from personal entanglements that could compromise the mission."

She squeezed his hand gently, her thumb tracing the back of his. "When Morwenna performed her ritual, she was alone. Not just physically, but energetically. She had to be. The nature of her sacrifice, of drawing that encroaching void into herself to mend the town's weave, required an absolute purity of focus, an untainted channel. Any significant personal attachment could have acted as a magnet for the darkness, a way for it to latch onto her, or even to use her loved ones as a point of leverage against her."

Pete pulled his hand away, a sudden chill settling over him that had nothing to do with the damp air of the chamber. He stood, pacing a few steps, the confined space amplifying his growing unease. He had been so focused on understanding the history, on supporting Aine in her present struggle, that he hadn't truly considered the personal ramifications for them. He had assumed that their bond would be an asset, a source of mutual strength. Now, he was being told it could be a liability.

"So, what are you saying, Aine?" he asked, his voice tight with a mixture of frustration and dawning fear. "Are you saying I have to... disappear? That this connection we're building... it has to stop?" The thought was a physical blow, a negation of the hope that had begun to bloom amidst the ancient stones and shadowed histories. He had found a rare connection with Aine, a shared understanding that transcended the ordinary, and the idea of severing it, of returning to a world devoid of her presence, was a bleak prospect indeed.

Aine watched him, her expression a complex blend of sorrow and a quiet, resolute strength. "I'm saying, Pete, that you need to understand the full scope of what this guardianship entails. It's not a role you can simply step into as an ally or a supportive partner in the conventional sense. My family's work has always been about protecting Kilkenny from forces that are unseen and often incomprehensible to outsiders. It requires a life lived on a different plane, a constant vigilance that often means personal sacrifice, and yes, sometimes, a deep and isolating solitude."

She took a deep breath, the air seeming to shimmer around her as she spoke. "The problem, for me, is that the threat to Kilkenny isn't just a theoretical or historical one anymore. It's present. It's active. And the measures needed to combat it, as Morwenna's experience and the accounts of others before her demonstrate, can be... demanding. They can require a profound personal commitment, and a willingness to endure things that are not easily shared or understood."

"And you believe," Pete interjected, his voice laced with a desperate need for clarification, "that my presence here, our relationship, somehow makes that task harder? That it makes you more vulnerable?"

"Not necessarily 'harder' in terms of the actual mechanics of the defense," Aine clarified, her brow furrowed in thought. "But it changes the dynamic. It introduces an element of... entanglement. My ancestors' approach was to maintain a clear, uncompromised channel for their work. They learned that the more deeply they were connected to individuals outside their immediate circle, the more they risked drawing attention, or worse, creating a point of entry for the very forces they sought to repel. The Shadow-Weave, or any similar influence, thrives on discord and distraction."

She sighed, a soft, weary sound. "Imagine trying to contain a wild, volatile energy within a specific area. The more conduits you have, the more potential points of leakage there are. My family has always strived to minimize those conduits, to create a singularity of focus. My involvement with you, Pete, naturally creates a dual focus. It's not a criticism of you, or of us. It's simply a statement of fact, based on generations of experience."

Pete ran a hand through his hair, the complexity of the situation pressing down on him. He felt a growing sense of dread, not just for the potential dangers Aine faced, but for the potential end of whatever was developing between them. "So, this is where I have to make a choice then, isn't it? You're telling me that for you to do what you need to do, for your family's legacy, I either have to step back entirely, or... or what? Accept a role that might actually put you in more danger?"

"It's not about you stepping back entirely, Pete, not necessarily," Aine said, her voice gentle, but firm. "It's about you understanding the depth of what this means. My family's duty is not a hobby; it's a life sentence, a sacred trust that has often demanded immense personal sacrifice. It means periods of intense focus, of withdrawal, of facing dangers that most people cannot even conceive of. It means that sometimes, the weight of it all can be incredibly isolating."

She met his gaze directly, her eyes holding a depth of emotion that spoke volumes. "And if you are to be a part of my life, you need to understand that this isolation, this constant vigilance, is an intrinsic part of it. You need to understand that there will be times when I must prioritize the safety and energetic well-being of Kilkenny above all else, even above our personal needs or desires. You need to decide if you are truly prepared to accept that reality, not just as an interesting historical footnote, but as the fundamental truth of my existence, and by extension, potentially yours."

The silence stretched between them, heavy with unspoken implications. Pete felt a profound sense of being adrift, caught between the allure of their burgeoning connection and the stark reality of the ancient, perilous path Aine walked. He had come seeking answers, seeking to understand the past, but he had stumbled into a present that demanded a choice, a choice that would undoubtedly redefine his future, and perhaps, his very sense of self.

He thought of Morwenna, her lonely struggle, the fragment of her light that remained a dim ember. He thought of the unseen forces she battled, the pervasive void that sought to consume Kilkenny's spirit. And he thought of Aine, a modern-day guardian, facing a similar, perhaps even more insidious, threat, burdened by a legacy that demanded so much, offered so little in return, and required an almost supernatural strength to endure.

"You're asking me to accept a life that's... inherently dangerous and isolating," Pete stated, his voice quiet, the bravado of their earlier explorations replaced by a sober introspection. "A life where our connection might be a vulnerability, rather than a strength. A life where I might have to watch you carry this immense burden, and perhaps, be unable to truly share in it, or even worse, inadvertently make it heavier."

Aine nodded, her expression unreadable, waiting for his response. The subterranean chamber, with its echoes of the past, now seemed to amplify the starkness of the present decision. It was a crossroads, a point where the weight of ancestral duty collided with the tentative shoots of a new, unexpected intimacy.

"And if I can't accept that, Aine?" he asked, the question hanging in the air, heavy with unspoken consequences. "If I can't reconcile myself to being a potential liability, or to a relationship that's so... conditionally focused?" The answer, he knew, would be devastating, not just for him, but for the fragile hope that had begun to flicker between them.

Aine's gaze softened, a hint of the profound affection he had come to cherish surfacing in her eyes. "Then, Pete, you would have to make a choice too. A choice about what you are willing and able to accept, to bear. My family's duty is paramount. It's a commitment that transcends personal desires, a responsibility that is etched into our very being. If your presence, or our connection, genuinely compromises that, then for the sake of Kilkenny, and for the sake of my ancestors' work, difficult decisions would have to be made. Decisions that would affect both of us, deeply."

The implication hung in the air, stark and unyielding. It wasn't a threat, but a statement of fact, a brutal honesty born of necessity. Pete felt a wave of conflicting emotions – a profound admiration for Aine's unwavering dedication, a desperate longing for the connection they shared, and a growing fear of the insurmountable chasm that seemed to be opening between them. He had stepped into a world of ancient magic and ancestral burdens, but the most profound challenge he now faced was not in deciphering lost texts or understanding arcane rituals, but in confronting the very real possibility that the burgeoning love he felt for Aine might be incompatible with the very essence of her existence.

He looked at her, really looked at her, seeing not just the keeper of Kilkenny's secrets, but a woman wrestling with a legacy that demanded an almost impossible balance. He saw the sacrifices she had already made, the isolation she must have endured, and the potential future sacrifices her path demanded. The choice, he realized, was not just hers; it was his as well. He had to decide if he was willing to embrace a reality where his presence could be a complication, where their relationship might be a point of contention for the very forces Aine fought to keep at bay. He had to decide if love was enough to bridge such an extraordinary divide, or if the weight of her inherited duty was a burden too great for their nascent bond to bear. The echoes of Morwenna's solitary struggle seemed to whisper a warning, a chilling reminder of the profound personal cost of safeguarding a town's very soul. Pete knew, with a heavy heart, that he stood at a precipice, the future of their connection hanging precariously in the balance, dictated by the ancient, unforgiving demands of Kilkenny's enduring guardianship.

A MOMENT OF SHARED RESOLVE

The weight of Aine's words, the stark reality of her lineage's perpetual vigil, settled around Pete like the damp chill of the ancient stone chamber. He had walked into this expecting a history lesson, perhaps a ghost story or two. He had found himself instead standing at the precipice of a life he could barely comprehend, a life intrinsically bound to the very fabric of Kilkenny, to its unseen currents and shadowed threats. The air thrummed with unspoken anxieties, with the ghost of Morwenna's solitary struggle and the echoing weight of generations of sacrifice. Yet, amidst the chilling truths, a different kind of energy began to stir within him, a defiant ember against the encroaching shadow of doubt.

He looked at Aine, truly looked at her, past the quiet composure, past the ancient knowledge that resided in her eyes. He saw the young woman who had guided him through forgotten passages, who had shared whispers of secrets buried deep within the town's heart. He saw the vulnerability beneath her strength, the immense burden she carried not just as a duty, but as an intrinsic part of her very being. And in that moment, the complex interplay of ancestral obligation and nascent affection crystallized into a singular, unshakeable truth. His feelings for her were not a distraction, not a potential liability to be managed and minimized. They were, in fact, a source of solace, a human anchor in the vast, often terrifying, sea of the unknown.

"Aine," he began, his voice steady, a stark contrast to the tremor he felt within. He took a step closer, the space between them suddenly charged with a different kind of energy, one that spoke of connection rather than complication. "I hear you. I understand the risks, the isolation, the sacrifices. It's... it's a lot to take in. More than I ever imagined." He paused, searching her eyes, seeking to convey the sincerity that bloomed within him. "But I need you to know this: my feelings for you, my desire to be here, to understand, to help... that's not going to change. If anything, knowing what you carry, what your family has faced, it only deepens that. It makes me... admire you more. It makes me want to be closer, not further away."

He reached out, not to touch her, but to hold the space between them, a silent offering of his presence. "You spoke of clarity, of needing a clear channel. I understand that. I respect that. But I don't believe that love, or genuine connection, inherently creates a weakness. Perhaps it's a different kind of strength. Perhaps it's about having someone to share the burden with, even if they can't carry the weight in the same way. Someone who sees the full scope of what you do, and chooses to stand beside you anyway."

He met her gaze directly, his own filled with a quiet resolve that mirrored the resilience he saw in her. "I'm not asking to become a guardian, Aine. I'm not claiming to understand the intricacies of the Shadow-Weave or the specifics of your family's defenses. But I am asking you to accept my support, my loyalty, and my belief in you. I believe that our connection can be a source of strength, a counterpoint to the isolation you've spoken of. If there are vulnerabilities, then perhaps together, we can find ways to mitigate them, to strengthen those points rather than severing the connection altogether."

Aine watched him, her expression shifting, the guardedness in her eyes softening, replaced by a flicker of something akin to surprise, then tentative hope. She had braced herself for withdrawal, for the inevitable fear that would lead him to retreat. But Pete, with his grounded perspective and unwavering conviction, was offering something entirely unexpected. He was offering not just understanding, but a willing participation, an acceptance of her reality that transcended the ordinary.

"You believe that?" she whispered, her voice barely audible, as if testing the truth of his words. "That our connection... could be a strength?"

"I do," Pete affirmed, his voice resonating with absolute certainty. "Morwenna's journal, her sacrifices... they were immense, and they were solitary. But she also wrote about the weight of that solitude, didn't she? About the longing for shared understanding. What if, by allowing yourself to be connected, to trust someone outside of your lineage, you aren't creating a weakness, but building a new kind of resilience? What if that shared intent, that mutual understanding, acts as its own form of protection?"

He took another step closer, his gaze unwavering. "I am here, Aine. I am committed to understanding this, to helping you navigate it in any way I can. My presence here isn't about altering your path, or about disrupting the balance you strive to maintain. It's about walking beside you, about offering whatever strength I possess, in whatever capacity you deem it useful. I want to be a safe harbor, not a storm. And if that means learning to be more vigilant, more aware of the subtle energies, then I am willing to learn. I am willing to be that clear channel, not just for you, but with you."

The air in the chamber seemed to shift, the oppressive weight of the past momentarily lifting, replaced by the burgeoning warmth of shared purpose. Aine's gaze, which had been fixed on him with a mixture of caution and weary resignation, now held a spark of nascent hope. She saw in Pete's earnest gaze not the recklessness of an outsider, but the genuine desire of a partner, someone who saw the immense value in her work and was willing to contribute to it in his own unique way.

"Pete," she began, her voice now infused with a new timbre, a blend of gratitude and a profound sense of relief. "What you're saying... it means more than you know. For generations, my family has operated under the assumption that any outside connection, any entanglement, was a direct risk. It was the bedrock of our practice, the cautionary tale etched into every ritual, every decision." She looked down at her hands, as if seeing the phantom imprints of ancestral anxieties. "Morwenna's words about 'clouding the intent' and 'diverting the flow of protective energies' were not just warnings; they were the distilled wisdom of survival."

She looked back up at him, her eyes shining with an emotion that was both beautiful and deeply moving. "But you are right. She also wrote, in the quieter moments, of the profound loneliness, of the yearning for a kindred spirit. Perhaps the wisdom of the past, while vital, also needed a new perspective, a re-evaluation in the context of a changing world, and changing... connections."

A small, almost imperceptible smile touched her lips. "You are offering a different kind of strength, Pete. One that isn't about isolation, but about shared resilience. You are offering a belief that perhaps the forces we face can be met not just with solitary vigilance, but with a unity of purpose, a shared intent that is amplified by mutual trust and affection." She took a deep breath, the resolve hardening within her, not out of resignation, but out of a newfound sense of possibility. "If you are truly willing to understand, to learn, to be a part of this... not as a passive observer, but as an active supporter, then perhaps we can face this together. Perhaps this connection, this shared resolve, can be our strength."

The unspoken question hung in the air: What does that look like? It was a question that still held a degree of uncertainty, a path yet to be fully illuminated. But the foundation had shifted. The fear of his presence being a liability had begun to recede, replaced by the burgeoning hope that it could, in fact, be an asset. Pete felt a surge of profound relief wash over him, a warmth spreading through his chest that chased away the lingering shadows of apprehension. He had feared that his deepest feelings for Aine would be the very thing that would push them apart, that his desire to connect would be a fatal flaw in the ancient tapestry of her duty. Instead, it seemed, it might be a thread that could strengthen the weave.

"It looks like this," Pete said, his voice filled with quiet determination. He finally closed the small distance between them, his hand gently reaching out to cup her cheek. Her skin was cool beneath his touch, a faint tremor running through her as he made contact. He saw a flicker of apprehension, then a yielding, a quiet acceptance of his gesture. "It looks like me, understanding that your life is extraordinary, and that it demands extraordinary things. It looks like me supporting you, believing in you, and trusting that you will guide me in how I can best be here, for you and for Kilkenny. It means I accept the risks, and I'm willing to learn how to manage them, not by stepping away, but by stepping closer, with awareness and respect."

He leaned in, his forehead resting against hers, their breaths mingling in the still air. "It means that whatever happens, whatever challenges we face, we face them together. Your fight is becoming my fight, Aine. Not to take it from you, but to stand beside you, to share the burden, and to remind you, in those moments of isolation, that you are not alone." The shared resolve that passed between them was palpable, a silent vow exchanged in the heart of the ancient earth. It was a promise that, despite the immense weight of her legacy, their budding connection had not only survived the truth, but had been forged into something stronger, something more resilient, ready to face whatever ancient shadows still lurked beneath the surface of

Kilkenny's history. The path ahead was still shrouded in mystery, the true nature of the threats still unfolding, but now, they would walk it not as two separate entities, bound by circumstance, but as a united front, their shared determination a beacon against the encroaching darkness. This moment, pregnant with unspoken futures and unwavering commitment, marked not an end, but a profound new beginning.

Chapter Ten: The Looming Challenge

A SIGN OF IMBALANCE

The air in Kilkenny had taken on a peculiar quality in the days following Pete's conversation with Aine. It wasn't a sudden, dramatic shift, but a subtle, pervasive alteration, like a symphony's harmony fraying at the edges. Pete, whose senses had always been attuned to the nuances of his surroundings, found himself increasingly unsettled by these almost imperceptible changes. It began with the weather. A town known for its temperate climate, nestled in the valley, found itself buffeted by unseasonable gusts of wind that seemed to carry a mournful howl, rattling windows and whipping leaves into frenzied dances. Then came the rain. Not the gentle, life-giving showers that nourished the surrounding countryside, but sudden, violent downpours that appeared without warning, transforming cobbled streets into miniature rivers, only to dissipate as abruptly as they arrived, leaving behind an unnatural stillness and a lingering dampness that clung to everything.

He found himself observing the townspeople with a renewed curiosity, searching for any outward signs of shared unease. Yet, for the most part, life continued its predictable rhythm. People hurried to work, children's laughter echoed in the market square, and the familiar clang of the blacksmith's hammer still rang out from his forge. It was as if Kilkenny itself was holding its breath, a vast organism subtly reacting to an unseen ailment. Pete recalled Aine's description of the Shadow-Weave, the invisible currents of energy that flowed through and around the town, a protective shield woven by generations of her lineage. He had understood it intellectually, as a historical fact, a burden of duty. Now, he began to feel it, to sense its potential fragility. The uncharacteristic weather felt less like a meteorological anomaly and more like a symptom, a visual representation of a deeper imbalance.

His walks through the town became more deliberate, his gaze lingering on details that might have previously escaped his notice. He observed the birds, usually abundant and vocal, now conspicuously absent from the skies, their usual chirping replaced by an unnerving silence. Even the stray cats, typically bold and visible, seemed to have retreated into the shadows, their emerald eyes occasionally flashing from hidden alcoves, filled with a primal wariness that mirrored his own growing apprehension. One afternoon, while browsing in O'Malley's bookshop, he overheard a hushed conversation between two elderly women. They spoke of a peculiar chill that had settled deep within their bones, a cold that no amount of fire could seem to dispel. Another mentioned her prize-winning roses, usually robust and blooming, now inexplicably withered and brown, their petals brittle and dry despite meticulous care. These were not isolated incidents; they were threads in a growing tapestry of strangeness, and Pete felt a prickle of alarm crawl up his spine.

He sought out Aine, finding her in the familiar quiet of the old library, the late afternoon sun casting long, dusty beams through the arched windows. She was poring over an ancient tome, her brow furrowed in concentration, a faint, almost imperceptible line etched between her eyebrows. He recounted his observations, the odd weather, the silent birds, the whispers he'd overheard. As he spoke, he watched her closely, searching for a reaction, a confirmation of his own disquiet.

Aine listened intently, her gaze shifting from the pages of the book to meet his. A shadow of concern flickered in her eyes, a subtle confirmation that his instincts were indeed accurate. "You've noticed it too," she stated, her voice soft but laced with a new gravity. "The shifts are becoming more pronounced."

She closed the book, its heavy leather cover falling with a soft thud that seemed to punctuate her words. "The Shadow-Weave is a delicate equilibrium, Pete. It's not a static barrier, but a living, breathing network of energy. It requires constant attunement, a mindful presence from those who are bound to it. When that balance is disturbed, when the protective measures falter, the effects are not confined to the metaphysical realm. They manifest in the mundane, in the very fabric of our reality."

She gestured towards the window, where the late afternoon light seemed to be fading prematurely, casting the library into an early twilight. "The unseasonable winds are a disruption in the atmospheric currents that are subtly influenced by the Weave. The silence of the birds... they are sensitive creatures, attuned to shifts in energy that we cannot perceive. Their retreat is a sign of unease, of something 'wrong' in the natural order."

Pete leaned against a towering bookshelf, the scent of old paper and dried ink filling his nostrils. He understood the concept, but the tangible evidence was far more unsettling. "What's causing it, Aine? What's disturbing the balance?"

Aine's gaze drifted to a faded tapestry depicting a scene from Kilkenny's distant past, figures cloaked and watchful. "That is the challenge," she admitted, her voice barely above a whisper. "The journal entries, my family's histories, they speak of cyclical periods of vulnerability. Times when the ancient wards, the very essence of the Weave, are tested. It could be a natural ebb and flow, a consequence of celestial alignments or terrestrial energies. Or," she paused, her eyes meeting his, the unspoken implication hanging heavy in the air, "it could be an external force. Something actively seeking to unravel the Weave, to exploit its weakened points."

The word "external" sent a shiver down Pete's spine, a visceral reaction that had nothing to do with the library's temperature. He thought back to his initial skepticism, his dismissal of the supernatural as mere folklore. Now, the whispers of ancient threats and unseen forces felt chillingly real. "Are you saying someone or something is deliberately trying to break through?"

"It's a possibility we cannot afford to ignore," Aine replied, her voice steady, betraying none of the fear that he suspected she harbored. "The strength of the Weave lies in its continuity, in the unbroken chain of vigilance passed down through generations. Any disruption, any lapse, creates a vulnerability. And vulnerabilities, as we both know, attract attention."

She picked up a slender, silver letter opener from her desk, turning it over and over in her fingers. "The stories of the 'Whispering Sickness' in the 17th century, the 'Long Winter' of the 19th century—these were not mere historical footnotes. They were periods where the Weave was severely tested, where the veil between our world and what lies beyond thinned dangerously. The consequences were... dire." She didn't elaborate, but the unspoken horrors conjured by her words were enough.

Pete's mind raced, trying to reconcile the mundane reality of Kilkenny with the profound, almost terrifying, implications of Aine's words. The subtle anomalies were more than just coincidences; they were early warning signs, the first tremors of a potential earthquake. He thought of the growing unease he'd felt himself, the almost subconscious awareness that something was not quite right. It wasn't just his imagination. It was the subtle hum of the Weave, its protective song beginning to falter.

"So, this imbalance... it's a sign that the defenses are weakening?" he pressed, needing to grasp the full scope of the predicament. "That whatever your family has been guarding against is... getting closer?"

"Precisely," Aine confirmed, her gaze unwavering. "It's like a crack in a dam. The water pressure might seem manageable at first, but if left unchecked, that crack will widen, eventually leading to catastrophic failure. The subtle signs are the early indicators. The intensified atmospheric disturbances, the animal behavior... these are the pressure points showing strain. The greater the strain, the more susceptible the Weave becomes to a breach."

She walked over to a large, antique map of Kilkenny displayed on an easel, her finger tracing the ley lines that Aine had shown him before, invisible threads of energy that crisscrossed the town. "My ancestors established numerous points of warding throughout the town, each one anchored by a specific ritual and a deep connection to the land. These points, when functioning in harmony, create the intricate network of the Shadow-Weave. But if even one of these anchors is weakened, or if the energy flow between them is disrupted, the entire system begins to falter. The 'imbalance' you're sensing is the ripple effect of such a disruption."

Pete felt a knot of anxiety tighten in his stomach. He had come to Kilkenny seeking a quiet life, a respite from the stresses of his own world. Instead, he found himself drawn into a battle that had been waged for centuries, a silent war fought in the shadows, its consequences now seeping into the everyday. The responsibility Aine carried was immense, a legacy of vigilance and sacrifice that stretched back into the mists of time. And now, he was inextricably linked to it, a willing participant in a challenge that threatened not just Aine, but the very soul of Kilkenny.

"What are we going to do?" he asked, his voice hushed with a dawning sense of urgency. "How do we strengthen it? How do we stop it from getting worse?"

Aine turned from the map, her expression resolute. "We need to identify the source of the disruption," she stated, her eyes locking onto his. "We need to understand why the Weave is faltering. Is it a decay of the ancient wards, a slow erosion over time? Or is it something more... active? Something that has found a way to interfere with the flow of energy?"

She walked back to her desk, retrieving a small, leather-bound notebook, its pages filled with her elegant script. "Morwenna's journal detailed some of the early signs of weakness, the subtle anomalies that preceded major disturbances. She also spoke of 'sensitive anchors,' points where the Weave was particularly susceptible to external influence. We need to re-examine those records, to cross-reference them with what you've been observing. We need to become attuned to the rhythm of the town, to discern the whispers of unease from the ordinary occurrences of life."

Pete nodded, a surge of determination replacing his apprehension. The weight of the looming challenge was undeniable, but so was the quiet strength he saw in Aine, the unwavering commitment that mirrored his own burgeoning resolve. He had pledged to stand by her, to understand, to help. Now, the abstract promise was solidifying into a concrete, urgent task. The subtle signs of imbalance were no longer just curiosities; they were a stark reminder of the stakes, a palpable call to action. The quiet vigilance of generations was being tested, and it was a test they would have to face together. The normalcy of Kilkenny, he was beginning to understand, was a fragile construct, meticulously maintained by a hidden, ongoing effort. And that effort was faltering. The true nature of the challenge was no longer just a question of historical record; it was a present, growing danger, manifesting in the very air they breathed, the very ground beneath their feet. The equilibrium was shifting, and the implications for both Aine and Kilkenny were profound and deeply unsettling. He felt the nascent stirrings of a deeper understanding of the immense pressure Aine lived under, a pressure that was now becoming his own to share. This was no longer an academic pursuit of knowledge; it was a vital, immediate fight for the town's very soul.

AINES PREPARATIONS

Aine's preparations were methodical, born from a lineage that understood the necessity of preparedness. She moved through her ancestral home with a quiet efficiency, each action deliberate, imbued with the weight of generations of responsibility. The faint scent of aged parchment and dried herbs that permeated the air seemed to deepen, a testament to the ancient knowledge she was now actively engaging with. Pete watched, a silent observer to a process that felt both deeply personal and profoundly significant, a ritualistic unfolding of a sacred duty.

Her first stop was the family library, a sanctuary of accumulated wisdom. Not the public library of Kilkenny, which she had visited with Pete, but a more intimate, hidden space, its existence known only to those initiated into the lineage. Dust motes danced in the slivers of light that pierced the heavy velvet curtains, illuminating rows upon rows of leather-bound tomes, their spines embossed with faded gilt lettering and symbols that spoke of forgotten languages and arcane practices. Aine's hands, usually so graceful and fluid, seemed to possess a heightened dexterity as she navigated the shelves, her fingers tracing the contours of ancient bindings with an almost reverent touch. She wasn't merely selecting books; she was communing with her ancestors, seeking their guidance in the face of this encroaching threat.

She pulled down a particularly heavy volume, its cover a deep, cracked leather, bound with tarnished silver clasps. The title, written in an archaic script, was barely discernible: 'Chronicles of the Weave's Vigil'. This was not a book meant for casual perusal; it was a sacred text, detailing the history, the maintenance, and the defense of the Shadow-Weave. Aine carried it to a large oak table, its surface scarred with the marks of countless hours of study and meticulous work. She opened it with a gentle reverence, the pages crackling like dry leaves under her touch. The script within was dense, a fascinating mix of flowing calligraphy and sharp, angular runes, interspersed with intricate diagrams and celestial charts.

As she began to read, her lips moved silently, mouthing the ancient words. Pete could see the concentration etched onto her face, the way her eyes scanned the pages, absorbing not just the literal meaning but the underlying intent, the subtle currents of power that were meant to be conveyed. She paused frequently, making notes in a slim, vellum-bound journal of her own, using a quill pen that seemed to hum with a faint, resonant energy. Her notations were terse, abbreviations and symbols that only she would understand, capturing the essence of the ancestral wisdom.

"Morwenna wrote of the 'Luminous Threads'," Aine murmured, her voice a low hum that seemed to resonate with the energy of the room. "She described them as conduits, the very pathways through which the Weave draws its strength. She believed that disruptions often occurred at these junctions, places where the threads were most vibrant, and thus, most vulnerable."

Pete watched her, fascinated. He saw a flicker of something in her eyes – not fear, but a deep, abiding sense of purpose, the quiet resolve of someone who understood the stakes and was prepared to meet them head-on. Her dedication was palpable, a stark contrast to his own initial hesitancy. He had been drawn into this world by circumstance, but Aine was its custodian, its guardian.

She then moved to a different section of the library, one that housed an array of intricately carved wooden chests. With a practiced hand, she opened one, revealing a collection of artifacts, each one nestled in layers of faded silk. There were polished stones that seemed to hold an inner light, vials containing liquids of unidentifiable hues, and intricately woven cords made from materials he couldn't readily identify. These were not mere trinkets; they were tools, imbued with generations of ritual and purpose, instruments meant to aid in the maintenance and defense of the Weave.

Aine carefully selected a small, obsidian disc, its surface polished to a mirror-like sheen. She held it up to the light, and for a moment, it seemed to absorb the very rays, growing darker, more intense. "The 'Scrying Mirror'," she explained, her voice gaining a touch of quiet authority. "It allows us to perceive imbalances, to see the 'fraying' of the Weave, as it were, in its truest form." She then picked up a set of thin, silver needles, each one etched with a different protective rune. "These are the 'Stabilizing Needles'. They are used to mend tears, to reinforce weakened points in the energetic fabric."

She laid them out on the table, meticulously arranging them in a specific pattern, a sequence dictated by ancient practice. Each movement was precise, economical, devoid of any wasted energy. Pete felt a growing admiration for her, for the immense burden of knowledge and responsibility she carried with such grace. He was witnessing not just the preparation for a challenge, but the embodiment of a legacy.

Her preparations extended beyond the library. She spent time in the gardens, her movements slow and deliberate as she examined the ancient standing stones that dotted the landscape surrounding her ancestral home. These were not merely decorative elements; they were integral to the Weave, anchors that drew power from the earth and channeled it into the town's protective network. Aine ran her hands over their moss-covered surfaces, her touch tracing the faint carvings that had been weathered by centuries of sun and rain. She was checking their integrity, ensuring their connection to the land remained strong.

She spoke softly to the stones, her voice barely audible above the rustling leaves and the distant murmur of the river. It was a form of communion, a reaffirmation of the pact between her lineage and the natural world. Pete saw her pause at one particular stone, larger and more imposing than the others, situated at a confluence of what he now understood to be ley lines. She knelt before it, placing her palm flat against its cool surface. A faint luminescence seemed to emanate from beneath her hand, a subtle exchange of energy.

"This is the Heartstone," Aine explained, turning to Pete with a look of quiet intensity. "It's the primary nexus of the Weave in this area. Its strength directly impacts the flow of energy throughout

Kilkenny." She withdrew her hand, and the luminescence faded. "It feels... sluggish. As if something is impeding its natural resonance."

The concern in her voice was evident, and Pete felt a corresponding surge of unease. The subtle signs he had observed were now being corroborated by Aine's more intimate knowledge and sensory perception. The unseasonable weather, the silent birds – these were not abstract anomalies; they were symptoms of a deeper malaise affecting the very energetic framework of Kilkenny.

Aine then produced a small, intricately carved wooden box from her satchel. Inside, nestled on a bed of dried heather, was a single, iridescent feather. "This belonged to a Sky-Watcher," she explained, her voice tinged with a mixture of reverence and melancholy. "A creature of immense sensitivity, attuned to the slightest shift in the atmospheric currents. They were once common in this valley, their calls a constant reminder of the Weave's vitality. Their silence now is a grave indicator." She carefully placed the feather into a small pouch made of woven silver threads. "We may need to consult with the whispers of the past, to seek out echoes of what the Sky-Watchers might have witnessed."

The meticulousness of her preparations was staggering. It wasn't just about gathering tools; it was about immersing herself in the ancient practices, about aligning herself with the energies she was meant to steward. Pete felt a profound sense of respect for her unwavering commitment. She was not driven by fear, but by a deep-seated sense of duty, a quiet determination to protect the legacy entrusted to her. He saw the weight of her inherited role, the centuries of vigilance compressed into her present actions, and it only served to deepen his admiration and his own burgeoning resolve to stand beside her.

"The balance," Aine continued, her gaze sweeping across the ancient landscape, "is not merely a matter of mystical forces. It is woven into the very fabric of Kilkenny, into the land, the air, the stones. To protect it, we must understand its deepest roots, its most vulnerable points." She then turned her attention back to the 'Chronicles of the Weave's Vigil', her fingers tracing a particularly complex diagram. "Morwenna's writings suggest that certain celestial alignments can amplify the Weave's natural defenses, but also make it susceptible to external interference. We need to pinpoint the exact nature of this current vulnerability."

She spoke of "harmonic resonance" and "energetic decay," terms that were foreign to Pete's everyday vocabulary but which, in Aine's context, took on a chillingly tangible meaning. He understood now that the challenge facing Kilkenny was far more complex than he had initially imagined, a subtle interplay of forces that required not just courage, but deep knowledge and a profound connection to the past. Aine's preparations were not just a practical response; they were a testament to her profound understanding of her lineage, her unwavering dedication to her ancestral duty, and her quiet strength in the face of an unknown, looming threat. He knew, with a certainty that settled deep within his bones, that he was witnessing something extraordinary, the unfolding of a responsibility that had been passed down through countless generations, a duty that now rested, in part, upon his own shoulders. The quiet ritual of her preparations was a powerful declaration, a promise of resistance against whatever was seeking to unravel the delicate tapestry of Kilkenny's protective energies. He felt a profound sense of being on the precipice of something significant, a battle waged not with swords and shields, but with ancient knowledge and unwavering will.

THE ROLE OF THE ANCESTRAL HOME

The weight of the 'Chronicles of the Weave's Vigil' settled not just on the oak table, but within Aine's very being. The library, with its hushed reverence and the scent of ages, was more than a repository of knowledge; it was a sanctuary, a physical manifestation of her lineage's enduring commitment. But Aine knew that theoretical understanding, however deep, was insufficient. The tangible application of that wisdom, the practical execution of rituals and the channeling of energy, required a specific locus, a place attuned to the subtle currents she now needed to command.

"There's another place," Aine said, her gaze distant, as if already seeing beyond the confines of the library. "A place that predates even this house, in a sense. It's where the initial binding of the Weave was anchored." She closed the heavy tome with a soft thud, the sound echoing in the stillness. "My great-grandmother, Elara, always spoke of it as the 'Heart of the Hearth'. It's a small, unassuming cottage, nestled deep in the western woods. It's been in our family for generations, passed down not for its monetary value, but for its intrinsic connection to the Weave."

Pete listened intently, absorbing her words. He was beginning to grasp the layered nature of Aine's world, a reality interwoven with elements he had never imagined. The idea of a 'Heart of the Hearth' conjured images of a place imbued with primal energy, a foundational point from which the town's protective shroud emanated. "A cottage? In the woods?" he repeated, picturing a rustic, perhaps isolated dwelling.

Aine nodded, her brow furrowed slightly. "It's more than just a cottage, Pete. It's a conduit. The very foundations are laid with stones that were charged with the earth's energy at the time of the initial enchantment. The central hearthstone, in particular, is said to be a fragment of a much older, sacred monolith. It's the nexus where the land's inherent power is most readily accessible, and where the most potent rituals can be performed to reinforce the Weave." She gestured towards a faded, hand-drawn map tucked within the pages of the 'Chronicles'. "This shows its approximate location. It's deliberately remote, designed to be shielded from casual observation and external interference."

The map, a delicate tracery on brittle parchment, depicted a winding river, dense woodlands, and a single, marked clearing. The 'cottage' was represented by a small, stylized symbol, its placement suggesting a deliberate isolation, a deliberate focus of power away from the bustling centre of Kilkenny. Pete studied the lines, trying to orient himself within its ancient geography. It looked like a place untouched by time, a sanctuary of raw, untamed energy.

"So, this cottage is... important?" he asked, the understatement hanging in the air. He already knew the answer, but he wanted to hear Aine articulate its significance.

Aine met his gaze, her eyes clear and resolute. "It is paramount. The library provides the knowledge, the artifacts are the tools, but the Heart of the Hearth is the crucible. It's where the Weave can be actively strengthened, where its frayed edges can be meticulously re-woven. Without it, our efforts will be like trying to repair a sail with thread alone, without the mast to support it." She paused, her voice dropping to a more serious tone. "The challenges we face are not merely passive threats that can be countered with ancient texts. They require active engagement, a channeling of power that can only be effectively facilitated at such a nexus point."

She carefully extracted the map, along with a small, intricately carved wooden key that had been nestled in a velvet pouch within the 'Chronicles'. The key was surprisingly heavy, its wood dark and polished, inlaid with symbols that seemed to subtly shift and shimmer in the low light. "This key," she explained, turning it over in her fingers, "opens the main door. But more than that, it's said to resonate with the very spirit of the place, to signal to the land that its chosen custodian has arrived."

Pete found himself imagining the journey. The 'western woods' implied a distance, a journey away from the familiar streets of Kilkenny, into a realm that was increasingly becoming his own through Aine's revelations. He pictured the ancient trees, the filtered sunlight, and the solitary cottage standing as a silent sentinel.

"What kind of rituals?" he asked, his curiosity piqued by the mention of active engagement. He was no longer just an observer; the urgency of Aine's task was becoming his own.

Aine carefully re-secured the map and key into a specially designed compartment within her satchel, a discreet feature that spoke of the long lineage of preparation. "The rituals vary depending on the nature of the imbalance. They can involve the placement of specific stones, the chanting of ancient verses to harmonize with the earth's vibrations, or the focusing of personal energy through meditation and visualization techniques. The Heart of the Hearth amplifies these actions, making them exponentially more effective." She drew a deep breath, the scent of aged paper and dried herbs momentarily replaced by a faint, earthy aroma that seemed to emanate from the satchel. "It's where we will need to work directly on reinforcing the Weave, on countering whatever is attempting to unravel it."

The concept of actively reinforcing the Weave resonated with Pete. It implied a proactive stance, a direct confrontation with the encroaching darkness. He understood then that Aine's preparation was not a passive act of gathering information, but a dynamic process of readying herself and her tools for a vital undertaking. The cottage was not just a location; it was an operational base, a sanctuary from which the counter-offensive would be launched.

"Is it safe?" he asked, the question a natural extension of his growing understanding of the potential dangers. The very concept of 'protective energy' implied the existence of forces that sought to breach it.

"Safety is a relative term in our world, Pete," Aine replied, a hint of a smile touching her lips. "The cottage itself is designed to be a place of immense natural protection. The land around it is saturated with the Weave's energy, acting as a natural deterrent. However, the act of reinforcing the Weave, of actively engaging with it, can sometimes draw the attention of those who would seek to exploit its vulnerabilities. It's a delicate balance, and our presence there will need to be conducted with the utmost discretion and respect for the energies we are manipulating."

She then rose, her movements fluid and deliberate, and began gathering some of the smaller artifacts she had laid out earlier. The obsidian scrying mirror was carefully wrapped in a soft cloth, and the silver needles were returned to their protective case. Each item seemed to hum with a latent power, waiting to be deployed.

"The approach to the cottage is also significant," Aine continued, her voice thoughtful. "The path itself is subtly woven into the natural landscape, designed to guide those who know the way while deterring those who do not. It requires a certain attunement, a recognition of the land's subtle signs. My grandmother taught me the markers, the subtle shifts in the foliage, the specific calls of certain birds that indicate the correct route."

Pete nodded, picturing himself following Aine through an ancient, mystical forest, guided by signs imperceptible to the uninitiated. The journey to this ancestral property was becoming more than just a means to an end; it was an integral part of the process, a ritual in itself, designed to ensure that only those with the right intention and connection could reach the heart of their power.

"It's also where many of the original protective wards were established," Aine added, placing a small, polished stone, radiating a soft, internal warmth, into her satchel. "Wards that have, over time, become integrated with the very essence of the land. They are not static barriers, but living energies that respond to the state of the Weave. If the Weave is healthy, they are potent. If it is weakened, their efficacy diminishes."

The implications were clear: the cottage wasn't merely a focal point for applying energy; it was a place where the health of the Weave could be most directly assessed and, by extension, where its decline would be most keenly felt. This made the cottage not just a tool, but a barometer, a vital early warning system.

"So, if the wards are weakening," Pete mused aloud, trying to connect the dots, "that would be another sign that something is wrong?"

Aine confirmed this with a grave nod. "Precisely. The resilience of the wards is a direct reflection of the Weave's overall integrity. If they falter, it indicates a significant strain, a deeper disturbance than we might otherwise perceive." She then lifted a small, leather-bound pouch, its contents rustling softly. "Inside this are several seeds from the 'Whispering Willow' that grows near the cottage. It's a tree that has a unique relationship with the Weave, its roots entwined with the energy ley lines. Planting these in specific locations around the cottage can help to re-establish and strengthen the subtle energetic pathways that lead to it."

The 'Whispering Willow' – another element of this hidden world, a sentient or semi-sentient guardian of the Weave's pathways. The more Aine revealed, the more intricate and interconnected this system of protection became. It was a tapestry woven from nature, ancient knowledge, and the dedicated actions of her lineage.

"It sounds like the cottage is central to everything," Pete stated, his voice firm with newfound understanding. "Not just for reinforcing the Weave, but for understanding its current state."

"It is," Aine agreed, her gaze meeting his. "It's where the ancient heart of Kilkenny's protection beats. It's where the most profound work must be done. The knowledge in these books," she patted the 'Chronicles' gently, "guides us. The artifacts give us the means. But the Heart of the Hearth is where the true battle will be waged, the place where we can most effectively mend what is broken and defend what is sacred."

The importance of this secluded property was now undeniably clear to Pete. It wasn't just an ancestral dwelling; it was the linchpin of Aine's ancestral responsibilities, the place where the abstract concepts of energy and protection would coalesce into tangible action. Accessing it, understanding its secrets, and harnessing its power were not merely optional steps; they were the very core of their looming challenge. He understood that his role, however it was defined, would inevitably involve this journey, this immersion into the heart of Aine's ancient duty. The cottage, a place he had never seen, was already beginning to feel like a critical destination, a focal point for the escalating situation in Kilkenny.

EXTERNAL INFLUENCE DETECTED

The air in the library, once a comforting balm of aged paper and quiet contemplation, now felt charged with an unspoken anxiety. Aine's words about the Heart of the Hearth and the vital rituals that needed to be performed there had settled deep within Pete, grounding him in the immediate, tangible nature of their task. Yet, as he absorbed the significance of the ancestral cottage, a prickle of unease, a phantom echo of a recent encounter, began to surface. It was a subtle discord in the otherwise harmonious narrative of lineage and duty.

He remembered the man from the previous day, the one who had seemed so out of place on the cobbled streets of Kilkenny. There had been an intensity in his gaze, a detached curiosity that had felt more like assessment than casual observation. At the time, Pete had dismissed it as the natural wariness one felt towards a stranger in a small town. But now, with the weight of Aine's revelations pressing down, that memory began to morph, taking on a more sinister hue. The man's lingering presence, his unnervingly direct questions about the town's history, seemed less like innocent inquiry and more like probing.

"There was someone," Pete began, his voice hesitant, choosing his words carefully. He didn't want to alarm Aine unnecessarily, but the memory felt too pertinent to ignore. "Yesterday, near the market square. A man... he struck me as being out of place. He asked a lot of questions about the town, about its founding, its old families." Pete paused, searching Aine's face for any flicker of recognition or concern. "He had a... a strange intensity about him. He wasn't just a tourist."

Aine's hand, which had been tracing the intricate carving on the lid of the 'Chronicles', stilled. Her gaze, which had been fixed on the aged text, slowly lifted, meeting Pete's with a newfound gravity. The casual ease that had permeated their discussion moments before seemed to evaporate, replaced by a sharp awareness. Her eyes, usually so full of a quiet, deep strength, now held a glint of something more guarded, a subtle tightening around the edges.

"Tell me more about him," she said, her voice remarkably even, betraying none of the inner turmoil that Pete suspected was now stirring. "What did he look like? What did he say specifically?"

Pete recounted the details as best he could – the man's nondescript clothing, the keenness of his eyes, the way he'd steered the conversation towards the older districts, the forgotten corners of Kilkenny's history. He mentioned the man's unnerving persistence, his almost predatory focus when Aine's family name had been inadvertently brought up by a passing shopkeeper. "He seemed particularly interested when the topic of old traditions and local folklore came up," Pete added, the memory now sharper, more defined. "He asked if there were any families that still... held onto the old ways. As if he were looking for something specific."

As Pete spoke, Aine's expression grew increasingly somber. She closed the 'Chronicles' with a soft, decisive click, the sound resonating in the sudden, heavy silence. Her fingers moved with practiced grace as she carefully secured the map and the wooden key back into her satchel, her movements now imbued with a sense of urgency that hadn't been present before. The library, which had felt like a safe harbor, now seemed to hold an unseen vulnerability.

"You are right to be concerned, Pete," Aine said, her voice barely a whisper, yet it carried the weight of a pronouncement. "Your instincts are keen. The description you give... it aligns with certain individuals who operate in the periphery of our world. Those who are drawn to places of power, to ancient energies, not out of reverence, but out of a desire to exploit them. They are often... scavengers of the unseen."

She rose from her chair, her posture straightening, radiating a quiet resolve. "The timing is... concerning. We are preparing to engage with the Heart of the Hearth, to reinforce the Weave. This is precisely the kind of activity that can draw unwanted attention. If someone is actively seeking to disrupt Kilkenny's balance, or to siphon its energies for their own purposes, then our efforts to strengthen it could be seen as a direct challenge. It's like tending a flame; it might attract moths, or it might attract those who wish to extinguish it."

Pete felt a knot of apprehension tighten in his stomach. The 'looming challenge' had just become significantly more concrete, more personal. It wasn't just a matter of ancient magic and forgotten lore anymore; it was about active opposition, about individuals who might actively seek to undermine their work. "Exploit its hidden energies?" he echoed, the concept chillingly alien yet suddenly very real. "What does that even mean?"

"Kilkenny, like many places steeped in ancient lineage and connected to natural ley lines, possesses a unique energetic signature," Aine explained, her gaze distant as if she were peering into the very fabric of the town's unseen currents. "The Weave is not merely a protective shroud; it's a manifestation of the land's vitality, its connection to the earth's inherent power. Those who understand these principles, or who have developed a sensitivity to them, can seek to manipulate these energies. They might attempt to drain them for their own purposes – to enhance their own abilities, to gain an advantage, or perhaps even to cause widespread disruption for the sake of chaos."

She walked over to a tall, narrow window, looking out at the ancient stones of Kilkenny bathed in the afternoon sun. The peace of the scene seemed almost a mockery of the unseen currents that were now at play. "The man you saw, if he is indeed what I suspect, might have been drawn by the subtle shifts in the Weave, perhaps sensing that something significant is about to happen. Or, he might have been sent. There are those who operate in factions, each with their own agenda, often seeking to control or neutralize sources of power that they cannot comprehend or that threaten their own clandestine operations."

The idea of factions, of organized groups seeking to manipulate such forces, was a disturbing escalation. It painted a picture of a clandestine world, far more complex and dangerous than Pete had initially imagined. His involvement, which had begun as a reluctant curiosity, now felt like a plunge into a deep, shadowed ocean.

"So, this person... he might be trying to stop us?" Pete asked, the question hanging heavy in the air. The notion of actively being targeted, of having their efforts actively thwarted, was a new and terrifying dimension.

Aine turned back from the window, her expression unreadable for a moment. "It is a distinct possibility. If he is working for someone who wishes to see the Weave weakened or even broken, then our preparations to reinforce it would be seen as a direct impediment. He might be here to observe, to gather intelligence on our plans, or even to interfere directly. The more potent the ritual, the greater the risk of attracting such attention."

She paced the length of the library, her footsteps soft on the thick rug, a silent testament to her controlled anxiety. "My great-grandmother Elara always warned about this. The act of maintaining the Weave is not a solitary, hidden endeavor. It is a constant vigilance against those who would seek to exploit its existence, or its absence. The Heart of the Hearth, being a nexus of such potent energy, is a prime target for such individuals. If they can disrupt the rituals performed there, or worse, seize control of its power, they could destabilize the entire region."

The 'scavengers of the unseen' – the phrase conjured images of shadowy figures lurking in the fringes of reality, drawn by the scent of power like predators to prey. Pete found himself replaying the man's features, the unnerving stillness in his eyes, trying to discern any tell-tale sign that he was more than he appeared. Had that intensity been a sign of supernatural sensitivity, or merely the cunning of a determined antagonist?

"What can we do?" Pete asked, the question a natural response to the escalating threat. The safety of the library, and by extension, the safety of Kilkenny, suddenly felt precarious.

Aine stopped pacing, her gaze settling on Pete with a renewed intensity. "First, we must proceed with our plans to reach the Heart of the Hearth. Delaying will only allow any potential adversaries more time to solidify their position or to discover our intentions. The cottage remains our most secure and effective base of operations." She then picked up a small, obsidian pendant that had been resting on the table, its surface polished to a mirror-like sheen. "This," she said, her voice dropping, "is an amulet of warding. It offers a degree of protection against certain forms of subtle intrusion and divination. I will give it to you. It may help shield you from unwanted attention, or at least alert you if you are being observed or... probed, energetically."

She held out the pendant. It was cool to the touch, and as Pete took it, he felt a faint, almost imperceptible thrumming beneath its surface, a whisper of latent power. The intricate symbols etched into its surface seemed to catch the dim light, hinting at their protective purpose.

"Thank you," Pete said, his voice earnest. He fastened the pendant around his neck, the cool metal a stark contrast to the growing heat of his apprehension. It felt like a tangible piece of Aine's own defense, a shared burden.

"We also need to be more cautious," Aine continued, her brow furrowed in thought. "Our movements, our discussions... they must be conducted with the utmost discretion. If this individual is indeed observing us, any hint of our destination or our plans could be detrimental. The journey to the Heart of the Hearth, which we hoped to undertake with a degree of privacy, now carries an added element of risk. We cannot afford to be followed, nor can we afford for our location to be compromised before we can secure it and begin the necessary work."

The path to the cottage, which Aine had described as subtly woven into the landscape, designed to deter the uninitiated, now seemed to hold an additional purpose: a natural defense against those who were actively seeking to track them. If this man or his associates were indeed looking for them, their ignorance of the true path could be their undoing. But the thought also carried a chilling implication: if they did find the way, the confrontation would be unavoidable.

"Did he say anything that might indicate his intentions?" Pete asked, recalling the brief, unnerving conversation. "Anything at all that seemed like a threat?"

Aine shook her head slowly. "Not directly. But the way he asked questions can be as revealing as the questions themselves. A genuine interest in local history is one thing; a probing, almost invasive questioning, especially when directed towards families with particular lineages or traditions, suggests a motive beyond mere curiosity. It suggests he is looking for leverage, for a weakness, for a point of entry."

She returned to the table, her gaze falling on the detailed map of the western woods. "The isolation of the Heart of the Hearth is its greatest strength, but it also makes it vulnerable if its location becomes known to those with malicious intent. The wards that Elara and her predecessors established will undoubtedly offer a measure of protection, but their effectiveness relies on our ability to reinforce them. If they are weakened by external forces before we even arrive..." she trailed off, the unspoken consequence hanging heavy in the air.

Pete felt a surge of protective instinct, not just for Aine, but for the town, for the very concept of the Weave that was becoming increasingly real to him. He was no longer a detached observer; he was becoming an active participant in this hidden struggle. "What if he's already trying to find it?" Pete asked, the question a stark realization. "What if he knows about the cottage?"

Aine's eyes narrowed, a flicker of steel in their depths. "That is a distinct possibility, and one we must prepare for. If he is aware of the cottage, or if he is attempting to locate it, then our presence there will be met with immediate opposition. It means the challenge is not merely looming; it has already arrived, and it has identified us as the primary threat to its agenda."

The library, once a sanctuary of knowledge, now felt like a command center in a brewing conflict. The delicate balance of Kilkenny's protection was not just threatened by an abstract imbalance in the Weave; it was actively being undermined by external forces. This man, this stranger, was the first concrete manifestation of that threat, a harbinger of the danger that lay ahead. Their mission to the Heart of the Hearth had just become a race against time, a delicate dance between reinforcing their defenses and confronting an encroaching enemy. The challenge was no longer just about preserving the Weave; it was about protecting it from those who sought to tear it asunder. The weight of their task, already immense, had just doubled.

PETES DETERMINATION

The hushed sanctuary of the Kilkenny library had transformed in Pete's mind, from a place of quaint historical discovery to a strategic outpost in a clandestine war. Aine's words, once a gentle unfolding of family lore, now echoed with the urgency of an impending battle. The 'scavengers of the unseen,' the 'factions,' the 'exploitation of energies' – these were not abstract concepts from a forgotten grimoire; they were the tangible threats now circling Kilkenny, and by extension, Aine herself. The unsettling encounter with the stranger had been the catalyst, transforming his casual visit into a commitment he hadn't anticipated, a commitment forged in the crucible of growing unease and a burgeoning sense of responsibility.

He looked at Aine, her face etched with a quiet determination that was both inspiring and deeply concerning. The responsibility she carried was immense, a burden passed down through generations, now resting on her young shoulders. He couldn't simply return to his mundane life, to the predictable rhythms of his own world, knowing she was facing such profound dangers. His initial fascination with Kilkenny's history had morphed into something far more profound: a deep-seated desire to protect not just the town's ancient secrets, but the person who was safeguarding them.

"Aine," he began, his voice firm, cutting through the lingering silence that had settled after their discussion about the shadowy figures. He met her gaze directly, the obsidian amulet cool against his skin, a tangible reminder of the risks they now faced. "I... I can't just go back to my normal life. Not after this. You're facing something... immense. And I want to help."

He saw a flicker of surprise, quickly followed by a nuanced understanding in her eyes. She knew his journey to Kilkenny had been one of tentative exploration, a chance to escape the predictable confines of his own routine. He had been an outsider, an observer. But that had changed. The revelations about the Heart of the Hearth, the encroaching threat, and the very real danger she was in, had irrevocably altered his perspective. He was no longer merely a visitor; he was a participant.

"Pete," she replied, her voice soft but steady, "I appreciate that. More than you know. But this is... it's not a simple matter. It's dangerous, and it requires a deep understanding of things that are not easily grasped." She gestured around the library, at the ancient tomes and maps spread across the tables. "This is my heritage, my duty. I wouldn't ask you to step into this if I didn't have to."

"But you are facing it," Pete countered, his resolve hardening. He found himself speaking with a conviction that surprised even himself. The fear was still there, a cold knot in his stomach, but it was being steadily overridden by a fierce protectiveness. "And if that stranger yesterday was any indication, you might not be facing it alone. If there are people out there trying to exploit or disrupt what you're doing, then I want to be on your side. I want to learn. I want to understand. Whatever I can do to help, I will."

He stepped closer, leaning over the table, his focus entirely on her. The afternoon sun, which had seemed so peaceful earlier, now illuminated the subtle lines of worry around Aine's eyes. He saw not just the weight of responsibility, but also the underlying vulnerability of someone carrying such a profound legacy. He felt a surge of genuine affection, a desire to shield her from the darkness that was beginning to gather.

"I'm not afraid of a little danger," he said, a small, almost defiant smile touching his lips. "I mean, I'm a little afraid, but... it's not going to stop me. You talked about needing to reinforce the Weave, about the rituals. If there's anything I can learn, any task I can undertake, anything at all... just tell me. I'm not a scholar, I'm not a historian, but I'm resourceful. And I'm loyal. And I believe in what you're trying to do."

He knew he was stepping into uncharted territory. His life, up to this point, had been defined by predictable parameters. He had never encountered anything like the 'Weave,' or the 'Heart of the Hearth,' or the tangible threat of individuals who sought to manipulate unseen energies. Yet, the prospect of learning, of being a part of something so ancient and vital, was compelling. More compelling, however, was the thought of Aine facing these challenges alone.

"You speak of learning," Aine said, her voice tinged with a mix of gratitude and caution. "This is not something that can be taught in a few lessons, Pete. The understanding of the Weave, the attunement to the energies of Kilkenny, the knowledge of the ancient rituals... it takes years, lifetimes, of dedication." She paused, her gaze drifting to the intricately carved wooden key nestled beside the 'Chronicles.' "And the dangers are not merely physical. There are mental and spiritual tolls as well. Those who seek to exploit these forces are often... insidious. They play on weaknesses, sow discord, and can corrupt even the most well-intentioned."

"I understand that," Pete insisted. "I'm not under any illusions. I know this is way out of my league. But I can learn. I can be careful. I can follow your lead. Think of me as... an extra pair of hands, or an extra set of eyes. Or even just someone to stand beside you, to watch your back. You said yourself that your great-grandmother warned about this. It's a constant vigilance. Maybe I can help with that vigilance."

He looked down at the amulet Aine had given him, its subtle thrumming a constant reminder of the unseen forces at play. He could feel its faint energy, a protective whisper against the growing unease he felt. It was a tangible link to her world, a symbol of his commitment. He imagined wearing it not just for protection, but as a badge of his newfound dedication.

"You're talking about a commitment that could change everything, Pete," Aine said, her tone serious. "If you truly mean it, if you're ready to step into this world, there's no turning back. It's not just about helping me with a specific task. It's about understanding that this existence, this... struggle, is ongoing. It's woven into the very fabric of Kilkenny, and by extension, into the lives of those who are connected to it."

"I know," Pete said, his voice resonating with a quiet conviction. "And I'm ready. I've spent enough time being a spectator. This... this feels real. It feels important. And you, Aine... you're important. I care about what happens to you, and to this place. If I can contribute in any way, then I have to try." He thought about the stranger, his probing questions, his unnerving intensity. The thought of that man, or others like him, preying on the delicate balance of Kilkenny, on Aine's efforts, ignited a fire within him.

"So," Pete continued, pushing aside the lingering apprehension, focusing on the immediate task at hand. "The cottage. The Heart of the Hearth. What's the plan? How do we get there? What do we need to do? I might not know anything about the Weave, but I can learn the practicalities. I can help with supplies, with scouting, with... anything that needs to be done. Just point me in the right direction."

Aine studied him for a long moment, her gaze penetrating, searching for any sign of wavering. She saw the earnestness in his eyes, the sincerity in his voice, and the quiet strength that had begun to emerge in him since their first meeting. He was no longer the lost tourist seeking directions; he was a willing ally, stepping willingly into the shadows.

"The journey itself is not straightforward," Aine began, her focus shifting, a new purpose in her tone. She reached for the map once more, her fingers tracing a path through the dense woods to the west of Kilkenny. "The cottage, the Heart of the Hearth, is not marked on any modern map. Its location is protected by a series of subtle wards, layered over centuries. Elara designed them to deter the uninitiated, to ensure that only those with a true connection, or those who are specifically guided, can find their way."

"Wards?" Pete echoed, the word still carrying a sense of the fantastical, yet now grounded by Aine's serious demeanor.

"Yes," Aine confirmed. "They are not visible barriers, but rather energetic deterrents. They can cause disorientation, lead seekers astray, or even instill a profound sense of unease, encouraging them to turn back. They are designed to be subtle, to work with the natural landscape rather than against it, making them difficult to detect by conventional means." She looked at Pete. "Your pendant is a form of warding as well, a personal one. It will help you to feel if you are being... observed, or if something is attempting to probe your intentions."

Pete touched the amulet again, feeling a subtle warmth emanating from it. The idea of unseen protections, of energetic defenses, was still astonishing, but he was beginning to accept it, to integrate it into his understanding of this hidden world. He was willing to trust Aine's knowledge implicitly.

"So, how do we navigate these wards?" Pete asked, his mind already whirring with practicalities. He thought of GPS, of maps, of compasses, and wondered how they would fare against such ancient protections.

"The 'Chronicles' holds some clues," Aine explained, tapping the worn leather cover of the ancient book. "And the wooden key is more than just a key; it's also a conduit, a way to acknowledge and pass through certain protections. But the most crucial element is understanding the intent. The wards are sensitive to the motivations of those who approach. They are designed to test sincerity and to repel those with malice." She paused, her gaze thoughtful. "This is where your presence might be invaluable, Pete. Not as a detractor, but as an anchor. Your... grounding in this world, your lack of inherent connection to the deeper workings of the Weave, might, paradoxically, make you less of a target for the wards' disorienting effects. You are not seeking power for yourself; you are seeking to support. This can be a form of clarity that even the most attuned might struggle with."

Pete considered this. He was an outsider, yes, but his intentions were pure, driven by a desire to help Aine and a growing fascination with the stakes involved. It was a strange thought: that his very ordinariness, his lack of deep magical or historical lineage, might be an asset. It made him feel less like a liability and more like a potential, albeit unconventional, asset.

"So, you're saying I might be able to... walk through some of the protections without being affected?" Pete asked, a flicker of hope mixed with his usual apprehension.

"It's a possibility," Aine conceded. "Elara's wards are sophisticated. They react to patterns of thought and intent. If your intent is clear and your focus is on assisting me, you might pass through certain deterrents more easily than someone who is trying to find this place for their own gain. We will need to be observant, to read the subtle shifts in the environment, the way the land reacts to our presence."

She turned her attention back to the map, her brow furrowed in concentration. "Our immediate goal is to reach the cottage without being followed. The stranger you saw, if he is indeed a harbinger of others, could be actively seeking to track us. We need to be discreet. The path we will take is not the most direct route, but it is the one that offers the most concealment. It winds through older growth forests, areas less frequented and more difficult to navigate for those who do not know the terrain."

Pete felt a jolt of adrenaline. The journey itself was becoming a mission, a test of their ability to evade detection. The idea of being hunted, of having to move with stealth and caution, was a stark reality of the danger they were in.

"What about supplies?" Pete asked, his mind immediately jumping to practical necessities. "We'll need food, water, some way to signal if we get separated, maybe... some kind of protection, even if it's just something to defend ourselves with?" He felt a bit foolish asking about self-defense, but the threat felt so potent.

Aine nodded, a faint smile touching her lips at his pragmatism. "Your foresight is commendable, Pete. We will need to pack provisions, of course. And a means of communication, though it will be limited by the natural environment. As for defense... the wards themselves offer a degree of protection against immediate, aggressive intrusion. But they are not foolproof against determined individuals. I will bring certain items, tools that have been passed down. And perhaps," she added, her gaze lingering on him, "you can be a strong and steady presence. Your resourcefulness might prove more valuable than any weapon."

He understood. His value lay not in his ability to fight, but in his steadiness, his willingness to learn, and his unwavering support. He was a partner, not a warrior, but in this world of unseen forces, perhaps that was precisely what was needed. He was a grounding presence, a reminder of the tangible reality they were fighting to protect.

"I'll do my best," Pete said, his voice firm. "I'll help gather whatever we need. Just tell me what to look for, what to bring. I'll be ready." He met her gaze, a silent promise passing between them. He was committed, not just to Aine, but to the cause, to the ancient legacy she carried. The challenge was immense, the path fraught with unknown dangers, but he was ready to face it, to learn, to assist, and to stand by her side, no matter what lay ahead. The ordinary tourist had found a purpose, and he wouldn't falter. His determination was now as unyielding as the ancient stones of Kilkenny.

Chapter Eleven: The Ritual Site

JOURNEY TO THE SACRED GROUND

The air in the library, once thick with the scent of aged paper and polish, now felt charged with an electric anticipation. Pete's offer, a lifeline cast into the swirling currents of her family's ancient responsibilities, had settled deep within Aine. He was an anomaly, an unexpected beacon of unwavering support in a world she had long believed she must navigate alone. His acceptance wasn't born of a scholar's curiosity or a thrill-seeker's ambition, but of something far more profound – a genuine desire to stand beside her. This realization, a fragile bloom in the arid landscape of her duties, offered a sliver of hope.

"The journey itself is not straightforward," Aine began, her voice low and resonant, drawing Pete's attention back to the worn map spread between them. She traced a route with her finger, a winding path leading away from the familiar embrace of Kilkenny town, towards the west, where the land began to fold and whisper its older secrets. "The cottage, the Heart of the Hearth, is not marked on any modern map. Its location is protected by a series of subtle wards, layered over centuries. Elara, my great-grandmother, designed them to deter the uninitiated, to ensure that only those with a true connection, or those who are specifically guided, can find their way."

Pete leaned closer, his eyes following the intricate lines on the parchment. "Wards?" he repeated, the word still tinged with a sense of the arcane, yet now grounded in the tangible threat that had brought them to this point.

"Yes," Aine confirmed, her gaze steady. "They are not visible barriers, but rather energetic deterrents. They can cause disorientation, lead seekers astray, or even instill a profound sense of unease, encouraging them to turn back. They are designed to be subtle, to work with the natural landscape rather than against it, making them difficult to detect by conventional means." She glanced at the obsidian amulet, cool against Pete's skin, a tangible reminder of the unseen forces at play. "Your pendant is a form of warding as well, a personal one. It will help you to feel if you are being... observed, or if something is attempting to probe your intentions."

Pete touched the amulet, a faint warmth emanating from it, a silent testament to its protective properties. The concept of unseen defenses, of energetic barriers woven into the very fabric of the land, was still astonishing, but he found himself accepting it, integrating it into his burgeoning understanding of this hidden world. He trusted Aine implicitly. "So, how do we navigate these wards?" he asked, his mind already a whirl of practicalities. He thought of GPS, of compasses, of satellite imagery, and wondered how they would fare against such ancient, sentient protections.

"The 'Chronicles' holds some clues," Aine explained, tapping the worn leather cover of the ancient book. "And the wooden key is more than just a key; it's also a conduit, a way to acknowledge and pass through certain protections. But the most crucial element is understanding the intent. The wards are sensitive to the motivations of those who approach. They are designed to test sincerity and to repel those with malice." She paused, her brow furrowing in thought. "This is where your presence might be invaluable, Pete. Not as a detractor, but as an anchor. Your... grounding in this world, your lack of inherent connection to the deeper workings of the Weave, might, paradoxically, make you less of a target for the wards' disorienting effects. You are not seeking power for yourself; you are seeking to support. This can be a form of clarity that even the most attuned might struggle with."

Pete considered this, a strange mix of apprehension and a burgeoning sense of purpose swirling within him. He was an outsider, yes, but his intentions were clear, driven by a desire to help Aine and a growing fascination with the stakes involved. It was an almost absurd thought: that his very ordinariness, his lack of deep magical lineage or arcane knowledge, might be an asset. It made him feel less like a liability and more like a potential, albeit unconventional, participant. "So, you're saying I might be able to... walk through some of the protections without being affected?" he asked, a flicker of hope battling with his ingrained skepticism.

"It's a possibility," Aine conceded, her gaze thoughtful. "Elara's wards are sophisticated. They react to patterns of thought and intent. If your intent is clear and your focus is on assisting me, you might pass through certain deterrents more easily than someone who is trying to find this place for their own gain. We will need to be observant, to read the subtle shifts in the environment, the way the land reacts to our presence. It is a dance, of sorts, a negotiation with the ancient spirits of this place."

She turned her attention back to the map, her brow furrowed in concentration. "Our immediate goal is to reach the cottage without being followed. The stranger you saw, if he is indeed a harbinger of others, could be actively seeking to track us. We need to be discreet. The path we will take is not the most direct route, but it is the one that offers the most concealment. It winds through older growth forests, areas less frequented and more difficult to navigate for those who do not know the terrain. It's a journey that requires patience and a deep respect for the natural world."

Pete felt a jolt of adrenaline, a primal awareness of the potential for danger. The journey itself was becoming a mission, a test of their ability to evade detection. The thought of being hunted, of having to move with stealth and caution, was a stark reminder of the gravity of their situation. "What about supplies?" Pete asked, his mind immediately shifting to practical necessities. "We'll need food, water, some way to signal if we get separated, maybe... some kind of protection, even if it's just something to defend ourselves with?" He felt a bit foolish asking about self-defense, but the threat felt so potent, so insubstantial yet so utterly real.

Aine nodded, a faint smile gracing her lips at his pragmatism. "Your foresight is commendable, Pete. We will need to pack provisions, of course. Water purifiers, nutrient-rich rations that are light and easy to carry. And a means of communication, though it will be limited by the natural environment. I have some specialized items, small stones that can resonate with each other over a short distance, but their range is uncertain. As for defense..." She hesitated, her gaze lingering on him. "The wards themselves offer a degree of protection against immediate, aggressive intrusion. But they are not foolproof against determined individuals. I will bring certain items, tools that have been passed down, imbued with the energies of our lineage. And perhaps," she added, her voice softening, "you can be a strong and steady presence. Your resourcefulness might prove more valuable than any weapon."

He understood. His value lay not in his ability to fight, but in his steadiness, his willingness to learn, and his unwavering support. He was a partner, not a warrior, but in this world of unseen forces, perhaps that was precisely what was needed. He was a grounding presence, a reminder of the tangible reality they were fighting to protect. "I'll do my best," Pete said, his voice firm, cutting through any lingering self-doubt. "I'll help gather whatever we need. Just tell me what to look for, what to bring. I'll be ready." He met her gaze, a silent promise passing between them. He was committed, not just to Aine, but to the cause, to the ancient legacy she carried. The challenge was immense, the path fraught with unknown dangers, but he was ready to face it, to learn, to assist, and to stand by her side, no matter what lay ahead. The ordinary tourist had found a purpose, and he wouldn't falter. His determination was now as unyielding as the ancient stones of Kilkenny.

The following morning, under a sky still bruised with the remnants of dawn, Aine led Pete away from the quiet streets of Kilkenny. Their destination was not a place easily found on any map, nor one that shouted its significance to the casual observer. It was a place of profound stillness, a pocket of ancient earth preserved from the relentless march of time. Their journey began on the outskirts of the town, where the tarmac gave way to a narrow, overgrown track, leading them into the embrace of the countryside. The air grew cooler, carrying the damp scent of moss and decaying leaves, a potent perfume of the wild.

"We're heading towards an old monastic site, though little remains above ground," Aine explained, her voice barely a whisper, as if not to disturb the sleeping earth around them. "It was founded in the early days of Christianity in Ireland, built on a site already considered sacred long before that. My ancestors, even before they took on the role of guardians for Kilkenny itself, were connected to places like this. They understood that the energetic currents of the land were strongest in these ancient, undisturbed locations."

Pete followed her, his eyes scanning the dense foliage that pressed in on either side of the narrow path. The trees here were ancient, their branches gnarled and twisted like arthritic fingers, draped with trailing ivy and lichen. Sunlight dappled through the thick canopy, casting shifting patterns of light and shadow on the forest floor. The silence was profound, broken only by the crunch of their footsteps on fallen leaves and the occasional call of a distant bird. It was a silence that felt heavy with unspoken history, a silence that seemed to listen as intently as they did.

"The 'Chronicles' speak of this place as a nexus," Aine continued, her voice gaining a hushed reverence. "A point where the different threads of the Weave converge, making it a place of immense power, but also one that requires careful tending. My family's duty isn't just to Kilkenny's present, but to its past and its future, a continuous thread woven through generations. This site is integral to that weaving. Elara used to bring me here when I was very young, not to teach me about the wards, but to help me understand the feeling of the land, the silent language it speaks."

As they ventured deeper, the terrain became more challenging. The path, barely discernible now, wound its way up a gentle incline, leading them towards a slight rise in the land. Pete felt a subtle shift in the atmosphere, a prickling sensation on his skin, not entirely unpleasant, but certainly noticeable. He instinctively reached for the amulet, its cool surface a comforting presence against his chest.

"The wards are beginning to stir," Aine said, her eyes fixed on the path ahead, a subtle alertness in her posture. "They are not malicious, but they are watchful. They are assessing our presence, our intent. Try to keep your thoughts clear, Pete. Focus on why we are here."

Pete took a deep breath, deliberately pushing aside any stray anxieties or distractions. He pictured Aine, her quiet determination, the weight of her inherited responsibility. He focused on his own resolve – to help, to learn, to support. It was a surprisingly effective exercise. The prickling sensation on his skin seemed to lessen, replaced by a faint sense of calm.

They emerged from the denser woods into a small, overgrown clearing. Before them stood the skeletal remains of a stone structure, a testament to the passage of centuries. Low, crumbling walls, barely hip-high, marked out the footprint of what had once been a small monastic cell or chapel. Moss and vibrant green ferns carpeted the stones, reclaiming them for the earth. In the center of the ruins, a single, ancient yew tree stood sentinel, its dark foliage creating a dense canopy overhead, even in the dappled sunlight. The air here felt different, thicker, humming with a subtle, resonant energy.

"This is it," Aine whispered, her gaze sweeping across the scene with a mixture of familiarity and deep respect. "The heart of this place. Even in its ruin, the essence remains. Elara believed that the true sanctuary wasn't the stone, but the spirit of the location itself, anchored by the land's natural energy. The cottage, though it's some distance from here, is where the more tangible rituals are performed, but this... this is where the connection is deepest."

Pete walked slowly around the perimeter of the ruins, his senses alert. He could feel it now, a palpable thrumming, like the silent vibration of a plucked string. It wasn't an aggressive energy, but it was undeniably powerful, ancient, and aware. He understood, in a way that mere words could never convey, why Aine felt such a profound connection to this place and to her lineage. It was more than just history; it was a living, breathing heritage.

"The energy here is very... pure," Pete observed, the word feeling inadequate to describe the profound stillness he felt.

"It is," Aine agreed, running her hand gently over a moss-covered stone. "It's a place where the veil between our world and others is thinner. For centuries, my family has used sites like this to attune themselves to the Weave, to draw strength and clarity for their duties. The rituals performed at the cottage are an extension of the energy of places like this, amplified and directed."

She pointed towards the ancient yew tree. "That tree is as old as the monastic settlement, perhaps even older. It's deeply rooted, not just in the earth, but in the energetic pathways of this region. It acts as a natural conduit, helping to stabilize and channel the energy that flows through this nexus. The wards are layered around this entire area, not just the ruins themselves, but extending outwards, a protective embrace."

Pete looked at the yew tree, its dark, almost black foliage a stark contrast to the vibrant green of the ferns. He could feel a faint pulse emanating from it, a slow, steady beat that seemed to resonate with the very earth beneath his feet. "It's incredible," he murmured, genuinely awestruck. "I've never felt anything like it."

"It's a reminder of what we're protecting," Aine said softly, her gaze distant, as if she were seeing not just the ruins, but the generations of her ancestors who had walked this ground. "Kilkenny is not just a town with a rich history. It's a place where the ancient currents of life are particularly strong. My family's role, for centuries, has been to act as custodians of these currents, to ensure they remain balanced and pure, uncorrupted by those who would seek to exploit them for their own gain."

She then turned her attention to a specific point at the edge of the clearing, where the ruins met the wilder undergrowth. "The path to the cottage doesn't begin here, but this is where we must now prepare ourselves. The next stage of the journey requires a different kind of awareness, a deeper immersion into the Weave's more subtle pathways. The wards here are designed to guide us, but also to test our resolve and our focus."

Aine knelt beside a large, flat stone, its surface worn smooth by centuries of weather. She carefully placed the ancient 'Chronicles' and the intricately carved wooden key upon it. "The 'Chronicles' provides the knowledge, the history, the understanding of how to navigate these energetic currents. But the key... the key is the acknowledgement. It's a symbol of our lineage, of our right to pass through these defenses." She picked up the key, its polished wood warm in her hand. "It's not just a physical key; it's a key to intention, to purpose."

As she spoke, Pete noticed her movements becoming more deliberate, more focused. She was entering a state of deep concentration, her connection to the place deepening. He felt a sense of calm descend upon him, a stillness that mirrored hers. He understood that this was not merely a trek through the woods; it was a sacred pilgrimage, a rite of passage into a hidden world.

"Before we move on," Aine said, her voice a low hum, "there is something I must show you, something that will help you understand the nature of the energies we are dealing with, and the importance of what we are doing." She carefully opened the 'Chronicles' to a specific page, its parchment brittle and discolored with age. The script was elegant, flowing, and ancient.

"This passage," she explained, her finger tracing the faded ink, "describes the 'Heart of the Hearth.' It's not just a physical object, though it is housed within the cottage. It is the embodiment of Kilkenny's life force, the central point of balance for the energetic currents that flow through the region. It's what gives this place its unique character, its vitality, its resilience against the forces that would seek to drain or pervert it."

Pete peered at the text, catching fragments of meaning. Words like 'nexus,' 'conduit,' and 'equilibrium' jumped out at him. He looked at the illustration on the page, a stylized depiction of interwoven lines, radiating outwards from a central point. It was abstract, yet somehow conveyed a sense of immense, flowing power.

"The 'Heart' is not something that can be seen or touched by ordinary means," Aine continued, her gaze intense. "It is perceived through the Weave, felt as a warmth, a pulse, a living presence. It's what my family has sworn to protect, to maintain its balance, to ensure its light continues to shine. If the Heart were to be corrupted, or its energy siphoned off, the consequences for Kilkenny would be devastating. Not just physically, but spiritually, culturally. The very essence of the town would begin to wither."

The gravity of her words settled heavily upon Pete. He thought of the stranger, of his unnerving intensity, his probing questions. He was one of those who would seek to exploit, to drain, to corrupt. The thought sent a shiver down his spine.

"And the rituals?" Pete asked, his voice hushed. "The ones you were preparing for?"

"The rituals are designed to reinforce the Heart's natural defenses, to strengthen its connection to the land, and to purify any dissonant energies that may have begun to gather," Aine explained. "They are ancient practices, passed down through generations, drawing upon the energies of places like this, and channeling them through the Heart. It requires a deep understanding of the Weave, and a clear, unwavering intention. And it's becoming increasingly difficult, especially with others now showing an interest in Kilkenny's hidden energies."

She looked at him, her eyes reflecting the ancient wisdom of her lineage and the present danger they faced. "This journey to the cottage is a crucial part of the preparation. It's a pilgrimage to a sacred ground, a place where the power that fuels the rituals can be truly felt and understood. It's a necessary step to ensure that the Heart is ready, and that I am ready, for what may come."

With a final, lingering glance at the ancient yew tree and the crumbling stones, Aine rose. The parchment of the 'Chronicles' was carefully folded, and the wooden key was tucked securely into a pouch at her belt. Pete felt a renewed sense of purpose. He was not just a bystander anymore. He was a participant in something ancient and vital, a silent guardian alongside a lineage of protectors.

"Come," Aine said, her voice clear and firm, breaking the reverie. "The path ahead is not marked, but it is known. We must move with respect, with awareness, and with a clear heart. The journey to the sacred ground has truly begun." She turned and stepped towards the dense undergrowth, a figure of quiet resolve against the backdrop of the ancient forest. Pete followed, his gaze fixed on her, ready to embrace whatever lay ahead, his own path now irrevocably intertwined with the hidden heart of Kilkenny.

PREPARING THE RITUAL

The air, already alive with the hushed secrets of the ancient wood, seemed to thicken as Aine began her preparations. They had reached a secluded dell, a natural amphitheater cradled by ancient oaks, their branches reaching skyward like supplicating arms. Sunlight, filtered through the dense canopy, painted shifting patterns on the mossy ground, lending an ethereal glow to the scene. This was not merely a resting place; it was a prelude. Aine moved with a quiet grace, a practiced reverence that spoke of countless generations who had performed similar rites.

She knelt first, her fingers sifting through the rich, dark soil. From a worn leather pouch, she produced a series of small, smooth stones, each one unique in its subtle coloration – earthy browns, deep greens, and flecks of almost imperceptible silver. These were not ordinary pebbles. They were talismans, imbued with the essence of specific ancestral places, each carrying its own resonance, its own protective quality. With meticulous care, Aine placed them in a precise circle, forming a boundary around the clearing. Her movements were deliberate, her breath steady, as if she were weaving an invisible tapestry upon the very fabric of the earth.

"These are Boundary Stones," she explained, her voice a low murmur that seemed to blend with the rustling leaves. "Each one carries the protective energy of a place significant to my family's guardianship. They create a sacred space, a sanctuary from which to perform the ritual. They also serve as a gentle warning, an indication that an area of focused intent is being established."

Pete watched, his own hands stilling, a profound sense of being an observer, yet also a participant, washing over him. He understood, with a clarity that transcended logic, that every action Aine took was imbued with purpose. He felt the weight of this history, not as a burden, but as a profound legacy. He was here to assist, to learn, and to bear witness to a power that had long been hidden from the world.

As the circle of stones was completed, Aine rose and turned her attention to the central space. From her satchel, she produced a finely woven linen cloth, embroidered with symbols that Pete vaguely recognized from the 'Chronicles.' It depicted the intertwined roots of trees, the flow of rivers, and celestial patterns, all converging on a single, radiant star. This cloth was laid carefully in the very center of the stone circle, its intricate patterns facing upwards, awaiting its purpose.

"This is the Hearth Cloth," Aine stated, her voice imbued with a gentle solemnity. "It represents the grounding of our intent, the connection between the earthly and the celestial. The symbols are an invocation, a drawing down of the energies that sustain Kilkenny, and a fortification of its inherent strength."

She then produced a small, intricately carved wooden box. Its surface was smooth and dark, bearing the faint scent of ancient cedar. With a soft click, she opened it. Inside, nestled on a bed of dried herbs, lay a single, unblemished raven's feather, its sheen a deep, iridescent black, and a shard of polished obsidian, so dark it seemed to absorb the very light around it.

"The feather," Aine began, her fingers hovering over the delicate quill, "is a messenger. It carries the intent of our actions outwards, to the unseen watchers, and can also bring back whispers of awareness. It is a conduit for communication beyond the spoken word. The obsidian, on the other hand, is for reflection. It absorbs any negativity that might be directed towards this space, and purifies it."

Pete's gaze was fixed on these objects, each imbued with a significance that far surpassed their material form. He felt a growing sense of awe, mixed with a prickle of apprehension. He was stepping into a world governed by principles he was only beginning to grasp, a world where the mundane and the mystical intertwined seamlessly.

"And the ritual itself?" Pete asked, his voice hushed, not wanting to break the sacred atmosphere. "What exactly will you be doing?"

Aine looked at him, her eyes holding a deep well of ancient knowledge, yet also a vulnerability that spoke of the immense responsibility she carried. "The ritual is a recalibration, Pete. It's about reinforcing the natural energetic flow of Kilkenny, the 'Weave' that sustains its essence. The Heart of the Hearth, which we seek to protect, is the focal point of this Weave. Over time, external influences, even the passage of seasons, can cause subtle shifts, imbalances. This ritual is designed to correct those imbalances, to ensure the Weave remains pure and strong."

She paused, her fingers gently stroking the raven's feather. "It involves chanting, yes, but also a channeling of personal energy, a focused intention to mend and strengthen. It's a dedication of my lineage's purpose to the continued well-being of Kilkenny. The 'Chronicles' provide the framework, the ancient words, but the true power comes from the heart, from the conviction of the one performing it."

She then reached for a small, smooth stone from her pouch, a pale grey one this time, streaked with faint white lines. She held it out to him. "I need your help, Pete. This ritual requires an anchor, someone whose presence can offer a different kind of grounding. The wards are designed to protect, but they are also sensitive to intent. Your intent here is to support, to protect, to be steadfast. This stone will help you focus that energy."

Pete took the stone, its surface cool and smooth against his palm. He could feel a faint warmth emanating from it, a subtle vibration that seemed to mirror the pulse of the earth beneath them. He gripped it tightly, focusing on Aine, on the task ahead, on his commitment to her and to this hidden world. He felt a sense of immense purpose coalesce within him, a quiet strength that surprised him.

"What do I do?" he asked, his voice firm, his gaze unwavering.

Aine smiled, a rare, genuine smile that lit up her face. "Simply stand here, beside me. When I begin to chant, focus on this stone, and on your intention to be a steady presence. Imagine a strong, unwavering line of connection between you, me, and the land. Your presence, your grounding, will lend a stability that even the most potent ancestral magic can sometimes lack."

She then carefully placed the obsidian shard beside the Hearth Cloth, its dark surface facing outwards. She took a deep, centering breath, her eyes closing for a brief moment. When she opened them, they held a newfound intensity, a reflection of the ancient power that was beginning to stir.

"The first part of the ritual is to establish the clarity of purpose," Aine explained. "To speak the intent aloud, so that the land, and any who might be listening, understands why we are here." She then began to speak, her voice starting as a soft hum that gradually deepened, taking on a rhythmic, resonant quality. The words were ancient, flowing from her lips with an ease that spoke of deep familiarity. Pete couldn't understand the exact meaning of the archaic dialect, but he felt the power behind it, the sheer weight of intention woven into each syllable.

"Terra firma, flumen aeternum, caelum semper spectans," she chanted, her voice resonating through the clearing. "Sanctitatem hanc custodire venimus, lucem perpetuo servare."

As she spoke, Pete focused on the stone in his hand, its subtle warmth spreading through his fingers. He pictured a strong, unyielding root system spreading from his feet, anchoring him firmly to the earth. He visualized a steady, golden light emanating from his chest, a beacon of calm and unwavering resolve. He felt the energy of the clearing intensify, the faint thrumming he had felt earlier growing stronger, almost palpable. The air around them seemed to shimmer, and the leaves on the surrounding trees rustled with a sound that was more than just wind.

Aine continued her chant, her voice rising and falling with the ancient cadence. She then produced a small vial filled with a luminous, viscous liquid – a substance that seemed to glow with an inner light. This, she carefully poured onto the Hearth Cloth, allowing it to soak into the embroidered symbols.

"This is Lumin," she explained, her voice still melodic, yet now carrying a slight strain from the vocalization. "A sacred oil derived from moon-kissed herbs and blessed spring water. It awakens the latent energies within the cloth and amplifies the intention of the ritual."

As the Lumin spread, the symbols on the cloth seemed to glow more brightly, the interwoven patterns pulsing with a soft, ethereal light. Pete felt a surge of warmth pass through him, a sensation of being deeply connected, not just to Aine, but to the very life force of the land itself. He felt the forest breathing around them, a slow, rhythmic inhalation and exhalation that seemed to synchronize with his own heartbeat.

Then, Aine reached for the raven's feather. She held it aloft, its dark tip pointing towards the sky. Her chanting shifted, becoming more incantatory, more focused on drawing power from above, from the unseen currents that flowed through the ancient woods.

"Per pennam noctis, nuntius ascendat, veritas revelatur, custos fidem tenet." Her voice was clear and strong now, cutting through the ambient sounds of the forest. "Audi vocem nostram, terra sacra. Accipe intentionem nostram. Confirma custodiam."

As she spoke, Pete felt a subtle shift in the air. It was as if an invisible net were being cast, not to trap, but to encompass, to delineate. He realized that the wards, subtle as they were, were now actively participating in the ritual, responding to Aine's focused intent. He felt a gentle pressure, like a soft breeze against his skin, as if the very air were assessing his presence, confirming his role as a supportive observer.

He kept his gaze steady, his grip firm on the stone. He pictured himself as a strong, ancient oak, its roots deep, its branches reaching towards the sky, unwavering in its strength. He focused on his desire to protect Aine, to ensure the safety of Kilkenny, to preserve the delicate balance that her lineage had maintained for centuries. The weight of history settled upon him, not as a burden, but as a shared responsibility. He understood that this moment, this carefully orchestrated ritual, was a testament to the enduring power of commitment and the deep-seated need to protect what is precious.

Aine then lowered the feather, her chant softening as she brought her attention back to the immediate surroundings. She picked up the obsidian shard, turning it over in her fingers. She spoke a few words, a murmur of gratitude and acknowledgement, and then placed it at the edge of the Hearth Cloth, its dark surface absorbing the ambient light.

"The obsidian acts as a shield," she explained, her voice now lower, more introspective. "It will absorb any stray energies, any unintended ripples from our actions, and neutralize them. It's a safeguard, ensuring that the focus of the ritual remains pure."

She then reached for the wooden key, which she had placed carefully beside the Boundary Stones. She held it in her palm, its familiar weight a comfort. "The key is the final affirmation," she said, her gaze meeting Pete's. "It is the tangible symbol of our connection to this place, and of our right to perform this rite. It is an acknowledgement of the ancient pacts that bind my family to Kilkenny's heart."

With a deliberate movement, Aine placed the wooden key on the Hearth Cloth, its carved surface resting on the luminous symbols. The combined energies seemed to hum, a low, resonant vibration that seemed to emanate from the very core of the clearing. Pete felt a sense of completion, of a sacred task begun, of a lineage honored. He looked at Aine, her face serene, her body radiating a quiet strength. He understood then that his role, though seemingly passive, was vital. He was a silent pillar, a steady presence that allowed the more intricate and potent energies of the ritual to flow unimpeded. He was not just assisting; he was contributing, his unwavering intent a crucial component in this ancient, sacred dance. The weight of history, the significance of this moment, settled upon him not as a burden, but as a profound honor. He was a part of something ancient, something vital, something that held the very essence of Kilkenny within its carefully constructed circle of power.

THE SYMBOLS AND THEIR MEANING

Pete watched as Aine continued to prepare the ritual site. His gaze drifted to the Hearth Cloth, the finely woven linen spread at the center of the Boundary Stones. He'd noticed the intricate embroidery before, a tapestry of interwoven roots, flowing rivers, and celestial patterns converging on a single, radiant star. Now, with the Lumin oil soaking into the fabric, the symbols seemed to pulse with an inner luminescence, their significance no longer merely visual but almost tangible. He recognized some of the patterns from the 'Chronicles,' those faded pages he'd pored over, images that had seemed like abstract designs then, but which now resonated with a profound, living meaning.

"The symbols on the Hearth Cloth," Aine began, her voice a soft melody that wove through the hushed clearing, "are more than just decorative. They are a language, a direct communication with the energetic currents of Kilkenny. Each line, each curve, is imbued with a specific purpose, a carefully chosen representation of the forces we seek to harness and protect." She gestured towards the interwoven roots depicted at the bottom of the cloth. "These represent the ancestral grounding, the deep connection to the earth that sustains this land. They speak of stability, of resilience, and of the enduring strength drawn from generations past. They are the roots of Kilkenny's being, anchoring its very essence."

Pete leaned in, tracing the lines of the roots with his eyes. He could almost feel the ancient earth beneath the moss, the hidden network of life that pulsed unseen. "So, it's about history, then?" he asked, his voice hushed with respect.

Aine nodded, her gaze moving to the flowing rivers depicted next. "History, yes, but also the continuous flow of life. These rivers are not just water; they symbolize the ceaseless movement of energy, the cycles of renewal and change that are vital to Kilkenny's health. They represent adaptability, the ability to flow around obstacles and to nourish the land. Think of them as the lifeblood of the 'Weave,' carrying vitality and purpose." She then indicated the celestial patterns above the rivers, stars and crescent moons intricately woven into the fabric. "And these," she continued, her voice gaining a slightly more reverent tone, "are the whispers of the cosmos. They represent the celestial influences, the cosmic alignment that plays a part in the balance of all things. They are about guidance, intuition, and the connection to a power far vaster than ourselves. The convergence of roots, rivers, and stars at that central point," she pointed to the radiant star emblem, "is the Heart of the Hearth, the nexus of all these energies, the very core of what we are safeguarding."

He understood then that his earlier fascination with the 'Chronicles' had been a subconscious recognition of these symbols, a faint echo of a connection he hadn't yet fully grasped. The stylized trees, the swirling water motifs, the distant stars—they were all pieces of a grander design, a sacred geometry that underpinned the very existence of Kilkenny.

"The entire cloth," Aine explained, her hands hovering over the embroidered surface, "acts as a focal point, a beacon that draws and concentrates the protective energies. It is a map of the forces at play, and a diagram of how to harmonize them. When we apply the Lumin, and when I chant the ancient words, these symbols become conduits, channeling the intended power."

She then picked up one of the small, smooth stones from her pouch, a deep green one this time, flecked with what looked like tiny specks of gold. "These stones, the Boundary Stones, are also imbued with symbolic meaning, though their primary function is to create the sacred perimeter. Each stone represents a specific type of ward, a particular facet of protection. This green stone, for instance, resonates with the earth's vitality and the resilience of the ancient forests. It's a ward against stagnation, against any force that would seek to drain Kilkenny of its natural life."

She placed it carefully back in the circle, its position precise. "The earthy brown ones," she continued, holding up a rounded, matte stone, "are for grounding and stability. They anchor the ritual, preventing the energies from becoming too dispersed or chaotic. They represent unwavering strength, a deep connection to the land's physical form."

Pete nodded, feeling a new understanding dawn. The meticulous placement of each stone wasn't just about creating a boundary; it was about layering defenses, each stone a unique guardian. He thought back to the stories he'd read, tales of ancient peoples who communicated with the land through intricate patterns and sacred objects. He was witnessing such a practice firsthand, a living testament to a tradition stretching back through the mists of time.

Aine then reached for the raven's feather again, holding it gently. "The feather, as I mentioned, is a messenger. Its symbolism is deeply rooted in the lore of many cultures. For us, the raven represents perception, adaptability, and the ability to traverse unseen realms. It is a symbol of the intermediary, the bridge between the seen and the unseen. When used in this ritual, it carries our intentions to the spirit of

Kilkenny, and can also bring back subtle warnings or insights from the land itself. It's a channel for that subtle communication, that deeper dialogue."

She then brought her attention to the obsidian shard, its dark, polished surface reflecting the dappled sunlight. "The obsidian," she said, her voice tinged with a solemn respect, "is a powerful purifier and protector. It's known for its ability to absorb negativity, to draw out and neutralize harmful energies. In ancient times, it was often used in scrying mirrors, to reveal truths, but also to reflect back the darkness from which it was born, rendering it inert. Here, it acts as a shield, a focal point for any stray or malevolent influences that might be drawn to the energy of the ritual. It is a powerful ward against disruption, ensuring the purity of our intent and the sanctity of this space."

He watched as she placed the obsidian shard at the edge of the Hearth Cloth, its dark sheen stark against the luminous fabric. It was a stark reminder of the dual nature of power – the need for both attraction and repulsion, for both harnessing light and warding off darkness.

"The wooden key," Aine continued, her fingers closing around the small, carved object, "is perhaps the most personal symbol in this array. It represents lineage, authority, and the inherent right to perform this duty. It's a tangible connection to the ancient pacts, a physical manifestation of the trust bestowed upon my family to safe-guard Kilkenny. The carvings on it are not arbitrary; they are a condensed form of the same protective symbols found on the Hearth Cloth, a miniature representation of the entire safeguarding philosophy. When placed on the cloth, it signifies the culmination of intent, the affirmation of our role as custodians."

He felt a surge of understanding. Each object, each symbol, was a carefully chosen piece of a much larger, intricate puzzle. They weren't just tools; they were active participants in the ritual, each contributing its unique energy and meaning to the overall purpose. It was a symphony of intention, a meticulously orchestrated performance designed to resonate with the very soul of the land.

"The combination of these elements," Aine explained, her gaze sweeping across the prepared site, "creates a multifaceted system of protection. The Boundary Stones define the sacred space and offer an initial layer of defense. The Hearth Cloth acts as the central focus, amplifying and directing the energies, while its symbols represent the forces we are working with. The Lumin oil awakens and enhances these energies, making them receptive to our intent. The raven's feather serves as a communicator, bridging the gap between our actions and the unseen world. The obsidian shard acts as a purifier and a shield, absorbing and neutralizing any harmful influences. And the key," she held it up for a moment, the light catching its polished surface, "is the final affirmation, the seal of authority and connection."

She paused, her eyes meeting Pete's, a quiet intensity in their depths. "These symbols, Pete, are the distilled wisdom of centuries. They are not static pronouncements, but living energies that respond to focused intent. They are the language of preservation, the grammar of guardianship. My ancestors understood that protecting Kilkenny required more than just physical barriers; it required a deep understanding of its energetic heart, and the ability to communicate with and influence the subtle forces that sustained it."

He found himself nodding slowly, a profound respect for Aine and her lineage growing with each explanation. He had always believed in the power of stories, in the weight of tradition, but this was something more tangible, something rooted in a direct, almost visceral connection to the world around them. The symbols were not just abstract representations; they were active agents, imbued with the power to influence, to protect, to maintain the delicate equilibrium of Kilkenny.

"The 'Chronicles'," he mused aloud, "they were more than just history books, weren't they? They were guides, handbooks of these ancient practices."

Aine smiled, a gentle, knowing expression. "Precisely. They contain the knowledge, the lineage's understanding of these symbols and their application. But knowledge alone is not enough. It requires the will, the dedication, and the personal resonance of the one who wields it. The symbols are the framework, but the intent, the focused energy of the practitioner, breathes life into them. Without that, they are merely ink on parchment, or carvings on wood."

She then began to gather the Lumin vial and the embroidered cloth with a practiced grace, her movements still economical and deliberate. The air in the clearing felt charged, alive with a subtle hum that Pete could now more readily attribute to the carefully arranged elements and the focused intent of Aine. He felt a profound sense of privilege, not just to be present, but to be learning the deeper truths behind the ancient practices, truths that were etched not just in texts, but in the very fabric of Kilkenny itself. The symbols, once abstract images, were now revealed as the keystones of a living, breathing tradition of protection, a testament to the enduring power of intentionality and the deep, spiritual bond between humanity and the natural world. He understood that the ongoing safeguarding of Kilkenny was an active, continuous process, woven from the threads of history, the flow of natural energies, and the unwavering commitment of those who understood its true, ethereal worth.

AINES ANCESTRAL CONNECTION

Pete watched, mesmerized, as Aine's hands moved with an almost ethereal grace, tracing unseen patterns in the air above the Hearth Cloth. The Lumin oil shimmered, catching the dappled sunlight and refracting it into a kaleidoscope of muted colors. He felt a strange, resonant hum in the air, a subtle vibration that seemed to emanate from the very earth beneath his feet. It wasn't just the carefully chosen objects or the intricate symbols on the cloth that held his attention; it was Aine herself, her posture, the focused intensity in her eyes, the way her breath seemed to synchronize with the gentle rustling of the leaves overhead.

"Can you feel it, Pete?" Aine's voice, barely a whisper, cut through the quietude. "The echoes?"

He wasn't entirely sure what she meant, but he felt... something. A heightened awareness, perhaps. A subtle shift in the atmosphere, as if the veil between worlds had thinned, allowing a different kind of presence to seep into the clearing. He nodded, unable to articulate the vague, stirring sensations within him.

Aine closed her eyes, her brow furrowed slightly in concentration. Her lips moved, forming words that were too soft to be understood, yet carried an undeniable power. It was as if she were speaking a forgotten language, one that resonated with the ancient stones and the deep, pulsating heart of Kilkenny. Pete watched as her shoulders relaxed, a subtle softening in her expression.

"They are here," she murmured, opening her eyes and looking not at him, but towards the ancient trees that ringed the clearing. Her gaze seemed to pierce through the foliage, as if beholding something far beyond the physical realm. "My ancestors. They are watching. They are... lending their strength."

He could almost see it – a subtle shimmer around her, like heat rising from a summer road, but cooler, imbued with an ancient wisdom. It was as if the very air around Aine was alive, vibrating with a borrowed energy, a heritage made manifest. The symbols on the Hearth Cloth, which had seemed to pulse with their own inner light moments before, now seemed to draw even more intensely from her presence. The interwoven roots, the flowing rivers, the celestial patterns – they all seemed to deepen in their luminescence, their significance amplified by the spiritual current she was tapping into.

"It's like... a conversation," Aine continued, her voice filled with a quiet awe. "A continuation. They walked this land, they felt its pulse, they understood its needs. And they passed that understanding down, generation after generation. This ritual, these symbols, this place... they are not merely remnants of the past, Pete. They are living continuations. Their wisdom isn't confined to the 'Chronicles.' It flows through me, through my blood, through the very act of performing this duty."

He understood then, with a clarity that struck him like a physical blow, that his earlier fascination with the 'Chronicles' wasn't just a casual interest in history. It was a subconscious recognition of a living legacy, a faint echo of a connection that transcended mere textual knowledge. The stylized trees, the swirling water motifs, the distant stars he'd seen depicted in faded ink – they were more than just illustrations; they were signposts, pointing towards this very moment, this very communion. They were part of a grander design, a sacred geometry that underpinned the existence of Kilkenny, a design that was not static but dynamically maintained by those who understood its energetic heart.

"When I touch these symbols," Aine explained, her voice growing stronger, more resonant, "I feel their presence most keenly. The roots... they are my grandmother's hands, steady and sure, grounding me. The rivers are the guidance of my mother, flowing with intuition and adaptability. The stars... they are the ancient ones, the first custodians, their wisdom a beacon from across the ages."

She looked at Pete, her eyes alight with a profound understanding. "It's not just about performing the actions, Pete. It's about embodying the intent, channeling the inherited knowledge and the collective strength. My ancestors are not ghosts watching from afar; they are present, participating. They are lending their energy, their experience, their very essence to this task. It's a shared guardianship, a living pact renewed with each ritual."

The intricate embroidery on the Hearth Cloth suddenly took on a new dimension for Pete. He saw not just patterns, but a tapestry of lineage, each thread representing a life lived, a duty fulfilled, a connection forged. The Lumin oil wasn't just an enhancer; it was a bridge, making the spiritual conduit more permeable, allowing the energies of the past to flow more freely into the present. The 'Chronicles' hadn't just been a repository of information; they were a testament to this ongoing, unbroken chain of guardianship, a detailed map of how to maintain that vital connection.

"The stones," Aine continued, picking up a smooth, grey stone, its surface cool and worn by time. "These are not just rocks. This one... this speaks of my great-uncle. He was a man of immense patience, of unwavering steadfastness. He understood the importance of holding firm, of providing a stable foundation, even when storms raged. He would have placed this stone here, feeling the strength of the earth beneath him, drawing on its resilience."

She placed the stone with deliberate care, her movements imbued with a reverence that transcended mere ritualistic action. It was an act of remembrance, an act of communion, an act of continuous stewardship. Pete watched as she picked up another, a reddish-brown one, and then another, a pale, almost white quartz. Each stone seemed to evoke a different feeling, a different resonance within her, and within him.

"The earthy brown ones," she said, holding one up, "are for grounding, for stability. They represent the strength of those who built, who labored, who made this land their own through sheer grit and determination. They are the unyielding roots, anchoring Kilkenny. My father's hands," she added, a fond smile touching her lips, "were strong and sure, like these stones. He understood the importance of a solid foundation, of building with purpose and integrity."

Pete found himself understanding the meticulous placement of each stone in a completely new light. It wasn't just about creating a perimeter; it was about layering defenses, each stone a unique guardian, imbued not only with symbolic meaning but with the essence of the ancestors who had understood and utilized those meanings. He recalled the stories he'd read in the 'Chronicles,' tales of ancient peoples who communicated with the land through intricate patterns and sacred objects, individuals who were not just storytellers but practitioners, weavers of energy and intent. He was witnessing such a practice firsthand, a living testament to a tradition stretching back through the mists of time, a tradition that was not dead and buried but vibrantly, powerfully alive.

"And the raven's feather," Aine murmured, her fingers brushing against its dark, glossy surface. "The raven. It's a symbol of keen perception, of the ability to see what others miss, to navigate the liminal spaces. My aunt, she possessed such a gift. She could sense shifts in the land, subtle warnings, whispers of change. She was the one who taught me to listen, truly listen, to the quiet voices that speak from the heart of Kilkenny. This feather is her connection, her ability to bridge the unseen realms, to carry our intentions and to bring back understanding."

She held it aloft, and Pete felt a faint breeze stir, though the leaves above remained still. It was as if the very air acknowledged the feather's purpose, the subtle communication it facilitated. The raven, in its symbolism, was not merely an observer but an active participant, a messenger that carried the weight of intention across the boundaries of perception.

"The obsidian shard," Aine continued, her voice taking on a more solemn tone as she handled the dark, volcanic glass. "A powerful purifier, a shield against negativity. This belonged to my great-grandmother. She faced immense challenges, darker times when Kilkenny's very essence was threatened. She understood the need for protection, for absorbing and neutralizing harm. This obsidian is her strength, her resilience made manifest, a ward against any force that would seek to disrupt the balance, to sow discord. It's a reflection of the darkness, but also its antidote."

He watched as she placed the obsidian shard at the edge of the Hearth Cloth, its dark, polished surface a stark counterpoint to the luminous embroidery. It was a powerful visual reminder of the duality inherent in safeguarding any place of power – the necessity of both attracting positive energies and repelling those that were harmful. It was a tangible manifestation of the ancient wisdom that protection required not just fortification, but also purification and discernment.

"And finally," Aine said, her gaze lingering on the small, carved wooden key, "the key. This is the most personal, the most direct link. It was passed down through my family for generations, a symbol of lineage, of trust, of the sacred duty we bear. The carvings on it are a condensed form of the very symbols on this cloth, a miniature representation of the entire safeguarding philosophy. When I place this here," she held it over the central star of the Hearth Cloth, "it is an affirmation. It is the seal of authority, the tangible expression of our inherited right and responsibility. It signifies the culmination of intent, the binding of our will to the ancient pacts that protect Kilkenny."

Pete felt a profound sense of understanding wash over him. Each object, each symbol, was not merely a component of the ritual; it was a living link to his ancestors, a conduit through which their strength, their wisdom, and their lived experience flowed. They were not static reminders of the past, but dynamic participants in the present, actively lending their energies to the ongoing task of safeguarding Kilkenny. The entire setup was a symphony of intention, a meticulously orchestrated performance designed not just to channel energy, but to resonate with the very soul of the land, a soul that was interwoven with the lives and spirits of those who had come before.

"The combination of these elements," Aine explained, her gaze sweeping across the prepared site, her voice gaining a quiet power, "creates a multifaceted system of protection, a living legacy. The Boundary Stones define the sacred space, each one a guardian imbued with the spirit of those who understood the land's needs. The Hearth Cloth is the heart, the nexus where all these energies converge, its symbols a map of Kilkenny's energetic essence and a diagram of its preservation. The Lumin oil awakens and enhances these energies, making them receptive to our intent. The raven's feather serves as a messenger, bridging the gap between our actions and the unseen world, carrying whispers of guidance and warning. The obsidian shard acts as a purifier and a shield, absorbing and neutralizing any harmful influences, a testament to the resilience of those who faced darkness. And the key," she held it up for a moment, the light catching its polished surface, "is the final affirmation, the seal of authority, the tangible connection to the unbroken chain of custodianship."

She paused, her eyes meeting Pete's, a quiet intensity in their depths. "These symbols, Pete, are the distilled wisdom of centuries, not just knowledge but living energies that respond to focused intent. They are the language of preservation, the grammar of guardianship, passed down through generations. My ancestors understood that protecting Kilkenny required more than just physical barriers; it required a deep understanding of its energetic heart, and the ability to communicate with and influence the subtle forces that sustained it. They understood that the past was not a history to be read, but a living force to be continually channeled and integrated into the present."

He found himself nodding slowly, a profound respect for Aine and her lineage deepening with each word. He had always believed in the power of stories, in the weight of tradition, but this was something far more tangible, something rooted in a direct, almost visceral connection to the world around them, a connection that spanned across time. The symbols were not just abstract representations; they were active agents, imbued with the power to influence, to protect, to maintain the delicate equilibrium of Kilkenny, each one a testament to the enduring power of intentionality and the deep, spiritual bond between humanity and the natural world, a bond that was actively maintained and renewed by the living legacy of her ancestors.

"The 'Chronicles'," he mused aloud, the pieces clicking into place with a satisfying finality, "they were more than just history books, weren't they? They were guides, handbooks of these ancient practices, a testament to the living lineage of protection."

Aine smiled, a gentle, knowing expression that seemed to hold the warmth of generations. "Precisely. They contain the knowledge, the lineage's understanding of these symbols and their application.

But knowledge alone is not enough. It requires the will, the dedication, and the personal resonance of the one who wields it, the one who embodies the lineage. The symbols are the framework, the inherited structure, but the intent, the focused energy of the practitioner, breathes life into them. Without that, they are merely ink on parchment, or carvings on wood, echoes without a voice."

She then began to gather the Lumin vial and the embroidered cloth with a practiced grace, her movements still economical and deliberate, the air in the clearing feeling charged, alive with a subtle hum that Pete could now readily attribute to the carefully arranged elements and the focused intent of Aine, a hum that was amplified by the palpable presence of her ancestors. He felt a profound sense of privilege, not just to be present, but to be learning the deeper truths behind the ancient practices, truths that were etched not just in texts but in the very fabric of Kilkenny itself, truths that spoke of a living, breathing tradition of protection, a testament to the enduring power of intentionality and the deep, spiritual bond between humanity and the natural world, a bond that was actively woven, thread by thread, by those who understood its true, ethereal worth. The ongoing safeguarding of Kilkenny was an active, continuous process, a dialogue between the present and the past, a testament to the enduring strength found in connection, both to the land and to the generations who had sworn to protect it.

THE EXTERNAL OBSERVER

The air, still vibrating with the residual energy of Aine's communion, seemed to crackle with an unspoken awareness. Pete, his senses still heightened from the ritual, felt it first – a prickling on the back of his neck, a subtle shift in the periphery of his vision. He turned his head slowly, scanning the dense foliage that bordered the clearing. It was then he saw him.

Deeper within the shadows cast by the ancient oaks, a figure stood, almost unnervingly still. The distance obscured any clear features, but the posture was unmistakable: an observer, rooted and watchful. The way the individual was positioned, partially obscured by the gnarled branches, spoke of deliberate concealment, a desire not to be seen, yet an undeniable presence that couldn't be ignored. The dappled sunlight, which had moments before seemed to illuminate the sacred nature of their undertaking, now served to highlight the enigmatic intruder, casting them in a disquieting chiaroscuro. There was no overt aggression in their stance, no aggressive posture, yet the sheer fact of their silent vigil was more unnerving than any shouted challenge could have been. It was the quiet, unwavering gaze that Pete felt most acutely, a sensation of being scrutinized, measured, and cataloged from a distance.

Aine, her own focus momentarily broken, followed Pete's gaze. A subtle tension entered her shoulders, a minute tightening around her jaw that betrayed her own awareness of the intrusion. Her eyes, so recently filled with the light of ancestral connection, now held a flicker of appraisal, a cautious assessment of this uninvited witness. She didn't speak, her silence a testament to the gravity of the situation. The ritual had been about connection, about the tangible presence of the past lending strength to the present. This new presence, however, was an unknown variable, a disruption to the carefully orchestrated harmony.

The observer remained at the treeline, a silhouette against the vibrant green. Their stillness was profound, as if they were as much a part of the ancient woods as the trees themselves. Pete tried to discern any details – clothing, equipment, anything that might offer a clue to their identity or purpose. But the shadows and the distance were too effective a shroud. Whoever it was, they were skilled in remaining unseen, their observation a deliberate, calculated act. The thought that their entire ritual, their sacred communion, had been witnessed by a stranger, an outsider whose intentions were completely unknown, sent a shiver of unease down Pete's spine. This was not the welcoming embrace of the ancestral spirits; this was the unblinking eye of the present, or perhaps something else entirely.

"Who is that?" Pete's whisper was barely audible, the question feeling both urgent and futile. The figure offered no response, no movement that could be interpreted as acknowledgment or threat. They simply continued to watch, a silent sentinel in the encroaching twilight. The clearing, moments before a sanctuary of inherited power and spiritual communion, now felt exposed, vulnerable. The ancient stones, the Hearth Cloth, the very air that had thrummed with the presence of Aine's ancestors, now seemed to hold a new kind of tension, one born of external scrutiny.

Aine finally broke the silence, her voice low and measured, devoid of the earlier awe. "Someone who has found us. Or perhaps, someone we have alerted them to." She didn't elaborate on the latter, but the implication hung heavy in the air. Had the very act of channeling such potent energy, of opening such a deep connection to the land and its guardians, drawn unwanted attention? The power they had invoked, the intimate dialogue with the past, was now laid bare to an unknown entity. It was a stark reminder that their work, however vital, was not conducted in a vacuum. The threads of connection they wove with the past were also visible, perhaps even tangible, to those who knew where and how to look in the present.

The observer's stillness was almost defiant. They weren't attempting to hide any longer; their concealment was now a statement, a declaration of their detached, yet undeniably present, observation. It was the kind of stillness that suggested patience, an unhurried assessment. They were not here to rush, nor to provoke. They were here to witness, to understand, or perhaps, to wait for the right moment. The ambiguity was the most unsettling aspect. Was this a scout for an opposing force, someone seeking to understand their methods and identify vulnerabilities? Or was it a neutral party, perhaps another practitioner of ancient ways, drawn by the surge of energy, seeking to understand the nature of the ritual without interfering? The possibilities, each laced with potential danger or intrigue, churned in Pete's mind.

He tried to re-focus on Aine, on the ritual site. The meticulously placed stones, the luminous oil, the intricate embroidery of the Hearth Cloth – they were all meant to be anchors, conduits. But now, a new element had been introduced, an external observer whose very presence seemed to warp the atmosphere, injecting a subtle paranoia into the sacred space. Were the protective wards, the energetic defenses Aine had so carefully constructed, capable of repelling or even deterring this silent watcher? Or had the openness of the ritual, the very act of reaching out to the ancestors, inadvertently lowered their defenses, making them visible to eyes they had not intended to meet?

Aine, however, seemed to regain a measure of composure, her gaze still fixed on the treeline. Her hand, which had been resting near the obsidian shard, moved almost imperceptibly, not in a gesture of aggression, but perhaps as a subtle reinforcement of intent, a reaffirmation of the wards in place. Her expression was no longer one of surprise, but of a deep, focused resolve. She understood that this was not a moment to falter. The ritual was not complete; its purpose was not yet fulfilled. The presence of the observer was simply another layer of complexity, another challenge to navigate.

"They are not interfering," Aine stated softly, more to herself than to Pete, her voice a low hum that seemed to resonate with the very earth beneath them. "Not yet. They are... observing. Testing the currents, perhaps." She finally shifted her gaze to Pete, her eyes carrying a weight of unspoken understanding. "This is not uncommon, Pete. When significant energies are drawn upon, especially those connected to the land and its ancient guardians, there are always those who are sensitive to such shifts. They are drawn to the confluence, much like moths to a flame, but not all moths are harmless."

Her words, while attempting to normalize the situation, only amplified the underlying tension. The idea that their powerful, ancestral-infused ritual was like a beacon, attracting attention from forces unknown, was a sobering thought. It transformed the intimate act of communion into something far more precarious, a public display of power that could invite both admiration and antagonism. The very depth of their connection, the very reason for performing the ritual, now seemed to be the source of their potential vulnerability.

Pete's mind raced through the possibilities. Was this observer an agent of some clandestine organization, tasked with monitoring or even disrupting such practices? Was it a solitary individual, a rogue practitioner who viewed their lineage and their duty as a threat or an opportunity? Or could it be something else entirely, something connected to the ancient forces Aine so carefully navigated? The mystery of their identity and intent cast a long shadow over the clearing, a disquieting counterpoint to the luminous glow of the Lumin oil and the earnest devotion etched on Aine's face.

He found himself instinctively taking a step closer to Aine, a protective instinct he hadn't realized he possessed. Their shared experience, the journey that had brought them to this hidden clearing, had forged a bond between them, a silent pact of mutual reliance. Whatever this observer represented, they would face it together. The carefully arranged components of the ritual site – the boundary stones, the Hearth Cloth, the potent symbols – were not just for communing with the ancestors; they were also a form of defense, a testament to the need for safeguarding not only Kilkenny's spirit but also their own actions and their lineage from prying eyes and potentially hostile forces.

Aine, sensing his subtle shift in posture, offered a small, almost imperceptible nod. Her focus returned to the task at hand, but a new layer of vigilance had been added to her movements. Each placement of a stone, each touch of the embroidered cloth, was now performed with a heightened awareness of the unseen eyes upon them. The ritual was no longer just about invoking the past; it was also about demonstrating resilience, about showing that even under observation, their purpose remained steadfast and their connection to Kilkenny's ancient protectors was unwavering.

The observer remained a silent statue at the edge of the woods. Their stillness was so profound that Pete began to doubt his own senses. Had he imagined it? Was it merely a trick of the light, a shadow cast by the setting sun? But then, he saw it – a subtle inclination of the head, a movement so slight it could easily have been missed, yet it was unmistakably an acknowledgement of their presence, a confirmation that they were indeed being watched. It was a silent, chilling communication that passed between the observer and the observed, a recognition of shared space and unknown intentions.

The ritual continued, the rhythm of Aine's actions a steady counterpoint to the unnerving stillness of the observer. Each chanted word, each carefully placed object, felt like a deliberate statement, a reaffirmation of their right to be there, to perform this sacred duty. The strength Aine drew from her ancestors was not just for the task of safeguarding Kilkenny; it was also for meeting this unexpected challenge, for holding firm against the unseen pressure of being watched. The 'Chronicles,' Pete realized, had likely detailed such occurrences, perhaps even provided strategies for dealing with external scrutiny. This was not just an ancient practice; it was a living tradition, one that encountered challenges as dynamic and unpredictable as the present day.

He wondered what the observer saw. Did they perceive the subtle luminescence of the Lumin oil, the faint shimmer that emanated from the Hearth Cloth? Did they feel the shift in the air, the hum of ancestral energy that Pete himself could now sense so acutely? Or were they merely seeing a woman performing a series of seemingly arbitrary actions in a secluded clearing? The observer's perspective was a complete mystery, and that, Pete found, was the most unsettling aspect of all. Their motivations were as opaque as the shadows that concealed them, their purpose as unreadable as the ancient symbols Aine so reverently handled.

The silence stretched, punctuated only by the soft sounds of the ritual and the rustling of leaves that seemed to whisper secrets of their own. Pete found himself stealing glances towards the treeline, his gaze drawn to the solitary figure. There was a strange duality to the situation: the profound intimacy of Aine's communion with her ancestors, and the cold, detached presence of the outsider. It was a potent reminder that even in moments of deep spiritual connection, the physical world, with its unpredictable elements and its hidden observers, continued to exert its influence.

Aine, having completed the final placement of an object – a small, intricately carved bird of wood – took a deep, steadying breath. Her eyes, however, remained fixed on the treeline, her posture radiating a quiet strength, an unwavering commitment to the completion of her duty, regardless of the watchful eyes upon them.

The energy within the clearing felt amplified now, not just by the ancestral presence, but by the deliberate defiance of this intrusion. It was as if the ritual itself was becoming a declaration, a testament to their resilience and their unwavering purpose in the face of unknown scrutiny. The observer was a silent challenge, and Aine was meeting it with the quiet, unyielding power of her lineage. The ritual, and their vigilance, was far from over.

Chapter Twelve: The Unseen Force

THE MANIFESTATION OF ENERGY

The air in the clearing, which had only moments before been charged with the solemnity of Aine's communion with her ancestors, began to acquire a new quality. It was a subtle, almost imperceptible shift at first, like the faintest whisper of a vibration felt deep within the bone. Pete, his senses still acutely attuned to the spectral echoes of the ritual, registered it as a peculiar pressure, an invisible weight pressing in from all sides. It wasn't a force to be reckoned with in terms of physical resistance, but rather a sensory anomaly, a disturbance in the usual fabric of reality that made the hairs on his arms stand on end. He glanced at Aine, seeking confirmation, and saw in her eyes a mirroring of his own apprehension, a shared awareness of this burgeoning, uninvited presence.

This burgeoning energy was unlike the vibrant, ancestral power that had flowed through Aine, a power that felt ancient and deeply rooted, like the very earth beneath their feet. This new sensation was different. It was less a tangible presence and more an atmospheric anomaly, a distortion in the ambient light that made the dappled sunlight filtering through the oak leaves seem to flicker and waver, as if viewed through rippling water. A low, resonant hum, almost subliminal, began to weave its way into the background noise of the forest, a sound that seemed to emanate not from any specific source, but from the very air itself. It was a sound that vibrated not in the ears, but in the chest, a deep thrumming that spoke of unseen currents stirring.

Aine, her gaze still fixed on the treeline where the silent observer remained, slowly shifted her weight. Her movements were fluid and deliberate, a testament to her ingrained practice of maintaining composure in the face of the unexpected. "It is manifesting," she murmured, her voice barely a breath, yet carrying the weight of profound understanding. "The confluence is growing stronger. This is the energy that Kilkenny itself emanates, a life force that has always been present, but which our lineage has learned to interact with, to channel." She paused, her eyes scanning the clearing as if tracing invisible lines of power. "It is not inherently good or evil, Pete. It simply is. A testament to the land's unique nature, its connection to the ethereal."

Pete tried to process her words, his mind struggling to reconcile the esoteric with the tangible. He could feel it now, more strongly. The prickling on his skin intensified, evolving into a sensation akin to a mild static shock, a tingling awareness that permeated his entire being. The very air seemed to thicken, to become more viscous, as if he were wading through a subtly resistant medium. He found himself unconsciously flexing his fingers, as if trying to grasp or understand this intangible force. It was as if the world, for a fleeting moment, had been rendered more... potent. The familiar sights and sounds of the forest were still there, but they were overlaid with this new, vibrant sensory experience. The green of the leaves seemed more vivid, the scent of damp earth more pronounced, the silence between the chirps of birds more resonant.

"It feels... alive," Pete managed to articulate, his voice hushed with awe and a touch of trepidation. He looked at his own hands, expecting to see some visible aura or emanation, but there was nothing. It was an internal sensation, a profound shift in his perception of the world around him. He could sense the latent power in the stones, the residual energy clinging to the Hearth Cloth, but this was different. This was a more pervasive, all-encompassing energy, an emanation from Kilkenny itself, a confirmation of its ancient, mystical heart.

Aine nodded, her focus unwavering. "Kilkenny is not merely a place, Pete. It is a nexus, a point where the veil between worlds is thin. Our ancestors understood this. They didn't just protect the land; they protected the very essence of its spiritual vibrancy. This energy... it is the echo of that protection, and of the inherent power that draws people like our observer, and forces like the ones we must guard against." She gestured subtly towards the treeline. "The summoning of ancestral power, the opening of these channels, it does not occur in a vacuum. It draws attention. It makes the inherent magic of this place more... manifest."

He watched as Aine traced a complex pattern in the air with her fingertip, a movement that seemed to create invisible ripples. The hum in the air seemed to respond, to momentarily intensify before subsiding back into its steady thrum. It was as if she were interacting with the energy, not just observing it. He wondered what she saw, what she felt in those subtle movements. Was she reading the flow of power, gauging its intensity, or perhaps attempting to shape it in some way? The thought that she could manipulate such an elemental force, that it was intrinsically linked to her lineage and her very being, was both humbling and deeply impressive.

The observer, still a silent sentinel at the edge of the woods, seemed to be a focal point, a silent anchor for this ambient energy. Pete wondered if their presence was a deliberate act of drawing upon this power, or if they were simply a sensitive recipient, a witness to its unfolding. The stillness of the figure was almost a testament to their own inner resilience, their ability to withstand the surge of raw, untamed energy that was now making the clearing feel both sacred and potentially volatile. It was a raw display of Kilkenny's unique nature, a reminder that its history was not solely etched in stone and parchment, but also in the very energetic currents that flowed through it.

"The 'Chronicles'," Pete mused aloud, his gaze drifting back to the ancient stones that marked the perimeter of their ritual space, "they must speak of this, of how this energy manifests. How to interpret it, how to use it, or perhaps, how to shield against it." He felt a surge of intellectual curiosity, a desire to understand the mechanics of this phenomenon, to place it within a framework of knowledge, however ancient and esoteric. The idea that a place could possess such a palpable, living energy was a concept that his rational mind was still grappling with, but his senses were in full agreement.

Aine met his gaze, a faint smile touching her lips. "They do. And much more. The manifestation of this energy is not merely an observation, Pete. It is a constant factor in our work. It is the foundation upon which all other protective measures are built. Think of it as the very air that Kilkenny breathes, the lifeblood that nourishes its ancient spirit. Our rituals, our wards, they are all designed to work in harmony with this energy, to harness its protective qualities, and to prevent it from being exploited or corrupted." She then gestured towards the Hearth Cloth, its intricate embroidery seemingly glowing with an inner light. "The patterns on the cloth, the oils we use, the stones we place – they are all attuned to this specific energetic signature. They act as conduits, amplifiers, and shields, all at once."

The observer remained, their stillness a stark contrast to the dynamic energy now suffusing the clearing. Pete found himself observing them with a renewed sense of purpose. Were they drawn by this very energy? Was their presence an attempt to understand, to replicate, or perhaps even to control it? The ambiguity of their motives, coupled with the tangible presence of this powerful, elemental force, created a potent blend of intrigue and unease. He felt a sense of responsibility settling upon him, a dawning realization that his role was not just to assist Aine, but to be a conscious witness to the fundamental forces at play, and to the individuals who sought to interact with them.

"It's... like Kilkenny is singing," Pete whispered, the analogy feeling strangely apt. The low hum had deepened, and the prickling sensation on his skin had intensified, coalescing into a warm, vibrant buzz that seemed to emanate from within his own body. He could feel a connection forming, not just to Aine, but to the very essence of the place. It was a subtle, almost imperceptible joining, a thread of awareness woven into the larger tapestry of the clearing's energy. This was the "unseen force" the chapter title hinted at, not a singular entity, but a pervasive, elemental power that permeated every aspect of Kilkenny's existence.

Aine's gaze softened as she met his. "A beautiful way to describe it, Pete. And it is our duty to ensure that the song remains harmonious, that it is heard by those who respect its ancient melody, and that it is protected from those who would seek to twist its notes into discord." She then turned her attention back to the ritual space, her movements becoming more purposeful, more charged with intention. The subtle gestures she made seemed to coax the very air around them, the energy responding to her unspoken commands. It was a silent dialogue between a guardian and the spirit of the land, a testament to generations of stewardship. The energy wasn't just a passive phenomenon; it was a responsive force, capable of being influenced by those attuned to its frequencies. This made their task all the more daunting and, in a way, exhilarating. The act of protection was not just about erecting barriers, but about actively engaging with and guiding the intrinsic powers of Kilkenny.

The observer remained a shadow at the periphery, their stillness a constant, unnerving presence. But now, Pete felt less afraid and more determined. The palpable energy humming around them was not a threat; it was a validation. It was proof of the ancient power they were safeguarding, the very reason for their presence in this secluded clearing. This was not just a historical duty; it was a living, breathing responsibility, intrinsically tied to the very essence of Kilkenny. The manifestation of this energy was a clear sign that their work was indeed vital, and that the forces they guarded against were real. The raw, vibrant power of Kilkenny was now a tangible, undeniable presence, and Pete felt a new sense of purpose solidify within him. He was no longer just an observer; he was becoming a participant, a protector of this ancient, unseen force.

AINES CHANNELING ABILITIES

The air crackled around Aine, not with the volatile, untamed energy Pete had initially sensed, but with a focused, disciplined power. Her stance shifted, becoming more rooted, more grounded. It wasn't just physical posture; Pete sensed a deeper anchoring, as if her very essence had sunk tendrils into the earth, drawing strength from Kilkenny's ancient heart. Her hands, which had been held loosely at her sides, now moved with an almost balletic grace, tracing arcs and patterns in the air that seemed to ripple the very atmosphere. These weren't random gestures; each movement was imbued with intention, a silent language spoken to the forces that were now so palpably present.

"This," Aine began, her voice a low, resonant hum that seemed to blend with the ambient thrum of the clearing, "is what my lineage has always been attuned to. It's not merely about sensing the energy, Pete. It's about understanding its nature, its ebb and flow, and learning to guide it, to shape it for a purpose." She paused, a faint smile gracing her lips as she drew a shimmering thread of light from the air between her palms, coiling it like a luminous rope. "It's an inheritance, yes, but one that requires constant refinement, ceaseless dedication. My ancestors didn't just pass down the knowledge; they passed down the responsibility of mastering it."

Pete watched, mesmerized. He had witnessed rituals before, the careful preparation, the invoking of ancient rites, but this was different. This was Aine not just performing a ritual, but embodying the power. The energy wasn't something she was merely touching; it was flowing through her, a conduit for something vast and profound. He could see the strain, the immense focus required, etched faintly on her brow, but beneath it was an unwavering strength, a deep well of resilience that spoke of generations of practice. The sheer force she wielded, the control she exerted, was breathtaking. It was as if she were a conductor, and the very essence of Kilkenny was her orchestra, responding to her every subtle cue.

"The 'Chronicles' detail the initial discovery of this connection," she continued, her eyes now glowing with a soft, internal light, "how our forebears first learned to perceive and interact with Kilkenny's inherent vibrance. They speak of the early struggles, the mistakes, the price of even the slightest miscalculation. It's a history written not just in ink, but in the very energetic imprints left upon the land, imprints that I can now read, and, to some extent, influence." She then gestured with her free hand, and the luminous thread she held pulsed, sending ripples of warmth through the clearing. "This isn't magic in the way most people understand it – spells and incantations conjured from nothing. This is about recognizing the latent power that exists, understanding its composition, and then carefully, precisely, redirecting its flow."

He felt a surge of awe mixed with a profound sense of humility. He had always seen Aine as a scholar, a guardian of ancient lore, but this revealed a dimension to her he hadn't fully grasped. Her strength wasn't just intellectual; it was primal, elemental. She was a living testament to the enduring power of lineage, a bridge between the past and the present, carrying the weight of centuries of knowledge and practice. The sheer responsibility of it all, the constant vigilance required to wield such forces without succumbing to their potential for destruction, settled upon him with a new, palpable weight. He understood now, on a deeper level, why she dedicated her life to this place, to this sacred duty.

"The way you manipulate it... it's like you're breathing it in and out," Pete ventured, struggling to find words adequate to describe the spectacle. "It doesn't seem like you're forcing it, more like... coaxing it. Persuading it." He watched as she gathered more of the ambient energy, weaving it into the luminous thread until it pulsed with a brilliant, steady light. The hum in the air seemed to harmonize with her actions, a subtle crescendo that resonated deep within his bones. It was as if the very fabric of reality was bending to her will, not out of subservience, but out of a shared understanding, a harmonious accord.

Aine offered a wry smile. "Coaxing and persuading are indeed good words, Pete. Force, in this context, is often counterproductive. It's akin to trying to dam a river with your bare hands – you might momentarily hold it back, but the pressure will build, and the eventual surge will be far more destructive. My training involved learning to understand the river's natural course, to build channels and redirects that guide its power safely, efficiently." She then brought the glowing thread closer, and he could see intricate patterns swirling within its luminescence, like miniature constellations. "Each energy signature, each vibration, has its own unique rhythm. My task is to identify those rhythms, to attune myself to them, and then to interweave my own intent with theirs."

He felt a pang of concern. The focus and effort required were clearly immense. He wondered if she ever felt overwhelmed, if the sheer scale of the forces she commanded ever threatened to consume her. But then he saw the unwavering resolve in her eyes, the steady set of her jaw, and he knew that her commitment was absolute. She had accepted this burden, not with reluctance, but with a profound sense of purpose. It was a duty she embraced, a legacy she honored with every fiber of her being. The ancient wisdom wasn't just in the texts she studied; it was in the very way she moved, in the quiet confidence with which she navigated these unseen currents.

"And this is what the observer is watching?" Pete asked, his gaze drifting towards the treeline where the silent figure remained, a stark silhouette against the dappled sunlight. "They are witnessing you, essentially, interacting with the soul of Kilkenny?"

Aine nodded, her focus shifting momentarily to the observer, then back to the energy she was shaping. "They are witnessing one aspect of it. My channeling of Kilkenny's energy is a fundamental part of our protective work, a way to understand and reinforce the wards that safeguard this place. But it is also a demonstration. A declaration, if you will. A clear signal to those who might seek to exploit this power that it is actively guarded, and that its guardians are deeply attuned to its every nuance." She tightened her grip on the luminous thread, and it seemed to condense, becoming more solid, yet retaining its inner radiance. "The more adept one becomes at channeling, the more visible the energy becomes to those sensitive to it. It's a way of saying, 'We are here. We are strong. And we are watching.'"

The implications of her words settled heavily on Pete. This wasn't just an academic exercise; it was a high-stakes game of influence and protection, played out on a battlefield of unseen forces. Aine's abilities were not merely a tool; they were a statement of intent, a powerful deterrent. The clarity with which she demonstrated her control was a message in itself, a testament to the depth of her understanding and the formidable power she could command. He felt a renewed appreciation for the vigilance and dedication required to maintain the balance, to protect Kilkenny from forces that would undoubtedly seek to corrupt or consume its unique essence.

"It's... incredible, Aine," Pete admitted, his voice barely above a whisper. "The depth of your connection, the sheer force you can wield. It's far more than I could have ever imagined." He felt a growing sense of respect, not just for her knowledge, but for the immense personal strength and discipline she possessed. This was a power that could easily corrupt, a path that could lead to arrogance or obsession, but Aine navigated it with grace and unwavering purpose. She was a protector, a guardian, and her abilities were the very embodiment of that role.

She finally released the channeled energy, allowing it to dissipate back into the ambient atmosphere, leaving behind a faint, pleasant warmth. The intense hum subsided to its previous, more subtle thrum, but the air still felt charged, invigorated. Aine took a deep, steadying breath, her gaze serene yet sharpened by the exertion. "The power of Kilkenny is a gift, Pete, and like all gifts, it comes with profound responsibilities. My ancestors understood this, and it is my duty to continue that understanding, to ensure that this unique vitality is preserved, and that its song remains a melody of protection, not a siren's call to those who would seek to exploit it." She met Pete's gaze, her eyes reflecting a quiet strength and an ancient wisdom that transcended mere years. "This is not a burden, Pete. It is my life's work. And it is a work that requires constant vigilance, unwavering commitment, and a deep understanding of the unseen forces that shape our world."

THE THREAT MATERIALIZES

The clearing, moments before a sanctuary of focused energy and ancient power, now felt... sullied. Pete's senses, still buzzing from the residual charge of Aine's channeling, prickled with a new, unwelcome sensation. It wasn't the raw, vibrant pulse of Kilkenny that he had become accustomed to, but something discordant, a subtle dissonance that grated against his very nerves. Aine, too, seemed to sense it. Her serene expression tightened, her eyes, moments ago alight with the internal glow of her lineage's power, now narrowed, scanning the periphery of the clearing with a hunter's keenness. The rhythmic thrum of the land, which had harmonized with her actions, now seemed to falter, as if a discordant note had been struck in a symphony.

A sudden, unnatural chill swept through the clearing, a gust of wind that seemed to originate from nowhere and everywhere at once. It rustled the leaves overhead with a dry, papery sound, devoid of the gentle breath of nature. Pete instinctively pulled his jacket tighter, not from the cold itself, but from the palpable wrongness of its intrusion. It wasn't the bracing air of a passing cloud, but a frigid breath that seemed to carry an alien intent. It swirled around Aine, a predatory caress that seemed to probe and test her defenses, seeking a weakness. She didn't flinch, but her stance subtly shifted again, her feet a fraction wider apart, her hands now held in a defensive posture, palms outward as if warding off an unseen blow.

"It's here," Aine murmured, her voice a low, dangerous whisper that cut through the unnatural silence. The luminous thread she had previously held had dissipated, its energy reclaimed by the land, but the air around her remained charged, not with her own power, but with a heightened alertness, a readiness for confrontation. Pete's gaze darted towards the treeline, his heart thudding a frantic rhythm against his ribs. He saw nothing, yet he felt a presence, a heavy, observing weight that settled upon the clearing like a shroud. It was the feeling of being watched, not by curious eyes, but by something ancient and calculating.

"What is it?" Pete asked, his voice rough with apprehension. He felt a primal urge to find cover, to retreat to the safety of numbers, but Aine's unwavering focus held him rooted, a reluctant witness to this escalating tension. He trusted her implicitly, but the sheer palpable wrongness of this new presence sent a tremor of fear through him. It was a stark contrast to the comforting, if powerful, energy of Kilkenny that Aine had been channeling. This was an invasive force, unwelcome and menacing.

Aine didn't answer immediately. Her head tilted slightly, as if listening to something beyond the range of normal hearing. Her brow furrowed, not in confusion, but in deep concentration, her mind actively engaging with this intruder. "It's not a raw force," she finally said, her voice tight with a controlled intensity. "It's... directed. Intentional. Someone knows we're here, Pete. And they don't like it." The implication hung heavy in the air. Their actions, Aine's demonstration of her power and her connection to Kilkenny, had not gone unnoticed. The silent observer from before, the one Aine had gestured towards, was no longer the only unknown element in this equation.

He scanned the dense foliage again, his eyes straining to pierce the verdant curtain. Was the observer the source of this disruption, or were they merely a scout for a larger, more sinister force? The chilling wind picked up again, this time swirling more insistently, carrying with it the faint scent of damp earth and something else... something acrid and metallic, like stale blood. Pete swallowed, the metallic tang on his tongue a physical manifestation of his growing unease. He found himself instinctively checking the ancient pocketknife he carried, a pathetic defense against whatever this unseen enemy might be, but a gesture of ingrained habit nonetheless.

"What do they want?" he pressed, his gaze locked on Aine's face, searching for any hint of fear, any crack in her formidable composure. He found only a steely resolve, a quiet acceptance of the challenge that had materialized.

"That's the question, isn't it?" Aine replied, her voice regaining some of its earlier resonance, though now laced with a steely edge. "They want to disrupt. To interfere. Perhaps to test our defenses. Or perhaps..." She trailed off, her eyes narrowing further as a flicker of movement caught her attention at the very edge of the clearing, a shadow detaching itself from the deeper gloom beneath the ancient oaks. It was too quick, too fluid to be an animal. It moved with a deliberate, almost predatory grace, a phantom darting through the undergrowth, its form indistinct, as if the very light refused to fully illuminate it.

"A fleeting shadow," Pete breathed, a knot of dread tightening in his stomach. He had seen shadows before, of course, the natural play of light and darkness, but this was different. This shadow possessed a velocity and a purpose that defied natural explanation. It seemed to glide rather than run, a smear of darkness against the vibrant green, vanishing and reappearing with disconcerting speed. It was as if the forest itself was a cloak for this entity, a living shroud that concealed its true form.

Aine raised a hand, palm outstretched, as if to calm him, or perhaps to focus her own awareness. "It's a scout," she confirmed, her voice barely audible above the rising murmur of the wind, which seemed to echo the stealthy movements in the trees. "They're assessing. Gathering information. The energy I was channeling... it was too potent, too visible to certain sensitivities. It announced our presence, and our strength." The realization struck Pete with the force of a physical blow. Aine's demonstration of power, meant to assert their protective vigilance, had inadvertently served as a beacon, drawing the very attention they sought to elude. The irony was as bitter as it was dangerous.

"So, we've walked into a trap?" Pete asked, the words tumbling out before he could censor them. The situation had escalated with terrifying speed, from a demonstration of esoteric power to a clandestine confrontation with an unknown enemy. The serene clearing had transformed into a potential battlefield, and they were woefully exposed.

Aine shook her head, her gaze unwavering as she tracked the fleeting movements of the shadow. "Not necessarily a trap. More of an... unwelcome intrusion. They're testing the boundaries, seeing how we react. Their objective is likely to gauge the strength of Kilkenny's defenses, and perhaps to sow discord, to create a vulnerability we can exploit." She gestured subtly, and Pete noticed the leaves around them, those not touched by the unnatural chill, seemed to rustle more purposefully, as if responding to her unspoken command. "They're probing. And we need to show them that their probing will be met with resistance."

The shadow paused for a fleeting moment at the edge of Aine's line of sight, a deeper patch of darkness against the dappled shade. Pete couldn't discern any features, any discernible form, but he felt an intense, almost suffocating sense of malevolence radiating from it. It was a primal fear, the instinctual terror of prey sensing a predator. He wondered if this was what Aine experienced when she first sensed the 'unseen force' – a vague, unsettling awareness that slowly solidified into a concrete threat.

"What kind of resistance?" Pete whispered, his eyes fixed on the spot where the shadow had been. "We can't see them, Aine. How do we fight something we can't even properly perceive?"

A faint, almost imperceptible smile touched Aine's lips, a glint of defiance in her eyes. "We don't need to see them to feel them, Pete. Their presence is a vibration, a disruption. And just as I can attune myself to Kilkenny's energy, I can also sense the discord they bring." She closed her eyes for a brief moment, and Pete saw the faintest tremor pass through her, as if she were calibrating herself to this new, hostile frequency. The air around her seemed to shimmer, not with the gentle light of Kilkenny's power, but with a sharper, more focused energy, like heat haze rising from asphalt.

"They're trying to sow doubt," she continued, opening her eyes, which now held a determined glint. "To make us question ourselves, to make us falter. They're using the very essence of Kilkenny against us, amplifying the natural unease that any ancient place can inspire, twisting it into fear." The chilling wind seemed to gust with renewed vigor, pushing against them, trying to unbalance them. Pete felt a growing unease, a subtle whisper of doubt in the back of his mind, a suggestion that perhaps they were out of their depth, that this was a game too dangerous to play. He consciously pushed the thoughts away, focusing on Aine's steady presence, her unwavering calm.

"They are trying to break the harmony," Aine stated, her voice gaining strength and clarity. "To shatter the resonance. My earlier channeling was about reinforcing that harmony, about demonstrating its resilience. Now, it's about defending it." She took a step forward, her movement fluid and deliberate, and the ground beneath her feet seemed to hum with a latent power, a silent answer to the encroaching disruption. The subtle interference wasn't just a matter of physical sensations; it was a spiritual and energetic assault.

Pete watched, a growing sense of awe mixed with fear. Aine wasn't just a scholar or a guardian; she was a warrior, defending a sacred trust with every fiber of her being. The forces at play were far more complex and dangerous than he had ever imagined. This wasn't just about ancient lore; it was about the present, about a tangible threat that sought to exploit the very essence of the land he had come to know and respect. The stakes had indeed been raised, and the quiet clearing had become the focal point of a silent, unseen war.

He noticed a subtle shift in the atmosphere. The invasive chill didn't entirely recede, but it seemed to be countered by a warmer, more protective aura emanating from Aine. It was as if she were creating a pocket of calm within the encroaching storm. The leaves that had been agitated by the unnatural wind now seemed to settle, their rustling taking on a more natural cadence. The unseen force was still present, its pressure palpable, but Aine's defiance was an anchor, holding steady against the tide of disruption.

"They are assessing the effectiveness of their initial probe," Aine explained, her gaze sharp and focused. "They'll try to escalate, to find a point of fracture. They might try to isolate us, to sow confusion, or even to directly confront us if they believe they have an advantage." The mere thought of a direct confrontation with whatever this shadow represented sent a shiver down Pete's spine. He tried to picture it, to give it form, but it remained stubbornly elusive, a phantom woven from darkness and ill intent.

He felt a growing sense of responsibility, a desire to contribute, to be more than just an observer. "Is there anything I can do?" he asked, his voice firm, betraying none of the fear that still gnawed at him. He wasn't a conduit for ancient energies, but he was resourceful, and he was loyal. He needed to find a way to be useful.

Aine's gaze softened for a fraction of a second, a flicker of gratitude in her eyes. "Your presence here, Pete, is already a form of strength. You are a grounding influence, a witness. But more than that," she continued, her focus returning to the perimeter, "you can be my eyes and ears on the physical plane. Be aware of your surroundings. Notice anything that seems out of place, any disturbance that doesn't quite fit. The unseen force may operate on a different level, but it still interacts with the physical world. A displaced stone, a disturbed patch of earth, a sound that shouldn't be there – these can all be indicators."

Pete nodded, his senses sharpening. He began to meticulously scan the clearing, his gaze sweeping over every detail. The fallen leaves, the gnarled roots of the ancient trees, the faint pathways worn by centuries of wind and rain. He was no longer just appreciating the natural beauty of Kilkenny; he was searching for anomalies, for the subtle signs of intrusion that Aine had described. The unnatural chill was still present, a constant reminder of the hostile presence, but he was also looking for anything that felt wrong on a purely physical level.

Suddenly, his eyes caught on something near the base of a large oak, a few yards from where he stood. It was a disturbance in the moss, a small patch that looked as if it had been recently scraped away, revealing the dark earth beneath. It was subtle, easily missed, but it was undeniably out of place in the otherwise undisturbed ground.

"Aine," Pete said, his voice low and urgent, pointing towards the anomaly. "Look here. This moss... it's been disturbed. Like something was dragged across it, or perhaps something was planted or removed."

Aine turned, following his gaze. Her eyes, still sharp with focus, narrowed as she took in the detail. She moved towards it with a quiet swiftness, her movements economical and precise. She knelt beside the disturbed earth, her fingers hovering just above it before gently touching the exposed soil. She didn't need to excavate; her connection to the land allowed her to perceive far more than mere visual cues.

"You're right," she confirmed, her voice taut with renewed intensity. "This is not natural erosion. It's recent. And it carries a residue... faint, but present. It's the same signature as the wind, the same discordant vibration. They're not just observing, Pete. They're actively interfering. They're leaving their mark, attempting to anchor themselves here, or perhaps to disrupt the existing energetic flows."

The realization that their intrusion was more than just a passive observation, that it involved active manipulation of the physical environment, sent a fresh wave of unease through Pete. This wasn't just a game of psychic warfare; it was a tangible intrusion, a violation of the sanctity of Kilkenny. The threat was materializing, becoming more concrete, and the stakes were rising with every passing moment. The unseen force was no longer a vague presence; it was a tangible enemy, leaving its mark upon the land.

PETES PROTECTIVE INSTINCTS

The subtle disturbance in the moss, a fresh scar on the ancient forest floor, sent a visceral jolt through Pete. It wasn't just the violation of the land itself that struck him, but the stark realization of his own perceived helplessness. Aine was the conduit, the one attuned to the ethereal currents and the whispers of Kilkenny. She could sense the discord, the intentionality, the probing nature of this unseen force. But Pete? He was the earthbound observer, the one tethered to the tangible, the one whose primary defense was his own two feet and a growing, desperate instinct to protect.

He felt it then, a primal urge that resonated deeper than any intellectual understanding. It was the instinct of a guardian, a protector, a desperate need to stand between the one he cared for and the encroaching darkness. Aine, with her quiet strength and the immense power she wielded, was still human, still vulnerable to forces that operated beyond the purely physical. The thought of her being harmed, of that serene focus being shattered by an unseen attacker, ignited a fierce, protective fire within him. He might not possess the ability to manipulate energy or commune with ancient spirits, but he had a body, a will, and a growing, unshakeable commitment to Aine and to the sanctity of Kilkenny.

"Is there anything I can do?" he asked again, the words a low rumble in his chest, his voice devoid of its earlier apprehension, replaced by a steely resolve. His gaze was fixed on Aine, not just searching for answers, but offering a silent, unwavering promise of support. He had always been a follower in these matters, a witness to Aine's extraordinary abilities. But this... this felt different. This felt like a call to action, a demand for him to step out of the shadows and become something more. He would not be a passive spectator to Aine's potential endangerment.

He watched as Aine continued her careful examination of the disturbed earth, her brow furrowed in concentration. The invisible pressure in the air seemed to intensify, a tangible weight pressing down on the clearing, as if the very atmosphere was holding its breath, waiting for a move, a reaction. Pete felt an almost overwhelming urge to physically place himself between Aine and the treeline, to become a living shield, however inadequate. He shifted his weight, his muscles tensing, ready to react to any immediate threat, his eyes scanning the dense foliage with a renewed intensity, searching for any flicker of movement, any anomaly that might betray the unseen enemy's position.

"You are doing what you can, Pete," Aine replied, her voice calm, though the underlying tension was unmistakable. She looked up at him, and for a fleeting moment, he saw a profound depth in her eyes – a mixture of gratitude, concern, and perhaps a touch of regret that he couldn't share the full burden of her abilities. "Your awareness is our first line of defense on this plane. You are my anchor to the physical reality, a reminder of what we are defending."

He understood. His role wasn't to replicate her power, but to complement it. To be the eyes and hands in a world that was suddenly imbued with unseen dangers. He clenched his fists, the rough leather of his gloves a familiar, grounding sensation. He was a stranger to this world of subtle energies and ancient powers, a world that Aine navigated with innate grace and formidable skill. Yet, he was here, standing beside her, drawn into the heart of a conflict he barely understood but felt compelled to be a part of.

The thought solidified: he wasn't just a companion anymore. He was a guardian. It was a role he had never consciously sought, but one that now felt undeniably his. The responsibility settled upon him, not as a burden, but as a commitment. He would not falter. He would not retreat. He would stand with Aine, drawing strength from her resilience, and offering whatever he could – his vigilance, his resolve, his unwavering presence.

"What are we defending, exactly?" he asked, his voice lower now, more introspective. The question wasn't born of ignorance, but of a deeper desire to grasp the magnitude of what was at stake. He had seen Aine's connection to Kilkenny, felt the vibrant pulse of the land itself. But to have an external force actively seeking to disrupt it, to leave its mark, suggested a deeper, more personal antagonism.

Aine's gaze returned to the disturbed patch of earth. "Kilkenny is more than just a place, Pete. It's a nexus of ancient power, a conduit for life energy, a place where the veil between worlds is thin. It's a sanctuary, a source of balance for this region, and perhaps for much more. What we are defending is its integrity, its purity, its ability to remain a place of strength and healing, rather than becoming a weapon or a battleground for... others."

The implication hung heavy in the air. "Others." It was a vague term, but in this context, it evoked a chilling image of beings or entities that operated with intent, with motives that directly opposed their own. The disturbance in the moss was a physical manifestation of their desire to tamper with this ancient power, to perhaps siphon it, corrupt it, or twist it to their own ends.

Pete felt a surge of anger, a hot, protective fury that momentarily eclipsed his fear. To violate such a sacred place, to attempt to manipulate such fundamental energies for selfish or malicious purposes, felt like an ultimate betrayal. He looked at Aine, her silhouette etched against the dappled sunlight filtering through the trees, and he saw not just a powerful individual, but a guardian of something precious and ancient. His commitment deepened, solidifying from a nascent concern into a fierce, unyielding resolve.

He began to actively scan the periphery of the clearing, his eyes no longer just searching for movement, but for subtle signs of disturbance. He noted the way the leaves on one particular bush seemed to be splayed outwards unnaturally, as if something had brushed past with considerable force. He observed a small patch of dry, brittle leaves that seemed out of place amongst the damp, vibrant undergrowth, a small anomaly that suggested a disruption in the natural moisture levels. He cataloged these details, filing them away, ready to report anything that felt even slightly amiss to Aine. His protective instinct wasn't just about shielding her physically; it was about providing her with every possible advantage, about being her vigilant sentry in the physical realm.

The chilling wind, which had seemed to recede momentarily, gusted again, carrying with it a faint whisper that sounded almost like distorted words. Pete strained to hear, but it was just beyond his comprehension, a garbled murmur that seemed to weave through the rustling leaves. It was unsettling, designed, he suspected, to sow unease and doubt, to fray his nerves and perhaps Aine's focus. But it had the opposite effect. It solidified his determination.

"They're trying to unnerve us," Pete stated, his voice steady, betraying none of the disquiet the whisper had attempted to instill. "To make us second-guess, to make us hesitate." He looked at Aine, a silent question in his eyes. Are you alright?

Aine met his gaze, a flicker of acknowledgment in her eyes. "They are testing our resolve, Pete. My own resolve, and yours. The discordant energy is meant to amplify any latent anxieties, any doubts about our purpose or our abilities. But," she added, her voice gaining a subtle strength, "it also reveals their own limitations. They rely on brute force, on disruption, on fear. They lack the deep, resonant harmony that Kilkenny possesses, the interconnectedness that we are working to preserve."

He took a deep breath, the scent of damp earth and ancient trees filling his lungs. He was not a scholar of ancient energies, but he was a student of human nature, of intent, and of resilience. And he could see the resilience in Aine, the unwavering core that refused to be swayed by the unseen pressures. He felt a mirror of that resilience begin to form within himself. His protective instinct wasn't a blind reaction; it was a conscious choice to stand firm, to support the greater cause that Aine represented.

He continued his vigil, his senses heightened, his focus sharp. He became acutely aware of the subtle shifts in the environment – the way a bird's call suddenly ceased, the unnerving silence that descended upon a section of the clearing, the almost imperceptible tremor in the ground beneath his feet. Each anomaly was a piece of a larger puzzle, a clue to the movements and intentions of their unseen adversaries. He realized that his role was not simply to react to threats, but to anticipate them, to provide Aine with the early warnings she needed to effectively counter them.

The feeling of being watched persisted, a constant, prickling sensation on the back of his neck. He resisted the urge to constantly look over his shoulder, knowing that such actions would only serve to break his focus and play into the enemy's hands. Instead, he channeled that awareness into a more proactive vigilance, scanning the immediate surroundings, looking for anything that felt out of place, anything that deviated from the natural order of the clearing. He was learning to 'read' the environment in a new way, to interpret the subtle language of the land as it responded to the unseen force.

He observed a spiderweb, glistening with dew, strung between two low-hanging branches. It was a delicate, intricate structure, a testament to nature's quiet persistence. He noted how the dew drops were catching the sunlight, creating tiny rainbows. Then, he saw it. A single, almost invisible strand of silk, not part of the web, stretched tautly from one branch to another, just above the main structure. It was so fine, so out of place, that it was almost imperceptible. It looked like a tripwire, a subtle snare designed to catch an unwary foot or perhaps to alert someone to a disturbance.

"Aine," he murmured, pointing subtly with his chin towards the anomalous strand. "That... that looks deliberate. A tripwire, maybe?"

Aine followed his gaze, her eyes narrowing. She didn't need to touch it to understand its purpose. A faint tremor ran through her as she sensed the residual energy clinging to the almost invisible thread. "You are perceptive, Pete," she said, her voice quiet but firm. "It is indeed a trap. Not for physical entrapment, but for energetic resonance. It's designed to amplify the discordant vibrations when disturbed, to send a surge of disruptive energy through the immediate area. A crude method, but effective for those who rely on brute force."

Pete felt a surge of satisfaction, a quiet triumph that he had been able to identify such a subtle threat. It reinforced his belief in his own ability to contribute, to be a true partner in this endeavor. He wasn't just a bystander; he was an active participant, a vital component in their defense. His protective instinct had evolved from a raw, emotional reaction to a more strategic, observant stance. He was learning to fight for Aine, and for Kilkenny, in his own way.

He continued his search, his focus sharpening with each successful observation. He noticed a patch of earth where the fallen leaves seemed to have been meticulously swept aside, revealing bare soil. It was too precise, too clean to be natural. It suggested an area of focused activity, a point where the unseen force had perhaps been concentrating its efforts, or leaving its mark.

"That patch of earth," he indicated, his voice low and urgent. "It looks like someone cleared it. Carefully."

Aine moved towards it, her senses already extended. She knelt, her fingers tracing the outline of the cleared area. "You are correct. This is where they attempted to anchor a... a minor warding, or perhaps a listening post. It's weak, easily disrupted, but it shows their intent to establish a more permanent presence, to monitor our activities more closely." She reached out, her fingers hovering over the soil, and Pete watched as a faint, golden light seemed to emanate from her fingertips, subtly shifting the energy of the spot. It wasn't a destructive act, but a recalibration, a gentle pushing back against the intrusive force.

He felt a profound sense of respect for her calm, deliberate actions. Even in the face of such unsettling intrusion, she remained centered, focused on preserving the integrity of Kilkenny. His own protective instincts surged again, a powerful wave of emotion that solidified his commitment. He would not allow this place, or the woman who guarded it, to be violated. He would stand guard, not just with his eyes, but with his unwavering presence, a silent testament to his devotion and his growing understanding of what was truly at stake. He was no longer just Pete, the companion. He was Pete, the protector.

A MOMENT OF DOUBT AND REASSURANCE

As Aine straightened, her gaze met his, and in that shared look, Pete saw a flicker of something he hadn't anticipated – a shadow of doubt, a brief, almost imperceptible wavering in her usually resolute demeanor. It was subtle, so subtle that he might have missed it entirely if his own heightened senses weren't so finely tuned to her in this charged environment. Her shoulders seemed to slump just a fraction, her brow furrowed not just with concentration, but with a weariness that went beyond the physical.

"Pete," she began, her voice softer now, the earlier tone of command giving way to something more vulnerable. She turned away from the disturbed earth, her gaze drifting towards the dense, shadowed woods that bordered the clearing, as if seeking answers from the ancient trees themselves. "Sometimes... sometimes I wonder if I'm enough. If I'm truly capable of holding this against them. They're more... persistent than I anticipated. More cunning. It feels like every time we push them back, they find a new way to infiltrate, to sow discord."

The words hung in the air, heavy and unexpected. Pete felt a pang in his chest, a visceral reaction to seeing Aine, this beacon of strength and ancient wisdom, express such vulnerability. He had come to see her as an almost unwavering force, a guardian whose power was as natural to her as breathing. But in that moment, he saw the immense pressure she was under, the sheer weight of responsibility that rested upon her slender shoulders.

He stepped closer, his movements deliberate, non-threatening. He didn't rush to offer platitudes or dismiss her feelings. Instead, he reached out, his gloved hand gently covering hers where it rested against the rough bark of an oak tree. Her skin was cool beneath the leather, and he felt a faint tremor pass through her.

"Aine," he said, his voice a low, steady rumble, deliberately pitched to be both reassuring and firm. He met her gaze, his own eyes holding hers, trying to convey the depth of his belief in her. "Look at me."

She turned fully towards him, her eyes, usually so full of ancient light, now holding a hint of a storm. "I'm trying, Pete. But the sheer scale of it... the ancientness of the forces we're up against. And the way they target this place, this nexus..." She trailed off, a sigh escaping her lips. "It's a lot. And sometimes, I feel like I'm just a single candle flame against a hurricane."

"That candle flame," Pete countered, his thumb stroking the back of her hand, "is the strongest flame I've ever known. You're not just a candle, Aine. You're the hearth fire that has kept this land warm for centuries. You are the lineage of protectors, the keepers of its secrets. You've faced challenges before, haven't you? You've felt the whispers of Kilkenny, its joys and its sorrows, its strength and its vulnerabilities. This is a test, yes, but it's a test you've been preparing for your entire life, in ways you might not even realize."

He saw a flicker of something shift in her eyes, a subtle change as his words began to penetrate the veil of her doubt. "But this feels different, Pete. This feels like an organized, targeted assault, not just random incursions. They are seeking to unravel what has been woven over millennia."

"And you are the weaver," he pressed gently. "The one who knows the threads, who understands the patterns. I see your strength, Aine. I've seen it in how you move, in how you interpret the subtle shifts in energy, in how you can calm a restless spirit or draw strength from the earth. Don't let the noise of their discord drown out the song of your own power. Remember who you are. Remember why you do this."

He squeezed her hand, offering a silent promise of his presence, his unwavering support. "And you're not alone in this. You have me. I may not be able to wield the ancient energies like you do, but I'm here. I'm your anchor, like you said. I'm your shield. I'm the one who will stand by your side, no matter what. If you feel like a single candle flame, then I'm the wind at your back, pushing you forward, keeping you lit. I'm the one who will remind you of your own brilliance when the shadows try to obscure it."

He watched her closely, searching for any sign that his words were having the desired effect. He saw her take a deep, steadying breath, her shoulders relaxing almost imperceptibly. The tension around her eyes seemed to ease, replaced by a returning spark of determination.

"A hearth fire..." she murmured, a faint, almost melancholic smile touching her lips. "That's... a beautiful way to put it, Pete." She looked at him then, her gaze piercing but also softening, a gratitude that went deeper than mere words. "You see things so clearly, even when I'm lost in the fog of it all. You remind me of the strength I possess, the strength that comes not just from my abilities, but from the very essence of Kilkenny itself."

She brought his hand up to her cheek, pressing it there for a moment. "My lineage, my attunement to this place... it's a gift, yes, but it also carries an immense burden. The weight of responsibility can be crushing, especially when facing an enemy that seems to relish in inflicting that weight. There are moments, in the quiet between their attacks, when the fear can creep in, the doubt about whether I'm truly strong enough to protect all that is sacred here."

"You are," Pete said, his voice unwavering. "You are more than strong enough. And even if there are moments when you doubt, I won't. I'll be the one to hold onto that belief for you, to remind you of your own power, your own worth. Your strength isn't just in your magic, Aine. It's in your courage, your resilience, your deep connection to this land, and yes, even in your moments of vulnerability. Those moments don't diminish you; they make you more human, more real, and all the more admirable."

He stepped back slightly, giving her space, but his gaze remained fixed on her, a silent testament to his unwavering support. He saw the change in her then, a subtle but profound shift. The weariness hadn't vanished entirely, but it was no longer an overwhelming force. It was tempered by a renewed sense of purpose, a rekindled inner fire.

"You're right, Pete," Aine said, her voice regaining a measure of its former strength, though still with that underlying tenderness. She met his gaze, and the storm in her eyes had receded, replaced by a calm, resolute clarity. "I can't let fear dictate my actions, or doubt paralyze me. Kilkenny needs me, and you are here, reminding me that I am not fighting this alone. Your presence, your belief in me... it anchors me. It gives me the fortitude to face whatever comes next."

She reached out again, this time taking his hand, her fingers intertwining with his. "Thank you. For seeing past the power, and for seeing me. For being my strength when mine wavers. You are more than a lover, Pete. You are my partner, my confidant, my fiercest ally."

Pete felt a warmth spread through him, a deep satisfaction that his words had reached her, that he had managed to bolster her spirit. It wasn't about being the one with the power, but about being the one who supported the one with the power. It was about standing together, two halves of a whole, facing an unseen enemy. His protective instinct was no longer just a reactive force; it was a proactive commitment, a conscious decision to nourish and sustain Aine's own strength.

He squeezed her hand in return. "Always, Aine. Always."

The air in the clearing seemed to lighten, the oppressive weight lifting slightly, as if their shared moment of vulnerability and reassurance had itself pushed back against the encroaching darkness. The whispers of the unseen force still lingered at the edge of their perception, but they no longer held the same power to sow doubt. They were now met with a unified resolve, a bond forged not just in shared danger, but in mutual trust and unwavering support. Pete understood now, more profoundly than ever, that his role was essential, not in mimicking Aine's abilities, but in being the bedrock upon which she could stand, firm and unyielding. He was her earthbound anchor, and in that strength, they would face whatever unseen force Kilkenny had to offer.

Chapter Thirteen: The Climax Approaches

THE FOCAL POINT REVEALED

The ancient oaks surrounding the clearing seemed to exhale a collective sigh, their leaves rustling as if in hushed agreement with Aine's words. The intensity of the encroaching presence had receded, not vanished, but subtly shifted, as if the unseen assailants were regrouping, recalculating their approach. Pete watched Aine, her gaze now fixed on a point beyond the immediate clearing, her brow furrowed in deep concentration. The fleeting vulnerability he had witnessed earlier had been replaced by a steely resolve, a rekindled flame that burned brighter than the encroaching shadows. His own resolve, bolstered by their shared moment of connection, felt equally unwavering.

"You speak of a focal point," Pete began, his voice low, deliberately cutting through the lingering quiet. He wanted to anchor Aine, to bring her focus back to the tangible, to the mission at hand.

"The heart of it all. Where is it, Aine? What is this thing that draws their attention, that makes Kilkenny so vital?"

Aine turned back to him, a subtle smile gracing her lips, a flicker of the ancient light returning to her eyes. "It's not a singular 'thing,' Pete, not in the way one might think of an artifact. Kilkenny's power isn't concentrated in a single object, but rather... channeled. Imagine the land itself as a vast, intricate network, a living tapestry of energy. Kilkenny, and specifically a place within it, acts as the nexus, the central hub where the threads converge, where the life force of this region is amplified and harmonized."

She gestured outwards, encompassing the entire valley, the rolling hills, the winding river, the very air they breathed. "This energy isn't confined to mystical realms or ethereal planes. It permeates everything. It influences the growth of the flora, the flow of the water, the very well-being of the inhabitants, even those who are unaware of its existence. My family's duty, for generations, has been to maintain the purity and balance of this nexus. To ensure that the energy flows unimpeded, nurturing and sustaining, rather than becoming corrupted or exploited."

Pete listened intently, the pieces of the puzzle beginning to align, though the full picture remained shrouded in mystery. "So, they're not trying to steal an object, but to disrupt the flow? To divert or corrupt the energy itself?"

"Precisely," Aine confirmed, her gaze now drifting towards the distant, imposing silhouette of Kilkenny Castle, its ancient stones bathed in the soft, late afternoon light. "And the focal point, the heart of that nexus, is located deep beneath the castle grounds. It's a place of immense power, a convergence of ley lines that have been active for millennia. It's where the natural energies of the land are most potent, most accessible. My ancestors discovered it, and through generations of careful stewardship, they learned to channel and regulate its output, ensuring it remained a source of balance, not chaos."

The revelation sent a ripple of understanding through Pete. Kilkenny Castle. It was an obvious, yet somehow elusive, answer. He had spent weeks exploring the outer reaches of Kilkenny, its charming streets, its ancient churches, its windswept hills, all the while the true source of its power lay hidden, perhaps just meters beneath his feet. His investigation had been guided by whispers, by fragmented legends, by Aine's intuition. Now, the objective was becoming terrifyingly clear.

"Beneath the castle," he repeated, the words tasting strange on his tongue. "How... how do they intend to corrupt it from there? And why is it so important to them?"

Aine's expression turned grim. "They seek to invert its purpose. To twist the life-giving energy into something... harmful. Imagine turning a healing spring into a poisoned well. Their goal is not simply to disrupt, but to fundamentally alter the nature of Kilkenny's power, to harness it for their own nefarious designs. Designs that involve not just this region, but potentially far beyond."

She paused, her eyes darkening with a concern that went beyond the immediate threat. "The threat isn't merely an external force seeking to conquer. It is an insidious corruption, a perversion of something sacred. They are not here to seize power, but to twist it, to defile it. They want to turn Kilkenny into a conduit for their own brand of dominion, to poison the very essence of life it embodies."

Pete felt a cold knot form in his stomach. He had understood the threat as an external force, an invading army. But this... this was far more unsettling. A perversion, a corruption from within. It was like watching a beautiful melody twist into a cacophony of discord.

"And this place beneath the castle," he pressed, his mind racing. "Is it something they can access directly? Or do they need to manipulate the energies from afar?"

"They can't directly access the heart of the nexus without first weakening the existing wards and fortifications," Aine explained, her voice regaining its steady, informative tone. "That's what they've been attempting with these smaller incursions, these subtle disturbances. They are probing, testing our defenses, seeking any vulnerability. The disruption in the moss, the anomalies you've identified – these are all attempts to weaken the energetic barriers that protect the nexus. They are trying to create tiny fissures, through which they can then inject their corrupting influence."

"Like that tripwire you sensed?" Pete asked, recalling the almost invisible thread.

"Exactly. Or the subtle redirection of natural currents. Or the introduction of dissonant energies. Each action, no matter how small it may seem, is a step towards their ultimate objective: to create a pathway, a breach, through which they can inflict their will upon the nexus. They are gradually unraveling the ancient tapestry, thread by thread."

Pete's mind went back to his initial arrival in Kilkenny, to the pervasive sense of peace and well-being that had drawn him in. He had felt a connection to the place, an almost palpable sense of vitality. Now, he understood why. It was the power of the nexus, humming beneath the surface, an unseen force that nurtured and sustained. And now, that very force was under attack.

"So, our objective is to reinforce those defenses? To undo what they've done?"

"More than that, Pete," Aine said, her gaze meeting his directly, her eyes alight with a fierce determination. "We must not only reinforce, but recalibrate. Their attempts to corrupt the nexus have already caused subtle shifts, imbalances. We need to not only push them back, but to actively restore the natural flow, to realign the converging energies. It's a delicate dance, a precise recalibration, to ensure the nexus remains a source of harmony, not a conduit for their discord."

She turned her attention back towards the castle, her gaze seemingly piercing through the stone and earth, as if she could see the very heart of the nexus pulsating beneath. "The true focal point isn't just a location; it's the convergence itself. The point where the ancient earth energies meet the energetic imprint of generations of my family's lineage, their dedication to protecting this place. That convergence, that living harmony, is what they seek to shatter."

Pete felt a surge of adrenaline, a renewed sense of purpose. He had come to Kilkenny seeking answers, chasing shadows and whispers. He had found Aine, and in doing so, he had found a cause. He understood now the true nature of her family's duty, the immense responsibility that had been passed down through the ages. This wasn't just about preserving a historical site; it was about safeguarding a fundamental source of life and balance.

"What needs to be done?" he asked, his voice firm, devoid of any trace of his earlier uncertainty. He had moved past simply wanting to help; he now felt a deep-seated need to be an active participant in this defense. His role as Pete, the protector, solidified with every passing moment.

Aine turned to him, her expression softened by a profound gratitude. "The wards beneath the castle are complex, Pete. They require a deep understanding of the ancient symbols, the resonant frequencies, and the specific energetic signatures of Kilkenny. My ancestors developed a series of intricate energetic patterns, woven into the very fabric of the nexus, to protect it. These patterns need to be reactivated, re-tuned to counter the specific frequencies our adversaries are employing."

She paused, her gaze thoughtful. "The primary objective now is to reach the chamber where the oldest and most potent of these patterns are anchored. It's a place sealed by a series of energetic locks, keyed to my family's lineage. Once there, I can begin the process of recalibration. But the path to it is not without its challenges. They will undoubtedly have anticipated our move, and will have bolstered their efforts to impede us."

Pete nodded, his mind already assessing the implications. The castle. It was a formidable structure, steeped in history, and now, it seemed, a battleground for forces he was only beginning to comprehend. He pictured the ancient stones, the winding corridors, the hidden chambers. He had explored much of the accessible parts of the castle during his initial investigations, drawn by its grandeur, by an unspoken pull. Now, he understood that he had been unknowingly drawn towards the very heart of the mystery.

"What kind of challenges?" he asked, his gaze fixed on the distant battlements of the castle. He could almost feel the ancient energies thrumming beneath its foundations, a silent testament to the forces at play.

"They will attempt to amplify the existing defenses, to make them turn against us," Aine explained, her voice low and measured. "The wards are designed to repel intrusions, but if they can manipulate the frequencies, they can make those very protections perceive us as the threat. They may also try to sow further discord, to create illusions, to misdirect us, or to directly confront us with manifestations of their power. Their ultimate aim is to prevent me from reaching the anchor point, and from re-establishing the true harmony."

Pete felt a chill run down his spine, not of fear, but of grim determination. This was no longer a theoretical puzzle; it was a tangible threat, a race against time. He looked at Aine, her slender frame conveying a quiet strength, a deep-seated knowledge that transcended his own understanding. He was drawn into the ancient traditions of her family, into a duty that had been upheld for centuries.

"When do we go?" he asked, his voice firm. He was ready. He understood his role now. He was not just an observer, but a participant, a shield, a steadfast ally.

Aine met his gaze, a flicker of warmth in her eyes, a shared understanding passing between them. "Soon. The approaching twilight often amplifies the energies, both natural and unnatural. It is when the veil between worlds thins most significantly. We will go under the cover of dusk, when their influence is at its strongest, but also when our own abilities can be most effectively utilized without undue observation."

She reached out, her fingers tracing the outline of a small, almost invisible symbol etched into the bark of a nearby tree, a symbol he hadn't noticed before. "This nexus is not merely a point of convergence," she murmured, her voice filled with a deep reverence. "It is the beating heart of Kilkenny, the source of its resilience, its magic, and its enduring spirit. What they seek to corrupt is the very essence of life that flows through this land. And we, Pete, are its guardians."

He felt a profound sense of purpose settle over him. He had stumbled into a world far beyond his initial understanding, a world of ancient powers and hidden battles. But in Aine, he had found not just a woman, but a beacon of strength, a guardian of something sacred. His initial confusion and apprehension had given way to a fierce protectiveness, a deep-seated commitment to her and to Kilkenny.

"So, the castle is the key," Pete stated, his mind already formulating strategies, considering the practicalities of infiltrating such a place under the cover of darkness. "The focal point. And their goal is to corrupt it, to twist its power."

"Yes," Aine confirmed, her gaze unwavering. "The nexus beneath Kilkenny Castle is the lynchpin. It is the heart of Kilkenny's energetic being. And its corruption would have far-reaching consequences. It would not simply silence the pulse of this land; it would fundamentally alter it, turning a sanctuary into a weapon. That is why it is so crucial we reach it, Pete, and reinforce the ancient protections before they can succeed."

The shadows of the clearing began to lengthen, the golden light of the setting sun casting long, distorted figures across the mossy ground. The air, once filled with a subtle tension, now felt charged with an almost palpable anticipation. Pete felt it too, a primal instinct that recognized the approaching confrontation. He was no longer merely an outsider investigating a strange phenomenon; he was a defender, standing shoulder-to-shoulder with Aine, ready to face whatever lay hidden within the ancient stones of Kilkenny Castle. The focal point revealed, the objective clear, the stakes higher than he could have ever imagined. The true battle for Kilkenny was about to begin.

THE OUTSIDERS TRUE MOTIVES

Pete watched the last sliver of sun dip below the horizon, painting the sky in hues of bruised purple and dying embers. The air grew colder, carrying with it the damp scent of earth and the whisper of unseen things. He felt Aine's presence beside him, a steady anchor in the swirling uncertainties of the coming night. He understood now that his journey to Kilkenny had been a convergence of threads, much like the nexus Aine described, leading him to this precipice, this imminent confrontation. The abstract pursuit of a mystery had coalesced into a tangible threat, embodied by the unseen enemy and their shadowy motives.

"You said they want to corrupt the nexus," Pete began, his voice barely a murmur against the rising wind. "But why? What would be the ultimate gain for them in turning a source of life into something destructive?" He felt a prickle of unease, a sensation that went beyond the immediate danger. To truly counter an enemy, one had to understand the heart of their ambition. Exploiting Kilkenny's power was too vague; he needed to grasp the nature of that exploitation.

Aine turned, her face illuminated by the faint starlight beginning to pierce the gathering gloom. Her expression was one of profound contemplation, as if sifting through layers of ancient knowledge. "It is rarely as simple as mere acquisition, Pete. Power, especially power of this nature, can be a tool for many ends. For some, it is about control. For others, chaos. And for a select few, it is about a twisted form of correction, a desire to reshape the world according to their own flawed vision."

She paused, gathering her thoughts. "Imagine a river that irrigates vast fields, sustaining life. Now imagine diverting that river, not to water other lands, but to flood and destroy the very fields it once nourished. Their objective is not to possess Kilkenny's energy, but to pervert it. To weaponize it."

"Weaponize it how?" Pete pressed. He visualized the nexus as a vibrant wellspring, its energy flowing outwards, nurturing the land. The thought of that same energy being turned into a destructive force was chilling. What form would such destruction take? Would it be a localized blight, or something with a far wider reach?

"The nexus harmonizes the natural energies of this land, promoting growth, balance, and well-being," Aine explained. "If corrupted, it could foster decay, discord, and imbalance. Think of it as introducing a virus into a perfectly functioning ecosystem. The very forces that sustain life could be twisted to promote its opposite. This could manifest in subtle ways at first – a creeping malaise, a wilting of crops, a growing unease among the populace. Or, if they are powerful enough, it could be a more immediate and devastating force, capable of unleashing destructive energies upon the land itself."

Pete's mind immediately went to the seemingly minor anomalies he had cataloged during his investigation – the peculiar wilting of certain plants, the inexplicable shifts in localized weather patterns, the subtle feeling of dread that had occasionally settled over him in certain parts of Kilkenny. Were these the early signs of this corruption, nascent whispers of the destructive force they sought to unleash?

"And what drives them to this?" Pete asked, his gaze sweeping across the darkening landscape, imagining unseen forces at work, weaving their insidious plans. "Personal gain? A desire to see this place crumble?"

Aine's eyes narrowed, a flicker of something akin to ancestral anger crossing her features. "There are those who believe certain energies are too potent to be left unchecked, or that they belong to those who can wield them with 'greater purpose.' Some seek to impose their own order, their own ideology, upon the natural flow of things. And then there are those who are simply drawn to power, regardless of its origin or its cost to others. They see this nexus, its inherent goodness and life-giving properties, as an affront. They want to prove that even purity can be defiled, that even life can be twisted into death."

"So, it's not just about Kilkenny, then," Pete mused, the scope of the threat broadening in his mind. "If they can corrupt this nexus, could they do the same elsewhere? Is this a test run?"

"The potential is certainly there," Aine confirmed, her voice grave. "Kilkenny's nexus is particularly potent due to its ancient lineage and the long stewardship of my family. Its corruption could serve as a demonstration, a blueprint for others. It could weaken the collective energetic defenses of the land, leaving other places vulnerable. Their ambition, I fear, extends far beyond this valley."

He pondered the implications. This wasn't just a localized territorial dispute; it was a potential harbinger of a wider conflict, a struggle for the very essence of the natural world. The outsider, whoever or whatever they were, possessed a vision that was not merely territorial, but ideological.

"Have you encountered their kind before?" Pete asked, a new layer of urgency entering his voice. "Have others sought to manipulate the nexus?"

"My family has guarded this place for generations, and for centuries, there have been attempts to access or influence the nexus," Aine admitted. "But these have typically been individuals seeking personal power, or small cults drawn to the potent energies. They were driven by greed or a misguided sense of spiritual pursuit. What we face now, however, feels different. It is more organized, more deliberate, and carries an aura of ancient malice. It suggests a deeper understanding, a more profound connection to the darker currents that can flow through such places."

"And this connection... is it tied to a particular group? A lineage?" Pete's mind flashed back to the cryptic symbols he had found, the recurring motifs that hinted at a hidden history.

Aine hesitated for a moment, her gaze drifting towards the imposing silhouette of Kilkenny Castle, now a dark monolith against the star-dusted sky. "There are... whispers. Legends of ancient societies that sought to master not just the visible energies, but the very fabric of existence. Societies that believed the natural order was flawed and sought to impose their own dominion, to 'perfect' the world through control and manipulation. My ancestors' records speak of such groups, but they were always elusive, operating in the deep shadows."

"So, the outsider could be part of something much older," Pete surmised. "A lingering threat from history, resurfacing now?"

"It is a possibility that cannot be dismissed," Aine conceded. "They possess knowledge that suggests a long-standing awareness of this nexus, and a patient, strategic approach to its exploitation. The disruptions you've observed, the subtle weakening of the wards – these are not the actions of a novice. They are the calculated steps of someone with a history, and perhaps a grievance, tied to this place, or to my family's role in its protection."

Pete felt a profound sense of weight settle upon him. He had initially viewed his investigation as an attempt to uncover a hidden truth, a personal quest for answers. Now, he understood that he was stepping into a conflict that was far older, far more complex than he had imagined. The "outsider" was not merely an anonymous antagonist; they were likely a product of history, their motives perhaps rooted in ancient conflicts or forgotten injustices.

"A grievance," Pete echoed, turning the word over in his mind. "Do you think this is personal, Aine? Is it about you, or your family's lineage, specifically?"

A faint tremor ran through Aine's hand as she reached out, her fingers brushing against his. "It is difficult to say with certainty. For generations, my family has been the custodian of this nexus. We have stood as a barrier against those who would seek to exploit its power. It is possible that this animosity is a continuation of ancient feuds, a deep-seated resentment against my bloodline for thwarting their ancestral ambitions."

She looked at him, her eyes reflecting the starlight, a depth of sorrow and resilience mingling within them. "Or perhaps, it is simply about the power itself. The desire to control such a vital source, and to see those who have protected it for so long removed from their guardianship. The specific motive, whether personal or systemic, matters less than the immediate threat they pose. But understanding it... it can help us anticipate their next move."

Pete nodded, processing her words. A personal vendetta could manifest in unpredictable ways, driven by emotion and a desire for revenge. A systemic ideology, however, would likely follow a more rigid, predictable pattern of expansion and control. He needed to consider both possibilities.

"If it's a historical grievance," Pete mused aloud, his thoughts racing, "then their actions might be calculated to dismantle not just the nexus, but the very foundation of your family's legacy, the symbols of your guardianship. It could be about severing the connection between your lineage and the land, breaking the chain of responsibility."

"That is a chilling, yet accurate, assessment," Aine replied, her voice hushed. "The wards and the patterns I mentioned are not merely physical or energetic barriers; they are also imbued with the history and intent of my ancestors. To disrupt them is to attack the very essence of our lineage's purpose, to erase generations of dedication. If they can break that connection, they can truly claim dominance over the nexus."

He thought about the symbols he'd seen, the faint markings on ancient stones, the subtle alterations in the earth's patterns. Were these deliberate attempts to deface or corrupt the signs of his family's stewardship? To erase their presence from the land?

"So, their goal might be to desecrate the very markers of your family's connection to Kilkenny," Pete reiterated, trying to pin down a tangible objective. "To sever the historical and energetic ties that bind your lineage to this place."

"Precisely," Aine confirmed. "And in doing so, to claim the nexus for themselves, to rewrite its purpose and its history. They are not just trying to steal power; they are attempting to steal legitimacy, to erase the rightful guardians and replace them with their own agenda. It is a form of spiritual and historical conquest."

The concept resonated deeply with Pete. He had always been drawn to the tangible evidence, to the logical progression of events. But here, in Kilkenny, the lines between the tangible and the intangible were blurred. History, lineage, and energetic patterns were all interwoven, forming the complex tapestry of the conflict.

"What if their motive is more about control through chaos?" Pete ventured, shifting his perspective. "Kilkenny's nexus is about balance. Perhaps they don't want to steal its power, but to simply shatter that balance, to unleash uncontrolled energy. A force that disrupts everything, creating a void that they can then fill with their own order, or simply revel in the ensuing destruction."

Aine nodded slowly, considering his words. "That is also a distinct possibility. Some entities thrive on discord. They find strength in entropy. If they could unravel the harmonious flow of the nexus, turning it into a source of unpredictable, chaotic energy, they could sow widespread disruption. Imagine a perpetual storm, a constant state of upheaval. That, too, would be a form of dominion, albeit one based on destruction rather than construction."

He pictured a world plunged into perpetual unrest, where the very foundations of natural order were shaken. It was a terrifying thought, and one that felt chillingly plausible in the face of the encroaching darkness.

"So, we're looking at a few possibilities for their ultimate aim," Pete summarized, cataloging the potential motives. "Exploitation for personal gain, a historical grievance aimed at dismantling your family's legacy and connection to the nexus, or a desire to sow chaos and embrace destruction. Or, of course, a combination of all three."

"The underlying thread, however," Aine said, her voice firm, "is their desire to fundamentally alter the nature of Kilkenny's energetic heart. Whether for personal power, to correct perceived historical wrongs, or to simply unleash unbridled chaos, their intent is to subvert its purpose. They seek to twist the life-giving pulse of this land into something that serves their own destructive agenda."

Pete felt a surge of resolve. The more he understood their potential motives, the clearer the path forward became. Knowing their 'why' allowed him to better anticipate their 'how.' If they sought to dismantle his family's legacy, their actions would target the ancient markers and ancestral protections. If they aimed for chaos, they might focus on creating imbalances and disruptions. If personal gain was the driving force, their strategy might be more focused on direct control of the nexus's output.

"And we need to stop that from happening," Pete stated, his voice resonating with a newfound clarity. He was no longer just helping Aine; he was actively engaging in a defense of something ancient and vital. His own motivations had shifted, from simple curiosity to a deep-seated commitment to protecting this place and its guardian.

"We do," Aine agreed, her gaze locking with his. "And to do so, we must understand their ultimate goal. If they are driven by a desire for control through historical grievance, then reinforcing those ancestral connections becomes paramount. If they seek chaos, then we must focus on restoring and stabilizing the inherent harmony. And if it is personal gain, we must anticipate their most direct attempts at manipulation."

She took a deep breath, the air crisp and cold. "The approach we take to the castle, the way we navigate its defenses, and the specific counter-measures I employ will all depend on their precise objective. Their motives are the key to unlocking their strategy, and their strategy is the key to our success."

Pete felt a sense of grim determination solidify within him. He had come to Kilkenny seeking a story, a mystery to unravel. He had found himself thrust into the heart of a battle for the very soul of the land. The outsider's motives were no longer an abstract concept; they were the driving force behind a tangible threat, a threat he was now committed to confronting, armed with a deeper understanding of what was truly at stake. The approaching night, once a symbol of encroaching danger, now represented an opportunity – an opportunity to confront the outsider and thwart their ultimate, destructive ambition. The path to the castle was fraught with peril, but the clarity of their purpose, illuminated by the potential motives of their adversary, offered a guiding light.

AINES FINAL PREPARATION

The air in the ancient chamber, usually thick with the scent of dried herbs and forgotten lore, now crackled with a different kind of energy. Aine moved with a purpose that transcended mere physical action; it was a ritual, a testament to generations of knowledge distilled into a single, critical moment. Pete stood by the arched doorway, a silent witness to her profound undertaking. The flickering torchlight cast dancing shadows across her face, deepening the lines of concentration etched around her eyes, yet also illuminating a core of unwavering resolve. He had seen her fierce determination before, in the heat of their pursuit, but this was something deeper, a communion with an ancestral power that felt both sacred and terrifying.

Before her, laid out on a worn velvet cloth, were the elements of her final preparation. Not merely tools, but components imbued with the very essence of Kilkenny, each chosen with an exacting precision that spoke of a deep, intuitive understanding. There was a vial of dew, collected from the petals of moon orchids that bloomed only in the deepest parts of the valley, their luminescence a captured fragment of starlight. Beside it lay a handful of soil, not just any soil, but earth drawn from the very heart of the nexus, rich with the accumulated life force of centuries. And nestled amongst them, a single, perfectly formed quartz crystal, pulsing with a faint, internal light, a conduit for the energies she intended to channel.

Aine reached for the dew first, her fingers tracing the cool glass of the vial. "This," she murmured, her voice a low hum in the quiet room, "holds the purity of a night untainted by shadow. It is a cleansing agent, a reminder of the natural order we must strive to preserve." She uncorked it with deliberate slowness, allowing the subtle, sweet fragrance to mingle with the chamber's existing atmosphere. A single drop, glistening like a tiny diamond, fell onto the quartz crystal. Where it landed, the crystal's inner light seemed to intensify, a ripple of pure energy expanding outwards.

Next, her attention turned to the soil. She cupped a small amount in her palm, her fingers sifting through the dark, fertile earth. "This is the blood of Kilkenny," she explained, her gaze fixed on the grains. "The very essence of its resilience, its history, its enduring spirit. It remembers all that has been, and anchors us to what must be." She placed a pinch of the soil at the base of the crystal, forming a small, dark circle around its luminescent core. The crystal seemed to absorb the earth's stillness, its light becoming more grounded, more stable.

Pete watched, a knot of apprehension tightening in his chest. He understood, intellectually, that Aine was preparing to defend Kilkenny, to reinforce its natural defenses against the encroaching threat. But witnessing the tangible, almost alchemical nature of her preparations evoked a deeper, more primal sense of unease. This was not a battle fought with conventional weapons; it was a confrontation on a plane of existence he was only beginning to grasp, a struggle for the very soul of the land.

Aine's gaze finally settled on the quartz crystal, now resting on its bed of ancient earth, kissed by the moon orchid dew. Her hands, steady despite the immense weight of her task, hovered above it. "And this," she whispered, her voice tinged with a profound reverence, "is the heart of the convergence. It will amplify, it will focus, and it will act as a beacon." She closed her eyes, and for a long moment, the only sound was the faint whisper of the wind outside, carrying with it the distant calls of night creatures.

Then, she spoke again, her voice taking on a different quality, resonating with an ancient power that seemed to emanate from the very stones of the chamber. "I offer myself. My lineage, my strength, my unwavering commitment to this sacred trust. Let the echoes of my ancestors guide me, and let their purpose fuel my resolve. I will stand against the corruption, against the imbalance, against the shadow that seeks to devour the light."

It was a pledge, a vow, a profound personal sacrifice. Pete felt a prickle of something akin to fear, not for himself, but for Aine. The dedication she spoke of was absolute, her willingness to put herself on the line absolute. He saw the flicker of exhaustion in her posture, the subtle tremor in her hands, and knew that this act of preparation was not without its toll. She was pouring not just elements of the land into this defense, but fragments of her very being, her life force, her ancestral legacy.

He took a step forward, his instinct to offer support overriding his desire to remain a silent observer. "Aine," he began, his voice raspy, "what exactly are you doing? And... is there anything I can do?" The question felt inadequate, a pathetic offering in the face of such immense dedication, but he had to ask. He couldn't simply stand by and watch.

Aine opened her eyes, and they were different now, deeper, infused with a fierce, ancient light. She offered him a small, weary smile. "You are doing what you can, Pete. By being here. By understanding. Your presence is a strength, a counterpoint to the isolation that often accompanies this duty." She gestured to the crystal. "I am weaving the protective energies. The dew is to purify the point of contact, the soil to ground the power, and the crystal to act as a focal point for a shield. A shield woven from the very essence of Kilkenny, amplified by my lineage's connection."

She then carefully placed the crystal into a small, intricately carved wooden box, its surface adorned with symbols that Pete vaguely recognized from his studies of the ancient markings. "This box," she explained, her movements precise and economical, "is designed to contain and amplify the focused energy. It will be the centerpiece of our defense at the nexus itself."

Her preparations weren't confined to this single chamber. He knew, from earlier conversations, that she had spent days meticulously gathering these components, consulting ancient texts, and performing smaller, preparatory rituals in the hidden groves and along the ley lines of the valley. She had visited the ancient standing stones, tracing their worn carvings, drawing upon their silent, enduring power. She had even communed with the oldest trees, their roots delving deep into the earth's secrets, their branches reaching towards the heavens, seeking their silent, grounding wisdom. Each action was a thread, meticulously woven into the larger tapestry of her defense.

As she continued her final adjustments to the crystal within its protective box, Pete's mind drifted back to the magnitude of the task ahead. The outsider, whoever they were, was preparing their own offensive. They would not be waiting idly. This was not merely a matter of reinforcing a location; it was about anticipating an assault, about being ready to meet a force that sought to unravel the very fabric of life in this valley.

He watched Aine's focused expression, the slight tension in her shoulders, and felt a surge of empathy. The burden she carried was immense, a legacy passed down through countless generations, each guardian facing their own trials. This wasn't just about Kilkenny; it was about her family, their history, their very identity. She was the culmination of their efforts, the last line of defense. The thought of what she might have to endure, the personal cost of this confrontation, gnawed at him. Was there a point beyond which even her resolve could not hold?

She meticulously checked the seals on the wooden box, her fingers brushing against the ancient wood. The symbols seemed to glow faintly under her touch, responding to her intent. "The wards around the nexus are weakening," she said, her voice low, almost a lament. "The outsider has been probing them, finding the cracks. My preparations are to reinforce those weaknesses, to weave a stronger, more resilient barrier."

She then retrieved a small, tarnished silver pendant from beneath her tunic. It was simple, almost crude in its craftsmanship, yet it radiated a quiet power. "This," she explained, holding it out for Pete to see, "was worn by my grandmother when she faced a similar threat. It's not a weapon, but a focus. It helps me to channel the intent of my lineage, to draw upon their collective strength when my own falters." She hesitated, then closed her hand around it, drawing it back against her skin. It was a deeply personal gesture, a silent acknowledgment of the isolation inherent in her role, and her subtle request for connection, even across the veil of time.

The finality of her preparations settled upon the chamber like a shroud. She had gathered her components, performed her rituals, and made her profound commitment. The stage was set, the players were in position, and the antagonist, though unseen, was a palpable presence, a shadow looming over the valley. Pete felt the weight of the approaching climax, a heavy, expectant silence that preceded the storm. He met Aine's gaze, and in her eyes, he saw not just the guardian of Kilkenny, but a woman facing an immeasurable challenge, a challenge that demanded everything she was, and perhaps more. He knew, with a certainty that chilled him to the bone, that this was the moment she had been preparing for her entire life. The nexus was her sanctuary, and she would defend it with every fiber of her being.

PETES UNWAVERING SUPPORT

He watched Aine, the guardian of Kilkenny, meticulously preparing her ancient defenses. The air in the chamber, once alive with the scent of herbs and lore, now thrummed with an energy that was both sacred and unnerving. He felt like a spectator at a ritual he barely understood, a spectator who desperately wanted to be more than just a witness. The weight of the approaching confrontation pressed down on him, a silent testament to the immense burden

Aine carried. Her every movement, from the delicate handling of the moon orchid dew to the grounding of the nexus soil around the quartz crystal, spoke of a lineage steeped in duty and sacrifice. He saw the weariness beneath her fierce determination, the subtle tremor in her hands that betrayed the immense strain she was under. This was not just a battle for the valley; it was a battle for her very essence, a pouring of her life force into the land she was sworn to protect.

Aine's final words, her pledge to stand against the encroaching shadow, echoed in the silent chamber. It was a vow that resonated with the raw power of generations, a commitment that transcended the ordinary. Pete felt a prickle of unease, not for himself, but for her. The depth of her dedication was absolute, her willingness to put herself on the line absolute. He understood, in that moment, that his role could not be that of a passive observer. He couldn't simply stand by and watch her face this alone. The thought of the personal cost, the toll this would take on her, was a cold dread that settled in his gut.

He took a step forward, his voice a low rumble that dared to break the sacred silence. "Aine," he began, the word feeling impossibly small against the backdrop of her monumental task. "What exactly are you doing?" The question was born of a desperate need to comprehend, to grasp the reality of the threat they faced. He knew, intellectually, that she was reinforcing the valley's defenses, weaving a shield against an unseen enemy. But witnessing the almost alchemical nature of her preparations, the tangible elements imbued with the very spirit of Kilkenny, felt like stepping into a realm far removed from his own understanding. It was a confrontation on a plane he was only beginning to perceive, a struggle for the very soul of the land.

Aine opened her eyes, and they were different now. Deeper, infused with an ancient light that spoke of a connection to something far greater than herself. A faint, weary smile touched her lips. "You are doing what you can, Pete," she said, her voice carrying a quiet reassurance. "By being here. By understanding. Your presence is a strength, a counterpoint to the isolation that often accompanies this duty." She gestured to the crystal, now nestled within its carved wooden box. "I am weaving the protective energies. The dew is to purify the point of contact, the soil to ground the power, and the crystal to act as a focal point for a shield. A shield woven from the very essence of Kilkenny, amplified by my lineage's connection."

Her explanation, though delivered with a weariness that tugged at his heart, offered a sliver of clarity. He understood the components, their purpose. But the magnitude of her undertaking, the sheer weight of responsibility she bore, was still almost incomprehensible. She was not merely performing a ritual; she was channeling the very life force of the valley, amplifying it with her own ancestral power, creating a bulwark against an encroaching darkness. He knew, with a certainty that chilled him, that this was more than just a physical defense. It was a spiritual, energetic stand against something that sought to corrupt and destroy.

He watched her carefully check the seals on the wooden box, her fingers brushing against the ancient wood, seemingly making the etched symbols glow faintly. "The wards around the nexus are weakening," she murmured, a hint of lament in her voice. "The outsider has been probing them, finding the cracks. My preparations are to reinforce those weaknesses, to weave a stronger, more resilient barrier."

Then, she retrieved a small, tarnished silver pendant from beneath her tunic. It was simple, almost crude in its craftsmanship, yet it radiated a quiet power, a silent testament to generations of guardians. "This," she explained, holding it out for him to see, "was worn by my grandmother when she faced a similar threat. It's not a weapon, but a focus. It helps me to channel the intent of my lineage, to draw upon their collective strength when my own falters." A flicker of vulnerability crossed her face as she closed her hand around it, drawing it back against her skin. It was a deeply personal gesture, a silent acknowledgment of the isolation inherent in her role, and a subtle plea for connection, even across the veil of time and lineage.

It was at that moment, witnessing her vulnerability and her unwavering resolve, that Pete knew he could no longer stand idly by. His love for Aine, deep and abiding, had evolved beyond the simple romantic affection he had felt upon meeting her. It had deepened into a fierce protectiveness, a profound respect for the strength of her spirit. He realized that his presence in her life, his support, was not just a comfort; it was a necessity.

"Aine," he said, his voice firm, cutting through the reverent silence. "Tell me what I can do. Anything." The question was not one of casual inquiry; it was a heartfelt plea, a declaration of his commitment. He had no arcane abilities, no ancient lineage connecting him to the land's defenses. His strengths lay in his resilience, his loyalty, and his willingness to face any challenge head-on, no matter how daunting. He was prepared to stand by her side, to be her shield if necessary, to face the outsider himself if it meant easing her burden, even by an iota.

Her gaze met his, and in her eyes, he saw a mixture of surprise and a flicker of something akin to relief. She had been preparing for this for so long, carrying this weight almost entirely alone. To have someone offer unwavering support, someone willing to stand by her without question, even without understanding the full scope of her powers, was a rare and precious gift.

"Pete," she began, her voice softer now, tinged with a deep gratitude. "Your willingness to stand with me, to offer your strength, is more than I could have asked for. You are not just a witness, you are my anchor. Your belief in me, in what we are fighting for, is a power in itself." She paused, considering his words, the genuine depth of his offer. "The preparations I have made are for the nexus itself. My fight will be there, at the heart of Kilkenny's defenses. But the outsider... they are a tangible force. They will seek to exploit any weakness, to disrupt the balance."

She looked at the intricately carved box containing the crystal, then back at him. "If they attempt to breach the valley's perimeter before I can fully manifest the shield, or if they try to create a diversion, you will be on the front lines. I need you to be my eyes and ears, to be the shield on the ground should anything break through. You will have to be ready to face them, Pete. Not with magic, but with everything you have. Your courage, your determination, your very presence will be a bulwark."

The words settled on him, heavy with consequence. He was not just a supportive companion; he was being asked to be a warrior, a defender in his own right. The prospect was daunting, a primal fear churning in his stomach. He had faced danger before, but this was different. This was a confrontation with an unknown entity, an entity that threatened not just his life, but the very fabric of this magical valley. Yet, looking at Aine, at the absolute conviction in her eyes, he felt a surge of strength, a readiness he hadn't known he possessed.

"I understand," he said, his voice steady, betraying none of the apprehension that churned within him. "Tell me what to do. Where to go. I will not fail you, Aine. I will stand with you, no matter what. Even if it means facing them myself." He meant it with every fiber of his being. His love for her had transformed him, pushing him beyond his perceived limits. He was no longer the outsider looking in; he was a part of this struggle, a vital ally in a battle for survival.

Aine reached out, her fingers brushing his cheek, a gesture of profound tenderness. "I know you will, Pete," she whispered, her eyes conveying a depth of emotion words could not capture. "Your unwavering support is a testament to your strength, a strength that resonates even here, in this place of ancient power. You are more than a romantic interest, Pete. You are my partner in this. My ally."

She then turned back to her preparations, her focus returning to the task at hand, but there was a new sense of resolve in her movements, a quiet confidence born from knowing she was not alone. Pete watched her, a fierce determination hardening his own gaze. He would be ready. He would do whatever it took to protect her and to protect Kilkenny. His love for her had made him strong, made him willing to face the unknown, to stand against the encroaching shadow, not with magic, but with the unwavering power of his heart. He was ready to play his part, whatever that might be, to ensure that Aine's sacrifice would not be in vain. The climax was approaching, and he was ready to meet it, not as a bystander, but as a defender, standing shoulder-to-shoulder with the woman he loved. His commitment was absolute, his support unwavering, a silent vow echoing the ancient pledges of Kilkenny's guardians. He would be her strength when hers faltered, her shield against the storm.

THE CONVERGENCE OF FORCES

The air in Kilkenny had reached a palpable saturation point, a humming tension that vibrated in the very stones of the ancient buildings and whispered through the rustling leaves of the surrounding forests. Pete felt it acutely, a prickling awareness that extended beyond the ordinary senses, as if the entire valley had collectively inhaled, waiting for the exhale that would herald the storm. He had spent the hours since his conversation with Aine in a state of heightened vigilance, his gaze constantly sweeping the horizon, his ears straining for any anomaly in the familiar sounds of the countryside. He understood, with a clarity that had solidified his resolve, that his role was no longer that of an observer, but of an active participant, a bulwark against whatever forces sought to breach the valley's sanctity.

Aine's preparations had been a stark illustration of the stakes involved. The meticulous arrangement of lunar-infused dew, the grounding of the nexus soil, and the deliberate placement of the quartz crystal within its protective casing—each action had been a deliberate act of weaving a tapestry of defense, a conduit for the valley's inherent power. He remembered the faint, almost imperceptible glow that had emanated from the etched symbols on the wooden box, a testament to the ancient magic Aine commanded, a magic drawn from generations of guardians. It was a power that spoke of a deep, ancestral connection to the land, a lineage that had, for centuries, stood as a silent sentinel against encroaching darkness. Now, that sentinel was preparing for its most significant test, and Pete was to stand beside her, an unlikely guardian armed with something far more fundamental than arcane knowledge: unwavering loyalty and a fierce, protective love.

The ancient energies of Kilkenny were not merely abstract concepts in Aine's lore; Pete was beginning to feel their presence as a tangible force. It was a subtle hum beneath the surface of reality, a deep resonance that pulsed with the rhythm of the land itself. He imagined it as a vast, intricate network of life, intertwined with the history and the spirit of every living thing within the valley's embrace. Aine was not just defending a place; she was defending a living entity, a repository of stories, memories, and a profound, enduring strength. Her lineage, he realized, was not just a bloodline; it was a conduit, a sacred trust passed down through the ages, ensuring that this vital connection remained unbroken.

The outsider, the encroaching shadow Aine spoke of, remained an enigma in terms of its specific form and capabilities, but its intent was clear: disruption, corruption, and ultimately, annihilation. Pete understood that this was not merely a territorial dispute or a battle for resources. It was a fundamental clash between preservation and destruction, between light and an insidious darkness that sought to extinguish all that was sacred. The outsider's probing of the wards around the nexus was a calculated assault, a search for vulnerabilities, a testing of the valley's defenses before a full-scale attack. Aine's reinforcements were a direct response to this threat, an attempt to mend the breaches and strengthen the very foundations of Kilkenny's protection.

He recalled Aine's quiet confidence, the subtle shift in her demeanor after he had pledged his support. It wasn't just relief he saw in her eyes, but a shared burden, a flicker of hope that perhaps, just perhaps, this time the isolation of her duty might be lessened. He knew his role would be to guard the perimeter, to act as a buffer should the outsider's strategy involve a direct physical assault on the valley's borders, a diversionary tactic to draw Aine's attention away from the nexus. He had no illusions about his capacity to combat the outsider with any sort of magical prowess. His strength lay in his groundedness, his unwavering determination, and his ability to endure. He would be the visible defense, the tangible resistance that the outsider would have to confront if they sought to bypass Aine's primary defenses.

The convergence of these elements—the ancient energies of Kilkenny, the power of Aine's lineage, the palpable threat of the outsider, and his own unexpected but resolute presence—felt like the drawing of a bowstring taut to its breaking point. The entire narrative of Kilkenny, its hidden history and its enduring spirit, was coalescing into this singular, climactic moment. The town, usually a picture of quiet charm and historical resonance, now felt like the eye of a gathering storm, its ordinary facade masking an ancient power on the verge of being unleashed. Aine's destiny, inextricably linked to the valley she protected, was about to be irrevocably shaped by the events that were now unfolding with an almost terrifying inevitability.

Pete found himself standing on the edge of the ancient standing stones, the very place where Aine had spoken of the nexus. The air here was even more charged, carrying a faint, earthy scent mixed with something indefinable, something that hinted at the deep earth and the sky above. The stones themselves seemed to hum with a latent energy, their weathered surfaces etched with symbols that Pete could now vaguely recognize as patterns of protection and resonance. He could almost feel the echoes of past guardians who had stood on this very spot, their own courage and determination woven into the fabric of the place.

He looked towards the heart of the valley, towards the place where Aine would be enacting the final stages of her ritual. He pictured her, alone in her concentration, channeling the very life force of Kilkenny, weaving a shield that would hopefully hold against the encroaching darkness. The thought sent a fresh wave of protectiveness through him. He was not a warrior in any conventional sense, but he was fiercely loyal, and his love for Aine had forged a new kind of courage within him. He was ready to face the unknown, to be the point of resistance, to stand between the outsider and the woman he loved.

The anticipation was a physical sensation, a tightening in his chest, a heightened awareness of every sound, every shadow. The wind, which had been a gentle breeze moments before, now picked up, rustling the leaves with an almost urgent whisper. It felt as though the valley itself was acknowledging the impending confrontation, bracing itself for the inevitable clash. He ran a hand over the rough surface of one of the standing stones, feeling its solid permanence, its deep connection to the earth. This was what they were fighting for, this ancient, enduring spirit of Kilkenny.

He knew that the outsider would not be a simple adversary. If they were capable of probing and weakening magical wards, they would possess abilities far beyond his comprehension. Yet, his purpose was clear: to be a distraction, a nuisance, a tangible obstacle that would force the outsider to divert their attention, however momentarily, from Aine and the nexus. He was to be the shadow's first encounter with resistance, the unexpected grit in the gears of their plan.

Pete closed his eyes, focusing on the connection he felt to Aine, to the valley. It was a fragile connection, he knew, a mere whisper compared to the deep, ancestral link she possessed. But it was his, and he would use it. He would stand his ground, not with magic, but with his own inherent strength, his own will to protect. He thought of the pendant Aine wore, the focus for her lineage's power. He had no such artifact, no tangible link to ancient forces, but he had his own spirit, his own resolve.

The sun began its slow descent, casting long shadows across the valley floor. The light took on a different quality, more golden, more infused with the magic of the approaching twilight. It was a beautiful sight, a scene of serene natural grandeur, yet beneath the surface, the tension was mounting. The convergence of forces was not just an abstract notion; it was becoming a tangible reality. The ancient energies of Kilkenny were stirring, Aine's lineage was being called upon, and the outsider was poised to strike. Pete, the outsider in this ancient world, was now an integral part of its defense.

He drew a deep breath, the air cool and crisp against his lungs. He felt a sense of purpose, a clarity that had been absent for so long. He was no longer adrift, no longer merely a witness to events beyond his control. He was a participant, a defender, a crucial element in the unfolding climax. The weight of that realization was immense, but it was also invigorating. He was ready. He would stand with Aine, not just as a lover, but as an ally, a shield on the ground, prepared to face whatever came his way, fueled by a love that had transcended the ordinary and embraced the extraordinary. The destiny of Kilkenny, and the woman he loved, rested on this convergence, and he was determined to play his part, no matter the cost. His commitment was absolute, a silent echo of Aine's own pledge, a testament to the enduring power of courage in the face of overwhelming odds. The convergence was here, and he was ready to meet it.

Chapter Fourteen: Confrontation and Resolution

THE CONFRONTATION AT THE FOCAL POINT

The air around the ancient standing stones vibrated with an almost visible intensity. It was as if the very atmosphere had been compressed, saturated with an energy that pulsed in time with Pete's own thrumming heartbeat. He stood at the edge of the clearing, a solitary figure silhouetted against the deepening twilight, his gaze fixed on the nexus – the heart of Aine's power, and now, the epicenter of their impending confrontation. The stones themselves seemed to hum, their weathered surfaces holding the secrets of millennia, their presence a silent testament to the guardians who had stood watch before Aine, and before them, all those who had drawn strength from this sacred ground. The wind had died down, leaving an unnerving stillness, a pregnant pause before the inevitable storm broke.

Pete felt a profound connection to this place, a sense of belonging that had blossomed in the short time he'd been in Kilkenny, a connection forged in shared purpose and a burgeoning, unspoken love for Aine. He wasn't a part of her ancient lineage, nor did he possess the innate understanding of the earth's energies that flowed through her veins. Yet, he was here, a willing participant, a shield of flesh and bone against a threat he could only dimly perceive. His role, Aine had explained, was to be the anchor, the tangible presence that would draw the outsider's attention, a necessary distraction from the delicate ritual she was performing at the very core of the nexus.

He watched as Aine moved with deliberate grace amidst the ancient stones. The air around her shimmered, not with heat, but with a contained, incandescent power. She was a conduit, a living embodiment of Kilkenny's spirit, drawing upon the deep reserves of earth magic that had sustained this valley for centuries. The intricate patterns she traced on the ground with glowing chalk, the soft, rhythmic chant that was barely audible above the thrumming of his own blood – it was all a symphony of defense, a delicate dance against an encroaching darkness. He could see the faint luminescence of the quartz crystal, nestled at the nexus's heart, a beacon of pure, unadulterated power.

The outsider. The concept remained abstract, a nebulous threat. Aine had described it as a force of imbalance, a hunger that sought to consume and corrupt. It was not a creature of flesh and blood, but something far more insidious, an entity that preyed on the very essence of life, seeking to unravel the ancient tapestry of Kilkenny. Its probing of the wards had been subtle, a whisper at the edges of their defenses, but it was growing bolder, its intent to breach the nexus becoming increasingly manifest. Pete understood that whatever form it took, it would be drawn to the concentration of power Aine was currently wielding.

A faint ripple disturbed the air near the edge of the clearing, a subtle distortion that seemed to suck the light from the surrounding twilight. It was almost imperceptible, a mere shimmer on the periphery of vision, but Pete's heightened senses registered it instantly. The outsider. It was here. He felt a surge of adrenaline, a primal instinct to protect kicking in. He moved forward, positioning himself between the approaching anomaly and Aine, his body a shield, his resolve a bulwark.

The distortion intensified, coalescing into a more defined presence. It wasn't a physical form, not in the way Pete understood it. It was a void, a patch of unnatural darkness that seemed to absorb sound and light. A chilling cold emanated from it, a palpable emptiness that made the very air feel thin and brittle. He could feel its attention turn towards him, a predatory assessment, a silent acknowledgment of his presence as an obstacle. It was an awareness that sent a shiver down his spine, not of fear, but of a grim determination. He would not yield.

Aine's chanting deepened, the subtle variations in her voice speaking of immense effort. The light around her intensified, pulsing outwards in waves that seemed to push back against the encroaching darkness. Pete could feel the strain, the immense pressure she was under. He knew that if the outsider managed to break through her defenses, if it reached the nexus, Aine would be overwhelmed. His task was to ensure that never happened.

He focused on the outsider, meeting its silent gaze with his own. He wasn't armed with ancient incantations or mystical artifacts. His weapon was his unwavering presence, his refusal to break. He thought of Aine's face, her quiet strength, the trust she had placed in him. That was his power. He stood his ground, a single point of defiance against the encroaching nullity.

The outsider began to move, not walking, but flowing, a tide of darkness creeping towards the standing stones. It radiated an aura of despair, a subtle erosion of will. Pete felt a whisper of doubt try to insinuate itself into his mind, a suggestion of futility, of the inevitability of its victory. He pushed it back, focusing on the warmth of his own breath, the solidity of the earth beneath his feet, the very real, tangible love he felt for Aine. These were the anchors that kept him grounded.

He stepped forward, closing the distance between himself and the anomaly. He didn't know what would happen if he touched it, if he tried to physically interact with this non-physical threat. But he couldn't just stand there and watch. He needed to make himself a more significant obstacle, a more tangible problem for the outsider to overcome.

As he moved closer, the external force seemed to recoil slightly, the unnatural darkness shifting as if in annoyance. It hadn't anticipated this direct confrontation. Its strategy, Pete surmised, was likely to bypass the outer defenses, to focus its assault directly on Aine. His stepping forward was an unexpected deviation from its plan.

He reached out his hand, palm open, towards the swirling void. The cold intensified, an icy tendril reaching out to meet his touch. For a moment, his fingers brushed against the edge of the darkness. It felt like plunging his hand into absolute nothingness, a sensation that threatened to pull him apart at a molecular level. A searing pain, not of burning, but of utter dissolution, shot through his arm. He gritted his teeth, forcing himself to maintain his stance.

Aine's voice, strained but resolute, cut through the oppressive silence. "Pete! Stay focused! Don't let it consume your light!"

Her words were a lifeline. He pulled his hand back, flexing his fingers, a tremor running through them. The pain subsided, leaving a strange numbness, a feeling of being diminished. But he was still here. He was still standing.

The outsider pulsed, a silent acknowledgment of the resistance it had met. It seemed to pause, assessing this unexpected impediment. Pete knew this was his chance. He needed to be more than just a physical barrier; he needed to be a distraction, a problem that demanded its full attention, however briefly.

He began to speak, his voice rough but steady. "You think you can just waltz in here, into Aine's valley, and take what isn't yours? You're not welcome here." He knew the words were simplistic, almost childish against the immense power arrayed against him. But he also knew that this was not a battle of eloquent speeches. It was a battle of wills.

The anomaly remained silent, but Pete felt its awareness sharpen, its focus narrowing onto him. The subtle probing of Aine's defenses seemed to momentarily cease. It was intrigued, perhaps even angered, by his defiance.

He continued, drawing on every ounce of courage he possessed. "This place has a spirit. A life force. And Aine is its guardian. You can't break that. Not while we're both standing here." He met the heart of the darkness with his gaze, trying to project an unshakeable resolve. He channeled his love for Aine, his fierce protectiveness, his newfound sense of belonging into that unwavering stare.

A subtle shift occurred within the void. It wasn't a physical movement, but a change in its density, its composition. It seemed to be gathering itself, preparing to unleash something more potent. Pete could feel a building pressure, a surge of raw, uncontained energy.

Aine's ritual was reaching its apex. The light from the nexus pulsed stronger, illuminating the clearing with an ethereal glow. The standing stones seemed to hum with a deeper resonance, amplifying her power. Pete could see the intricate web of energy she was weaving, a luminous shield that was slowly but surely encompassing the nexus.

The outsider lunged.

It wasn't a directed attack on Pete, but a surge of pure, destructive force aimed at the nascent shield Aine was creating. It was an attempt to shatter her concentration, to break through the protective barrier before it was fully formed. Pete was caught in the periphery of this assault, the edge of the destructive wave washing over him.

He felt a searing heat, a violent expulsion of energy that slammed into him. He was thrown backwards, stumbling, his breath knocked from his lungs. He landed hard on the earth, the impact jarring him to the bone. For a moment, his vision swam, the world a blur of swirling light and darkness.

But he forced himself up, his muscles screaming in protest. He saw Aine, still standing at the nexus, though her form flickered, her concentration wavering under the immense onslaught. The shield was incomplete, a fragile dome of light with a gaping hole where the outsider's initial blast had struck.

The outsider, having expended its initial burst of energy, seemed to pause, observing the damage. It was a calculated maneuver, a strategic assessment of the situation. It knew it had weakened Aine. Now, it would press its advantage.

Pete's mind raced. He couldn't fight the outsider's raw power directly. But he could still serve as a distraction. He could draw its attention away from Aine, giving her the precious moments she needed to mend the breach in her defenses.

He staggered to his feet, ignoring the pain, the sheer exhaustion that threatened to pull him down. He walked towards the outsider, not with aggression, but with a stubborn refusal to yield. "You won't get to her," he rasped, his voice hoarse. "Not today."

He stopped a few yards from the anomaly, planting his feet firmly. He looked not at the void itself, but at the periphery, at the subtle distortions it caused in the air, in the light. He focused on these subtle disturbances, treating them as points of interaction. He began to move, not in a straight line, but in a series of unpredictable feints and sidesteps, trying to draw the outsider's gaze, its full attention.

It worked. The void began to shift, its focus returning to him. The chilling emptiness seemed to expand, its tendrils reaching out, not to strike, but to encompass, to draw him in. Pete felt the oppressive weight of its attention, the subtle erosion of his resolve again attempting to take hold.

He kept moving, his steps erratic, his movements designed to be frustratingly elusive. He imagined himself as a fly buzzing around a predator, a minor annoyance that demanded a response. He wasn't fighting; he was persisting. He was a testament to the idea that even in the face of overwhelming power, the will to protect could endure.

Meanwhile, Aine was working. Pete could sense it, a faint but growing pulse of stable energy emanating from the nexus. She was reinforcing the shield, weaving new strands of power into the broken sections. Each time the outsider's attention wavered, even for a fraction of a second, she seized the opportunity.

The outsider seemed to grow impatient. The chilling cold intensified, and Pete felt a pressure building around him, as if the very air was being squeezed. It was preparing another assault, and this time, it was clearly aimed at him.

Just as the pressure reached its unbearable peak, and Pete braced himself for a direct confrontation, something shifted. The outsider recoiled, not from him, but from the nexus. The light emanating from Aine's ritual had swelled, a blinding wave of pure, untainted energy that surged outwards, engulfing the clearing.

The outsider shrieked, a sound that was not of this world, a cacophony of pain and outrage. It contorted, its dark form thrashing as if caught in a vortex. The radiant light of the nexus was anathema to it, burning away its essence, unraveling its corrupting influence.

Pete watched, mesmerized, as the outsider was systematically dismantled by Aine's power. The dark void seemed to shrink, to fragment, its edges dissolving into nothingness. The chilling cold receded, replaced by the comforting warmth of the nexus's light.

The process was agonizingly slow, a testament to the outsider's resilience. But Aine's resolve was absolute. She stood firm, her arms outstretched, her chanting unwavering, channeling the very lifeblood of Kilkenny into a final, decisive push.

With a final, guttural shriek that echoed through the valley, the outsider imploded, collapsing in on itself, leaving behind only a faint shimmer in the air, a residual distortion that quickly dissipated. The oppressive darkness vanished, and the clearing was bathed in the soft, serene glow of the nexus.

Aine swayed, her strength visibly depleted. Pete rushed to her side, his own exhaustion forgotten. He reached out, his hands trembling, and gently cupped her face. Her eyes, when they opened, were filled with a profound weariness, but also with an immense relief, and a flicker of something more – a shared victory.

"You did it," he whispered, his voice thick with emotion. "You saved it. You saved us."

Aine managed a weak smile. "We did it," she corrected, her voice barely above a whisper. "You were my anchor, Pete. You held the line when I couldn't. You were more than I could have hoped for."

He felt a warmth spread through him, a sense of accomplishment far deeper than anything he had ever known. He looked around the clearing, at the ancient standing stones bathed in the soft twilight, at the nexus pulsating with a steady, vibrant energy. Kilkenny was safe. The balance had been restored.

The air, moments before thick with tension and the threat of annihilation, now felt clean, pure, and alive. The subtle hum of the earth's energy was no longer a prelude to conflict, but a gentle lullaby, a song of peace and renewal. Pete realized that he was no longer an outsider in this ancient land. He was a part of its story, a protector, an ally. He had faced the darkness and, standing beside the woman he loved, he had helped to banish it. The confrontation had been brutal, terrifying, and at times, it had felt as though all hope was lost. But in the end, the light, fueled by courage and a love that transcended the ordinary, had prevailed. The future of Kilkenny, and their own intertwined destinies, lay before them, bathed in the gentle, victorious glow of the nexus.

AINES ULTIMATE SACRIFICE OR TRIUMPH

The very fabric of reality seemed to stretch and strain around Aine as she drew upon the deep, ancient reserves of her lineage. It wasn't merely a physical exertion; it was a communion, a soul-deep connection to the pulse of Kilkenny, to the heartbeat of the earth that pulsed beneath the standing stones. The air crackled, not with the harsh, destructive energy of the outsider, but with a pure, incandescent luminescence that emanated from Aine herself. Her eyes, usually so full of warmth and a gentle wisdom, now blazed with an otherworldly light, reflecting the millennia of power that coursed through her veins. The chants she had begun earlier, once a whisper, now resonated with the power of a thousand voices, each syllable an invocation, a plea, and a command.

Pete watched, breathless, as the swirling vortex of darkness that was the outsider seemed to recoil from the escalating display of Aine's strength. It was as if the very concept of being – of existence, of light and life – was anathema to the void. Its tendrils of chilling emptiness lashed out, seeking to find purchase, to exploit any weakness in the burgeoning shield Aine was weaving. But Aine was no longer just Aine, the woman Pete had come to know and love. She was the guardian, the conduit, the living embodiment of the valley's enduring spirit. Her connection to the land was absolute, her purpose crystalline.

She raised her hands, palms open, and the quartz crystal at the nexus flared, not with a sudden burst, but with a sustained, unwavering radiance. It was the heart of the nexus, amplifying Aine's intent, channeling the raw power of the earth into a focused beam of pure energy. Pete felt a profound shift in the atmosphere. The air grew warmer, carrying with it the scent of damp earth and ancient moss, a comforting aroma that spoke of life and resilience. The whispers of doubt that had gnawed at the edges of his mind, subtle insinuations of the outsider's power, were silenced, drowned out by the undeniable force of Aine's will.

This was the culmination, the moment for which generations of her ancestors had prepared. It was a test not just of her power, but of her commitment, of her willingness to embody the sacred trust passed down through her bloodline. Pete saw in her eyes a flicker of something he recognized from their quiet moments together – a deep love for this place, for its people, and for him. But now, that love was transmuted, expanded into a fierce, protective embrace that encompassed everything and everyone.

The outsider, sensing the escalating threat, began to press its attack with renewed ferocity. It wasn't a physical lunge, but a more insidious attempt to corrupt, to poison the very energy Aine was wielding. Pete could feel it, a subtle discordance in the symphony of light and sound, a discordant note that sought to unravel the harmony. He knew that Aine's power was immense, but the outsider's nature was to consume, to distort. It was a force of pure, unadulterated entropy.

Aine responded not with force, but with wisdom. She didn't try to meet the outsider's aggression with brute strength. Instead, she shifted her focus, her energy. She began to weave the power of the nexus into a different form, a more intricate and subtle tapestry. It was as if she were taking the pure, raw energy and shaping it, giving it form and purpose, guiding it like a skilled artisan. The light didn't just push back; it began to flow around the encroaching darkness, not to destroy it, but to contain it, to absorb it, and to transform it.

This was where the true sacrifice lay, Pete realized. It wasn't a grand, dramatic act of self-immolation, but a profound act of will, a deliberate choice to embrace a burden that would forever change her. To absorb the outsider, to neutralize its corrupting influence, required a part of her own essence, a fraction of her life force. It was a dangerous gamble, a testament to her unwavering belief in the sanctity of Kilkenny.

The outsider, caught off guard by this unexpected maneuver, pulsed with what seemed like confusion. It had prepared for a battle, for a direct confrontation. It had not anticipated this quiet, inexorable absorption. Its form began to waver, the edges of its darkness blurring as Aine's radiant light enveloped it. Pete could hear faint, distressed whispers emanating from it, the desperate cries of a force that was being unmade, not through destruction, but through assimilation.

Aine's chanting grew more intense, her voice a steady anchor in the swirling energies. Her body trembled, not from weakness, but from the immense strain of channeling such power. The sweat beaded on her brow, and her knuckles were white as she gripped an invisible force. Pete wanted to rush to her, to offer his support, but he knew he was powerless to directly aid her in this, the most intimate of battles. His role as an anchor was complete; now, hers was to be the fulcrum.

He watched as the quartz crystal pulsed in time with her heartbeat, a rhythmic thrum that resonated deep within his own chest. He saw the intricate patterns of light that Aine was weaving, forming a cocoon of pure energy around the dissolving outsider. It was a thing of terrible beauty, a testament to the enduring strength of life. He felt a profound sense of awe, mixed with a deep, aching love for the woman who was undertaking this monumental task.

The process was slow, agonizingly so. Hours seemed to pass, though in reality, it was likely only minutes. The twilight deepened into night, and the stars began to prick the velvet sky, bearing silent witness to the struggle unfolding below. The very air seemed to hold its breath, waiting for the resolution. Pete remained a steadfast presence, his gaze never leaving Aine, a silent testament to his unwavering support.

As the last vestiges of the outsider's darkness were absorbed, Aine's body sagged. The radiant light that had enveloped her dimmed, returning to the soft, warm glow that was characteristic of her. She stumbled, her knees buckling, and Pete was there in an instant, catching her before she fell.

Her eyes fluttered open, and a weak smile touched her lips. "It's... done," she whispered, her voice raspy. "The balance is restored."

Pete held her close, his heart a mixture of relief and a dawning apprehension. He could see the toll this had taken. Her face was pale, and there was a weariness in her eyes that went beyond the physical. He knew, with a certainty that chilled him, that this act of absorption had cost her dearly.

"You did it, Aine," he murmured, his voice thick with emotion. "You saved us all."

She leaned her head against his chest, drawing strength from his embrace. "It wasn't just me, Pete. You were my anchor. You kept me grounded, focused. You reminded me what I was fighting for." She pulled back slightly, her gaze meeting his, and in her eyes, he saw not just exhaustion, but a profound acceptance. "I had to absorb its essence, Pete. To truly neutralize it, I had to take its potential for harm into myself. It's... a part of me now."

The words hung in the air, heavy with unspoken implications. Pete's brow furrowed. "What do you mean, a part of you? Will it... change you?"

Aine took a deep, shuddering breath. "It is a constant struggle, Pete. To hold onto its darkness without letting it consume my light. It is a vigilance I will have to maintain, a balance I must always strive for. It is the price of guardianship, the burden of my lineage." She looked out at the now serene clearing, the standing stones standing as silent sentinels, their ancient power now interwoven with her own. "This is my role. To protect Kilkenny, not just with my power, but with every fiber of my being. It is a sacrifice, yes, but it is also... my triumph."

He understood then. This wasn't a happy ending in the conventional sense. It was something more profound, more enduring. Aine had faced the ultimate threat and had not only repelled it, but had integrated it, neutralizing its destructive potential by taking it into herself. It was an act of immense courage, a testament to her deep connection to her heritage and her unwavering commitment to her duty.

He looked at her, at the woman who had just stared into the abyss and emerged, not unscathed, but unbroken. He saw the strength in her eyes, the quiet determination that had always drawn him to her. His love for her, which had felt so pure and simple before, now deepened, encompassing this new facet of her existence. He knew their path forward would not be easy. He would have to be there for her, to support her in this constant struggle, to remind her of the light within her when the shadows threatened to overwhelm.

"Then it is my triumph too, Aine," Pete said, his voice firm. "We will face this together. Whatever it takes."

Aine's smile returned, a genuine, radiant smile that chased away the shadows of weariness. It was the smile of a guardian who had fulfilled her sacred duty, of a woman who had made an ultimate sacrifice and found, in that act, her truest strength. The night was still, and the air was filled with the gentle hum of Kilkenny's renewed vitality. The confrontation had been fierce, the resolution profound, and Aine, the guardian of the valley, had emerged not diminished, but transformed, her legacy secured, her ultimate sacrifice a testament to her enduring triumph. The enduring power of the valley, now inextricably linked to her own, promised a future of peace, but one that would always be watched over by a guardian who carried the shadows within her light. The weight of centuries, and the responsibility for the present, rested on her shoulders, a burden she bore with grace and an unyielding spirit. The journey had been arduous, fraught with peril, but in its conclusion, Aine had solidified her place as the true inheritor of her ancestral destiny, a protector whose strength was amplified by the very darkness she had overcome.

PETES PIVOTAL ACTION

The residual energy of Aine's triumph still hummed in the air, a palpable thrum that Pete felt resonate through the very bones of the earth. He held her, the woman who had just woven herself into the fabric of Kilkenny's defense, a living shield against an encroaching void. Her words, spoken with a weariness that spoke of immense internal battle, echoed in his mind: "It is a constant struggle, Pete. To hold onto its darkness without letting it consume my light." He had agreed, a simple vow uttered in the quiet aftermath of an epochal struggle, "Then it is my triumph too, Aine. We will face this together. Whatever it takes." But as the initial wave of relief subsided, the weight of that promise settled upon him, heavier than he had anticipated.

He understood his role was no longer simply that of a lover, a confidante, or even an anchor. It had evolved, irrevocably, into something more. He was now the keeper of Aine's equilibrium, the one who would stand sentinel against the encroaching shadows that she had so bravely internalized. This wasn't just about supporting her emotional well-being; it was about actively participating in her defense, a silent, steadfast presence that would serve as a bulwark against the encroaching entropy she now carried. His gaze swept over the clearing, the standing stones now seeming to emanate a softer, more diffused light, reflecting the transformation that had occurred. The raw, untamed power that had pulsed from them earlier was now tempered, almost domesticated, by Aine's ultimate act of preservation.

He gently released Aine, who swayed slightly before regaining her footing, leaning against one of the ancient monoliths. Her eyes, though still carrying the fatigue of her ordeal, now held a new depth, a quiet understanding of the path ahead. He saw the subtle shift in her posture, a slight tension in her shoulders that hadn't been there before, the invisible weight of the absorbed darkness settling upon her. It was a constant, subtle effort, he realized, to maintain the delicate balance she had spoken of. This wasn't a battle won and forgotten; it was a perpetual state of being.

"What do we do now?" Pete asked, his voice low, searching. The question was deceptively simple, yet it encompassed the vast, uncharted territory that lay before them. The immediate threat was neutralized, the outsider vanquished, but the consequences of Aine's sacrifice were only just beginning to manifest. He needed to understand the practical implications, the day-to-day realities of her transformed existence. Was there a specific ritual she needed to perform? A regimen of focus and control? He was ready to learn, to adapt, to do whatever was necessary to support her.

Aine turned, her gaze meeting his, a faint, almost imperceptible tremor in her hand as she reached out to touch his arm. "We live, Pete," she said, her voice soft but firm. "We live, and I learn to navigate this new landscape within me. The stones... they still hold power. But now, so do I, in a different way." She gestured towards the nexus, where the quartz crystal still pulsed with a gentle, internal light. "This place is my anchor, and you... you are my constant reminder of what I am protecting, of the light that must always prevail."

He understood. The power was still there, but it was no longer solely an external force to be channeled. It was now intrinsically linked to her, a part of her very being. The vigilance she spoke of was a constant, internal struggle, a mental and spiritual discipline that would require unwavering commitment. And his role was to be the steadfast presence that would facilitate that discipline. He was to be the mirror that reflected her inner light, the quiet strength that would shore her up when the shadows within threatened to overwhelm.

He began to walk with her, away from the immediate vicinity of the standing stones, towards the faint glow of the distant village. The moon, a sliver of silver in the inky sky, cast long, dancing shadows that seemed to mimic the internal struggle Aine now faced. Pete felt a surge of protectiveness, a primal instinct to shield her from any potential harm. He knew, however, that the greatest threat now came from within, and his role would be to help her manage that internal battle.

"When you first absorbed it," Pete began, choosing his words carefully, "you said it was like... containing it. Not destroying it, but transforming it. How does that manifest, day to day?" He wanted to understand the nuances of her new reality. Was it a constant battle of wills? Did she feel its presence as a distinct entity, or was it more of a subtle influence, a whispering temptation? He needed to be able to recognize the signs, to offer support before it became a crisis.

Aine paused, a thoughtful expression on her face. "It's like having a second heartbeat, Pete," she explained, her voice quiet. "A faint, discordant rhythm beneath the song of my own life. Sometimes it's almost imperceptible, a mere whisper of unease. Other times, especially when I'm tired, or stressed, it becomes more insistent. It tempts me with power, with quick solutions, with the ease of succumbing to its nature." She met his gaze, her eyes filled with a mixture of vulnerability and resolve. "But I remember. I remember why I did this. I remember us, and Kilkenny, and the generations before me."

Pete stopped walking, turning to face her fully. He reached out, gently taking her hand. "And I will remind you," he said, his voice resonating with a newfound conviction. "Every single day, if need be. You don't have to carry this alone, Aine. Not anymore." He squeezed her hand, a silent promise that his commitment was absolute. He would be her unwavering support, her constant reminder of the light.

As they continued their walk, the quiet of the night was broken only by the chirping of crickets and the distant hoot of an owl. The air, once charged with volatile energy, was now imbued with a serene tranquility. Yet, beneath that surface calm, Pete sensed the undercurrent of Aine's internal struggle, a subtle tension that she held with remarkable grace. He was aware of his own role in this delicate dance. He needed to be perceptive, to anticipate her needs, to offer comfort and reassurance without being overbearing.

He remembered a conversation they'd had weeks ago, before the true danger had manifested. They had been sitting by the hearth, the flames casting flickering shadows on the walls of their small cottage, discussing the future. Aine had spoken of the weight of her lineage, the responsibility that rested upon her shoulders. He had listened, offering his own quiet strength, his unwavering belief in her. Now, that belief was amplified, transformed into a tangible force that would help her navigate the immense challenge she had undertaken.

"We should consider reinforcing the wards around the village," Pete suggested, his mind already shifting to practical matters. "The outsider's influence, even neutralized, might have left residual traces, or perhaps created vulnerabilities that we didn't anticipate." He was thinking ahead, looking for ways to actively contribute to their continued safety. His courage wasn't in wielding ancient powers, but in his unwavering loyalty and his practical approach to problem-solving. He was the steady hand, the grounded perspective that complemented Aine's extraordinary abilities.

Aine nodded, a flicker of gratitude in her eyes. "That is a good idea, Pete. Your foresight has always been invaluable. Even when I was focused on the immediate confrontation, you were already considering the aftermath." She leaned her head against his shoulder as they walked, drawing a measure of comfort from his presence. "It is reassuring to know that I have you by my side, not just as a lover, but as a partner in this new guardianship."

He felt a warmth spread through him at her words. He might not possess her ancestral power, but he had something equally potent: unwavering devotion and a keen mind. His actions during the confrontation, though seemingly passive, had been crucial. He had been her anchor, her constant presence, a grounding force that had allowed her to access and wield her power without being consumed by it. He had remained steadfast, a silent sentinel of support, and that had been instrumental in her ability to withstand the outsider's insidious attempts to corrupt her energy.

He recalled a specific moment, just as the outsider's corrupting influence began to weave its way into Aine's protective shield. He had seen the subtle faltering in her focus, the brief flicker of doubt that had crossed her face. In that instant, he had instinctively projected his own conviction, his absolute faith in her. He hadn't spoken aloud, but he had poured every ounce of his being into that silent affirmation. He had willed her to remember her strength, her purpose, and he believed, with all his heart, that his unspoken support had been a vital catalyst in her subsequent shift to containment.

"When it felt like it was trying to poison your energy," Pete said, his voice regaining some of the urgency he'd felt then, "I saw you hesitate for a moment. And in that moment, I... I just focused all my will on you. On reminding you of why you were doing this. On Kilkenny. On us." He hesitated, feeling a touch of awkwardness at confessing such an intimate, internal action. "I don't know if it made any difference, but I had to try."

Aine stopped again, turning to him with a soft, knowing smile. She raised her hand, gently tracing the line of his jaw. "It made all the difference, Pete," she whispered, her voice filled with a deep, profound sincerity. "You were my anchor. You were the reminder of the light when the darkness pressed in most fiercely. You gave me the strength to shift my approach, to move from brute force to something... more. Your presence, your unwavering faith, that is as potent as any ancient spell."

He felt a surge of emotion, a deep sense of fulfillment at her words. His contribution, though not flashy or overtly powerful, had been essential. It had been the human element, the raw, unadulterated courage of love and loyalty, that had tipped the scales. He had provided the emotional bedrock upon which Aine could build her extraordinary defense. He was a testament to the idea that even in the face of ancient, otherworldly powers, the strength of human connection and unwavering resolve could be the deciding factor.

As they neared the edge of the woods, the first lights of Kilkenny twinkled in the distance, a beacon of normalcy in the aftermath of such profound upheaval. Pete knew their lives had changed forever. Aine was no longer just the guardian; she was the embodiment of that guardianship, carrying its burdens and its triumphs within her very soul. And he, in turn, was no longer just her lover; he was her steadfast companion, her shield against the shadows, her constant reminder of the light.

"We'll need to be vigilant," Pete stated, his tone firm and resolute. "The outsider is gone, but the echoes of its presence might still linger. And now, with you carrying its neutralized essence, we have a new kind of vigilance to maintain." He was already planning, strategizing. His mind, usually so grounded in the tangible, was now attuned to the subtler forces at play, the intricate balance that Aine had so bravely forged. He saw their future as a shared endeavor, a continuous effort to maintain the peace she had fought so hard to secure.

Aine met his gaze, her own reflecting his determination. "And we will be vigilant, Pete. Together." She offered him a small, encouraging smile. "You have already proven how vital your presence is. Your courage is not in grand gestures, but in your unwavering steadfastness. You are the quiet strength that makes the extraordinary possible."

He returned her smile, a sense of purpose settling upon him. His pivotal action had not been a single, dramatic moment, but a sustained, unwavering commitment. It was the courage to stand by her side, to offer emotional support when it was most needed, and to face the future, whatever it might hold, with unshakeable loyalty. He understood now that his role, though different from Aine's, was no less critical. He was the human element, the grounding force, the constant reminder that even in the deepest of shadows, the light of love and courage would always find a way to shine through. The resolution of the immediate crisis was not an end, but a beginning, and he was ready to face it, hand in hand with the woman he loved, the guardian who had saved them all. The weight of her sacrifice was immense, but in his unwavering support, he aimed to lighten that burden, ensuring that her triumph, and theirs, would endure.

THE RESTORING OF BALANCE

The air in Kilkenny, which had been thick with an unsettling hum, a disquieting tremor that vibrated through the very foundations of the town, began to clarify. The unnatural chill that had seeped into the stone walls and coiled around the hearts of its inhabitants started to dissipate, like mist burned away by the morning sun. The eerie silence that had fallen upon the marketplace, where hawkers and villagers alike had been frozen in place by an unseen dread, now yielded to tentative sounds. A dog barked in the distance, a mundane sound that was, in its very ordinariness, a testament to the returning normalcy. The unsettling visions that had flickered at the periphery of sight, the whispers that had snaked through the quiet hours, all began to recede, drawing back into the hidden places from which they had emerged. Kilkenny breathed again, a collective sigh of relief that rippled through the streets and into the hearts of its people.

Pete watched the subtle shifts with a keen, almost painful awareness. He could feel the change in Aine beside him, a gradual easing of the tension that had been coiled within her. The fierce, protective aura that had blazed around her during the confrontation had softened, returning to its more familiar, gentle luminescence. The standing stones, which had pulsed with a raw, untamed energy, now seemed to settle, their ancient power retracting, becoming a part of the very earth they anchored. It was as if the land itself had exhaled, releasing the pent-up tension of the conflict. He saw it in the way the shadows lengthened and then began to recede from the edges of the clearing, no longer harbingers of encroaching darkness but simply the natural fading of the day.

"It feels... quieter," Aine murmured, her voice raspy with exhaustion, yet carrying a new note of profound peace. She leaned against Pete, her body a comforting weight against his. "The noise inside me has subsided. It's still there, of course, a presence I will always carry, but it's no longer screaming for release." She took a shaky breath, her gaze sweeping across the now still and silent landscape. The wild energy that had surged through her, the raw power that had been channeled and contained, was now a part of her, an integrated force, rather than a chaotic storm.

Pete held her close, his own heart gradually slowing its frantic beat. He had felt the raw power, had witnessed the immense struggle, and now, he was feeling the aftermath, the slow, steady return to equilibrium. The residual energy that had thrummed through him, a faint echo of Aine's internal battle, was fading, leaving him with a profound sense of quiet awe. He looked at the ancient monoliths, their grey surfaces no longer radiating a threatening luminescence, but a soft, enduring glow. They were the guardians of Kilkenny, and Aine, by her extraordinary act, had become their living embodiment, the conduit through which their power flowed and was, in turn, maintained.

"The balance," Pete said, the word carrying the weight of their shared understanding. "You've restored the balance." He felt a tremor run through her, a subtle shift of weight as she drew strength from his presence. It wasn't just about external forces being neutralized; it was about the internal recalibration, the delicate, intricate dance of power and control that Aine now orchestrated within herself. The world outside had reacted to the disruption, the strange phenomena that had plagued Kilkenny being outward manifestations of an inner turmoil. Now, with that inner turmoil soothed, the external world began to reflect that same restored calm.

Aine nodded, her forehead resting against his chest. "It's not just restored, Pete. I think... I think it might be stronger. The act of containing the outsider, of holding its essence without letting it corrupt me, has woven its way into the fabric of what I am. It's a part of me now, and in a strange way, that integration has solidified the wards, deepened the connection." She pulled back slightly, her eyes, though shadowed with fatigue, shone with a quiet, resolute light. "The stones are at peace. And Kilkenny is at peace."

He saw the truth of her words in the subtle yet significant changes around them. The oppressive atmosphere that had clung to the town like a shroud had lifted. The unnatural silence that had gripped the normally bustling streets was replaced by the sounds of life reasserting itself. He imagined the villagers, tentatively emerging from their homes, their faces etched with relief, their voices a hushed murmur of disbelief and gratitude. The strange occurrences, the whispers of fear that had spread like wildfire, were now just terrifying memories, stories to be recounted with a shiver and a thankful glance towards the silent guardians of the village.

"The energies," Pete mused, his gaze drifting towards the distant lights of Kilkenny, now a warm, welcoming glow in the deepening twilight. "They feel... settled. Like a river that has been dammed and then allowed to flow back into its natural course, but somehow, with a new strength, a new clarity." He felt it too, a profound sense of calm washing over him, a release of the tension that had been coiled in his own shoulders since the first inkling of danger. His role had been to support Aine, to be her steadfast human connection, and now, in the quiet aftermath, he felt the profound significance of that role. He had been the anchor, the steady hand in the storm, and that, he realized, was a power in itself.

Aine's hand found his, her fingers interlacing with his. Her touch was cool, a stark contrast to the residual heat he still felt from the intense energy that had coursed through her. "The outsider sought to unravel the threads of protection that have bound Kilkenny for generations," she explained, her voice soft but clear. "It fed on discord, on fear, on the disruption of the natural order. By absorbing its essence, by refusing to be consumed by its negativity, I have, in essence, rewoven those threads, but with a resilience born of overcoming its influence."

He understood. The ancient magic of Kilkenny, the intricate network of wards and protections that had safeguarded the town for centuries, had been tested. It had been assaulted by a force that sought to corrupt and dismantle it. Aine's act, while born of necessity and immense personal sacrifice, had been the ultimate act of preservation. She hadn't destroyed the threat; she had internalized it, transformed it, and in doing so, had inadvertently strengthened the very system she was sworn to protect. The residual darkness, once a beacon of danger, was now a testament to her strength, a hidden layer of fortification.

"So, the phenomena we saw," Pete continued, piecing together the fragments of their ordeal, "the shifting shadows, the whispers, the feeling of dread... those were all outward signs of its attempt to break through, to destabilize everything?" He wanted to fully grasp the nature of the threat they had faced, to understand the true scope of Aine's victory. It wasn't just a battle against an unseen enemy; it was a battle against the very fabric of their reality, a fight to maintain the delicate equilibrium that governed their world.

Aine nodded, her gaze distant as she recalled the terrifying moments. "Precisely. It was like a virus, attempting to corrupt the system from within. It amplified existing fears, preyed on anxieties, and sought to sow discord. But the core of Kilkenny, its heart, remained strong. And my connection to that heart, to its ancestral guardians, allowed me to channel that resistance, to absorb the corruption and transmute it." She paused, a faint smile touching her lips. "It was a risky gambit. One misstep, and I would have become the very thing I was fighting."

Pete's grip tightened on her hand. The sheer courage, the sheer terror of that possibility, struck him anew. He had seen her strength, but he hadn't fully grasped the razor's edge upon which she had walked. He felt a surge of protectiveness, a fierce desire to shield her from any future threats, any lingering shadows of their recent struggle. His own role, he knew, was to be that shield, that constant source of support and reassurance.

"But you didn't falter," he said, his voice filled with admiration. "You held strong. And now, Kilkenny is safe. The whispers are gone. The fear has subsided." He could almost hear the return of laughter to the village, the murmur of normal conversation, the simple, comforting sounds of a community at peace. The unnatural stillness that had descended upon the town was already a fading memory, replaced by the gentle hum of everyday life.

"The outsider's presence left a wound, but not a fatal one," Aine explained, her words measured and thoughtful. "The energies of Kilkenny are reasserting themselves, healing that wound. The strange occurrences you witnessed were manifestations of that wound, of the imbalance caused by its intrusion. Now that the source of that imbalance has been contained, the natural order is reasserting itself. The shadows retreat, the whispers fall silent, and the underlying calm returns."

Pete looked at her, seeing not just the woman he loved, but the embodiment of Kilkenny's enduring strength. Her sacrifice, her bravery, had not only saved them from immediate destruction but had, in a profound and unexpected way, fortified their defenses. The very act of overcoming the darkness had made the light stronger. The subtle disturbances that had plagued the town were like ripples on the surface of a deep, calm lake; now the lake was still once more, its depths undisturbed.

"It's like the land itself is breathing a sigh of relief," Pete observed, the imagery feeling acutely accurate. He could sense the subtle shift in the earth beneath his feet, a grounding, steady rhythm that hadn't been present during the height of the crisis. The very air felt cleaner, lighter, free from the oppressive weight of the encroaching void. Kilkenny, his home, was returning to its serene, ancient self, its hidden heart beating steadily once more.

Aine smiled, a genuine, unburdened smile that reached her eyes. "Yes, exactly. The land remembers its ancient rhythm, its innate harmony. My ancestors worked to maintain that harmony, and now, in a new way, I have done the same. The integration of the outsider's essence hasn't just protected Kilkenny; it has, in a sense, reinforced the very foundations of its magic, creating a new layer of resilience."

He felt a profound sense of gratitude, not just for Aine's strength, but for the enduring power of the lineage she represented. This was a legacy of protection, a continuous line of guardianship that had faced down countless threats, each time emerging stronger. He, in his own way, was now a part of that legacy, a witness and a supporter of its enduring strength. His place was beside her, a constant reminder of the human spirit's capacity for resilience and love, even in the face of overwhelming odds.

"And what of the residual energy you mentioned?" Pete inquired, his mind already moving towards the practicalities of their new reality. He understood that while the immediate threat was gone, the consequences of Aine's actions would require ongoing vigilance. "Will there be... aftershocks? Lingering effects we need to be aware of?"

Aine's expression turned more serious, though the underlying peace remained. "There will always be a... resonance. A subtle echo of what has transpired. The energy of the outsider, though contained, is still a part of me. It's like a scar, a permanent mark of the battle. But it is a scar that I have learned to integrate, to manage. It's a reminder, not a threat." She met his gaze, her eyes holding a newfound depth, a quiet wisdom born of her ordeal. "The key is vigilance, yes, but it is also about understanding. I must learn to live with this new facet of myself, to ensure that the light always remains dominant."

He understood her meaning. The vigilance wasn't just about watching for external threats; it was an internal discipline, a constant awareness of the delicate balance she maintained within. His role was to be a part of that vigilance, to offer his steady presence, his unwavering belief, and his practical insights. He was the grounding force that would help her navigate the subtle shifts, the quiet temptations that might arise from the integrated darkness.

"And I will be there, every step of the way," Pete vowed, his voice firm and unwavering. "We will face it together. Just as we faced the storm." He squeezed her hand, a silent promise that his commitment was absolute. He wouldn't let her face this internal battle alone. He was her partner, her anchor, her constant reminder of the light that burned so brightly within her.

As they began to walk back towards the sleeping village, the sounds of life, faint at first, began to grow. A window creaked open, and a cat meowed, a small, everyday occurrence that seemed, in that moment, like a miracle. The ancient stones stood sentinel, their purpose fulfilled, their energy now a quiet hum beneath the surface of the land. Kilkenny was settling back into its natural rhythm, its hidden heart beating steadily once more, a testament to the enduring strength of its guardians, and to the quiet, unwavering courage of love. The night was still and peaceful, but beneath that peace lay the promise of a new dawn, a dawn that Aine, with Pete by her side, would now help to usher in, stronger and more resilient than ever before. The profound stillness that now enveloped Kilkenny was not merely the absence of threat, but the palpable presence of restored harmony, a deep and abiding peace that resonated through the very soul of the town, a peace hard-won and now, profoundly cherished.

AINE AND PETES FUTURE

The lingering scent of ozone, a sharp, almost metallic tang that clung to the air, was the only immediate reminder of the cataclysmic forces they had just witnessed. Pete watched Aine, her profile etched against the deepening twilight, the residual glow from the standing stones fading into a soft, internal luminescence. The profound quiet that had settled over the landscape was no longer a silence born of fear, but one of deep, abiding peace, a stillness that spoke of equilibrium restored. He could feel the weight of her gaze as she turned to him, her eyes, though weary, held a new clarity, a depth that hadn't been there before.

"It's over," she said, the words barely a whisper, yet they carried the finality of a pronouncement. "The outsider is... contained. Within me." A shiver traced its way down her spine, not of cold, but of profound, existential realization. The immensity of what she had done, of what she had become, settled upon her like a cloak, heavy yet strangely comforting. She met Pete's steady gaze, searching for an understanding that went beyond words, a reflection of the unspoken questions that now hung between them.

"You did it, Aine," Pete said, his voice rough with emotion. He reached out, his fingers brushing against her cheek, tracing the delicate curve of her jaw. "You saved us. You saved Kilkenny." The words felt inadequate, a pale imitation of the monumental feat she had achieved. He saw the exhaustion etched around her eyes, the subtle tremor in her hands, but beneath it all, he saw an unwavering strength, a resilience forged in the crucible of the unimaginable.

Aine leaned into his touch, drawing a steadying breath. "It wasn't just me, Pete. You were there. Your presence, your unwavering belief... it was my anchor." She paused, her gaze drifting back towards the ancient stones, their silent sentinels bathed in the soft moonlight. "The power was immense. Overwhelming. But knowing you were beside me, that I wasn't alone in this... it made all the difference." Her hand found his, her fingers tightening around his as if seeking reassurance, a tangible connection to the world they had fought so hard to protect.

"We faced it together," Pete affirmed, his thumb gently stroking the back of her hand. He felt the slight tremor beneath his touch, a faint echo of the raw power that had surged through her. It was a power he now understood, a power that was now irrevocably a part of her. The implications of that realization, of the life they had always envisioned, began to surface, casting long shadows of uncertainty over their shared future. "But now... now that it's over... what does this mean, Aine? For us?"

The question hung in the air, heavy with unspoken fears and tentative hopes. Aine's gaze met his, her expression a complex tapestry of relief, apprehension, and a profound sense of responsibility. "That's the question, isn't it?" she murmured, her voice laced with a weariness that went beyond physical exhaustion. "I've... integrated the outsider. Its essence is a part of me now. It's a constant presence, a quiet hum beneath the surface of my being. It's not a threat anymore, not in the way it was, but it's... there."

Pete listened intently, his mind racing to process the enormity of her words. He had witnessed her strength, her courage, her extraordinary connection to Kilkenny's ancient magic. But this was a new dimension, a transformation that extended beyond anything he had ever imagined. He felt a surge of protectiveness, a primal urge to shield her from any potential harm, any residual darkness that might seek to exploit this new facet of her being.

"And that means...?" he prompted, his voice carefully neutral, though his heart pounded with a mixture of anticipation and dread. He knew that their future, the quiet life they had dreamed of, might now be fundamentally altered. He loved Aine, deeply and irrevocably, but he was also a man of the ordinary world, a world that, until recently, had seemed blissfully unaware of the ancient forces that governed Kilkenny.

Aine's sigh was soft, a sound of profound introspection. "It means I can't simply... go back. My connection to Kilkenny, to the standing stones, to the very energy of this place, has been... deepened. Amplified. The outsider's influence, though transmuted, has awakened something within me, a latent power that I now have a responsibility to understand and to wield." She looked at him, her eyes pleading for understanding, for acceptance. "My duties as guardian have not ended, Pete. In fact, they've become more complex, more... intimate."

He reached out, his hand covering hers, his touch a silent reassurance. "I understand that, Aine. I saw what you did. I felt the power. And I know that you are capable of incredible things." He paused, choosing his words carefully. "But can we... can we still have a life? A normal life? Can I be a part of that, or will I always be an outsider looking in on your world?" The question was difficult to voice, fraught with vulnerability, but he needed to know. Their shared ordeal had forged an unbreakable bond, but it had also exposed the vast chasm between their experiences, between their understanding of the world.

A faint smile touched Aine's lips, a bittersweet expression that acknowledged the truth of his words. "You're not an outsider, Pete. You were never an outsider. You're the one who saw me, truly saw me, even when I was afraid of what I was becoming. You stood by me, even when the world seemed to be unraveling around us." She squeezed his hand tighter. "The question isn't whether you can be a part of my world, Pete. The question is whether you can accept the totality of it. The magic, the responsibilities, the constant vigilance... and the fact that I am now, in a way I never fully anticipated, inextricably bound to Kilkenny and its secrets."

He met her gaze, his own resolve hardening. He had always been drawn to Aine, to her quiet strength, her inherent grace, and her deep connection to the land. He had chosen to stay in Kilkenny, to build a life with her, and now, he realized, that choice had led him to a crossroads he had never anticipated. He had been thrust into a world of ancient magic and hidden powers, and in doing so, he had discovered a strength and resilience within himself that he hadn't known he possessed.

"I came to Kilkenny seeking peace," Pete said, his voice steady and sure. "I found it, and I found you. I've seen the darkness, Aine, but I've also seen the light that you carry. I've seen the power that resides in this place, and I've seen your capacity to protect it." He took a deep breath, the words coming from a place of profound conviction. "My life is intertwined with yours, Aine. Whether it's within the ancient wards of Kilkenny or in some quiet cottage on the outskirts, it doesn't matter. What matters is that we are together. And if being with you means understanding and accepting this... this new reality, then so be it."

A soft gasp escaped Aine's lips, and a single tear traced a path down her cheek, catching the moonlight. It was a tear of relief, of gratitude, of an overwhelming sense of love and acceptance. "Pete," she whispered, her voice thick with emotion. "Are you sure? This isn't a fairy tale, you know. This is a life bound to ancient forces, to responsibilities that can be... demanding. There will be times when the weight of it all feels too much, when the echoes of what I carry might... intrude."

"I'm sure," Pete replied, his gaze unwavering. "I love you, Aine. And I choose this life, with you. We will face whatever comes, together. We'll learn, we'll adapt. I may not understand the intricacies of the magic as you do, but I understand commitment. I understand loyalty. And I understand love." He brought her hand to his lips, pressing a soft kiss to her knuckles, a silent vow of his enduring devotion. "You're not alone in this, Aine. Never."

Aine's shoulders relaxed, the tension that had been coiled within her for so long finally beginning to release. A genuine smile, radiant and pure, bloomed on her face. "Then we face it together," she said, her voice filled with a renewed sense of purpose and a quiet, unshakeable resolve. "We build our future, here, in Kilkenny. We find a way to balance the ordinary with the extraordinary, the love we share with the responsibilities I carry."

They stood in comfortable silence for a moment, the vastness of the night sky stretching above them, a silent witness to their shared commitment. The air, no longer charged with the raw energy of the outsider, was now filled with a different kind of power – the quiet strength of two hearts united, of a love that had been tested by fire and emerged stronger, more resilient than ever before. The path ahead was uncertain, undoubtedly filled with challenges they couldn't yet foresee, but they would face it side-by-side, their bond a beacon of hope in the deepening twilight.

As they began their descent from the hill, the distant lights of Kilkenny twinkled like scattered stars, a welcoming glow that promised sanctuary and a return to normalcy, albeit a normalcy forever altered by the events of the day. Aine leaned against Pete, her hand clasped firmly in his, the weight of her newfound power a palpable presence, yet it no longer felt like a burden. Instead, it felt like a sacred trust, a legacy she was now empowered to carry forward, with him by her side.

"What do you think it will be like?" Pete asked, his voice soft, a note of curiosity mingled with apprehension. "Our future, I mean. With... everything." He gestured vaguely, encompassing the ancient stones, the land, and the very essence of Kilkenny's hidden world. He was ready to embrace it, but the unknown still held a certain trepidation.

Aine smiled, a thoughtful expression gracing her features. "It will be... different. It will require patience, understanding, and a constant willingness to learn. There will be times when my focus needs to be solely on Kilkenny, on maintaining the balance. But there will also be moments of quiet normalcy, of simple joys, of building a life together, just as we'd always planned." She squeezed his hand. "We'll have to be adaptable, Pete. And we'll have to trust each other implicitly. Because the vigilance I speak of, it's not just mine. It's ours."

He nodded, the concept of their shared vigilance settling into his consciousness. It wasn't just about her being the guardian; it was about him being her unwavering support, her confidant, her human anchor in a world that often blurred the lines between the tangible and the mystical. His role might be less visible, less overtly powerful, but he understood its profound importance. He was the steady hand, the grounding force, the reminder of the ordinary world that Aine was fighting to protect.

"And the integration?" Pete inquired, returning to a more practical, yet deeply personal, aspect of their conversation. He remembered her words about the outsider's essence becoming a part of her. "How does that feel, day to day? Is it... a struggle?" He wanted to understand the personal cost of her extraordinary courage, the internal landscape she now navigated.

Aine considered his question, her gaze thoughtful. "It's... a duality. There are moments when I feel the echo of its power, its cold logic, its insatiable drive. It's a whisper that tempts, a subtle suggestion that can easily be mistaken for intuition if one isn't careful." She paused, her expression turning more serious. "But it's also a source of strength, a deeper understanding of the very forces I must contend with. It's like having an intimate knowledge of the enemy, Pete. And by understanding it, by not letting it consume me, I can anticipate its moves, its weaknesses."

"So, it's about control," Pete mused, the concept resonating with him. He thought of the immense control Aine had demonstrated during the confrontation, her ability to wield such raw power without succumbing to its corrupting influence. It was a testament to her character, her inherent goodness.

"Not just control," Aine corrected gently. "It's about integration. About weaving it into the tapestry of who I am, rather than letting it become the dominant thread. It's about finding the balance within myself, just as I maintain the balance for Kilkenny. It's a constant, conscious effort, but it's an effort I am willing to make." Her eyes met his, and in their depths, he saw not just the guardian of Kilkenny, but the woman he loved, a woman of extraordinary courage and unwavering resolve.

He pulled her closer, wrapping his arms around her, holding her tightly. "And I'll be here to help you find that balance, Aine. Every single day. We'll build our life here, in Kilkenny, and we'll make it work. Because what we have is worth fighting for. It's worth building, and it's worth protecting." The words were spoken with a conviction that resonated in the quiet night, a promise that echoed the enduring strength of the land around them.

Aine rested her head against his chest, a contented sigh escaping her lips. "Together," she whispered, the word a soft vow, a shared commitment that transcended the extraordinary circumstances that had brought them to this point. The future was unwritten, a vast expanse of possibilities, but with Pete by her side, she felt ready to face whatever lay ahead, to embrace the unique path that had been laid out for them, a path paved with love, resilience, and the enduring magic of Kilkenny. The subtle hum of ancient power beneath their feet felt less like a threat and more like a promise, a testament to the enduring strength of their bond, and to the life they were now ready to build, together. The darkness had been confronted, the resolution found, and now, in the quiet aftermath, a new chapter of their lives was just beginning, bathed in the soft glow of shared understanding and unwavering love.

Chapter Fifteen: Echoes and Endings

REFLECTIONS ON KILKENNY

The crisp morning air, usually a welcome caress after the humid embrace of the previous night, now carried a different sort of sharpness for Pete. It was the clarity that comes after a storm, but also the poignant awareness of an impending departure. His vacation, a planned escape from the mundane rhythm of his city life, had irrevocably transformed into something far more profound. Kilkenny, which he had initially seen as a charming backdrop for a restful break, now pulsed with a secret life, a hidden narrative woven into the very fabric of its ancient stones and winding lanes.

He stood on the ramparts of Kilkenny Castle, the stone cool and solid beneath his hands, a stark contrast to the ethereal energy he had witnessed just hours before. From this vantage point, the city spread out below him, a tapestry of ochre rooftops and shadowed alleyways. It was the same view he'd admired on his first day, but the lens through which he now saw it was entirely new. The seemingly placid flow of the River Nore, snaking its way through the heart of the town, no longer represented mere natural beauty; it felt like a conduit, a silent artery carrying the ancient lifeblood of the land. The very air seemed to hum with a subtler, more resonant energy, an echo of the forces Aine commanded, of the outsider she had so bravely contained.

He walked through the city's heart, his footsteps falling on cobblestones that had borne witness to centuries of history, both seen and unseen. The familiar chime of St. Canice's Cathedral, a sound that had once been a gentle reminder of the town's ecclesiastical heritage, now seemed to carry a deeper resonance, a call and response to the ancient powers that slumbered, and sometimes, awoke, within Kilkenny. He found himself lingering in the narrow streets, noticing details he had previously overlooked: the intricate carvings on ancient doorways, the weathered gargoyles perched precariously on building facades, the almost imperceptible patterns in the mortar of old walls. Each seemed to whisper fragments of a forgotten language, stories of protection, of warding, of the constant, quiet vigilance that Aine embodied.

The thought of leaving Kilkenny, of returning to his old life, felt like a jarring discord. The mundane concerns that had once occupied his mind – work deadlines, social obligations, the everyday anxieties of urban existence – now seemed distant, almost trivial. Kilkenny had not merely offered him a temporary respite; it had served as an unexpected crucible, forging a new awareness within him, an understanding of a reality that extended far beyond the tangible. He had come seeking peace, and he had found it, but it was a peace interwoven with a profound sense of responsibility, a quiet awe for the forces that shaped not just this ancient city, but perhaps, the very world.

The lively stalls of the farmer's market exerted a powerful pull on him, the atmosphere saturated with the rich aromas of ripe fruits, crisp vegetables, and fragrant pastries. The effortless rapport between the merchants and the community members, the very essence of their mutual exchange, seemed a valuable treasure, a powerful illustration of humanity's resilience and its innate craving for fellowship. He acquired a rustic loaf of bread from a woman whose radiant smile mirrored the sun's gentle morning glow. In that fleeting instant, a profound ache for permanence washed over him; he yearned to integrate, to belong not as a fleeting observer, but as an integral part of this locale, intimately acquainted with its unspoken rhythms and its quiet fortitude.

His exploration led him to the Kilkenny Design Centre, where its cutting-edge design stood in bold opposition to the timeworn fortifications it abutted. Within its walls, the ingenuity of current craftspeople was showcased, a lively declaration of the persistent drive for novelty that Kilkenny nurtured. He absorbed the painstaking artistry in every thread of fabric, the confident artistry in every ceramic piece, and the refined skill evident in each piece of adornment. A novel form of strength dawned on him – the force of human imagination and creative flair, a potency that, in its own unique fashion, enriched Kilkenny's character, offering a sophisticated harmony to the city's more primal energies.

Wandering the famously trod thoroughfare of the Medieval Mile, a route linking the city's most monumental historical landmarks, Pete experienced a profound surge of awareness regarding the immense historical resonance embedded within the very ground he traversed. The vast expanse of Kilkenny's historical narrative transformed from a detached, academic subject into a tangible reality, a vibrant force that breathed through the remnants of the Dominican Priory and reverberated within the somber alcoves of St. Francis's

Abbey. He envisioned the countless individuals who had journeyed these same routes, their aspirations, their anxieties, their arduous endeavors, all intermingled and accumulated, constructing the complex tapestry of the Kilkenny he encountered.

He returned to familiar locales, their former appeal now amplified into something reverent. The intimate alleys, once merely visually pleasing, now seemed imbued with unspoken histories, like stoic guardians of obscured wisdom. He followed the faded markings of indecipherable etchings, sensing a link to the primordial designs woven within, a purpose reaching beyond the confines of eras. Kilkenny itself appeared transformed into a living chronicle, and his recent encounters had granted him an insight into its profound underlying structure.

The imposing silhouette of Kilkenny Castle, the initial beacon drawing him to the locale, now resonated with a far richer meaning. Transcending its aesthetic splendor and historical weight, it felt like an intersection, a confluence of the ordinary and the enchanted. He recalled Aine's quiet fortitude and the weight of her newly assumed duties. The castle, with its formidable ramparts and ageless narratives, stood as more than a mere monument; it embodied custodianship, a tangible embodiment of the protective currents coursing through Kilkenny, currents that Aine now grasped and commanded with a power that left him awestruck.

Pausing at the ancient city ramparts, his fingers traced the rough, time-worn stone. To him, it wasn't merely an artifact of ages past, but a profound declaration of humanity's persistent yearning for security, for defined limits, and for a bulwark against threats aiming to shatter the existing framework. This sentiment struck a chord within him, echoing the conflict he had observed, the arduous fight to restrain a power that endangered the fragile equilibrium of their existence. Kilkenny's past, in essence, served as a narrative of such struggles, of perseverance against formidable challenges, and of the perpetual, often clandestine, labor required to preserve peace.

The knowledge of what lay beneath the surface, of the unseen forces that Aine now navigated, added a layer of profound melancholy to his impending departure. He knew that his understanding, though awakened, was still nascent. He had glimpsed the edge of a vast and ancient ocean, and he knew that Aine was now inextricably bound to its depths. His love for her, already profound, had deepened into a fierce protectiveness, a desire to shield her from the weight of her new responsibilities, even as he understood that his role was not to shield, but to support, to stand beside her.

As the afternoon waned, casting long shadows across the historic streets, Pete found a quiet bench overlooking the river. The water flowed onward, indifferent to the momentous events that had transpired. Yet, to Pete, it felt like a constant, gentle reminder of continuity, of the enduring nature of life, and of the cycles of change and renewal. Kilkenny, he realized, was not a place of static history, but a living, breathing entity, its past interwoven with its present, its future shaped by the courage and wisdom of those who understood its deepest secrets.

Once disregarded as mere atmospheric whims or flights of fancy, the fine gradations in the air, the nearly invisible flows of power, now resonated with him. He understood these as the very heartbeat of Kilkenny, the hushed exhalations of a locale imbued with enchantment. The city's appealing exterior, to his discerning gaze, had become a delicate membrane, and he perceived that beneath it resided a realm of immense consequence, a domain he had been blessed to glimpse, a realm that had reshaped his very being. His outlook had not merely altered; it had been profoundly enlarged, unveiling strata of existence previously unimaginable.

Contemplating Aine, her formidable resilience and the steadfast resolve she displayed in accepting her fate, stirred a potent blend of elation and a profound, persistent pang. Initially arriving in Kilkenny with detached curiosity, a sojourner in pursuit of fleeting respite, he departed transformed. He became a quiet observer, an integral participant in the unfolding saga, irrevocably altered by the enchantment he had witnessed and the remarkable woman who commanded it. His holiday concluded, yet his personal odyssey and evolving comprehension had merely commenced. Kilkenny transcended its status as a mere waypoint; it marked a pivotal juncture, an awakening, a location indelibly imprinted upon his spirit as the epicenter of his individual enlightenment. The resonance of the exceptional would accompany him, a perpetual testament to the veiled realm existing just beyond the mundane, a domain now recognized with unwavering conviction as profoundly tangible.

AINES LEGACY AND COMMITMENT

The weight of centuries settled upon Aine not as a burden, but as a finely woven cloak, each thread representing a generation, a guardian, a story. She stood at the edge of the River Nore, its waters reflecting the bruised twilight sky, and felt the deep, abiding connection to the land, to the very stones of Kilkenny. Her family's legacy was not a dusty collection of names in a forgotten ledger; it was a living pulse, a constant thrumming beneath the surface of everyday life, a responsibility she had inherited, yes, but one she now understood with a clarity that resonated through her very bones. The recent ordeal, the containment of the encroaching darkness, had been a baptism by fire, and she had emerged, not unscathed, but undeniably stronger, her resolve forged in the crucible of fear and unwavering determination.

She traced the intricate patterns etched into an ancient stone embedded in the riverbank, a familiar ritual that had been passed down from her grandmother. Each swirl, each curve, was a sigil of protection, a ward against the restless energies that Kilkenny had always been a beacon for. Her grandmother had spoken of the 'Guardianship of the Nore,' a mantle that had fallen upon the women of their line for generations untold. It was more than just a title; it was a calling, a sacred trust to maintain the delicate equilibrium between the seen and the unseen, to ensure that Kilkenny remained a sanctuary, not a conduit for chaos. Aine had always respected this heritage, but now, after facing the abyss and pushing it back, she embodied it. The power that had once felt like a whispered suggestion, a subtle inclination, now felt like an integral part of her being, as natural and necessary as breathing.

Her thoughts drifted back to the confrontation, to the chilling presence that had sought to breach the city's ancient protections. She remembered the surge of primal energy that had coursed through her, the instinctual understanding of how to weave the existing wards, to reinforce them, to channel the very essence of Kilkenny itself into a bulwark. It had been terrifying, yes, but there was also an exhilaration, a profound sense of purpose that had eclipsed any personal fear. She had not fought alone. She had felt the echoes of her ancestors, their strength lending itself to hers, their wisdom guiding her actions even when her own mind was a storm of adrenaline. It was a humbling realization, this interconnectedness across time, this vast reservoir of resilience upon which she could draw.

The challenge had tested her limits, pushing her beyond anything she could have imagined. There were moments, fleeting but sharp, when doubt had threatened to consume her. Could she, a woman who had lived a relatively ordinary life until recently, truly wield such ancient power? But then, she would remember her grandmother's steady gaze, the quiet confidence that had always emanated from her, and the answer would come, not as a loud declaration, but as a deep, unshakeable certainty. Yes, she could. She had to. Kilkenny deserved nothing less, and neither did the future she was now so fiercely determined to protect.

She looked up at Kilkenny Castle, its imposing silhouette stark against the darkening sky. It was more than just a historical landmark; it was a focal point, a nexus of the energies she now understood so intimately. Its ancient stones held the memory of countless lives, of battles fought and won, of periods of peace and prosperity. And woven within that history, unseen by most, was the intricate network of wards and enchantments that her family had established and maintained. She had learned to 'read' the castle now, to feel the subtle ebb and flow of its protective aura, to identify any dissonances, any points of weakness. It was a responsibility that weighed on her, but not unpleasantly. It was the weight of purpose, the affirmation of her place in a lineage that stretched back into the mists of time.

The city, too, had transformed in her perception. The familiar streets, the charming facades, now seemed to shimmer with an inner light, an unseen luminescence that spoke of a deeper reality. She could feel the ley lines, the invisible currents of energy that crisscrossed Kilkenny, and she understood how her family's work had always been about harmonizing these forces, about ensuring they flowed in beneficial ways. She saw the ordinary people of Kilkenny, going about their lives, blissfully unaware of the ancient battles waged on their behalf, and a profound sense of duty settled upon her. She was their silent guardian, their unseen shield.

A wave of gratitude washed over her for Pete. He had witnessed her struggle, had seen her at her most vulnerable, and had offered not judgment, but unwavering support. His presence, his simple, grounding humanity, had been a lifeline during the most intense moments. He had seen the magic, not with fear, but with a quiet awe that had touched her deeply. He understood, in his own way, the magnitude of what she had faced and what it meant for her future. His love was a quiet strength, a reminder that even in the face of overwhelming power, human connection remained a vital anchor.

She knew that her journey was far from over. The recent victory was significant, a testament to her growing strength and understanding, but the forces she contended with were ancient and persistent. There would be other challenges, other moments when the veil between worlds would thin, when the need for her vigilance would be paramount. But she no longer approached these possibilities with trepidation. Instead, she felt a quiet confidence, a deep-seated readiness. She had faced her deepest fears and emerged on the other side, transformed.

Her connection to Kilkenny was no longer just about duty; it was about love. She loved the feel of the ancient stones beneath her feet, the scent of the damp earth after a rain, the murmur of the river carrying whispers of the past. She loved the spirit of the city, its resilience, its enduring beauty, its capacity to hold both the mundane and the miraculous within its embrace. Kilkenny was her home, not just by birthright, but by a conscious, unwavering choice. She was its protector, and in protecting it, she had found a profound sense of belonging, a purpose that resonated with the deepest parts of her soul.

She turned from the riverbank, her gaze sweeping across the city, now bathed in the soft glow of streetlights. The darkness that had threatened to engulf Kilkenny had receded, pushed back by the combined strength of her lineage and her own newly awakened power. Aine felt a deep and abiding peace, a sense of completion for this particular chapter, but also an eager anticipation for what lay ahead. She was ready. Ready for the quiet vigilance, ready for the unseen battles, ready to continue the ancient tradition, to be the Guardian of Kilkenny, not just in name, but in spirit and in truth. Her commitment was absolute, her purpose clear, and as she walked towards the heart of the city, she felt the ancient magic of Kilkenny singing within her, a song of continuity, of strength, and of an enduring legacy.

The wind rustled through the leaves of the ancient trees along the river, a sound that now seemed to carry the voices of generations past, murmuring their approval, their encouragement. Aine paused, closing her eyes for a moment, allowing the symphony of the night to wash over her. She felt the presence of her grandmother, a gentle warmth, a silent acknowledgment of her success. She also felt the collective spirit of all the women who had stood in this place before her, their strength a palpable force that now bolstered her own. This was not a solitary burden she carried, but a shared inheritance, a lineage of resilience and unwavering dedication.

Her mind replayed certain moments from the recent ordeal, not with a sense of lingering trauma, but with a newfound analytical clarity. She understood the specific vibrational frequencies that had been used against the city's wards, the subtle manipulation of ambient energies that had almost succeeded. Her grandmother's teachings, once abstract concepts, now had practical applications, a framework for understanding and countering such incursions. She had learned to anticipate, to adapt, to weave counter-energies with a precision that surprised even herself. This was the evolution of her power, the maturation of a nascent ability into a formidable force.

She acknowledged the inherent risks involved in her role. Kilkenny, with its unique confluence of energies, would always be a magnet for those who sought to exploit or corrupt such power. There would be times when the stakes would be incredibly high, when the consequences of failure would be dire. But the fear that had once been a constant companion had been largely replaced by a quiet resolve. She had stared into the face of destruction and had found within herself the fortitude to stand firm. This was not recklessness; it was a calculated acceptance of her destiny, a commitment to fulfilling the role she had been born to play.

The city lights twinkled like fallen stars against the velvet backdrop of the night sky. Each light represented a home, a family, lives lived in the shadow of unseen protections. It was a responsibility that filled her with a deep sense of purpose. She was not merely defending buildings and historical sites; she was safeguarding the continuity of life, the simple, precious normalcy that allowed people to dream, to love, to build futures. This was the true essence of her legacy, to ensure that the light of Kilkenny, both literal and metaphorical, would never be extinguished.

She considered the future, not with anxiety, but with a sense of preparedness. She knew that her understanding of the forces at play would continue to deepen, that new challenges would undoubtedly arise. She was committed to continuous learning, to honing her skills, to staying attuned to the subtle shifts in Kilkenny's energetic landscape. She would revisit the ancient texts, seek out the hidden knowledge passed down through her family, and remain open to the wisdom that the land itself offered. Her commitment was not a static vow, but a dynamic, ongoing engagement with her heritage and her responsibilities.

The feeling of being deeply rooted in Kilkenny was stronger than ever. It wasn't just a place she lived; it was a part of her, and she, a part of it. The recent events had cemented this bond, transforming her awareness from a passive recognition of her lineage to an active, vibrant embodiment of her role. She was no longer merely the inheritor of a legacy; she was its active participant, its contemporary guardian, ready to face whatever the coming days, months, and years might bring, with a steadfast heart and an unyielding spirit. The echoes of the past had converged with the present, and in Aine's commitment, the future of Kilkenny found its unwavering strength. She breathed in the night air, a silent promise whispered on the wind – she would not fail.

THE ENDURING BOND

The shared ordeal had irrevocably altered the landscape of Aine and Pete's relationship. The veneer of normalcy had been stripped away, revealing a connection forged in the crucible of peril. Gone were the tentative inquiries, the hesitant steps towards understanding each other's hidden depths. In their place was a raw, unvarnished intimacy, born from confronting the unimaginable side-by-side. Aine found herself watching Pete, not with the eyes of someone merely acquainted, but with the profound recognition of a fellow traveler who had seen the same shadowed paths, who understood the silent language of fear and courage. He had seen her at her most elemental, her power surging through her like a tempest, and his reaction had not been recoil, but an unwavering acceptance that resonated deeper than any spoken word.

Pete, in turn, seemed to carry a new awareness of Aine. He still possessed his characteristic warmth and grounded humor, but now it was underscored by a quiet respect, a recognition of the ancient strength that pulsed beneath her surface. He no longer saw her solely as the woman he was falling for; he saw the Guardian, the inheritor of a legacy that defied ordinary comprehension. The deception, the secrets she had kept, were no longer barriers, but rather a testament to the immense pressure she had been under, a testament to the weight of her responsibilities. He had navigated the treacherous currents of her past, and in doing so, had become an integral part of her present and, she dared to believe, her future.

Their conversations had shifted, no longer confined to the mundane details of daily life. They spoke of the unseen currents that flowed through Kilkenny, of the subtle shifts in energy that only Aine could perceive. Pete, with his keen observational skills and intuitive understanding, often picked up on nuances that even Aine might have initially overlooked, offering a fresh perspective that enriched her own perception. He would ask questions not of disbelief, but of genuine curiosity, his brow furrowed in concentration as she explained the intricacies of wards, sigils, and the energetic resonance of ancient places. He listened with an attentiveness that spoke volumes, absorbing her words not as fantastical tales, but as vital pieces of a puzzle that was slowly unfolding before him.

One evening, as they sat by the river, the same river that had witnessed so much of Aine's awakening, Pete reached out and took her hand. His touch was firm, reassuring, a silent anchor in the swirling currents of her thoughts. "You know," he began, his voice low and contemplative, "I used to think I understood what it meant to be strong. To be brave. But seeing you... seeing what you carry, what you do... it's a different kind of strength entirely. It's not just about fighting back, is it? It's about holding on, about protecting something even when it terrifies you."

Aine squeezed his hand, her throat tight with emotion. "It's about believing in it, Pete. Believing in Kilkenny, believing in the people who live here, even when they don't know what's being done to keep them safe. And... believing in myself, even when the doubt tries to creep in."

"You never let it creep in when it mattered," he countered softly. "Not when it counted. And that's what I saw. That's what I'll always remember."

The shared experience had stripped away pretenses, leaving behind a vulnerability that was both terrifying and liberating. Aine found herself sharing parts of her past that she had long kept buried, fragments of loneliness and self-doubt that had punctuated her life before she fully embraced her heritage. Pete, in turn, opened up about his own past, the quiet struggles and aspirations that had shaped him, the moments of uncertainty that had often gone unseen. Their confessions were not grand declarations, but quiet revelations, woven into the fabric of their shared nights and contemplative days.

There was a moment, palpable and electric, when Aine realized that their connection had surpassed the boundaries of mere affection. It was a quiet understanding that bloomed in the shared silence, in the gentle pressure of his hand on her arm, in the way their gazes met and held, conveying a depth of shared knowledge that words could never fully articulate. The deception that had initially clouded their interactions now felt like a distant storm, a necessary tempest that had cleared the air and revealed the true, enduring foundation of their bond.

However, the question of their future remained, a delicate, unspoken query hanging in the air between them. Kilkenny was Aine's charge, her destiny intrinsically bound to its ancient stones and whispering winds. Her role as Guardian demanded a vigilance that was relentless, a commitment that often meant living on the precipice of danger. Could Pete truly find a place in such a life? Could their love, so potent and so real, thrive in the shadow of the unseen, in the constant awareness of forces that sought to disrupt the delicate balance?

Aine voiced this unspoken concern one evening, the words tumbling out before she could censor them. "Pete," she began, her voice a little shaky, "I... I don't know what this means for us. For you. My life... it's not a normal one. It's filled with responsibilities that can't be shared, with dangers that... that might be too much for anyone to bear, let alone someone who isn't bound to it the way I am."

Pete turned to her, his expression open and steady. He took both her hands, his thumbs tracing slow circles on her skin. "Aine," he said, his voice firm, "I know it's not normal. I know it's... a lot. But what we went through, it changed me too. I saw the darkness, yes, but I also saw the light. I saw what you are capable of, what you protect. And I don't want to be on the outside of that. I want to be with you, however that looks. I trust you. And I trust... us."

His words were a balm to her soul, a soothing counterpoint to the anxieties that had begun to gnaw at her. It wasn't just his declaration of love, but his acknowledgment of the reality of her life, his willingness to embrace it rather than shy away from it. He didn't offer easy platitudes or dismiss the inherent challenges. Instead, he offered his presence, his understanding, his unwavering commitment.

"It won't be easy," Aine admitted, her gaze searching his face. "There will be times when I have to be... distant. Focused. When I have to trust my instincts, even if they lead me away from... from ordinary life."

"I know," Pete replied, his grip tightening. "But you won't be alone. Not in here." He tapped his chest gently. "And if you need me, truly need me, I'll be there. I'll learn. I'll adapt. Because you... you're worth all of it, Aine. You're worth the extraordinary."

The weight of her responsibilities had always felt like a solitary mantle. She had accepted it, embraced it, but the thought of sharing even a fraction of that burden, of having someone by her side who understood the stakes, was a prospect that filled her with a quiet, profound joy. Pete's unwavering presence was not just a comfort; it was a revelation. It was the confirmation that love, even in the face of such unique and demanding circumstances, could find a way to flourish, to adapt, and to deepen.

They continued to navigate the complexities of their connection, not with a sense of obligation, but with a growing understanding of the unique tapestry they were weaving together. Aine recognized that her role as Guardian was paramount, that her commitment to Kilkenny was absolute. But she also recognized that Pete was not an impediment to that commitment, but rather a testament to its enduring power. He was a reminder that even amidst the ancient magic and unseen battles, the most potent force of all was the human heart, its capacity for love, for trust, and for unwavering support.

The future was still uncertain, its contours veiled in the same enigmatic mist that often enshrouded Kilkenny's ancient past. But as Aine looked at Pete, at the genuine affection and steadfast resolve in his eyes, she felt a burgeoning sense of hope. Their bond was not a fragile thing, easily shattered by the pressures of her extraordinary life. Instead, it was a deep, unbreakable tie, forged in the fires of adversity, strengthened by shared understanding, and illuminated by the promise of a love that dared to embrace the extraordinary. They had faced deception and danger, and in its wake, they had found something far more profound: a connection that was as enduring as

Kilkenny's ancient stones, as resilient as the river that flowed through its heart, and as true as the pulse of magic that resonated within Aine herself. The echoes of their shared experience had not led to an ending, but to the commencement of a new, more profound chapter, a testament to a bond that transcended the ordinary and embraced the eternal.

A FOND FAREWELL OR A NEW BEGINNING

The air in Aine's small cottage, once a sanctuary, now felt charged with an unspoken transition. The familiar scent of drying herbs and old parchment was now overlaid with the faint, lingering aroma of Pete's presence – a subtle, grounding scent of woodsmoke and something undeniably him. It was a fragrance that had, over the whirlwind weeks, become as comforting and essential as the ancient magic that pulsed through the very stones of Kilkenny. Now, that scent was slowly, irrevocably, beginning to fade.

Pete stood by the door, his worn leather satchel slung over his shoulder. The same satchel that had held unremarkable holiday souvenirs a few weeks prior now seemed to carry the weight of unspoken futures, of diverging paths. His gaze met Aine's, and in that shared look, a universe of emotions flickered – understanding, regret, a hesitant, determined hope. The world they had navigated together, a world of hidden dangers and ancient pacts, had irrevocably bound them. The casual acquaintance that had brought him to Kilkenny had dissolved like mist under a determined sun, replaced by a connection that felt as deep and enduring as the River Nore itself.

"So," Pete began, his voice deliberately even, a fragile attempt to anchor them both to a semblance of normalcy that no longer existed. "My train leaves in a couple of hours." He offered a small, tight smile that didn't quite reach his eyes. The easy banter, the quick wit that had always been a hallmark of their interactions, felt strained now, like a familiar melody played out of tune.

Aine nodded, her own throat feeling tight. She had prepared herself for this moment, mentally rehearsed the words, the gestures, the carefully constructed facade of brave acceptance. Yet, the reality of it felt like a physical blow. Every fibre of her being screamed against this departure. He had become more than just a companion; he had become her confidant, her anchor in the turbulent currents of her inherited responsibilities. He had seen her power, her fear, her unwavering resolve, and had not flinched. Instead, he had leaned in, his belief in her a palpable force, a silent testament to the depth of his feelings.

"I know," she managed, her voice barely a whisper. She hugged herself, her arms a futile barrier against the encroaching emptiness. The secret she carried, the ancient legacy that defined her existence, had always been a solitary burden. She had accepted its weight, understood its isolating nature. But Pete... Pete had, through sheer force of will and an undeniable capacity for love, managed to breach those self-imposed walls. He had seen the raw truth of her life, the constant hum of unseen forces, the quiet, ever-present danger, and had not turned away. Instead, he had offered his strength, his perspective, his unwavering presence.

"It's... it's been an incredible time, Aine," Pete continued, his gaze sweeping around the small, book-lined room, lingering for a moment on the arcane symbols etched into the wooden beams of the ceiling, symbols he now understood held a power far beyond mere decoration. He'd seen her wield that power, felt its energy surge through the ancient stones of Kilkenny, and it had fundamentally altered his perception of reality. "More than I could have ever imagined when I booked that train ticket for a... a quiet getaway." He chuckled, a low, self-deprecating sound. "Quiet was definitely not on the agenda."

Aine's lips curved into a weak smile. "No," she agreed. "It certainly wasn't. But... I'm glad it wasn't. I wouldn't trade any of it, Pete. Not the danger, not the... the revelations. Especially not you." The last part was spoken with a sincerity that left no room for doubt, a raw confession of the depth of her feelings, feelings she had once believed herself incapable of experiencing fully, tethered as she was to her duty.

He took a step closer, his eyes locking with hers. The space between them crackled with an unspoken understanding, a shared history forged in the crucible of shared peril. The casual, almost flirtatious banter that had marked their initial interactions now felt like a relic of a different lifetime. What had blossomed between them was something far more profound, a connection woven from threads of trust, mutual respect, and a love that had been tested and tempered by the extraordinary circumstances of her life.

"And I wouldn't trade you, Aine," he said, his voice rough with emotion. He reached out, his fingers brushing a stray strand of hair from her cheek, his touch a gentle, almost reverent caress. "You... you showed me a world I never knew existed. A world that's been hidden in plain sight all along." He paused, his gaze unwavering. "And you showed me... well, you showed me what it means to truly believe in something, and in someone."

The unspoken question hung heavy in the air between them. Was this goodbye? Was Pete's departure a definitive closing of this chapter, a return to his 'normal' life, leaving the magic and the danger of Kilkenny behind? Or was it merely a pause, a temporary separation before a new, perhaps even more entwined, beginning? He had seen the heart of her world, had walked beside her through its shadowed corners and its radiant power. He knew what she was, what she did, and he hadn't run. In fact, he had embraced it, in his own quiet, steady way.

"Pete," Aine began, her voice trembling slightly, the carefully constructed composure threatening to crumble. "What... what happens now? For us?" The question was raw, unvarnished, a reflection of the gnawing uncertainty that had been her constant companion since the true nature of her role had been revealed to him. She was bound to Kilkenny, her very essence intertwined with its ancient heartbeat. Her responsibilities were all-consuming, demanding a vigilance that often meant isolation, sacrifice, and a life lived on the precipice. Could he truly fit into that? Could their nascent love survive the constant shadow of the unseen, the ever-present threat that loomed just beyond the veil of ordinary perception?

Pete's hand lingered on her cheek, his thumb gently stroking her skin. He met her gaze with an honesty that bolstered her faltering spirit. "That," he said, his voice steady and calm, "is the million-dollar question, isn't it?" He took a deep breath, then let it out slowly. "I don't have a neat answer for you, Aine. I can't pretend that everything is going to go back to how it was before. You... you've changed me. Kilkenny has changed me. And I think," he added, a hint of a smile finally breaking through the tension, "you've changed me for the better."

He stepped back, giving her space, but his eyes never left hers. "I'm not a Guardian. I don't have your sight, your innate connection to all of this." He gestured vaguely, encompassing the cottage, the town, the ancient energy that pulsed beneath it all. "And I understand that. I'm not asking to be something I'm not. But I'm also not the same person who arrived here looking for a quiet break. I've seen what you do, Aine. I've seen the courage it takes, the responsibility you carry. And I... I want to be a part of it, somehow. Not as a participant, maybe, but as... as your support. As someone who understands."

His words were a lifeline, a beacon of hope in the swirling uncertainty. It wasn't a demand for integration, not a plea to be inducted into her world as an equal player. It was a quiet offer of partnership, a willingness to stand by her side, to learn, to adapt, to simply be there. This was a gift far greater than any magic could bestow – the gift of shared understanding, of unwavering support.

"But it's dangerous, Pete," Aine countered, the ingrained caution of her lineage resurfacing. "It's not just about understanding. It's about living with the constant threat. There will be times when I have to make decisions that... that are difficult, that might even put you at risk. Times when I have to disappear, when I have to focus solely on what needs to be done, and I won't be able to explain."

"I know," he replied, his gaze steady. "And I'm not naive. I saw the... the other side of it. I felt the fear. But I also saw your strength. I saw how you faced it, how you protected us. And I trust you, Aine. I trust your judgment. I trust your power. And I trust... us. Whatever 'us' turns out to be." He managed a more genuine smile this time, a flicker of the old Pete, tempered by the new knowledge he carried. "I'm not asking for guarantees. Just... for the possibility. The possibility of staying connected to this world, and to you."

He looked at his watch. "The train," he said, his voice tinged with a reluctant finality. He reached into his satchel and pulled out a small, intricately carved wooden bird. It was a familiar Kilkenny craft, but this one felt different, imbued with a special significance. He placed it in her palm. "Something to remember me by. Or...

something to remind you that there's a world outside of all this, a world I'm going back to. And it's a world I'd like to share with you, when you can. When you're ready."

Aine's fingers closed around the cool wood. It felt solid, real, a tangible reminder of their shared time. She looked up at him, tears pricking at the corners of her eyes. "Pete," she whispered, her voice thick with unshed emotion, "I don't want this to be a goodbye. I want..." She hesitated, the words catching in her throat. She wanted him to stay, to be a constant in her life, to share the quiet moments as well as the extraordinary ones. But she also knew the immense weight of her responsibilities, the fact that her life was intrinsically tied to the fate of Kilkenny.

Pete saw the unspoken plea in her eyes, the internal struggle she was waging. He stepped forward and gently cupped her face in his hands. "Then it's not a goodbye, Aine," he said softly, his gaze unwavering. "It's... a 'see you soon'." He leaned in, and for a long, breathless moment, their lips met. It was a kiss that held the bittersweet ache of parting, the desperate hope of reunion, and the profound understanding of a love that had found its footing in the most unlikely of circumstances. It was a promise, a silent vow exchanged between two souls irrevocably altered by their shared journey.

He pulled away, his eyes shining with a mixture of sadness and resolve. "Take care of yourself, Guardian," he murmured, his voice husky. He gave her one last, lingering look, a look that spoke volumes of the connection they had forged, before turning and walking towards the door.

Aine watched him go, her heart a heavy, aching weight in her chest. The cottage felt vast and silent without his presence, the air suddenly thin and cold. She clutched the wooden bird in her hand, its smooth surface a small comfort. Was this truly the end of their time together? Or was this parting a necessary prelude to something more? Had Pete's brief sojourn in Kilkenny merely been a holiday that had taken an unexpected turn, or had it been the catalyst for a profound life change, a decision to weave his own destiny with that of the woman who held the fate of an ancient city in her hands?

As the sound of his footsteps faded down the lane, Aine was left with a kaleidoscope of emotions. Sadness, yes, a deep and piercing sorrow for the absence of his warmth and laughter. But beneath it, a nascent hope, a quiet strength that had been ignited by his unwavering belief in her. He had seen her at her most vulnerable, her most powerful, and had offered not just acceptance, but a genuine desire to be a part of her world, however complex and perilous it might be. The future remained shrouded in the familiar mists of Kilkenny's ancient mysteries, its path uncertain. But for the first time in a long time, Aine didn't feel entirely alone in navigating it. Pete's departure was not simply a farewell; it was a question mark, an open door, a new beginning waiting to be written, a testament to the enduring power of connection, even when forged in the heart of the extraordinary. The echoes of their shared experience had not led to a final conclusion, but to a profound moment of introspection, a subtle yet significant shift in the trajectory of her solitary existence, a quiet affirmation that even for a Guardian, love could find a way.

THE LINGERING MYSTERY

The silence in Aine's cottage was a heavy, tangible thing now, a stark contrast to the vibrant, charged energy that had permeated its walls just hours before. Pete's departure had left an imprint, not just on the air, but on the very fabric of the space, a subtle shift in its familiar aura. The scent of woodsmoke and his quiet strength, once a comforting presence, now lingered as a poignant memory, a testament to the unexpected intimacy they had found amidst the ancient stones of Kilkenny. He had arrived a visitor, seeking respite from the mundane, and had stumbled into a world woven from myth and guardianship, a world that had irrevocably altered his perspective. As Aine stood by the window, watching the distant silhouette of the train disappear beyond the rolling hills, she knew that Kilkenny, too, had left its indelible mark on him. The whispers of its history, the subtle pulse of its magic, the quiet determination in her own eyes – these were not things easily forgotten.

The days that followed Pete's departure settled into a familiar rhythm, yet Aine found herself observing her world with a new lens. Kilkenny, always a place of profound depth and hidden currents, seemed to reveal itself in subtler ways. The ancient magic, a constant companion, now felt less like an external force and more like an intrinsic part of her own being, amplified by the knowledge that someone outside its immediate embrace had witnessed and understood, at least in part, its profound significance. The familiar hum of the city, the murmur of the River Nore, the very earth beneath her feet – each element held a newly perceived resonance. She found herself pausing more often, listening to the unspoken language of the stones, the silent stories carried on the wind. It was as if Pete's journey into her world had somehow deepened her own connection to it, highlighting the layers of history and power that lay just beneath the veneer of everyday life.

The threat, the immediate danger that had drawn Pete into her orbit, had receded, leaving behind a fragile peace. Yet, the nature of her guardianship was such that vigilance was an unceasing state of being. The residual energies, the subtle imbalances that marked the wake of any significant magical disturbance, required careful monitoring. Aine found herself drawn back to the ancient texts, the worn scrolls that detailed the ebb and flow of Kilkenny's mystical currents. It was a solitary pursuit, as it always had been, but the memory of Pete's quiet presence, his earnest attempts to comprehend the complexities of her world, lent a different quality to her solitude. He hadn't just been a witness; he had been a sounding board, a voice of grounding reason in the face of overwhelming ancient forces.

The town itself seemed to exhale, the collective tension that had gripped its hidden heart slowly dissipating. The residents, unaware of the magnitude of the events that had transpired, went about their lives with a renewed sense of normalcy, a testament to Aine's successful efforts. Yet, for Aine, the normalcy was tinged with a new awareness. She saw the subtle protective wards she had reinforced, the ancient symbols that still glowed faintly in certain forgotten corners, the quiet vigilance of the natural world that mirrored her own. Kilkenny was a tapestry of interconnected energies, and while the immediate unraveling had been averted, the threads of its ancient mystery remained, ever-present, ever-defining.

Pete's influence extended beyond the personal. His very presence had served as a catalyst, a disruption of the predictable flow, forcing a reassessment of familiar patterns. He had brought an outsider's perspective, a grounded curiosity that had, in turn, illuminated aspects of her own role that had become almost too familiar to notice. The intricate web of rituals, the subtle nuances of power, the silent pacts that bound her to Kilkenny – he had approached them not with fear or judgment, but with a quiet fascination, a willingness to learn. It was a rare gift, one that had made his departure all the more poignant. He hadn't just seen the magic; he had seen her, the woman behind the Guardian, and had found her worthy of understanding, of connection.

In the quiet evenings, Aine would find herself tracing the intricate carvings on the wooden bird Pete had left her. It was a simple object, a piece of local craftsmanship, yet it held the weight of their shared experience. It was a tangible reminder of his time in Kilkenny, a symbol of the world he belonged to, and the bridge they had built between their disparate realities. She wondered about him, about his return to his 'normal' life. Had the echoes of Kilkenny's magic followed him? Had the quiet intensity of her world imprinted itself upon his consciousness in a way that would forever alter his perception of the ordinary? She hoped so. She hoped that a part of Kilkenny, a part of her, would remain with him, a subtle current beneath the surface of his everyday existence.

The responsibility of her guardianship was a solitary path, often fraught with unseen dangers and profound isolation. She had always accepted this, had embraced the quiet burden of her lineage. But Pete's presence had offered a glimpse of something else – the possibility of shared understanding, of a connection that transcended the solitary nature of her duty. He had seen the weight she carried, the sacrifices she made, and had not flinched. Instead, he had offered his support, his belief, a quiet promise of companionship, however unconventional. It was a hope that, even in her most solitary moments, she would carry with her, a quiet testament to the transformative power of connection.

Kilkenny, in its ancient wisdom, held its secrets close, revealing them only to those who were attuned to its subtle vibrations. The immediate crisis had passed, but the underlying mysteries remained, woven into the very fabric of the city. Aine understood this inherently. Her role was not to conquer these mysteries, but to understand them, to live in harmony with them, and to protect the delicate balance that sustained Kilkenny. Pete's departure was not an ending, but a transition. He carried with him the echoes of his time in Ireland, a deeper understanding of the world's hidden heart, forever changed by his encounter with a Guardian and the ancient magic she protected. And Aine, left in the familiar quiet of her cottage, knew that she too had been changed, not by the passing of a threat, but by the unexpected blossoming of a connection that had dared to cross the boundaries of the ordinary, leaving behind not just memories, but a lingering sense of possibility, a quiet promise that even in a world of ancient secrets, love and understanding could indeed find a way. The lingering mystery was not in the passing of danger, but in the enduring power of the bonds forged in its wake. Kilkenny, as always, held its breath, its ancient heart pulsing with stories yet untold, and Aine, now with a renewed perspective, stood ready to listen, to protect, and perhaps, to await the return of the echoes she had come to cherish.

ACKNOWLEDGEMENT

My profound appreciation extends to the multitude of souls whose contributions were instrumental in bringing this novel to fruition. My heartfelt gratitude is directed towards my Family, whose perceptive judgment and constructive feedback proved absolutely vital in molding this narrative. To my trusted critique partners, I offer immense thanks for your steadfast encouragement and for challenging me to delve into previously uncharted emotional territories within the plot and its inhabitants. Particular commendation goes to the historical societies and the dedicated local historians of Kilkenny; their extensive archives and vibrant chronicles of the city's heritage furnished an irreplaceable bedrock for this undertaking. Furthermore, I am deeply indebted to my family and friends, whose enduring patience and spirited motivation served as an unwavering wellspring of resilience throughout this endeavor. Lastly, my deepest thanks belong to Kilkenny itself, for its persistent enchantment, its resonant stones, and the enduring sagas it continues to preserve.

GLOSSARY

This supplementary section is designed to deepen your immersion into the novel's narrative, offering illuminating details that expand upon its depicted reality and significant occurrences. Within these pages, you will discover:

Kilkenny's Ancient Lore: A brief overview of some of the lesser-known myths and legends surrounding Kilkenny and its environs, referenced in the text.

Guardian Lore: Details on the historical lineage and ongoing responsibilities of the Guardians of Kilkenny, including specific protective rituals and their symbolic meanings.

Symbolism of Natural Elements: Explanations of the significance attributed to certain natural phenomena and geological features within the mystical framework of Kilkenny.

This supplementary section delves deeper, illuminating the fictional realm and its unfolding narrative. Within its pages, you will discover:

Kilkenny's Ancient Lore: A brief overview of some of the lesser-known myths and legends surrounding Kilkenny and its environs, referenced in the text.

Guardian Lore: Details on the historical lineage and ongoing responsibilities of the Guardians of Kilkenny, including specific protective rituals and their symbolic meanings.

Symbolism of Natural Elements: Explanations of the significance attributed to certain natural phenomena and geological features within the mystical framework of Kilkenny.

This novel is deeply rooted in a vibrant confluence of historical fact and ancient lore. Though a work of fiction, its genesis blossomed from the fertile soil of Kilkenny's storied past and the enduring power of Irish legends. The author specifically recognizes the profound influence of:

* **Whispers of the Emerald Isle's soul:** An exploration of Irish folklore and mythology, with a special nod to localized tales and the subtle currents of magical traditions. * **Echoes from Kilkenny's stones:** Historical records and architectural analyses illuminating the city's venerable sites and iconic structures. * **Unseen forces shaping the land:** Scholarly investigations into energy fields and the intangible influences that permeate both historical landscapes and natural settings.

P. Hartwell, a fiction author, crafts complex mysteries, imbuing them with vibrant, historically resonant backdrops. Driven by a profound understanding of the subtle influences shaping our existence and the lasting strength of human bonds, he merges meticulous historical investigation with creative narrative in every piece. The city of Kilkenny, with its deep historical strata and tangible aura, proved an immense catalyst for this particular story. This setting enabled him to delve into the concealed streams of enchantment and custodianship that subtly underpin everyday reality. Hartwell makes his home in Buffalo, perpetually enthralled by the persistent enigmas of bygone eras and the boundless potential of what is yet to come.

P. Hartwell is a fiction mystery author drawn to the places where history falters and secrets endure. Raised along the windswept shores of Lake Erie and shaped by global travels and ancestral lore, he writes stories that stir beneath the surface—where grief haunts, truth hides, and the past refuses to stay buried. With a cinematic eye for atmosphere and a deep reverence for forgotten histories, Hartwell crafts mysteries steeped in emotional tension and elemental unease. His work invites readers into shadowy worlds where every clue carries weight, and every silence speaks volumes.